THE SKYBOUND SAGA

BOOK I: BLACK WINGS BEATING

BOOK II: RED SKIES FALLING

GOLD WINGS RISING

ALEX LONDON

THE SKYBOUND SAGA **BOOK III**

FARRAR STRAUS GIROUX NEW YORK

Farrar Straus Giroux Books for Young Readers
An imprint of Macmillan Publishing Group, LLC
120 Broadway, New York, NY 10271
fiercereads.com

Our books may be purchased in bulk for promotional, educational, or business use. Please
contact your local bookseller or the Macmillan Corporate and Premium Sales Department
at (800) 221-7945 ext. 5442 or by email at MacmillanSpecialMarkets@macmillan.com.

Library of Congress Cataloging-in-Publication Data is available.

First edition, 2020

Book design by Elizabeth H. Clark

Printed in the United States of America

ISBN 978-0-374-30689-2

1   3   5   7   9   10   8   6   4   2

To Grace Kendall, who made this trilogy—
and this author—soar.
—A. L.

LOWER JAW

SKY CASTLE

RISHL BRONZE PITS

PARSH DESERT

TALON FORTRESS

AN OLD SONG

THEY'D LOCKED THEMSELVES INSIDE CAGES BUILT FROM THE
wreckage of the world.

The occupants of the Six Villages had strung up heavy netting to cut off any open sky, from roof to roof and fencepost to chimney, layers of nets and bars and beams sagging over streets and courtyards, casting patchwork shadows. They tied lines to the half-crumbled barricades—structures left over from a half-won battle they'd only half given up fighting—and looped the opposite ends on boulders. Every rope that once held a kite to a war barrow had been repurposed to create a shield between earth and sky.

As if the sky could be kept out by nets of rope and wire.

As if the sky hadn't wanted this cage built in the first place.

As if a net could keep the sky from falling.

The ghost eagles did not know their own thoughts were anything other than the sky's. They believed themselves the sky's talons, the sky's will, the only beings truly beloved by wind and air. They believed humanity was exactly where it was meant to be: cowering inside a cage. The ghost eagles believed they were winning.

The ghost eagles were right.

When the ghost eagles flocked down from the high mountain peaks, the Sky Castle had sealed itself underneath nets and behind walls, cut off from its own army. No messages came in or out. Any stragglers on the plains or in the mountains or crossing the desert had been chased into shelters or torn to shreds. The Sky Castle took in no more frightened masses, closed its gates completely. Inside, the occupants were beginning to starve and, in desperation, beginning to riot.

The blood birch forest was quiet. None who entered left. The Owl Mothers had retreated, as they always did.

The ghost eagles attacked the Talon Fortress straightaway, leaving it abandoned and crumbling. They perched on the tops of its huge curved walls, which were shaped like talons breaking through the mountainside. They feasted on those who did not flee fast enough, and they built their eyrie from ruined stone and broken bones. This place had been theirs long ago, before the people, and now it was theirs once again. They perched by the hundreds and, from there, saw everything.

The flock of humanity scattered, and each settlement was its own cage, and each cage was all alone.

The ghost eagles ignored most of them but could never ignore the Six Villages. Through rage and hunger, the Six called them back, night after night after night, for reasons not even they could quite understand. The girl and her brother haunted their dreams. The ghost eagles saw memories, fragments of thought that were not their own, feelings so utterly human that they were incomprehensible to the convocation of ancient birds. They screeched back with their own voices, trying to chase out these thoughts that drew them, over and over, to the sky above the Six.

The once-broad main street of the Six Villages was clogged with tents and shacks, divided and subdivided into narrow twisting alleys and paths barely wider than a gull's wings. Awnings protruded at odd angles, crossbeams cutting this way and that. The bent shells of war barrows capped alley entrances, forming arches over which the inhabitants strung their nets and ropes—anything they thought might impede an attack from above. Everything was built with a bird's-eye view in mind.

What a person might consider laughter fluttered through the ghost eagles' thoughts.

People had no idea what a bird's-eye view entailed, nor what the eyes of these birds could see. One mind with a thousand eyes—they saw everything. They *thought* they saw everything.

In the Six, people fought over territory. Some lived in mountain caves just above the towns, stretched to the very limit of the nets' reach. The nets were strongest wherever they met stone.

Fights broke out, houses changed hands, and violence in the narrow lanes was as common as cardinals scuffling with blue jays. Survivors of Kartami violence attacked ex-Kartami warriors—or people they believed to be ex-Kartami warriors. Kartami warriors not ready to give up their cause slaughtered Uztari soldiers in their sleep or slit the throats of the precious hawks and falcons they still viewed as blasephemous.

Then there was the violence born not of ideology or grievance but of survival: new gangs extorting people over food and water, gangs competing with each other after the collapse of the Tamir family's control, freelance criminals, starved to the point of petty violence.

And, as in any society, there were people who loved

violence simply for its own sake, who ran fighting rings with both bird and human bouts, who jumped anyone they didn't like for any reason they could think up. There was too much ale and hunter's leaf in town, and also too little. Supplies were starting to run low. Prices were soaring. Some people always found ways to profit from pain.

Kyrg Birgund, the nominal defense counselor of the Sky Castle, tried to maintain order, but there'd been little respect for the authority of kyrgs before the current calamity, and the situation hadn't made anyone *more* respectful. Soon the soldiers would be hungry. Soon they would take what they needed from the people, who would, of course, fight back.

These were the thoughts that occupied the brother and sister, the thoughts the ghost eagles heard. The boy fretted. The girl plotted. The ghost eagles listened.

These human dramas played out in the crowded town during the day. Volunteers raced to patch tears in the nets, which the ghost eagles would then shred at night. It was endless maintenance. The people tired as they hungered.

The ghost eagles did not tire, though they did hunger as well. They could eat and eat, of course, but they would never be full. Want of meat was not what starved them. Still, at night, they ate.

Every morning the huddled multitudes of the Six Villages

tried to mend their barriers against wrath from the predators above, and every night, from the moment the sixth star appeared in the sky until the first red light of dawn, those same predators came screeching down upon them.

People waited out the long nights with wax stuffed in their ears. At first the wax was for keeping out the ghost eagles' cries, but it served a second purpose for the hard-hearted: not all the night's shrieking came from ghost eagles.

Each morning, more people were found missing. The ghost eagles snared lifelong falconers of Uztar. They grabbed Altari Crawling Priests who'd never so much as looked at a bird of prey, let alone captured or trained one. They seized ex-Kartami warriors stranded in the Six Villages after their army was crushed. They massacred Uztari foot soldiers and Uztari officers and Uztari traders and merchants and trappers and cooks. They took old and young, lovers and loners, sick and healthy—all forms of mind and body that the sky had ever seen. There was no discrimination. Death came for anyone unlucky enough to be caught.

Crowds gathered in the dawn sunshine each morning to breathe fresh air and share news about who had been taken in the night, how they had screamed, and what pieces of them might be found tangled in the web of ropes overhead. People placed bets on hands and limbs. The odds of a head were so low, a gambler would make a fortune if one were ever found.

The children sang new songs:

Fix the nets and tie your line
Or a ghost eagle will break your spine.
Every night they shriek and cry.
Who will live and who will die?
Me or you? You or I?
The eagle takes every-bod-die!

The last rhyme stretched thinner than the protective nets, but so it went with humanity. When happy, they sang; when sad, they sang; and when afraid, they sang. They were beings of song who knew well that song would not save them.

Sing on, rodents, sing on!

The ghost eagles had a song, too—an old, old song—and they'd sung it before and would sing it again. They sang this song every few generations, and it was always the same. They *thought* it would always be the same.

They wondered what might happen if it changed. They dared not wonder what might happen.

The song could never change.

The ghost eagles shrieked.

KYLEE

SHARING NIGHTMARES

1

EVERY NIGHT SINCE THE BURSTING MOON WAS A FINGERNAIL SLIVER, the ghost eagles had returned to test their defenses, and every night, Kylee watched Brysen toss and turn in his sleep, muttering in a long-dead language, mouth frothing and muscles taut near to tearing, until the dread flock left at dawn.

There was no amount of wax Brysen could stuff in his ears to block out the screeching, though for the first few nights he had tried. Nothing helped. Nothing calmed his dreams. Jowyn would hold him close, cover his ears with pale hands, rock Brysen in his arms, and whisper soothing words as though Brysen were a baby. But the screeching came from within and could not be stopped.

Kylee would sit stone-faced, watching. No one held her close. No one rocked her or whispered soothing words. She'd sit on the hard floor of the cave they now called home, jaw set tight, and show no sign that she heard the shrieking, too, that she saw the same visions her twin brother saw, asleep or awake, and that, when she did sleep, her nightmares were the same as his.

Kylee always woke before Brysen, and this morning, in the predawn stillness of the cave, Grazim told her she'd been muttering in her sleep, speaking words in the Hollow Tongue that neither of them recognized.

"You sounded just like him," she said. "I think you two never look more alike than when you're asleep."

"Don't watch me sleep," Kylee told Grazim, who shrugged. Kylee asked the girl to swear her silence. She didn't want her twin to know that she was experiencing the same nightmares.

"Keeping secrets from your brother?" Grazim shook her head. "That never works out well for you."

"Just swear," Kylee said.

And Grazim swore, and the moment Brysen woke, when the first feathering of morning sun fluttered through the cave's narrow open skylights, Kylee was at his side with the same question as the morning before and the morning before that and every morning for the last half turn of the swelling moon, ever since the convocation of ghost eagles had first descended on Uztar and begun to crush the world in their talons.

"What did you see?"

"Darkness and snow," Brysen whispered, his voice hoarse. "Just like every night."

"Anything else?" she asked.

His right eye met hers, sky-blue but cloudy from restlessness. The bronze patch he wore over his left eye had a dull patina to it, and his skin was still raw where it had been stitched with sparrow's tendon, but the wound was healing neatly. Jowyn regularly reminded Brysen to keep cleaning the wound and applying ointment to it at night, and so far, Brysen had obeyed. But now they were running low on the necessary herbs, which were becoming harder and harder to find. Foraging outside the protective nets was getting difficult, and some of the herbs could only be harvested at night, which was impossible. As it stood, what they had stored was all they would ever have, unless something changed. Unless they figured out how to fight back against the murderous sky.

When the wound finished healing and growing closed around the eyepatch, the bronze would be like a part of Brysen's face. Kylee was still not used to looking at her brother and seeing only one eye staring back. He was her twin, and somehow the change to his body made her cheekbone itch, like a reminder that, whatever happened to them, they would always be bound together. That was family: a leash or a tether, for good or for ill.

She'd have liked to tug at Brysen's leash, train him like he was a wild-caught falcon, keep him honest. She knew he was holding back what he dreamed. She raised an eyebrow at him.

"I saw footprints," he told her after it became obvious that she would wait for him to continue all morning if she had to. "Hundreds of footprints in a line that crossed over the whole world, then suddenly stopped. Empty snow ahead of them, and a shadow of wings. When the wings flapped, the snow was disturbed and the footprints vanished—all but two sets. Children's footprints. The wings flapped harder but couldn't erase them. There was a screaming regret."

"What does that mean?" Grazim scoffed. She stood against the smooth stone wall opposite Brysen's pallet, arms crossed, impatient for her morning tea. She made no secret that she found this whole exercise a waste of time, especially since she knew that Kylee already knew what Brysen had dreamed. "They showed you a 'screaming regret'?"

"Not everything that is shown can be seen," Jowyn interjected, his pale fingers lacing with Brysen's. "You ever try to describe a dream?"

"I don't share my dreams," Grazim told Jowyn, but she directed her next comment straight at Kylee. "They don't have anything useful to tell me."

"Some people just don't want to know themselves," Jowyn replied.

"Some people should mind their business," she snapped back. Grazim wasn't the type of person who tried to get along with others. She was a scholar and a warrior, and she didn't think making nice was a necessary part of either title. Kylee liked that about her. People pleasers exhausted her.

Kylee focused on getting information out of Brysen, ignoring the squabbling of her friends. "Where were the footprints leading?"

Brysen frowned and shook his head. "I don't know."

He was still holding back. She had the same dreams, saw the same line of footprints. She saw where the children's footprints led. She didn't ask him because she needed to know the answer; she asked him because she wanted to know if he would tell her.

The ghost eagles were putting these visions in their heads with their nightly shrieks, and Kylee hoped what they saw could be useful to destroy the flock. Brysen, who had healed a ghost eagle on the battlefield, didn't seem to want them destroyed. By holding back, by keeping information to himself, he revealed divided loyalties. Kylee wondered whose side he was on: hers, or theirs? How deep into his head had the ghost eagles penetrated? Could she trust her brother?

"Is there anything else you can tell me?" she asked, hopeful.

"No. Sorry," he said, wincing. "I've got a headache."

Kylee wanted to touch his shoulder or his hand, reassure him that it was okay, that it wasn't too late to do the right thing. It was, she believed, never too late to do the right thing. But urging Brysen to be his best self was Jowyn's job now. Brysen preferred the comfort Jowyn offered over hers anyway, and she, in fact, had little comfort to give him. If he was choosing to protect the ghost eagles, then he was beyond her help. She knew where the footprints in the dream led, and she would go there the first chance she had, with or without his help.

She had made a battlefield vow to the ghost eagles and to herself.

She was going to destroy them all.

2

"BREAKFAST!" MA CALLED, HER VOICE ECHOING THROUGH THE CAVERN, turning the simple sustaining noun into an imperative. *"Fast . . . fast . . . fast . . . fast . . ."*

With the surviving battle boys sharing the meal, it was an appropriate echo; if Kylee didn't get to breakfast *fast*, the boys would devour every scrap of food before she had taken her first sip of weak tea.

Grazim had already shoved off the wall to make her way toward the large kitchen chamber. "I'll save you some bread," she said, "if the vultures haven't snatched it all already."

"Thanks," Kylee said.

The Six Villages themselves were deeply overcrowded now

and desperately unsafe, and the caves set into the foothills above the village had become coveted property. The cave they lived in had once been a distillery for the Tamir gang's foothill gin, so it was fairly secure and easy to defend, which Kylee appreciated. Defending it, however, meant living with Brysen's old friends, the ragtag gang of battle boys who protected it and protected them. Just because the ghost eagles declared war on all humanity and united the different armies against a common enemy didn't mean they all suddenly got along. It didn't help that people blamed Brysen and Kylee for the ghost eagles' attacks in the first place. They had a lot of enemies in the Six now, and there was a need for friends with few scruples when it came to using violence to protect their own. Grazim described them as vultures, but Kylee thought of them as a mob of loud but loyal crows.

"You coming?" Kylee asked her brother. She wanted to keep an eye on him. If he was following the dream footprints, too, then she wanted to know about it.

"I'm not hungry," he replied.

She left him and Jowyn in their sleeping nook. She'd developed a rule for herself: to eat whenever she had the chance, because in war you never know when your next meal might come. She had the same rule about going to the bathroom. So much of survival is about the basics, and she made a point not to neglect them. Brysen, as usual, had different priorities.

He'd probably sleep through the end of the world, if it weren't for the nightmares. If the world hadn't, in fact, already ended.

The battle boys were already scarfing down breakfast when she reached the kitchen.

"It's real good, mem," Nyck told Kylee's mother as he shoved flatbread dusted with chili root into his mouth, then crunched on a handful of crisped river rice with charred sweetgrass. He looked up at Kylee when she came in but didn't stop eating. Ma was, it turned out, a decent cook.

"Your father never appreciated subtle flavors," she told Kylee as she gave her a smooth ceramic dish. "If there was no meat, he didn't think it was food."

"I remember," Kylee replied, and felt a jolt of pain as the memory yanked her backward, an entire history boiling up behind her eyes: the fervent prayers and dire curses Ma offered instead of affection; the retreat Ma took in the face of her violent husband; the suffering Brysen endured, from which Ma never once shielded him; the lack of comfort Ma offered, never once helping Kylee soothe him. Kylee had never been hit, but she felt the blows in her own way, even now, and they stung.

Kylee breathed through the memory, amazed that the simple act of remembering could make her body react so aggressively. She felt actual sweat beading in her hairline, and her heartbeat accelerated. She hated the power the past still held over her present.

Ma's mouth twitched at the corners. She wasn't asking forgiveness, and she wouldn't get it, but, of all the strange develop-
ments since the ghost eagles' return, her mother's transformation
was by far the strangest: She'd become an actual parent.

Kylee took her dish over to the mat where Nyck and three
other battle boys sat, glad for the distraction they'd provide.
Grazim preferred to sip her tea and eat a short distance away
from the others—she didn't like the sound of people
chewing—but she tossed Kylee a disc of flatbread she'd saved.
Her aim was good, and Kylee thanked her again. The constant
thank-yous made Grazim roll her eyes, but Kylee really was
grateful. It was nice to have a reliable ally in the house. It was
not something she was used to. Brysen had never been reliable, and his loyalty often caused more problems than it
solved. She wondered now if she could even count on that.

"Where's your brother?" Ma asked.

"Having a late morning with Jowyn?" Nyck smirked, eyebrows waggling with insinuation.

"Not every bird is a peacock," Grazim grunted.

"He's resting," Kylee said.

"*Resting* could be a euphemism," Nyck offered, which got a
well-aimed pebble winged at the back of his head. "Ow!"

"And that could be a sharper stone next time," Grazim
said.

Kylee smiled. This little community that surrounded her

had become something like she always imagined a family should be. They bickered and they bantered, and they ate together whenever they could, and even Ma, who never appeared to enjoy anything in their lives before now, appeared to enjoy providing for all these young people. All it had taken to find happiness was the fall of civilization.

"They caught one!" Jowyn came running into the cavern, still pulling a shirt on over his too-pale chest, which was covered with strange tattoos from his time in the blood birch forest, with the covey of the Owl Mothers.

"One what?" Nyck asked, but Grazim and Kylee were already on their feet.

"A ghost eagle," Jowyn said. "In the nets, last night. It's injured."

"How do you know?" Lyra asked. She was new to the battle boys, the daughter of a slain Altari grass merchant, and she hadn't known any of them before the war began. She didn't know the history of Kylee, Brysen, and the ghost eagles beyond what rumors carried on the wind and the hints and insinuations made around the cave. She asked questions no one else was fool enough to ask out loud, either because they already knew or because they didn't want to know the answers.

"Brysen can hear it," Jowyn explained, and tapped the side of his head. "Said it's being tortured, and he went to . . ." The sentence trailed off.

Kylee bit the inside of her cheeks. Was she angry that Brysen ran off without her? Or was she upset because he heard the ghost eagle's cries and she didn't?

And then she realized that she *did* hear them. The pain she felt when she remembered her father, remembered their lives before . . . that was the ghost eagle's pain, too, like two words that rhymed, sung in harmony. She didn't hear the ghost eagles because her own inner voice was too loud and indistinguishable from theirs.

It was not easy having the thoughts of giant killer birds echoing in your head, not easy to feel so much of what they did, half-tamed and enraged.

She was out the door before her plate finished rattling where she'd dropped it. The others ran close behind. The ghost eagles had already killed hundreds of Six Villagers, and she really hoped her brother wasn't going to run into a mob of the surviving friends and families just to do something stupid, like try to help this injured eagle.

She knew, of course, that helping the injured ghost eagle was exactly what he was going to do.

3

NEITHER KYLEE NOR HER BROTHER WERE SUPPOSED TO GO INTO THE crowded village lanes without at least two battle boys, and now Brysen had run, one-eyed, half-dressed, and all alone, into the heart of the village.

Brysen couldn't run very fast these days—he was still prone to tripping as his depth perception adjusted—but he was smart enough to know that Kylee would be after him, and he clearly did not want her to be.

The cave's entrance was hidden from outsiders by a large round stone set in a groove on a system of pulleys and ropes for easy opening and closing. Brysen had wedged a small stone in the groove, stopping the door stone from rolling open.

Kylee pulled against it, cursed, and pounded on the rock face in frustration.

"The scuzzard!" she shouted, then called for Nyck and the others to come help her. "You couldn't have stopped him?" she asked Jowyn.

"You ever stop Brysen from doing what he wanted?" he replied.

She grunted and leaned her weight against the huge round door. Together, Kylee, Grazim, Jowyn, Nyck, Lyra, and the last battle boy with them, Kheryn, all pushed and heaved together, but the stone barely moved at all.

"Why'd he shut us in?" Nyck wondered.

"Maybe he wanted to keep us safe from the captured ghost eagle?" Jowyn offered optimistically.

"He doesn't want me trying to stop him," Kylee said.

"From what?" Lyra asked.

"From helping a ghost eagle," she said.

Lyra began: "Why would he help a—"

"Not the time, Ly," Nyck interrupted her. "Just push."

Still the stone didn't move. Kylee cursed. She considered tying Brysen up and keeping him prisoner when he came back—*if* he came back—at least until she finished off the ghost eagles herself, but she imagined he wouldn't submit willingly. Jowyn and Ma might also offer some resistance.

There was no easy way for her to hold her brother against his will, even if it was for his own good.

"You all could take one of the smugglers' passages," her ma called from the hearth.

"Excuse me?" Kylee left the door and made her way back to her mother, who was rolling out some kind of sweet dough for dumplings.

"The smugglers' passages," Ma said. "There's one hidden in my sleeping niche. I'm sure there are others."

"That makes sense," Nyck interjected, plucking a piece of raw dough from the table with the dexterity of a cutpurse— which he had been. "When the Tamirs used this place, they'd have made all kinds of secret ways in and out. Can't run a criminal enterprise with only one exit, right?"

"Why are you only telling me this now?" Kylee demanded. "That's a major security risk!"

"I was . . ." Ma's voice trailed off, and Kylee knew. Ma hadn't told them about the passage because she was thinking about using it to sneak out. She'd prepared in the same way back at home, back before, when Da was still alive. Ma had kept a small bag hidden—in it were clothes for a desert crossing, an empty waterskin, and three and a half bronze rounds, the exact amount a long-hauler would charge someone to travel as a passenger. Even when bronze was tight and their bellies empty, Ma never revealed that hidden purse. She also never used it to leave them.

Ma wasn't aware that the twins knew, but they did. Kylee figured that Ma just liked having the option. Maybe that's what kept her going all those seasons, the idea that she *could* leave. This secret tunnel was the same thing: a possibility. Now that she'd shared it, Kylee wondered what her ma would cling to in the days to come.

"Thanks, Ma," Kylee said. She understood what revealing this information had cost her mother, but that was as much warmth as she had the inclination to give. Kylee rushed to her mother's sleeping niche, pushed aside an old knit that had been hanging there when they arrived, and found a round stone that rolled on a counterweight into a slot, like a smaller version of the cavern's main entrance.

She opened it and called over her shoulder to Nyck and the others: "If you're coming with me, make sure to plug your ears when we get close. The ghost eagle's cries can make you see things that aren't there, think things you shouldn't, and do things you wouldn't."

"We remember," Nyck said, and they were off, crouched low in a dark passage that smelled like old sweat, stale hunter's leaf, and the deep damp of the underground. The cave wound down, under the foothills, and there were metal grates along the way, which swung out. Those grates could be locked from the inside to prevent intrusion, a fact that made Kylee glad for the Tamir family's general mistrust of outsiders.

When they finally came to the end of the passageway and peered into the daylight, Kylee saw that they were far below the cave's entrance, concealed behind a boulder on a narrow slope near the Broken Jess. Inside a yard——what had once been the Tamirs' battle pits——were soldiers, milling about. Kyrg Birgund had turned the Broken Jess into his garrison, fortifying the nets above and the fencing around it. He had as much to fear from the people on the ground as from the ghost eagles above. Everyone knew that Birgund had stockpiles of food. Everyone cast hungry eyes in the direction of the Broken Jess.

Kylee gestured to the others to stay low and quiet. They were beyond the fence, and she hoped they could slip past it and onto the main street without being seen. She didn't like the soldiers knowing her comings and goings. Having abandoned the army of Uztar to save her brother——unleashing the ghost eagles on all of them in the process——Kylee wasn't exactly popular with the military.

Not popular with anyone but my friends, she thought to herself, which was, she figured, exactly the way it should be. Grazim rested a hand on her back, gave her a gentle nudge forward.

They crept past the garrison, listening to the shrieks of the birds kept inside. They were the last birds of prey in the Six, caged safely under nets and roofs. So far the ghost eagles hadn't taken them, but any bird that escaped the nets flew straight for the high mountains and away. No one knew if the birds made it or if the eagles took them down, but either way, no one saw them again.

"I'd love to get in there and snag a kestrel or two," Nyck whispered, ever the schemer. He and his battle boys were at their best with birds on the fist, and they were only half the gangsters they could be without them. Nyck had grand aspirations to be a leader of crooks.

"We don't need to bring Kyrg Birgund's attention down on us any more than it already is," Kylee told him. "No stealing."

Nyck whined. "But—"

"No. Stealing." Kylee was firm.

"Your friends are all miscreants," Grazim grumbled at her. Grazim had grand aspirations to be a leader of empires, and she didn't relish her current association with criminals and outcasts. Part of her, though, clearly enjoyed it, too.

"I know," Kylee replied, unable to stop herself smiling.

Once they'd passed the Broken Jess and made their way to what had once been the main thoroughfare, they stopped sneaking and instead walked with open confidence, as though they knew where they were going.

They did not.

Kylee didn't know where her brother had run off to, and

he'd had quite a head start. She tried to concentrate, to listen for the eagle's shrieks either in her mind or in reality, but there were too many other sounds all around them and too many distracting thoughts in her head.

She didn't recognize her hometown, and she felt countless strangers' eyes on her as she and the others weaved their way through the narrow alleys that extended from the main street like threads in a spiderweb.

Everyone knew who she was. Everyone knew she had commanded the ghost eagles in their own language, thinking she could control them, not realizing she and everyone else was being snared in their trap like a hawk diving for a tamer's lure. She'd thought the ghost eagle was her partner. She'd learned it was her enemy.

As she was passing a gin counter—many such stalls had sprung up to serve the frayed nerves of the masses—Kylee stopped. The owner, a former leather tanner named Nymaya, had always been kind to Kylee and Brysen.

"Did you see which way my brother went?" she asked Nymaya. Two customers were perched like kestrels at the counter, which was just a plank of wood the owner had fashioned into a makeshift bar. When Kylee spoke, both customers swiveled their heads to size her up.

Jowyn, Nyck, and the other two battle boys arrived just

then, and the customers returned their attention to their drinks.

"Into the Mutes," Nymaya said, pointing with the rag she'd been using to wipe out a cracked mug.

"Scuzz," Nyck muttered, then he picked up one of the women's cups and downed the gumroot gin in it. Nymaya glared at him, but he grinned.

Nyck's battle boys supplied much of the cheap gin to these little pop-up pubs, and you didn't cause trouble with him if you didn't want to risk living out the rest of your days dry as the Parsh Desert. Few wanted to take that risk, so they put up with the teenaged miscreant's presumptuousness. Also, Nymaya had a soft spot for Nyck.

Grazim frowned. She did not have a soft spot for Nyck or for Nymaya.

"What?" said Nyck. "If we're going into the Mutes, I need to preen my nerves."

Obviously, Kylee thought, *the Mutes are where Brysen would run to.* Whatever was the worst idea, whatever was the most reckless thing a person could do, that's what her twin brother would do. Whether it was fall in love or fall off a cliff, if it was an unnecessary risk, Brysen would take it.

And so into the Mutes they went. Kylee couldn't be sure they'd all come out again.

. . .

Mutes was an old falconers' word for bird scuzz. Skilled trappers studied the different kinds and qualities of mutes on tree branches and rock faces to lead them to prized hawks and falcons. Such care was not given by those who named the Mutes District. They just meant scuzz, and most wouldn't dare set the soles of their shoes within its boundaries.

Of all the new districts in the Six Villages, the Mutes was the worst for Kylee and her brother. The surviving Kartami warriors had settled there. Warrior pairs shared tents and shacks, four or six apiece. Converts and new fanatics and sympathizers had joined them, sleeping in the crowded lanes along with untold numbers of their former captives. Also in the Mutes were Crawling Priests and bird renouncers, repentant battle pit fighters and desperate migrants who couldn't find shelter in any of the less dangerous districts. This was a place where even a tan line from a falconer's glove or a trace of bird scuzz on your boot could get you killed. They certainly knew who Kylee, Brysen, and their friends were. They'd cursed every single one of them by name and marked every single one of them for death.

"Stay keen," Kylee warned. None of her friends needed to be told, and none of them hesitated to follow her.

The moment they crossed under the mounted metal war barrow that marked the entrance to the district, the whistling started, signaling who was coming in, how many of them there were, and where they were headed. If they ran into trouble, they would be outnumbered instantly. There were no birds of prey here to call upon for help. Other than the ghost eagles, the sky above stayed empty but for the hot wind off the desert. Any birds remaining in the Six were kept caged and far from this district.

"I swear, if we get out of here alive," Grazim whispered to Kylee as they walked shoulder-to-shoulder, "we should tie your brother to a wall."

"Isn't that Jowyn's job?" Nyck whispered over her shoulder. Kylee could hear the grin in his voice.

"Shut up," Jowyn grunted. He was usually the first to laugh at Nyck's bawdy sense of humor, but his eyes were darting from doorway to doorway, scanning every gap between buildings, and both his fist were balled. He wasn't an experienced fighter like Nyck, and he didn't know that tension wasn't the same as focus. He looked so tense, a hummingbird's fart could've snapped him in half.

"Breathe," Kylee urged him. "Brysen can handle himself."

Jowyn side-eyed her. Of course Brysen couldn't handle himself. They both knew that.

"Where'd he go?" Lyra wondered.

They got their answer from a ghost eagle's shriek: "REEEEEEE!"

They flinched like one exposed nerve in six bodies. The battle boys scrambled to put the wax plugs into their ears, but Nyck fumbled his and dropped them in the dirt. "REEEEE!" the eagle cried again, and Nyck collapsed to his knees, covering his ears with his hands, weeping.

Kylee couldn't see what Nyck saw. In her mind, she saw Brysen wandering off, alone, through high mountain snow, and she saw herself hovering over him, talons out. She was the ghost eagle; he was her prey. In the vision, her ghost eagle body shivered in the thin, cold air and shuddered with the thrill of a predator. In reality, she clenched her jaw and tried to push the illusion away.

"Stop it stop it stop it!" Nyck shouted on the ground. A pair of Kartami around his age watched from the open flaps of a tattered tent, laughing. One rested a red-wrapped fist lazily on the other's shoulder.

"What's wrong with her?" the other grunted. Their ears were plugged. "She don't like the music?"

Faster than a falcon diving at a hare, Grazim strode to the Kartami warrior, doubled him over with a punch in the gut, and put her blade to the other Kartami's throat. "Say another word and it'll be your last."

The young warrior swallowed but nodded, and Grazim

pulled the knife away from their throat. Lyra helped Nyck up, whispering something Kylee couldn't hear as she shoved wax into his ears. Nyck nodded and smiled, then made the broken-wing salute across his chest at the pair of warriors in the tent.

"Next time we talk, you'll be more respectful," he said. "If a ghost eagle doesn't devour you first."

They rolled their eyes and spat into the mud, then turned their backs on him and went inside. Kylee thought Nyck might chase them, but he had more sense. He knew how to hold a grudge until the right time to let it fly.

Around a corner, she found her brother exactly where she feared she would: in the middle of a crowd, surrounded on all sides. Above him, dangling over the street and dripping berry-black blood onto his shoulder, was an injured ghost eagle. The dread bird was ensnared in a rough tangle of barbed wire and netting.

"REEEEE!" it screamed.

"Gut them both!" the crowd bellowed, and she saw the pain on Brysen's face. She knew he heard the ghost eagle in his head, crying out over and over in a language that was more real than words could render, a language felt and seen and tasted more than heard. This wasn't the ghost eagle sending them a message; this was the ghost eagle screaming. What it screamed was this:

Pain pain pain pain pain.

Kylee, however, didn't wince like Brysen did.

She smiled. Though she could feel an echo of the ghost eagle's pain, it wasn't her pain, and she knew the ghost eagle deserved to hurt. It deserved to suffer. She *liked* that its agony was inside her mind. She wanted to know how much it hurt and, if she could, to figure out how to make it hurt worse.

"REEEEEE!" it screamed again. Suddenly, everyone in the crowd turned their heads toward Kylee. Even Brysen snapped his head around, and she covered her mouth with her hands.

She hadn't meant to, but when the ghost eagle cried out in agony, she'd laughed very, very loud.

4

BRYSEN'S EYE FIXED FIRM ON HER THROUGH THE SURROUNDING crowd, his forehead furrowed. His thick gray hair was grown out long enough to pull back behind his ears, but it still stood up, wild from sleep, and he stood out, shirtless in the crowd, in a way he never before would have dreamed.

Until Jowyn came into his life, Brysen was always afraid to let anyone see his chest and back. The left side of his body was covered in burn scars, from below the waist of his pants up to his neck. His back was a crisscross of whip scars and burns, woven in a pattern tighter than the Six's defensive nets.

Now, though, in this new world the ghost eagles had thrust upon them, he didn't seem the slightest bit concerned about anyone seeing him. If he'd not been wearing pants when he heard about the eagle, he'd probably be standing naked in the street without a second thought. Not everything that happened since the ghost eagles laid their wrath on humanity was awful, though Brysen's newfound body confidence probably wasn't a fair trade for the end of the world as they knew it.

You're at our mercy, she thought at the ghost eagle. *Tell me what you want from us.*

She hoped it could still see her thoughts. Lesser birds of prey could see heat coming off their quarry's body, but ghost eagles could see the thoughts in the minds of their prey— their hopes and fears, their memories. And they could twist them. A ghost eagle could drive a person mad before devouring them, *if* they chose to devour their victims at all. Alone among predators, the ghost eagles killed for sport.

Well, not among all predators. Humans did, too.

"REEEEEE!" the ghost eagle screamed, injured and afraid. Its wing was broken, and a matte-black foot was bent in the wrong direction with a talon the length of a hand dangling from a single bloody sinew. In its panic, the ghost eagle was crying out and sharing thoughts it couldn't control.

Kylee saw blades slashing feather and flesh. She saw pyres burning on icy slopes, bodies piled high in the flames. She also saw a six-talon whip cracking across her brother's back, saw her father's ice-blue eyes watching her witness Brysen's punishment. The ghost eagle was mixing its pain with her own, and Kylee wasn't sure where its memories stopped and hers started. She felt what it felt, and it, in turn, felt what she felt.

She wanted it out of her head. Just because it lost control didn't mean she had to.

"*Iryeem*," she said to the bird. The Hollow Tongue word meant *mercy*, but she was not asking for mercy. She was *offering* it.

The bird's big black eye, as large as a baby's fist, blinked at her, looked her up and down. It knew her, had known her all her life. She'd do anything to protect the people she loved and had no intention of forgiving the ghost eagle for a lifetime of manipulation and suffering, but if the ghost eagle pulled itself together, told her something she could use to end the nightly attacks, then she would end its pain. It was a trade. In exchange for humanity's chance at life, she would give this one a merciful death.

"*Iryeem*," she offered again. To speak the Hollow Tongue in a way that a bird of prey could understand, you had to mean it. It had to be your absolute truth. The bird knew she meant it. She thought of the place from her dream, the place she and Brysen had both seen. She knew where those footsteps were headed. She didn't need the dream to show her. She just knew. *What is in that place?* she wondered. *Why there?*

"REEEEEE!" the ghost eagle cried, and she flinched. She

40

didn't see snow or footprints or blades or blood. She saw Ma and Da, and they were younger, and each held a baby. Her scuzzard of a father had a smile on his face as he looked down at the swaddled infant in his arms. She felt a sudden swell of pure, unconditional love.

Brysen must see it, too. He looked absolutely startled. The bird's black eye brightened. It believed, Kylee knew, that it had done what she'd wanted. It believed it had shown her something useful.

But she hated riddles and wanted to rip its wings off. The vision vanished.

"Well, now the whole flock of filthy fledgling feather lovers is here," a thick-set older man shouted at Kylee, his voice loud enough to be heard through the wax in everyone's ears.

His face was red and puffy from drink, and his teeth were green from hunter's leaf. He didn't look like an ex-warrior, but she didn't recognize him, so he wasn't from the Six Villages. Maybe he was a trader who'd renounced his ways or an Altari long-hauler who'd finally found a community in which he could thrive, a place where it was safe to openly hate the people he'd always hated in secret. The hate between Altari and Uztari had always existed, but the collapse of Uztari society and the emergence of an extremist stronghold had given people like him free rein to speak openly—at least within the boundaries of the Mutes.

The man wore a red cloth on his left hand, wrapped around the palm and wrist. The red cloth was a symbol of loyalty to the lost Kartami cause, a visual reference to cutting off every falconer's fist. The cloth was a promise that, even in defeat, they had not given up their gruesome goals. They called themselves Redfists.

"And they brought their battle boys!" the red-fisted man exclaimed. "Y'all know these bird-battling gangsters are the reason we pay double for a drink?"

The crowd grumbled. Kylee saw dozens more red-wrapped fists in the throng, pressing in from all sides. The ghost eagle squirmed where it dangled in the net. Someone threw a rock that hit its broken wing.

More people arrived, surrounding Kylee's small group. Someone shoved at her shoulder. Someone else pushed Grazim into her. Jowyn made a move to get through the crowd, to Brysen, but Kylee put her hand out, stopped him. She shook her head a tiny bit, warning him not to do anything that might provoke the crowd.

It wasn't just for safety's sake—the ghost eagle was communicating, but these people were just a slight breeze away from hacking it to pieces. A dead ghost eagle could tell Kylee nothing about the convocation's plans, about their vulnerabilities, about how to defeat them. A dead ghost eagle was useless, but a *trapped* one was at their mercy. She had to learn what she could before the crowd killed it or before it tried to kill them. She had to get past its riddles.

Tell me more, she thought.

"REEEEE!" the eagle cried, and Kylee heard its voice inside her head.

Free us and I'll cut them all down for you. Free us and you'll fear no one ever again.

She knew the bird was lying. It might indeed do what it promised, but she would always have *it* to fear. It was not Kylee's servant—that much she had learned. Ghost eagles could use the truth to tell terrible lies, and they were on no one's side but their own.

Free us, she thought, curious about its use of the plural *us* instead of the singular *me*. This bird was part of a flock; maybe its thoughts were, too. In communicating with one ghost eagle, was she communicating with all of them? If she killed this one, she wondered, what would the others feel?

"REEEEEE!" the bird screeched, and Kylee pictured open skies, the feeling of soaring so high that her back was warmed by starlight. She felt herself gliding and diving and spreading her wings. She wanted to whoop with joy.

But it wasn't her joy. This was a ghost eagle, thrilling at the dive, diving straight for a small group of travelers somewhere in the foothills. She recognized one of them: her best friend, Nyall, far away and totally exposed.

The ghost eagle was threatening her. She'd scared it. This was interesting. When one bird hurt, they all hurt. Killing one wouldn't stop the whole—by sharing one mind, they made sure no one ghost eagle mattered more than any of the others—but that didn't mean the agony of losing one didn't matter. Knowing how to hurt the ghost eagles gave Kylee power. She had to figure out how to use it.

Just then, the puffy Redfist snatched a big battle spear someone else had been holding, the kind the Kartami had hurled from their war barrows before the ghost eagles tore their kites from the sky. The Redfist aimed the speartip at the ghost eagle's left eye and stabbed.

"REEEEEEE!" The ghost eagle released a cry so loud, not even the wax plugs could stop it, and everyone flinched, including Kylee. Her left eye filled with tears. This was not a trick; this was agony, whipping through her consciousness like a tornado. The ghost eagle couldn't help but share its pain, the spear still protruding from its eye socket.

Unlike before, it was Brysen who didn't flinch this time. This was a pain he'd already felt, already survived—his left eye had been cut out by the Kartami's leader, Anon, who was dead now. Brysen spun around to look up at the bird, his scar-crossed back facing Kylee, his arms raised. He said something Kylee couldn't make out, and the eagle calmed.

Brysen was sharing his own calm with the bird. "*Shessele*," he repeated.

"No, Bry!" Kylee shouted at him, but he ignored her and leaned in, whispered so she couldn't hear. Ever since the ghost eagles had spoken through him on the battlefield, he'd known fragments of the Hollow Tongue that not even Kylee and Grazim knew, though they had studied with the Owl Mothers, who knew more of the Hollow Tongue than anyone. He knew words that could calm a panicked bird, words that could ease its aching body, words that could heal a broken wing. Kylee had only ever used the Hollow Tongue to kill.

As he whispered, the eagle thrashed. Suddenly it broke from the net, shaking loose the spearpoint from its skull and flapping its mighty wings.

Healed.

"REEE REEE REEE!" the bird cried out, and it was grateful, but it was also smug. It was the one laughing now, as people scattered for cover.

Brysen stood below it, looking up at its wide wings beating against the golden morning sun, its black talons pointed down like it might seize him by the throat and finally take him away.

Finally? Kylee thought. Why would she think *finally*, as though it was inevitable that the ghost eagle would take Brysen, as though it was just a matter of time?

"Let's get out of here!" Nyck shouted, taking Kylee's hand. Jowyn ran for Brysen and grabbed him by the shoulders, pushed him forward so they could use the chaos of the ghost eagle's sudden freedom to get away from the Mutes before someone tried to show the sunlight all their insides.

"Leaving so soon, chickadees?"

The same puffy-faced Redfist stood in their way, flanked by the two teens who'd taunted Nyck before. The man had lost his spear but was wielding a jagged sword, and the two teens still had their spears from the war, clean and sharp and keen.

Kylee looked up to see the ghost eagle flap high, turn, and glide away, toward the nearby mountains.

"*Kraas*," she called after it. "*Raakrah!*" They were Hollow Tongue words for *kill* and *hunt*—words that worked for her in the past—but the bird flew away, unheeding. They'd get no help from above. They were on their own below.

Kylee pulled the curved black-talon blade from her belt. The knife had been her brother's, and before that it had been their father's, and now it was hers. It was the very blade the Kartami had used to take Brysen's eye. Brysen had been good with the blade, but he didn't want it anymore. They should've just gotten rid of the wretched thing, but Kylee'd had a feeling its work wasn't yet done, and she was glad for keeping it now.

"Bry, you really know how to start a morning," Nyck declared. The battle boys fanned out around them. "Couldn't you and Jowyn have just stayed in bed and snuggled or something?"

"Hey, I tried," Jowyn objected. "I'd do nothing but snuggle if the sky would let me."

"Don't blame the sky for Brysen's stupidity," Grazim snapped at him.

"Trying to help someone in need isn't stupid," Jowyn said back.

"The ghost eagles are not *someone*," Grazim told him.

"Sorry." Brysen finally spoke, his voice so quiet the others couldn't possibly have heard through their earplugs, but Kylee heard. "I had to."

"I know you *think* you did," she said.

"We can't kill our way out of this war," he told her, his eye darting from Redfist to Redfist.

"Maybe not this war," she grunted, "but definitely this alley."

5

THE TWO KARTAMI TEENS FANNED OUT FROM THE REDFIST WITH THE
sword, trying to flank Kylee's group. The crowd that scattered
when the ghost eagle broke free was returning, circling to
watch the fight, though some ignored the impending violence
and set directly to mending the net where the ghost eagle
broke it.

Grazim cursed. With the only possible opening to the sky
closing, their advantage was closed off, too. Grazim was bigger than Kylee, taller and thicker than Kylee, too, but she
didn't have much talent for physical fights. With her command of the Hollow Tongue, she saw no point in mastering
any other kind of combat.

Kylee, on the other hand, knew that creatures of the sky were unreliable allies. Sometimes a person could count on only two things: their own fists and the friends fighting beside them.

Kylee, Grazim, Jowyn, Brysen, Nyck, and his battle boys could probably cut through these three attackers, but Kylee had no doubt that the moment the fighting started, they'd find the entire Mutes rising against them. There were plenty of ex-warriors in the district who lost loved ones to Kylee and Grazim during the siege of the Six Villages, and plenty more had lost loved ones to the battle boys, who fought on the barricades. This wouldn't just be a random act of mob violence; this was revenge. Kylee wondered if, somehow, this encounter had been planned.

No, she thought. *Brysen came here on his own because of the ghost eagle. How could the Redfists plan for that?*

They couldn't, she realized.

But the ghost eagles could.

"Scuzz," she said out loud.

They'd been sent here just like a hawk from a tamer's fist. *Why* the ghost eagles would send them recklessly into the Mutes for a bloody brawl was a question for another time. The only question for the moment was how to get out of there.

A quick glance over the crowd revealed small weapons in red-wrapped fists. Tiny blunt-handled katar blades, thin stiletto daggers, metal clubs, carved bone knuckles, and six-talon whips—just like Da had been fond of using on Brysen's back.

Grazim and Nyck were taking in their surroundings, too. They both signaled a question to Kylee with their eyes: *Are we doing this?*

They couldn't kill their way out. They might neutralize a few of the people here, but they were outnumbered, deep in a hostile area. They'd never get out alive. And to fight would be to play exactly into the ghost eagle's plans—something Kylee refused to do.

Kylee hated this ability, her talent for quickly imagining the cascading consequences behind every action. It was a result of growing up with a brother who never thought about consequences and a father whose temper was violent and capricious. Brysen knew he'd be beaten no matter what he did, so he surrendered to the chaos, embraced it, even. Kylee always believed she could fix things, so she thought through every possible outcome and tried to mitigate the worst ones, always searching for some path to safety, if only she could find it.

She rarely found it, but she never stopped trying.

She belted her blade.

"Ky?" Nyck cocked his head at her.

"Put away your weapons," she told them.

Grazim's frown bent deep as an eagle's beak. Her fists were still balled, not that they'd have done much good.

The teens with their spears grinned. The Redfist spat a green glob on the ground and took a step forward. These three would have no hesitation in cutting down unarmed teenagers.

"We all live together in the Six now," Kylee told them. "We're going to have to learn to get along until the ghost eagles' siege is over. Why not start today?"

"This siege is your fault," the Redfist sneered. "You and your grub-sucking brother called down this curse upon all of us. Maybe if we kill you two, the ghost eagles'll leave us alone."

"If the ghost eagles wanted my brother and me dead, they'd have done it themselves by now. They've had plenty of chances."

"Maybe they want *us* to do it," the man said. "To prove we're worthy."

"It's dangerous to presume you know what the ghost eagles want," Jowyn interjected, "or that you could even begin to understand their minds."

Kylee kept to herself that the man might be completely correct. Even without access to the eagles' thoughts, he'd reached the same conclusion she had: The ghost eagles had created this situation on purpose.

"No one's talking to you, owl boy." The man spat again. "Go back to sucking sap from a rotten tree."

"Only a fool thinks a blessing is a slur," Jowyn answered calmly. "I'm proud of what I am and what the Owl Mothers made me."

"Throw a parade, then," the man grunted. "Doesn't mean you're welcome here. No wing-worshippers in the Mutes."

Around them, more knives were drawn from belts and robes. People pressed in closer.

"We trust you and all that, Kylee," Nyck said with a quiver in his voice. "But what's the plan?"

Jowyn stepped in front of Brysen slightly, as if a spear couldn't punch through both of them. Brysen then jostled to get in front of the pale boy, each of them trying to be the one to protect the other. Kylee didn't much understand lust and romance and all her brother's sweaty heartache, but this kind of loyalty she understood. She'd have stood in front of all of them if she could.

Instead, she made an offer.

"Let them *all* go," she said, "and I'll surrender to you."

"Who asked for surrender?" The Redfist took another step forward, flexed his fingers in the red fabric that gripped his sword hilt. "We want your heads in the mud, not your knees on the ground."

"You'll win that fight," Kylee said. "I mean 'you' *plural* will win." She looked at the angry crowd around them. "But *you*, specifically . . ." She locked eyes with the Redfist. "I will slit your neck open from ear to ear before they take me down, and then I'll shove that red rag so far down your open throat, you'll suffocate before you bleed out. I promise you that."

She couldn't do any of that, of course. She was making empty threats, but threats were pretty much the only negotiating tool she had. The man's sneer faltered.

The two teenage warriors beside him, however, weren't so easily intimidated.

"I don't think so," one of them said, and, without further preamble, threw their spear straight for her.

It was like time slowed. She saw the teen's muscles twitch, a ripple that extended from their thigh, up their side, to their throwing arm as it unwound and loosed the spear. The morning light gleamed off the spear tip as it flew toward her, slicing through air that suddenly felt thick as ice. Her own motions moved just as slowly; she flinched first, then prepared to dodge as Grazim and Brysen moved to protect her. Nyck switched his footing to knock her out of the way. Brysen lurched forward to shove her down. The other battle boys raised their blades to attack. None of them was moving fast enough. Kylee knew by the thud-thump of her heart that the three beats it took for the spear to reach her would be her last.

Thud-thump.

Thud-thump.

This must be how human movements look to ghost eagles, she thought. *So slow, so helpless.* An entire species trudging through mud, while the wide-winged birds soared above it all, dove and killed with the ease of a shadow falling at sunrise.

But a streak of white cut the thick air, emitting a loud *thwack* as the spear was knocked off course, which sent the crowd diving out of its path.

A pure-white gyrfalcon swooped up to the roof of the nearest wood-slat shack and perched there, tucking the foot it had just banged on the spear under itself. Its face snapped around to take in the crowd, the district, the net just above its head that severed it—and protected it—from the sky.

There was another heartbeat of slack-jawed silence, and then came a high squeal as three tiny kestrels sliced through the Mutes, circled the crowd, and perched opposite the gyr-falcon. A heavy-bodied tailor's hawk and a juvenile osprey flapped in next, then a half dozen hawks of different breeds and two more true falcons. Finally a tired, old berkut—a common golden eagle, as much like a ghost eagle as a mouse is like a bear, but still, a big bird with fearsome talons—set itself down on the ground right in front of Kylee. It tucked back its wings and lowered its head, side-eyeing the crowd like an ornery shopkeeper peering over a jar of candied ginger while children fogged the milk glass with their breath.

You? Kylee mouthed to Grazim, who shook her head. Kylee hadn't called these birds of prey. She hadn't even known there were this many birds of prey left in the Six Villages. They all wore dog-leather jesses on their ankles, and some had small brass bells that jingled when they moved. These were not wild birds. These were trained birds of the army of Uztar.

And now that they were here, Kylee and Grazim could command them.

The crowd backed away, tripping over one another to escape; Kylee's fame had its advantages. At her command, the ghost eagle had murdered hundreds, and no one quite knew the limits of her power.

"*Shyehnaah,*" she said, and every bird flexed and prepared to launch, as if for a hunt, then waited for her next command. "What do you think?" she asked Grazim, forcing her voice to sound casual.

Grazim picked up Kylee's cue, her tone easy. "We could take an eye from every one of them as an homage." She glanced at Brysen.

Brysen snorted. He'd always had a dark sense of humor.

"Or," Grazim continued, "a lot of Hollow Tongue commands would do here. There are words for *disembowel*, for

55

exsanguinate, and, of course"—she smiled at the puffy-faced Redfist in front of them—"for *castrate*. It's a creative language. I'm sure we could even combine a few."

The crowd backed off farther. The Kartami teens breathed loudly through their noses, one of them glaring at Nyck but then lowering their spear and tightening the red cloth around their fist.

Nyck blew that one a kiss.

"We walk away from here unharmed, and so do all of you," Kylee said. "It's that simple. We don't need to do the ghosts eagles' work for them, do we?"

She looked up at the nets, which made the whole village feel like a birdcage. Did the ghost eagles simply want humanity to exterminate itself? And, if so, could Kylee and her little band of misfits stop that from happening?

They could, at least for today. When the food ran lower and the fear grew hotter, they might not be able to, but for now, the crowd was parting.

"*Caleen*," Grazim whispered, and as one, the birds of prey took off, flapping just above their heads, scattering the crowd but not diving to attack. Kylee and her friends walked forward, paving a path through the crowd. As the group made their way, each bird simply flew alongside, moving from one perch to the next, escorting them through the maze of alleyways until they finally reached the district's boundary.

"I thought *caleen* meant *chase* or *pursue*," Kylee whispered to Grazim as they walked under the mounted war barrow that marked the edge of the district. The lookouts had retreated inside for cover, but Kylee was certain they were still watching, so she covered her mouth while she spoke, not wanting anyone to hear that her grasp on Hollow Tongue vocabulary was not quite up to the threats she'd issued.

"Words carry all sorts of weight," Grazim said. "I figure the only difference between *chasing* and *escorting* is intensity and intention, so I adjusted both."

"You're more poet than I thought you were," Kylee told her.

"All hunters are poets," Grazim replied, then bumped into Nyck's back when he and his battle boys stopped short in front of her.

"Some people just don't appreciate poetry," Nyck said.

Blocking every path and alley and rooftop beneath the netting—not including the route back into the Mutes—stood armed soldiers of Uztar, weapons drawn and gloved hands raised, expecting their birds of prey to return to them.

"Kyrg Birgund would like to see you," an officer announced.

6

"THE KYRG DOES NOT APPRECIATE YOU SNEAKING AROUND AND inciting violence." The officer looked over the battle boys. "Your criminal activity is tolerated as long as it does not cause real trouble."

"You call this real trouble?" Nyck puffed up with as much bravado as he could. "Nobody even got a bloody nose!"

"Shh," Kylee hushed him.

The officer stepped forward without the slightest fear of the battle boys, Grazim, Kylee, or the flock of raptors fluttering behind them. She wore thin, padded armor that had been patched in places, and on her left hand was a long falconer's glove, the leather grown shiny with use. Her belt was slung with knives, and she carried a heavy alloy mace strapped across her back. This was not show armor for a rear-guard officer—she'd seen combat. She had probably been on the battlefield when Kylee summoned the ghost eagle to massacre them, and when Brysen had somehow summoned hundreds more. A scar ran from her hairline to her collarbone. Its thickness was, in fact, close to that of a ghost eagle's talon.

"I am Ser Ygeva, lieutenant to Kyrg Birgund. After you release our birds back to us," she ordered, "you will follow us to the Broken Jess."

Ygeva whistled, and the berkut, perched on an upturned war barrow behind them, shook out its feathers. It looked at Kylee and Grazim, torn between the command of the primal Hollow Tongue language and a whistle from the master who'd tamed and trained her.

Grazim's eyes narrowed, and Kylee could tell she, too, was torn between her former loyalty to the army of Uztar and her extreme dislike of being told what to do.

Kylee, however, was determined to avoid bloodshed today. She needed everything to settle down if she was going to go to the place the trapped ghost eagle had shown her. She needed peace and quiet to figure out what it meant, but not the kind she'd find locked up in a kyrg's cell.

And after what she'd seen of Nyall, who was somewhere out on the open plains, she needed to move quickly. She wouldn't be able to keep him safe until she had leverage over these vicious birds, and to get that, she had to know what they wanted from her.

"*Fliss*," she said, releasing the army's raptors, who flew all at once to their startled tamers' fists, like crows frightened from a tree. It was an easy command, but the sudden explosion of feathers looked impressive, and she liked how the soldiers behind Ser Ygeva all flinched.

Kylee did not hate that people were afraid of her. She did not hate it at all.

"I . . . I have to . . . I don't feel well." Brysen suddenly groaned and pressed his palms against his temples, swaying on his feet as though he might pass out.

Oh, for cloud's sake, what was her brother doing now?

Jowyn immediately put a hand on Brysen's back to steady him. "You okay?"

Brysen gave a sad little nod, staring at his feet. "I just need to go home."

Kylee kept her face blank as she watched her brother, who stood on unsteady legs. The knee wobble was a bit much, in her opinion. Brysen was not a great actor, and this particular performance was one of his worst. Overwrought and cliché. No one who was actually sick acted like this. His overacting was like that of lovers in the popular tales churned out by story-sellers, always sighing and arching their eyebrows at each other.

The officer sighed and arched her eyebrows. "You're ill?"

"It's the strain of the morning," Brysen said pitifully. "I have to rest."

What is he up to? Kylee arched her own eyebrows, realized she was doing it, and set her face blank again. Was he trying to get away from the soldiers or from her? Was he going to follow the footprints in the dream without her? If so, what did he think he'd find there?

She tried to recall the details, to parse the images that had filled her dreams and his, but already they felt distant and hazy. Had there been a wing in the snow? Were the footprints leading *into* the mountains or down away from them? She wasn't much for remembering dreams and, like Grazim, had never taken them seriously before. She wished she'd just come clean with Brysen this morning so they could've talked about it together. Trusting him might've been the smarter choice, but Kylee needed to feel like she was in control, and anyway, it was too late now. Wherever he was going, it would be without her.

"You may take him," Ygeva said to Jowyn as if Brysen wasn't even there, dismissing them with a wave of her hand. "Your presence is not required."

"I hope Kyrg Birgund won't miss me too badly," Brysen added with a little too much bite. Even when feigning sickness, he couldn't resist snark. He and the kyrg had about as much love for each other as a river snake has for an osprey, though both probably thought themselves the osprey in this scenario.

"He's working very hard to forget you exist," the officer told Brysen. "Feel lucky you don't occupy more of his thoughts. He could have you in chains before sunset if he chose."

"Better men than him have tried to put me in chains." Brysen grinned, leaving behind the ruse of being sick altogether. "And I've even enjoyed it."

"Go," the officer snapped, and Brysen gave her a winged salute, thumbs hooked and fingers outstretched across his chest. Jowyn pulled him back and led him by the arm through the soldiers, who made no effort to move out of their way. Brysen made some effort to bump into as many of them as he could.

"Apologies," he muttered to each of them as he crashed his shoulders into their outstretched falcon arms, making the birds flap and screech at their tamers. "My eye . . . oops . . . my bad . . . my eye, you know?"

Kylee's jaw dropped a little. Her brother had lost his eye no more than a moon's turning ago, and he was already using the injury to annoy people he didn't like. Kylee'd have been impressed with the resilience of her brother's obnoxiouness if the people he was very obviously bumping on purpose weren't armed and looking for reasons to kill him.

Ser Ygeva stared straight ahead, stone-faced, waiting for Brysen to finish his show of leaving and working very hard not to give in to how much he was succeeding at annoying her.

"My eye . . . oops . . . apologies . . . my eye . . . war injury . . . oops . . . sorry . . . my eye . . ."

Kylee offered the officer a silent shrug, as if to say, *What can you do? Brothers, am I right?* She watched Brysen leave, hoping he wouldn't do anything else stupid that morning. She wanted a chance to talk to him later, to share what they knew, to work together instead of at arm's length from each other.

When Brysen was gone and the jostled soldiers and birds were calm again, Ygeva addressed Kylee. "Now, perhaps the rest of you would join us without all the drama?"

Kylee looked at the others, who gave her quick nods, and she gestured for the officer to lead the way. They followed Ygeva back through the winding streets and switchbacks and lanes of the vast shantytown that the Six had become. The Uztari falconers walked behind and among them, giving her no chance to talk with her friends.

While they walked, Kylee marveled at how she hardly recognized the Six Villages anymore. Devastating attacks from above had unleashed a flurry of creativity; new structures had risen, new business had flourished, and new slang had wormed its way into the everyday cacophony of the streets.

"You put that spoon down or I'll tie you to the wrong side of the nets!" someone yelled inside a patchwork shanty that smelled like boiled river moss.

"Your heart's black as a ghost eagle's talon!" the alleged spoon thief replied.

"Mud-biter!"

"Worm-worshipper!"

"Put it down or I'll tell the Redfists where to find you!"

"Take that back!"

"Put the spoon back!"

"Make me!"

The overcrowding had shortened tempers.

Kylee was surprised when they turned a corner and she found herself standing at the gates of the Broken Jess.

"I hate what you've done to the place," Nyck grumbled. He'd basically lived at the Broken Jess since leaving home as a child. He'd run the petty gambling operation at the battle pits for Goryn Tamir and had worked his way up to undisputed leader of his own little gang. The Broken Jess was the first place he'd been able to be himself and the first place he'd thrived, in his own unethical way. It must have hurt to see it turned into a military camp, run by people who wouldn't have even let him through the gate if he weren't with Kylee.

"There's still ale and hunter's leaf," Ser Ygeva said. She pulled a soft piece of slate from a rucksack and broke off a few chips, each engraved with Kyrg Birgund's seal. Military money. Vouchers they could use to keep order without spending bronze or anything of actual value. She handed the chips to Nyck and gestured to a tent surrounded by barrels. It was guarded by red-eyed soldiers holding red-eyed hawks on their fists. "Help yourself."

Nyck and the other battle boys hesitated, looked to Kylee.

"I'll be fine," she said. "Go."

Nyck, Lyra, and Kheryn left them as the officer led Kylee and Grazim inside the main stone building.

The central hall was the same as it had been before: long tables arranged in the middle, perches for birds behind the tables, with more cages along the far wall. Casks of ale and sacks of food were piled high below the balconies of what were once private booths. Those booths were now officers' billets.

They stopped at the bottom of twisted stairs leading up to a door. Kylee knew well where that door led. Beyond it was a small chamber attached to a pulley system. It lowered into a vaulted room below the Broken Jess, a room that had been the private office of the gangster Goryn Tamir.

Thanks to Kylee and Brysen, Goryn was now a prisoner of the Sky Castle; his sister, Yves Tamir, had been run off into the wilderness; and his mother, Cynari Tamir, erstwhile ruler of the Six Villages, had caught her last breeze in the talons of a ghost eagle. Still, even without the Tamirs, Kylee knew nothing good ever happened in fortified underground rooms.

On instinct, as they climbed the stairs and stepped into the dark chamber, Kylee reached back to take her brother's hand, forgetting he wasn't there. A quick glance at Grazim was met with a frown. They were friends, but they were more I'll-gut-your-enemies-and-watch-them-bleed-out-beside-you friends rather than I'll-hold-your-hand friends.

Kylee held her own hand, fingers laced together, as the chamber's inner cage slammed shut and the small room clanked and clattered down the shaft.

They passed the wall niche that held the gear crank. Soldiers turned it slowly, eyeing them as they slid by. The cage came to a shuddering stop, and the door slid open. Where Goryn held brutal banquets for attendants and hangers-on, Kyrg Birgund had set up a secure administrative outpost, neatly divided by curtains. He'd built mews to hold more trained raptors safely underground, where they could neither escape nor be attacked. Kylee recognized heavy chests from the military campaign. She knew they were filled with bronze. There were extra stores of food, water, ale, and weaponry, too. Most of the thick rugs on which Goryn entertained his guests—and under which he suffocated his prisoners—were rolled up and standing along the walls. Somehow, the simple efficiency of the space was just as frightening as the cruel opulence that filled it before.

A room was like a word, weighted with history and tethered to intention. This room had a history of torture and still held the same intention as always. It was a place in which to wield power.

As they entered, Kylee noticed that all the birds of prey in the room were caged and that a tamer stood beside each cage. She cast another look at Grazim, who nodded quickly. This wasn't a hand-holding look. This was a look that made its message quite clear to Kylee: Her friend was already plotting how to get one of those cages open.

They're scared of what we can do, Kylee thought. *Good.*

7

"DID YOU EAT BREAKFAST?" KYRG BIRGUND ROSE FROM HIS FIELD desk as they stood in the middle of the floor. He gestured to a rug where a feast was laid out: fresh flatbread with flameberry jam, an assortment of butter and cream that told of easy access to milk-producing animals, herb-crusted eggs, grain-stuffed greens dusted with chili powder, crisp-charred beans, and even some kind of meaty stew spiced with cardamom, which Kylee knew did not grow around the villages. "Young people need to eat."

One of their stomachs rumbled loudly, and Kylee was mortified to realize it was her own. Thanks to Brysen's escapade, she hadn't eaten breakfast, and the morning's events had made her hungry. But she knew that men like Kyrg Birgund didn't offer anything out of generosity. This meal wasn't a gift from a powerful adult to a hungry kid; this was a morsel from a tamer trying to bend a hawk to his will.

Kylee would not be bent, nor tamed. She declined.

The kyrg had access to smuggled food and was showing off. That meant he also had access to messages, incoming and out-going, and he might know what was going on back at the Sky Castle. He might know where Nyall was. He might even be able to send a message to him. That fact alone made him worth hearing out. That fact also made him dangerous. He wasn't nearly as cut off from the rest of the world as he seemed.

"Where's the boy?" one of the kyrg's valets sneered.

"You mean my brother?" Kylee answered coolly. "He wasn't feeling well, and Jowyn took him home."

The valet made a face like a sour apple—not like someone eating a sour apple but like the apple itself, bruised and shriv-eled and tart. "He should show more respect."

She ignored the valet and spoke directly to the kyrg. "Did you bring me here to talk about my brother's manners? Because I can promise you, after seventeen ice-wind seasons, he's not going to learn. You'd have more luck teaching a rooster a starling's song."

Kyrg Birgund snorted a small laugh. "It's best the boy hasn't joined us. He's never been much for delicate discussion, and this discussion demands . . ."

"Delicacies?" Kylee suggested with a gesture at the food.

"Relax," he told her. "We're all on the same side here. The ghost eagles are as much a threat to you as to the rest of us."

"Are you sure of that?" she offered, raising her eyebrows in just as theatrical a way as she could. The kyrg didn't say anything, and in his pause, Kylee felt her advantage grow. So what if she had no idea what the ghost eagles wanted or what they would do to her if given the chance? The kyrg didn't need to know that. "Anyway, you summoned us?"

"A thank-you would be appropriate." Birgund smiled at her, his grin like the talons of a hawk squeezing life from a hare. "I didn't have to risk my soldiers or their birds to save you this morning. I imagine the Mutes can get quite nasty for people as recognizable as yourselves."

"You did it for a reason," Kylee told him. "Or perhaps you've just grown fonder of us now that you've made yourself a home here in the Six?"

The kyrg's smile held but twitched at the edges. He was not a man used to defiance, and he had found nothing but defiance from Kylee since the moment she'd entered his life. She figured he would at least be used to it by now, but some people just can't let go of the status they think they've earned merely by existing. Kylee owed this man no respect and would offer him only the bare minimum of cooperation until she found out what he wanted.

"I am doing my best to keep order and safety here," he said. "You are not helping."

"Not our job," Kylee said.

The kyrg addressed Grazim directly: "You had, as I recall, wanted a seat on the Council? As the first Altari ever to be named a kyrg? Wasn't that your hope and your arrangement with the proctor?" Grazim sucked in her breath, hearing her own dreams spoken to her so plainly. "Of course, you failed your end of the bargain, keeping this one"—he waved the back of his hand at Kylee—"under control."

"I did as the situation demanded," Grazim said, betraying no sense of their new friendship or her loyalty to it, if such loyalty existed. Kylee began to wonder.

"It is, of course, possible to make amends," the kyrg continued, taking a bite of jam-coated flatbread and smacking his lips. Crumbs caught in his rough beard. "For both of you."

"I don't see what amends I have to make," Kylee told him.

"You don't?" The kyrg set the flatbread down and wiped his hands on a silk kerchief from his pocket. He looked at his feet and seemed to be . . . laughing? "You don't think you have any amends to make? For anything?" He looked up at her, and there was hate in his eyes, the kind of hate that burrows like worms into the laughter of cruel men. "You, who brought all this upon us, who summoned the ghost eagle and lost control, who inflicted your brother's lovesick stupidity on our entire civilization? Where are your tears for the dead children of this war? Or is their love not equal to the love you hold for your brother? Is your family more special than theirs, your story the only one under this blasted sky that matters?" His face was turning red as he yelled. "Your brother is a fool, which is almost forgivable, but *you*! Your entitlement and self-centered rage sickens me! You have no idea what it is to command an army, to take their lives into your hands and know that some will be lost based on every calculation you make. You're a petulant child who didn't get her way and has damned us all because of it, and yet you have the *audacity* to stand before *me* and say you have no amends to make! NONE!"

Kylee found that she was cringing in spite of herself, inchworming backward, toward the chamber door that was closed tight behind her. The birds of prey in their cages began rousing and screeching as the walls echoed with the kyrg's bellowing.

"You could spend the rest of your life making amends and never come close to easing the pain you have inflicted on Uztar!"

"It wasn't me," Kylee said, hating herself for how weak her voice sounded. "It was the ghost eagles."

She felt tears pressing against her eyes and fought them back. She cried when she was frustrated or angry, and it was a foolish man who took her tears for weakness.

"You're crying now?" The foolish man in front of her shook his head. "So defiant when there are talons to do the killing for you, but without them? Here you are, crying. Maybe I should have brought your brother down here."

Patience, Kylee told herself. *If we're patient, he'll reveal what he wants.* Desire can be both a source of strength and a source of weakness. *We're not so different from the ghost eagles*, she thought. *They're just better at this.*

"What do you want from me?" she asked him, wiping her eyes.

"You can still serve the Council of Forty," he said. "Your talents are still required."

"And why do you require our talents?" Grazim asked, uncrossing her arms and softening her stance. She remained fond as ever of having her talents admired, even by people she hated. Perhaps especially by people she hated. Kylee tried to catch her eye, to warn her from showing too much eagerness.

"Thirty-eight," Kylee interrupted their conversation.

"Excuse me?"

"Thirty-eight," she repeated. "The Council of Forty is down to thirty-eight. I helped remove Kyrg Ryven for treason, if you'll recall, and you are now stuck here with me. So it's a council of thirty-eight in the Sky Castle."

"They are *called* the Council of Forty," Birgund grunted.

"You'll excuse us if we're particular about words' meanings," Kylee told him. "We know the power that words can have when spoken accurately."

"I am not going to get into a semantic argument with some village girl and her Altari heretic," he said, giving Grazim a withering look. It didn't matter how powerful Grazim became, nor how much she lived like an Uztari. With that look, Birgund made it clear that Grazim would never belong among them.

Idiot, Kylee thought. *You could've driven a wedge between us, but with every sneer you keep Grazim on my side.*

"If you would like our help with something, perhaps you should show some goodwill to us," Kylee suggested.

"Goodwill?" Birgund brushed his hands along his formal officer's robe. "Do you have any suggestions?"

"Release my friend Nyall from the dungeons beneath the Sky Castle," Kylee said.

"That will not be possible," he replied.

"And why not?" Kylee demanded. "I see you've been able to get food from the outside, so you can certainly send a message. You want my help? Release my friend from your dungeons."

"It is not possible," the kyrg said, "because he already escaped."

Kylee couldn't help flinching this time. If Nyall was no longer in a cell, then what the ghost eagle had shown her could be real. He was somewhere in the open, outside the walls and the nets, exposed to threats from above, and if the ghost eagles hadn't already gotten him, he was in grave danger.

"I understand your predicament." The kyrg's voice softened. "You care about certain people and you want them safe, which is why I think you'll like my proposal. The Six Villages are crowded, will soon starve, and are filled to the brim with our enemies."

"The Mutes," Grazim noted.

"We have no duty to protect and support the people who hate us with the limited resources we have," the kyrg explained. "So my proposal is this: My soldiers will secure the perimeter of the Mutes. You and your sneaky little battle boys will cut open the nets, and then you will call down the ghost eagles and eliminate that portion of the population, which we no longer can or will support."

"You want us to murder innocent people?" Grazim grunted. "*That's* your offer?"

"They are hardly innocent"—he kept his eyes on Kylee—"as this morning surely shows."

Kylee stood up straight. She surprised herself by feeling no particular horror or shock at his proposal. She wasn't even surprised.

Birgund pressed his momentum: "It was the people in the Mutes who attacked your home and declared war on the ghost eagles. It was those same people who took your brother's eye, who would happily have gutted him in front of you, and might still. I know you like vengeance, Kylee, and want to protect your family. I am offering you a chance at both, and you'll earn the gratitude of the Council in the process."

"Earned by murdering people you'd rather not deal with when you restore power," Kylee said, "while avoiding any guilt for their extermination yourself."

The kyrg nodded. "That *is* the idea. I can hardly be seen as the people's savior if I personally supervise the murders of thousands. You two, however, will never be seen as saviors anyway. They already hate and fear you. Nothing lost."

"Except thousands of lives," Grazim said. "And our morality."

The kyrg waved his hand, as if neither of those were worth much anyway.

"What if that is exactly what the ghost eagles want?" Kylee asked him. "For us to destroy one another?"

The kyrg shrugged. "I am not going to let the ghost eagles' desires dictate my actions. If they want what I want, then I will use them, just as I will use you. Your motivations aren't my concern, either, as a matter of fact, so long as our empire is protected."

"You saw how easily ghost eagles can turn on you," Kylee said. "They will not be tamed. They're not interested in serving anyone but themselves and their own agenda, which we don't even understand."

"That is why I need you, Kylee," he said. "Anyone could cut open the nets to let death fly free. I need you to keep those dread birds under control and focused on the right people once they are inside."

"How should I do that?" Kylee asked him.

"I can't believe you're considering this!" Grazim exclaimed.

"You'll do it by taking what your brother is after at this very moment," another voice said, and this time, Kylee felt a chill race up the knobs of her spine, like a nightmare climbing a ladder.

Kyrg Ryven stepped out from behind one of the dividing curtains, his bearing just as haughty and graceful as it had been before Kylee foiled his attempted coup and had him thrown in the dungeons. His black clothes were simpler than any he'd worn in the Sky Castle, and he had a bruise on his cheek that had healed to yellow and brown, but he was, otherwise, the same as ever. Kyrg Ryven was the only person besides Kylee and Brysen who could command a ghost eagle. Or, at least, the only person whom the ghost eagles allowed to believe was commanding them.

"Yes," Ryven told her, "I've had some interesting dreams of late myself, and I'd love to discuss them with you."

"But how . . . ?" Kylee began, but she didn't even know what question to start with. Her eyes darted between the treacherous young lord and the self-satisfied general.

"There will be time for questions later," Ryven said. "Right now I want to help you chase your dreams, as they say. Or in this case, chase the ghost eagles' dreams."

Kylee swallowed. "Those aren't the ghost eagles' dreams," she said. "They're its nightmares."

GOING, GOING, GONE

NYALL'S JAILBREAK WAS NOTHING TO GLOAT ABOUT. TECHNICALLY he'd broken out of his cell, dispatched and taken the knife off a guard, and even discovered three high-value prisoners that the proctor of the Council had locked up beside him, but those were just about the last things that broke his way.

His plan had fallen apart nearly the moment they'd stepped out of the dungeons.

He'd opened their cell doors in reverse order of how dangerous he thought they were, starting with Goryn Tamir, former scion of the Six Villages' most powerful family and a self-styled monster. Far from his family and his attendants, half-starved, and wearing ankle chains, Goryn had lost all of the menace he'd once worn like a rooster's crown. He'd jumped at the chance to be Nyall's hostage if it meant going home.

Next Nyall had opened the Owl Mother's cell. Üku had been locked up because of Kylee, and she had no love for Nyall. She was a master of the Hollow Tongue, a leader of her people, and a truly dangerous woman. Nyall had entered her cell quickly and put a heavy leather jailer's hood directly over her head. That way she couldn't call down an owl to attack him the moment they got outside.

Last he'd freed Kyrg Ryven, a deposed lord from the Council of Forty who conspired with Üku to stage a coup. Kylee'd also had him locked up, which was a relief, because Nyall had been irked by the young kyrg's attempts to seduce her. It was some comfort that Kylee had no interest in him, either, but Nyall still didn't like the kyrg's presumptuousness. The moment he had a hood over Ryven's handsome face, he'd knocked it hard into the stone wall.

"Oops, my bad," he'd said. He couldn't make out the fallen nobleman's muffled curses.

With two prisoners hooded and Goryn willing to escort them out of the Sky Castle, Nyall had been confident that he might make it all the way back home unharmed. He'd use Üku to bargain safe passage through the Owl Mother's territory in the blood birch forest, and returning Goryn unchained to his mother back in the Six might buy him some goodwill from the Tamirs, which Nyall figured couldn't hurt. Ryven would stay a prisoner. Kylee would know what to do with him.

The thought of Kylee quickened his heart. He hoped she was okay. Whatever had happened to him because of her, he loved her unconditionally. If the Kartami had captured or killed her, there would be no telling what Nyall would do. He was risking a jailbreak for her, to make sure she was free to do what needed to be done without worrying that he was being held hostage by the Council.

Goryn was able to lead them out of the Sky Castle through a system of tunnels. The man managed a smuggling empire, after all. After what felt like hours, they popped out of a drainage tunnel, easily removing its rusted grate covering. They found themselves on the exterior of the Sky Castle, downslope from its westernmost gate and thankfully at an optimal point from which to begin their trek through the mountains and back toward the Six Villages. The group paused to take a breather; so far it had been slow going with two bound prisoners, and there was steep climbing ahead.

It was morning; the sun was still rising in the sky. At this vantage point, he could nearly see the Six . . .

Suddenly a great, writhing cloud of darkness had come sweeping down from the far mountains, circling the sky over the Six Villages like a giant cyclone of black feathers. Every bird in the vicinity fell into silence. Even from so far away, Nyall knew what that cloud was.

No one had ever seen more than one ghost eagle before. Now there were hundreds in the distant sky.

Nyall felt a lump the size of an ostrich egg in his stomach, then felt that egg crack and splatter in his guts as the huge convocation dropped down upon his hometown like a collapsing eclipse. He couldn't make them out anymore, not across this distance and from where they stood below the cloud line. He couldn't know what horror they were unleashing on every single person he had ever cared about. If Kylee was in control, maybe she'd be okay. Maybe this was the moment they won the war, and he was watching it from afar. But if she'd lost control . . .

From underneath his hood, ex-Kyrg Ryven laughed.

Nyall, without thinking, snatched off the lord's hood and got right into his face. "What's so funny?" he demanded.

The handsome young lord laughed so hard, crow's-feet etched themselves next to his eyes and his body shook. He doubled over like he'd been punched.

"Careful . . . ," Goryn warned Nyall.

"They've done it . . ." Ryven laughed. "They've done it . . ."

"Done what?" Nyall demanded.

Ryven's head snapped up. "They moved us all, like pieces on a game board," he said. "Put everyone where they wanted them for *just* this moment."

"What moment?" Nyall squeezed the hood in his fist. He considered shoving it back onto the deposed kyrg's head and then shoving the deposed kyrg himself off the side of the mountain.

"The moment they spring their trap," he said. "The moment they tear our world apart. Your friend Kylee? She was never in control."

"You lie."

Ryven shrugged. "I don't need to lie."

"Put his hood back on," Goryn told Nyall. "All we can do is keep moving. You and I've got people back in the Six, and the sooner we move, the sooner we can help them."

"Too late," Ryven said, and then, so fast Nyall didn't have time to shut his mouth with a fist—though he did get a punch in after the fact—the kyrg spoke.

"*Tuslaash*," he said before Nyall knocked him off his feet and thrust the hood back on.

At first nothing happened. Goryn and Nyall froze. They listened but only heard the high mountain wind.

Then something fluttered nearby.

Nyall darted his head around, didn't see anything. He listened, but every creature on the mountainside had gone quiet.

Nothing chirped or squawked or sang. The silence unnerved him. What was his world without birdsong in it?

Another flutter. Goryn spun toward the sound but saw nothing.

"We need to get inside somewhere," Nyall said.

"Back into the Sky Castle?" Goryn suggested. "We can hide out for days if we need to. Weeks, even. I know people."

Nyall shook his head. "We have to get home."

Another fluttering of wings, this time accompanied by a whistle, like a lark's. Both Nyall and Goryn turned. Nyall, the only one with a weapon, drew out the knife he'd taken from the guards.

The attack came from the other direction. An avalanche of rock gulls burst from behind a boulder and flew low, snapping their beaks at him and at Goryn.

Nyall dove to the ground, covering his head as the birds pecked and flapped over him, screaming and screeching. Glancing up through the crook of his elbow, Nyall watched a gull swipe the hood off Ryven's head and then saw another free his wrists. They did the same for the Owl Mother, whose face, when it emerged from the hood, was furious. She looked toward the Villages and said something to Ryven that Nyall couldn't hear over the din of the gulls. He tried to stand but was knocked back down just as Üku and Ryven ran off in opposite directions. To his surprise, Üku headed back toward the Sky Castle.

He felt blood trickling down his forehead where a bird had cut him. The entire flock rose straight up at once. Nyall looked up at the colony, flapping, hovering above, preparing to dive once more.

"They're going to kill us!" Goryn shouted, scrambling for cover.

Nyall, however, was frozen to the spot. He felt certain that if he moved, they'd attack sooner. He simply waited, knowing his life hung in the balance of a single twitch of his muscle, feeling that the end was about to come down on him in a flurry of white feathers and thin black beaks.

Instead, the birds turned and flapped away, flying over the Sky Castle, and then rising past the mountains beyond. Gone.

"What the scuzz?" Nyall muttered, looking for Goryn, who'd managed to run halfway up the rocky slope before stopping to watch the colony leave. Nyall looked the other way, searching for Ryven, but he'd already managed to disappear. Üku had, too. Nyall had managed, in the span of a few heartbeats, to lose all his prisoners.

"A soaring success," he grunted as he stood to brush himself off and think about his next move, Nyall saw the great convocation of ghost eagles rise again, ascending into the clouds over the Six and circling once more before breaking away, screeching. They flew in a mass that blotted out the horizon—and they were heading straight in his direction.

Goryn saw this, too, and he screamed and sprinted toward the drainage tunnel, all concern for the fate of the Six Villages left in the dirt he kicked up running for safety. But Nyall couldn't risk going back to the Sky Castle. He couldn't risk leaving Kylee and Brysen's fate unknown. If they needed help, he needed to be there to help them. If they were beyond help, he needed to be there to mourn them. Either way, he needed to keep going forward.

He stayed low, trying to keep under whatever cover he could find, and picked his way down the mountain, praying to every star in the sky that the ghost eagles would leave him be.

Which they did, over a dozen days of hard travel.

On the thirteenth day, he crossed a rocky, dried lakebed that was maybe halfway along his journey to the Six. It was morning, and he was starving, having found no game to hunt and only the paltriest smattering of edible plants. He needed water, too, and knew there had to be a meltwater stream somewhere ahead. There was still snow on the highest peaks, and he was sweating like a pack mule below—nature dictated that he would find drinkable water down here somewhere. He just had to get to it.

Instead, while the sun was just rising, casting speckled

gold over the valley, he heard a screech from above, a screech that made the marrow in his bones ache. Suddenly, he had a terrible vision of Kylee surrounded by an enraged mob, of Brysen wearing an eyepatch, separated from her. A ghost eagle hung suspended in a net. What was he seeing? Was this a memory? Was this happening now?

He looked up just in time to see huge black wings spread above him, black talons outstretched, and then, with sharp pains in his neck and chest, he felt his feet leave the ground.

"I'm sorry, Ky," he groaned. "I tried to—" But he couldn't finish the sentence. The air was squeezed from his lungs, and the ghost eagle hauled him up and up and up, toward the silent sunrise.

Gone, he thought. *This is me, gone.*

BRYSEN

WAXWINGS

8

BRYSEN FOLLOWED THE NARROW LANE AWAY FROM THE MUTES UNTIL
his sister and the soldiers who rescued them were out of sight,
then he turned left where he should've turned right. He
quickened his pace, forcing Jowyn to jog to keep up. He still
held Brysen's arm, and Brysen felt bad hauling Jowyn along
with him like this, but he found it much easier to navigate the
crowded lanes and alleys with the other boy to help him. He'd
nearly fallen flat on his face a dozen times while running down
here. Now, though, he thought maybe he should've just gone
ahead alone and dealt with the inevitable stumbles and
premature turns as they came, because what would Jowyn say
when he saw where they were headed?

Jowyn kept pace with him. "So our place is back that way, you know?" He pointed over his shoulder, toward the sloping foothills on the other end of town. Brysen didn't slow, and Jowyn obviously knew something else was going on after the fake sickness and now this brisk walk in the wrong direction. "You want to at least go back there and get a shirt?"

"It's pretty warm out," Brysen offered, trying to sound casual, though Jowyn knew him too well to fall for his bad acting. Kylee did, too. He wasn't worried about her with Kyrg Birgund; she could handle that blowhard. He was more worried about the way she'd questioned him this morning, like she knew more than she was letting on. Like she knew he was holding back. It was for her own good, of course, but she'd never understand that. She thought everyone was either on her side or against her, and she didn't leave much room for gray areas. She was willing to do anything if it was for what she thought was right, but once she decided something was wrong, that was the end of it for her. Kylee would definitely think that what Brysen was doing was wrong.

"What's going on, Bry?" Jowyn asked him. "You have that look you get sometimes."

"What look?" Was Brysen feigning innocence because he thought it would work, or did he just like hearing Jowyn call him out? Did he like the reminder that, in spite of everything he'd ever done and risked and lost, he was still known? That he was still worth knowing?

Before Jowyn, he chased love the way waxwings chase gnats—twisting and turning in the desperate hope that he could eat his fill—but love and hunger are not the same. No one could fill Brysen's rumbling hollows, but in Jowyn he'd found someone who saw his appetites and stuck around anyway.

Jowyn once recited to him, *Love is not a hunter's art, a snaring to devour. Love is sheltering a seed for someone else's flower.* The boy loved making up little poems. Whenever Brysen withdrew into himself, Jowyn produced little rhymes to draw him back out.

Now Jowyn nudged Brysen with his shoulder, stopping him in the middle of a narrow lane. Eyes peered out at them through the mismatched slats of quickly hewn homes. Everyone knew the one-eyed boy with the gray hair and the pale boy with the strange tattoos. Everyone knew to keep their distance from both. With Mama Tamir dead and Goryn Tamir a prisoner in the Sky Castle, Jowyn was the closest thing the once-feared Tamir clan had to an heir. And Brysen . . . well, he and his sister ignited a war with the sky. That sort of thing tended to make people wary.

"You're up to something," Jowyn said.

"You really think you've got me pegged, huh?" Brysen shook his head.

"Well, not right *here* in this dirty street, but maybe later . . ." Jowyn's bright grin broke wide open as he rested his wrists on Brysen's shoulders.

"Is that *all* you think about?" Brysen laughed. Jowyn really was shameless in the best possible way. It was contagious. Even as desperation stalked them and the sky fell night after night, Jowyn would not let misery crowd out joy. Brysen was learning that from him. He did wonder what Jowyn could possibly get from Brysen in return, unless he simply liked mopey, one-eyed boys with prematurely gray hair and unintentional killer-bird visions. If that was Jowyn's type, Brysen felt lucky to be it.

He looked back and forth between Jowyn's eyes and then down at his lips. Brysen's monocular vision made it difficult to judge how close Jowyn's face was to his. The degraded depth perception made tasks like picking up a plate or bringing a cup of hot tea to his mouth more difficult, but in this one instance, it created a thrilling uncertainty. Every kiss had the drama of a first kiss, because every kiss could go comically wrong.

"You going to tell me what you're up to?" Jowyn whispered, and when Brysen didn't immediately confess, Jowyn stepped back. "Suit yourself." He shrugged. "Sorry, folks!" he announced to the prurient eyes gazing between the cracks. "No show today. Nothing to see here!"

"Fine," Brysen groaned, and pulled Jowyn close again so he could whisper while they kept walking. "I'm going up to the old house."

"Why?"

"I'm looking for something," Brysen said. "I'd rather not say *what* until I find it."

"Something embarrassing or dangerous or both?" Jowyn asked.

Brysen shrugged. He wasn't going to give Jowyn anything to go on. He might know Brysen *too* well.

"You know I'll never find you embarrassing, right?" Jowyn told him. "I *couldn't* find you embarrassing."

How was Brysen supposed to respond to that?

"Uh-huh," he said, and walked on, weaving through the lanes, offering friendly nods to the slack-jawed people that he passed and trying very hard to look like he was not trying very hard not to trip. He was glad Jowyn had his arm. His head ached from the strain, and he tried to close the eye that he no longer had, which pulled at the stitching in the bronze and sent a sharp pain right to the center of his skull. He winced.

His gray hair fell over the eyepatch in a way that made people uncertain of what they were seeing. Now that he struggled with some kinds of perception, it felt good to know that people staring at him did, too.

"Okay, so it's not something embarrassing," Jowyn continued, "unless you shed all shame when you shed your shirt . . . not that I mind, of course." His nervous habit was his banter, and it worked well for him. He didn't even need Brysen to participate. He could amuse himself with witty repartee from sundown to sunup, which he had done for the first days after the battle of the Six Villages. Brysen had lain bloodied and insensate after the Kartami took his eye and his beloved goshawk, Shara.

Jowyn's babbling and rhymes and poems had called Brysen back to himself, like whistling down a hawk lost in a storm. Poetry wasn't just an amusing pastime Jowyn enjoyed; it was his falconer's call. Brysen was the hawk, hooded by his words, tethered safe and saved.

"If it's not embarrassing, and it is *you* we're talking about . . . ," Jowyn prattled on, helping Brysen navigate around some kind of kiln that had been built right in the middle of the lane. "Then it's dangerous, what you're after. It would have to be, to risk that kyrg's anger." Still Brysen said nothing. "And, these days, what's dangerous that doesn't flap and screech in the night?"

Brysen just pursed his lips. He liked the sound of Jowyn's rambling, wanted him to keep going while they walked. It made the walk up to the home they'd left behind in ruins far more pleasant. The place didn't have many good memories tethered to it—or *any* good memories, in fact. Maybe that was why he was having trouble remembering his way back there now.

He turned into what he thought was a series of connected alleys but instead found a dead end inhabited by at least two dozen people, sitting around a putrid fire under the flimsiest of tents. A wild-eyed man squatted by the fire, poking at the meat he'd just cooked.

It took Brysen a moment to realize it wasn't cooked meat—it was bird entrails, and the stick the man was using to poke them was covered in intricate carvings. This was an augur, a diviner trying to read the future in the blood and guts of slaughtered birds—one of the countless new practices that had sprung up in the aftermath of the ghost eagle attack.

In the wreckage that accompanied the end of the world, a lot of unexpected prayers rose. Some people rededicated to their old faith in the ruins, while others flew from everything they had once believed and instead embraced brand-new blasphemies. Empty-sky zealots gambled with the bones of falcons, and scar-pocked pit fighters became dawn-to-dusk devotees of bird worship, crawling in the dirt and lamenting their sins against the sky. And there were plenty of charlatans conjuring false hope in the ashes, claiming they could divine the will of the dread flocks that attacked each night . . . for a fee.

Brysen couldn't stand the ones who preyed on the scared

and the vulnerable. After all, who *wasn't* scared? Who *wasn't* vulnerable?

"Tell you your future!" the augur shouted at him. "For a half round, I'll tell you all your days to come. Want to know when you'll die? Your true love's secrets? Which way your greatness lies? I have it all right here!"

He poked again at the fire, and Brysen hesitated. What if he *could* tell those things? Yeah, the augur was probably a liar and a charlatan . . . but what if he wasn't? What'd Brysen need bronze for, anyway? He could part with a half round on the off chance this augur saw something useful in the bird guts.

"I—" he started, but Jowyn grabbed his arm and pulled him to the mouth of the alley.

"I'll tell you my secrets for less bronze than that," Jowyn said. "Come on. You know this guy's full of scuzz."

"Am I, owl boy?" The augur's voice rose to a high pitch. His bloodshot eyes locked on Jowyn, and he rose to his full height, which was not unimpressive. He was broad-shouldered and pale, and though his skin was scarred and pocked and stained with soot, there were visible tattoos all over it. The tattoos were just like Jowyn's, but they looked like they'd been rubbed and scratched and maimed, deliberately distorted to be nearly unrecognizable. Brysen heard Jowyn suck in air.

"You aren't the first boy the Owl Mothers have exiled," the augur said. "You aren't the first to have shed blood on their mountain, either." He pointed to a ring of crude tattoos around his neck, each in the shape of a person. There were a dozen. The augur laughed at Jowyn's obvious shock. "Difference is I loved the killing, so they cast me out for it. Now, if you want your future told, I'll tell you, free. You'll end up dead or just like me!"

Suddenly the augur leapt across the fire, brandishing his sharp stick like a club, screaming. Brysen reacted instantly, not sure he could land a counterpunch but certain he could put himself between Jowyn and this madman.

Before he had a chance, though, the augur stumbled and fell on his face in the dirt, bashing his lip. He rolled over onto his back, mouth full of blood, and laughed. "Your faces! Hahaha! You should see your faces!"

"Come on," Jowyn urged Brysen. "He's drunk."

"You okay?" Brysen asked Jowyn as they left the augur rolling on the ground, laughing near his pile of bird entrails. Jowyn's hand was shaking on Brysen's shoulder.

"Yeah," he said. "Fine."

"You don't always have to be okay," Brysen told him. "I'm not so fragile that you can't be upset."

Jowyn smiled at him. "I really am okay now," he said, but

there was a twinge in his voice that Brysen didn't like, the sound of something unsaid.

"You're nothing like that, you know," Brysen said.

"He rhymed," Jowyn said sadly. "Right before he attacked us, he spoke in a rhyme."

Brysen almost laughed, but Jowyn really was upset by that. "Don't let one random lunatic take your love of rhyming from you."

Jowyn shook his head. "Don't call him a lunatic," he said. "He just doesn't know how to live in exile, okay? Not everyone has someone to lean on."

For a moment Brysen didn't realize Jowyn was talking about him. *He* was the reason Jowyn hadn't gone mad in exile from the Owl Mothers. Brysen held Jowyn together. He'd never really held anyone together before. He could barely hold himself together.

"Um . . . okay," he said. "Lean on." Then he changed the subject. "So I guess I *do* need your help, after all. I'm a little lost. You figure out where we're going yet?"

Jowyn nodded. "Your old house."

"Yeah," Brysen said. "But I'm totally turned around."

"This way." Jowyn steered him, and they carried on through the narrow streets, looking for the right path to the bridge that led over the river and up the hill to the burned ruins of Brysen's old house above the Six Villages. They'd have to leave the cover of the nets, but the ghost eagles hadn't yet attacked in daylight, and Brysen felt confident they'd be safe under the open morning sky.

After all, it was a ghost eagle that had shown him where to go in the first place.

9

THE FOOTHILLS ABOVE THE SIX VILLAGES NEVER BUSTLED WITH
people—that was one of the reasons Brysen's father built
their home up there, outside of town—but now the isolation
made Brysen shudder. He started to wish he'd grabbed a
shirt or cloak or something on his rush out this morning,
though it was too late to go back now. They'd left the safety
of the protective nets, they'd crossed the footbridge, and
they were standing in the ashes of his old house, under an
open sky.

The wind swirled snow off the high peaks and made a low,
keening whine between the cuts and crags. Some people
thought the sound was the mountains groaning with the pain

of the world's existence, but Brysen had always taken comfort in the eerie noise. He thought it was more like a song—no matter how hurt he was or how alone he felt, the mountains were always there above, singing just as badly as he did.

But the mountain's sound had always been punched through with birdsong, the cries of high hawks and the cheeps of anxious wrens. Now the skies were mostly empty, save a lone vulture or two, and the scrubby trees on the slopes were silent as dried bones. He looked up toward the distant blood birch forest and wondered about the Owl Mothers, wondered if their owls had flown off, too, or if they were steady as ever, watching and waiting out the rise and fall of a civilization. Jowyn was looking up there, too, his face inscrutable.

"I'm sure they're watching all this," Jowyn said. "They'll find a way to survive. That was always their highest value—preserving the community. The community is more important to them than any one member. That's why they exiled me."

Left unsaid was the real reason they'd exiled him: Brysen.

Brysen looked around the small compound that had been his home. The hawk mews, where he'd kept his birds, had been burned completely. The house was made of stone, so the fire had burned away only the supports, toppling in the roof. Now it was a pile of charred rock, with four firm walls still standing. The gnarly ash tree peeked over one wall like a nosy neighbor. Brysen closed his eyes, tried to call up what he'd seen in his dreams.

Footprints in the snow. Wings desperately trying to beat away the tracks. That's what he'd shared with Kylee. But now he focused on what he hadn't said . . . *The footprints led here, to their old house, and a great black ghost eagle was perched on the ruins as though sitting on a nest. It screeched.* It was that screech that had pulled Brysen out of his dream.

He had a feeling about what it meant, but he wanted to be sure, wanted to see for himself. His feelings had led him astray before, had made him look ridiculous and had even hurt people. He'd learned to proceed carefully now. Blood and bruises were thorough teachers, and before he did anything based on a gut feeling, he needed to first confirm it in reality. If he was wrong about what he'd find, then he'd tell Kylee about the rest of his dream and they could try to work out the meaning together.

If he was right, though? What then?

If he was right, he had no idea what he would do.

He looked around the compound, searching for a sign. He had to use the mountains behind the house to adjust his sense of perspective. It was a new way of seeing depth, and it reminded him of all he'd given to the ghost eagles. He'd lost his eye, but he had not given in to self-pity or self-destruction— and not long ago, he probably would've. He'd trusted Jowyn

and opened up to him. He'd allowed himself to be seen, phys-
ically and emotionally, and he thought that maybe he would
be rewarded for all that personal progress. But suffering
wasn't a game of sticks and marbles with a prize for the win-
ner. There was no moral to the pain he'd suffered and no prize
for enduring it. That was just life.

He'd assumed it would be obvious when he got here, but
the ghost eagles only showed what they had to show in order
to bend a person to their will. Their promises were as hollow
as their bones. Why'd they lure him up here with visions just
to strand him under the sky?

Under the open sky.

No net.

No protection.

It was a trap.

He looked toward the far horizon but saw no flutterings of
black wings. He turned and looked at the cliff, at the high
ridges over his house, but saw nothing unusual. His single-eye
vision flattened the scene in such a way that any movement
stood out to him. The first few days, he'd flinched at everything, even the shadows of clouds. Now he was better at judging when something was actually moving toward him.

Nothing moved. This was not an ambush. He let the rush
of alarm pass away, took slow breaths in through the nose and
out through the mouth, and he thought.

They didn't send me up here to kill me. They showed me something in the dream. It wasn't random. It meant *something. Why would a ghost eagle sit on the ruins of my house?*

That was the key. It wasn't *perched* on the ruins. It was sitting . . . as though on a nest.

He stepped up to the base of the old ash tree that loomed over one of the standing walls, its branches beginning to bud in the warming air of the season. One of the branches had been stripped bare of bark in a series of stripes—the kind of scars that thick talons might make.

Brysen didn't wait for Jowyn to help him; he simply took off his boots, grabbed the tree's trunk, and started climbing. He'd been climbing this tree since he was old enough to stand. He knew every knot and branch by touch alone.

Of course they would choose this tree, he thought.

"Careful!" Jowyn warned, which made Brysen pause to look down at him. "Right, right," Jowyn mumbled. "I didn't actually need to tell you that. Still . . . try not to fall."

Brysen went back to climbing, hand over hand, reaching out wherever he expected a branch and finding it. He could never have climbed a less familiar tree with this much ease, but pretty soon he was on the thick branch that had been the ghost eagle's perch in his dream. He wrapped his legs around the branch and shimmied forward, inching over the ledge of his home's ruined wall.

And he found what the ghost eagles had wanted him to find.

On the ledge below him sat one huge black egg, snug in a nest of charred stones and scorched wood. Above him, the mountains groaned mournful music while his own heartbeat rolled thunder in his ears.

10

BRYSEN REACHED DOWN TO THE CHARRED ROCKS WHERE THE GHOST eagle had made its nest. The stones were sun-warm, and a thin coat of ash had settled over the large black egg, so that he had to brush it away with his fingers in order to see the shell clearly.

No one, as far as he knew, had ever seen a ghost eagle's egg before—at least, no one who'd lived long enough to tell. The stories all said that ghost eagles made their nests higher in the mountains than anyone could ever climb. Some believed the eagles didn't lay eggs at all, that they were born from ashes of wildfires on the other side of the mountains. Others said they were born from shadows or nightmares, or even one's own fears. As a boy, Brysen believed he created the ghost eagle himself, from every dark and selfish thought he'd ever had. He never fully let go of that childish belief, but here was a ghost eagle's egg, sitting in a nest just like any other bird egg.

Well, not *just* like any other egg. The egg was the size of a winter squash, and its shell was a matte black that would make a starless night jealous. It was marbled with other blacks: glossy blue blacks, glossy gray blacks, and black with a tinge of red, which veined the surface and made Brysen think of a poisoned heart's final beats. Looking at it, he became very aware of how loudly he was breathing, how his right leg quivered where it gripped the branch, how his whole fragile body was balanced on a tree limb, how he was seeing a thing no person was meant to see, and how open and exposed he was to the sky.

He reminded himself that the ghost eagles showed him this place, *chose* him to come here, after all. They weren't likely to attack him now for doing just what they wanted . . . unless, of course, they didn't actually want him to come here. After all, there was a different quality to the dreams, compared to what he saw when the ghost eagles spoke directly into his mind. The dreams were weirder, wilder, more untethered. They were more like what he experienced that morning, when the injured ghost eagle cried out, rather than when the ghost eagles tried to speak to him on purpose. Maybe they hadn't chosen him. Maybe they were just screaming and he alone could hear them.

"What is it?" Jowyn called up to him, and Brysen remembered that, even without his sister here, he was not, in fact, alone.

He had no way to carry down the egg, so he'd have to get Jowyn's help in catching it. This meant he actually had to tell Jowyn, but the words felt stuck in his throat. He wasn't quite ready to speak, not ready for this moment to become the next moment, when things would start happening. He'd have to explain, and then he'd probably have to calm Jowyn, and then he'd have to get the egg down safely and figure out what to do with it. He'd need to keep it hidden from the soldiers and the Six Villagers. Would the ghost eagles come looking for it, or would they want him to bring it to them? Was he supposed to wait for it to hatch and then parent a ghost eagle's baby eaglet? Would he chew up bits of human flesh and spit them into the baby monster's mouth until it grew strong enough to kill a man on its own? Could he raise a baby ghost eagle to be on his side? To be on humanity's side?

That future unfurled ahead of him like a flag in the wind— but he stopped himself. There was nothing else but now, this moment, the breeze rustling him along with the leaves, the smooth surface of the shell warming against his fingertips. He breathed deep and thought about the ghost eagle he'd healed that morning. As it fled the net with mended wings spread wide, he'd thought of a word, a Hollow Tongue word he didn't understand.

Touching the egg now, he understood. He whispered it aloud.

"*Zasaase*," he said. "*Zasaase*."

It meant safety. It meant *You are safe with me. For now you are safe.* It was the most he could promise.

"Brysen?" Jowyn called again. "Everything okay?"

"Do you trust me?" he called back.

"Are you really asking me that?"

"Yeah! I am!" Brysen peered down at him through the branches.

"Do *you* trust *me*?" Jowyn replied, and Brysen said yes, of course he did. He wondered how Jowyn could even doubt it. "Then *never* ask me that again," Jowyn said.

It was all the answer he needed. Brysen stretched, using both hands to scoop up the egg. Its shell was harder than he thought an eggshell could be, but ghost eagle eggs wouldn't have delicate shells, would they? He tried to imagine a ghost eagle sitting on it like a hen but couldn't quite make the image stick. Perhaps that wasn't how ghost eagles cared for their eggs, or perhaps he just lacked the imagination to imagine the creatures of his nightmares as parents. Then again, his parents were also the stuff of his nightmares, so perhaps he could cut the giant killer birds some slack. There were as many kinds of parents in the world as seeds on the wind. Some grew thorns and some grew flowers, but all took root in similar soil.

"Get under me and catch what I toss down *very carefully*," he told Jowyn. "I need you to tell me when you're ready, because I might not be able to see perfectly, and we cannot drop this, okay? I don't know what'll happen if we do, but I'm sure it's nothing good."

"I'm ready!" Jowyn called, and Brysen lined up the egg over where Jowyn stood. He let it fall.

It looked like the egg just shrank a little, and he couldn't tell precisely when it reached Jowyn, but barely a second passed before the boy's hands caught the egg, moving with it to ensure a soft landing. Jowyn cradled it into his side before he really registered what it was that he'd caught. Then he looked up at Brysen, stunned.

"Yeah," Brysen told him, climbing down as quickly as he could. "That."

"You know the old riddle? Which came first, the bird or the egg?" Jowyn asked him. "I never thought of it as terrifying before." Brysen hit the ground and walked over to him, but Jowyn didn't hand back the egg right away. "How did you know it was here?" Jowyn asked. When Brysen didn't answer, Jowyn understood. "Your dreams."

Brysen nodded. "The Hollow Tongue is more than a

language," he said. "It's, like . . . when you speak it, you *become* it. It absorbs you, but you absorb it, too. The words aren't separate from what they describe. They *become* what they describe. That's how I'm able to heal birds just by speaking and how Kylee can turn *her* anger into *their* anger. The Hollow Tongue erases all divisions between the one who's speaking and what is spoken. It's like wind through the air, or a ripple on water. It *is* the element it moves within."

"So what do the ghost eagles want you to do with this egg?" Brysen watched Jowyn turn it around in his hands, tracing the black-on-black swirls decorating its surface. "Nurse it? Raise it so it thinks you're its pa? That doesn't really fit their whole *we'll-kill-you-all* agenda."

"They never said *kill*," Brysen corrected Jowyn. His body felt cold just remembering the moment when the ghost eagles seized his mind on the battlefield and spoke through him. At the time, he'd been torn apart by grief for losing Shara, throbbing with pain from his gaping eye socket, and in shock from unexpectedly healing the ghost eagle. He'd thought about that moment every day since, and he remembered clear as a mountain lake the actual words the ghost eagles had said:

We will tame you all.

"They said *tame*," he told Jowyn.

"What does that mean? They're taming you by giving you an egg?"

He nodded, but Jowyn frowned. He didn't get it.

"How do you tame a bird?" Brysen asked.

"Me?" Jowyn said. "I never have."

"It takes time," Brysen said. "You hang around, get the bird used to you. You bind it to you, let it perch on your glove. You give it pieces of meat. You show it that you are reliable, that you will be there to nourish it so long as it returns to you. And then you trust it and let it fly, and if you put in the time and the effort to know it, then it will know you from all the falconers in the world, and it will do as you wish and return for as long as it can."

"Sounds like falling in love," Jowyn said, with a wry smile that made Brysen's heart spark like a damp log catching fire.

"You haven't tamed me yet," he said.

Jowyn passed Brysen the egg, gently setting it in his open hands. "No," he said. "But you've tamed me. I trust you completely and will return to you no matter what . . . and that does *not* sound like a ghost eagle."

"But it does," Brysen said. "They've been in my life since it began, in one way or another. They bound themselves to me and to my sister when we were children. They got us used to them, and they gave both of us morsels of what we most wanted: fame and purpose, protection and power. Even love." He met Jowyn's stare. "I wouldn't have met you if it weren't for capturing one of them."

"You would've," Jowyn disagreed. "One way or another, you would've. There's no world in which we don't meet. You could've been born one raven in a flock of thousands, and I could've been a mole in the dirt, but I'd still hear the beating of your battered heart from across the sky. I'd have found you."

"As a mole?" Brysen asked.

"I'd be a pretty mole," Jowyn replied.

"You'd have to be," Brysen said. "I'd be the best-looking raven, and terribly shallow."

"Moles don't see well," Jowyn said. "Your looks wouldn't matter."

"Yeah, but ravens *do* see well, so yours would . . ." Brysen laughed. "I don't date moles."

"Well, then I'd be a raven and look just like every other raven and *still* we'd find each other in the flock. We'd find each other in a hundred thousand flocks. That's just how our story goes." Jowyn pulled at the collar of his shirt, reminding Brysen of his newest tattoo: the two of them in silhouette on a mountain, shoulder-to-shoulder, staring at the moon. The outline of Brysen held a hawk on its fist—his hawk, Shara, who'd been killed too soon. He felt his eye dampen at the thought of her. Jowyn misread the sentiment, thought it was about them. He set his thumb gently below Brysen's eye, put his other hand on the back of Brysen's neck, and pulled their lips together for a kiss, the black egg pressed between their bodies.

Jowyn broke the kiss first, and Brysen cleared his throat. His palms were sweaty where they clutched the black egg, and he felt movement inside: the eaglet stirring in time with his heartbeat. He felt a surge of joy that enveloped him and the egg and even Jowyn, a joy that erased any distinction between them. He felt almost overwhelmed with care: how much he cared for Jowyn, how much he wanted no harm to come to him for as long as he breathed. And then he pictured Shara and how he had failed her, but the thought of his eaglet in its egg and that caring feeling swept back over him just as quickly. Looking down, he saw that the thin swirls of black on the shell's surface were flecked with tiny rivulets of gold. Had that gold color been there before? Had his thoughts changed the shell?

"*Zasaase*," he whispered again, and the gold brightened, and the joy he felt opened like a flower blooming. If the shell changed with his feelings, then could his emotions also change the ghost eagle inside? Would this eaglet be born full of the love he felt, full in the way the ghost eagles could fill a person's mind with rage? Was that his purpose here? To fill *one* tiny being with love and protect it from all who might wish it harm?

He wasn't really asking himself; he knew the answer. He'd

decided, and Jowyn must've seen the resolve change on his face.

"Shara died," Jowyn told him, bluntly. "She was your hawk, and she died. You can't replace her with this. You can't heal a wound with the thing that made it."

"This isn't about me," Brysen said, which he knew was a lie even as he said it. He didn't say the real reason aloud. He didn't say what he really meant, which was *What if I can protect this one the way I wish someone had protected me? What if I can protect this one the way I failed to protect Shara? What if I can be redeemed?*

Instead, he said, "What if I can change all the ghost eagles by changing this one? What if I can save us with this?"

"Bry . . . ," Jowyn began. Brysen looked up at the pale boy, preparing his argument, trying to convince himself that what he'd said was true—protecting this egg was about something bigger than his own longing—but Jowyn was looking past him, mouth open, eyes wide. "*Brysen* . . . ," he whispered.

Brysen craned his neck, followed Jowyn's gaze.

Three ghost eagles perched on the rocks above them, looking down.

Cast in shadow, the egg's shell blackened in his hands.

11

"REEEEE!" THE THREE GHOST EAGLES SCREECHED.

They lowered their heads, looking sideways at the two boys. Their feathers were blacker than a raven's, their huge hooked beaks just as black, and the crown of black feathers atop their heads didn't ruffle though the wind blew through it.

"REEEE!" they called again, and Brysen gasped at what he saw: Shara—his own hawk, tamed and nurtured since he was a boy—cut down by the Kartami army right before his eye, a memory from not even a full moon's turn ago.

The vision was so clear, so complete, he felt it again in his body, the way he had felt it on the battlefield. He could smell her blood. He wasn't just remembering; the ghost eagles were making him relive it, the violent death of the creature he loved most.

Next to him, Jowyn burst into tears and suddenly wrapped his arms around Brysen, squeezing him. His eyes were shut tight. "They cut you!" he yelled, and Brysen knew Jowyn was reliving the moment when the Kartami cut out his eye, when Jowyn had been helpless to stop them.

The three birds spread their wings, preparing to dive. The sun was at their backs, gleaming off their feathers like midnight lightning.

Visions cycled through Brysen's mind, every one depicting someone he had failed to protect. He assumed the same was true for Jowyn.

"They want their egg back," Jowyn said.

"They aren't going to hurt us," Brysen said.

He wasn't sure about that, but these visions lacked the calculated malice he so often felt from the ghost eagles. These were spontaneous memories bubbling up uncontrolled. He was used to this kind of memory, the kind that boiled up suddenly and took over his whole body, as though his skin had memories of its own. He'd been plagued by these sorts of memories since long before the ghost eagles came, and he recognized one when he felt it. It was fear. The ghost eagles were scared, although he couldn't be certain if it was their fear he was feeling or his own. "They're not going to attack as long as I have this."

"I thought they *wanted* you to find it," Jowyn said.

"I was wrong," he said.

"Well, give it back to them, then!" Jowyn yelled.

The birds hadn't attacked yet. He shifted positions so he was a little in front of Jowyn. If he was wrong and they did attack, they'd hit him first. Not that it would save Jowyn. Brysen was being selfish; if they were both going to die, he wanted to go first. He couldn't bear to see Jowyn die.

"I think holding it is the only thing keeping us alive," he said as he squeezed the egg tighter.

The ghost eagles screeched again, and this time, Brysen saw the blood birch forest, its trees swaying in a cool wind. He didn't know why, but the vision made him feel deeply sad. For some reason, he thought of a whining dog. Was this how the ghost eagles begged?

He thought about giving in, letting them have their egg, but the shell turned a deeper black. He changed his mind, held it close.

"*Shessele*," he said. "Stay calm." And the black shell glimmered again with flecks of gold. The ghost eagles seemed to hesitate. "*Zasaase*," he whispered. "You're safe with me."

The birds lowered their wings. They hesitated, shifting their huge taloned feet on the stone wall. Rocks crumbled and skittered into the yard, loose stones rolling to Brysen's feet. One of the eagles tilted its head back and screamed.

"REEEEEE!"

Brysen heard footsteps clicking on the loose stones in the yard behind him.

Click click. Click click. Click click.

There was a walkway between the house and the mews. The twins had loosened the stepping-stones to make them click when trod upon. That way they'd know when their da was coming and Brysen could hide or at least prepare for the beating he was about to suffer. To this day, the clicking sound filled his mouth with a bitter taste, and his whole body would tense. It was the purest form of fear, but it wasn't his anymore. He had nothing to fear from the stones or from his father.

Click click. Click click. Click click.

He breathed through the moment, calming his own nerves. He didn't want the eagles to be afraid, either. Fear wasn't very useful for taming a bird of prey—it usually led to the bird lashing out or falling sullen or flying away. It never got them or their tamer any closer to real partnership. Fear was as useless in falconry as it was between people. Brysen had been afraid of Da right up until the ghost eagle killed him, but he had hardly ever obeyed the man and had never respected him. Fear was fickle.

Understanding endured.

Brysen wanted to understand.

"What do you want?" he asked the ghost eagles. "Why did you show me this?"

The eagles stared down at him. They didn't screech. They didn't attack. They just watched. And then he felt it: confusion. The ghost eagles were confused.

"They don't know," he whispered, and felt Jowyn's fingers wrap around his waist. "They don't know what they want."

Suddenly the eagle in the center of the group bent its legs and launched from the rock, wings opening and flapping so hard that the breeze they made blew up dust. The two others followed. He and Jowyn ducked in unison, knocking their heads together as they each tried to cover the other.

"Oof!" Brysen grunted, seeing stars but still gripping the egg as tightly as he could. He expected talons to rake across his back at any moment, but instead the ghost eagle flew right over them, the other two flanking it. Brysen ran to the home's blackened doorway, watching as the birds swept down the slope. They soared over the charred ruins of Brysen's hawk mews and over the thorny fence that marked the edge of the compound, then dove behind a boulder along the path toward the Six.

A piercing scream rose a moment before the first eagle reappeared. Held in its talons was a figure, thrashing and crying out in its grip, one hand wrapped with red cloth but both hands holding the ghost eagle's ankles, trying to break free. The giant bird's talons dug into the figure's shoulders, staining their tunic redder than the cloth around their fist. Another of the eagles hoisted a second, identical figure. Both victims were carried, kicking and screaming, toward the house. The third eagle circled above, and Brysen turned, keeping his eyes on the eagles just as they dropped the two people right in front of him. Both rolled in the dirt, one's ankles obviously broken from the fall. The other yelled at Brysen as they tried to stand.

"Unholy scuzz-speaker! We'll die and live as air, but when justice comes for you, you'll rot in mud forever."

Brysen recognized them: the pair of teenaged Kartami warriors who'd attacked Kylee in the Mutes; they'd snuck out and followed Brysen and Jowyn.

The ghost eagles circled overhead in a perfect wheel, their wings like spokes. They cried out, and in his mind Brysen saw that morning, the spear heading straight for Kylee's heart, their smug faces as they mocked Nyck, and worse, from before . . . the battle boys they'd cut down during the siege of the Six Villages, the place they'd stood guard over while their leader cut out Brysen's eye, how they'd smiled at each other when they heard his blood-boiling scream. He even felt their joy at his pain, his eye socket twitching with the echo of what had been done to him. He was reliving his torture from their point of view.

A knife lay in the dirt right in front of Brysen—maybe one of the two warriors had dropped it, or maybe it was from the ghost eagle. Brysen wanted to pick it up. He wanted to slice both their throats, just as they'd have gladly sliced his.

He still held the egg in both hands. Its surface was black again. He'd have to let it go to pick up the knife. *It would be so easy to kill these two. It would feel so good.*

Instead he kicked the knife's handle so it skittered away, out of the house, disappearing into a nearby bramble thicket. He looked down at them. "You'll want to find shelter," he told them. "You're safe from me, but those three . . ." He looked up at the three ghost eagles. "I don't know what they'll do."

With that, he turned away, feeling Jowyn's hand on his back again, and walked as evenly and as calmly as he could down the slope toward the relative safety of the nets, still holding the egg to his warm skin. He didn't dare look down at it or up at the ghost eagles or even sideways at Jowyn. His mind was racing, and his eye was fixed forward.

He could feel that the ghost eagles were confused and afraid and unsure as to why he had their egg now, but Brysen wasn't unsure. He had a purpose. He was going to protect this egg until it hatched, come what may. Whether the ghost eagles thought he was a caretaker or a hostage-taker didn't concern him now. What did concern him was how to keep this fragile life safe from the people who'd surely want it for their own purposes. If the ghost eagles were afraid of the person who held the egg, then whoever held it would have power, and Brysen wasn't sure he trusted anyone with that kind of power, at least not now.

He was so focused on his thoughts that he hardly heard the ghost eagles dive at the two warriors behind him. Their blood soaked the same dirt where Brysen and Kylee used to play as children. The mountains echoed, as they had many times before, with sound of screaming.

But all Brysen could think about was this baby bird.

12

"SO . . . I DON'T HAVE A SHIRT," BRYSEN SAID WHEN THEY WERE BACK under the safety of the nets on the edge of the Six Villages. They'd nearly been caught putting the stake for the netting that they'd pulled up back into the ground, and they had to pretend to be having an emotional argument until the passerby kept going.

"If you actually hung your clothes up after you wore them, I wouldn't have to do it for you!" Jowyn pretended to yell, though his act had the sting of truth to it.

"You didn't have to steal my shirt," Brysen answered, unsure they were selling the drama. "Like you stole my heart," he added, feinging woe and anguish.

The passerby moved on, avoiding eye contact. No one likes walking into the middle of a couple's quarrel.

Now they were alone again, and Brysen gestured to his bare chest, the ghost eagle egg tucked under his arm. "I mean, the shirt thing is real."

Jowyn looked him up and down. "I noticed."

"No place to hide the egg," he said, and presented it to Jowyn, whose mouth hung open. "What? We can't just walk through the streets with it."

"You want me to *carry* a killer bird's egg for you?" Brysen tried his pleadiest pleading face, but Jowyn shook his head. "You're the one they're interested in. How do I know they won't show up and rip off my head the moment I take it from you?"

"The nets," Brysen said, hoping Jowyn wouldn't point out that the birds broke through the nets nearly every night.

"And what about your sister?" Jowyn wondered. "You'll tell her about it?"

Brysen kept his mouth shut.

"I'm not interested in lying to Kylee," Jowyn said. "I love you, but I do not want to get between you two. You want to hide it from her? That's going to have to be *your* problem."

"How am I supposed to carry it?" Brysen held up the egg, and Jowyn dropped his eyes ever so briefly, his gaze like a hummingbird visiting honeysuckle. He raised his eyebrows.

"My *pants?*"

Jowyn nodded.

Brysen tried being coy. "But I'm not sure there's room."

"Don't flirt," Jowyn said. "I'm preemptively mad at you for getting me killed, which still seems likely. If not by its parents, then by this baby when it hatches."

"That won't happen," Brysen said. "This will think *we're* its parents, like a duckling imprinting on the first face it sees when it breaks out of its shell. It'll be a ghost eagle on our side."

Jowyn shook his head at the absurdity of the idea, which Brysen knew was a totally reasonable response, but he wanted Jowyn to have faith in him—not in reason. Anyone could take a leap of faith into an idea that made obvious sense. This idea demanded Jowyn have bigger faith than that. This had suddenly become, in Brysen's head, about more than the egg. This was now about their relationship and whether Jowyn was really in it the way Brysen hoped.

Brysen just held the giant egg out to Jowyn, his head cocked in as charming a way as he could cock it, hoping the light was catching off his bronze eyepatch just so. He tried to look insouciant, but all he was thinking was, *Please, please, please . . . believe in me.*

And then Jowyn sighed and took the egg, hiding it beneath his loose shirt. Brysen's heart leapt like a flock of starlings bursting into a clear blue sky. He thought his smile might break open his face. Jowyn laughed and frowned at him simultaneously.

"What?" he asked.

Brysen shook his head and patted Jowyn's shoulder. He didn't want to ruin the moment by pointing it out. Jowyn believed in him. More didn't need to be said.

"More stomachache, less pregnant," he suggested instead, looping his arm through the crook of Jowyn's elbow to make the pose seem more natural. They began to pick their way through the winding alleys of the Six toward the cavern, where Brysen hoped his sister wouldn't ask too many questions.

"You went where?"

"He's with who?"

Kylee and Brysen's questions passed by each other like clouds above a fog bank, neither acknowledging the other.

Brysen had heard her talk about Kyrg Ryven before—he was the youngest member of the Council of Forty and the only other speaker of the Hollow Tongue who the ghost eagles had listened to—but the man had been deposed and was supposed to be in a Sky Castle dungeon.

At least his presence in the Six Villages gave Brysen an

excuse to ask a lot of questions, allowing Jowyn to hide the ghost eagle's egg under the blankets on their sleeping pallet. That was one place he was sure his sister wouldn't go rummaging. Even Brysen, who was usually not so fastidious, had noticed that his blankets smelled ripe.

"You said he's responsible for Vyvian's murder at the Sky Castle," Brysen said, "and he's here? We can bring him to justice."

"What does that even mean?" Kylee snapped at him. "What does justice look like to you?"

Brysen shrugged.

"Right now, I'm worried more about survival," she said, "which you keep making harder and harder. Tell me why you went up to our house."

Something in her tone told Brysen she didn't really need him to answer. Did she know already? Had she seen the same visions he had? If she had, then she'd been lying to him for days, pretending not to know what his dreams showed.

Well, he could be less than truthful, too, if that's how she wanted to play it.

"There's no privacy here," Brysen said, then lowered his voice to what he hoped sounded like a confessional tone. "Jowyn and I just wanted to be alone."

Jowyn wouldn't appreciate being brought into his lie, but Brysen didn't have many other good excuses. He expected his sister to roll her eyes, like she did whenever he talked about that sort of thing, but instead she dropped her head, letting her dark hair fall over her face. She rubbed her eyes with both her hands, then finally snapped up to look at him.

"Why do you make *everything* so much harder than it has to be?"

"Me!" Brysen said, raising his voice. Sure, he was lying, but so was she, and if she knew he was lying, then she knew he knew, too, so it was hardly fair for her to go on insulting him. "Having my own ideas is *not* making everything harder. Just because I don't always do what you want doesn't mean I'm some problem you have to solve."

"I didn't say that," Kylee said. "I just wish you'd be honest with me now. It's important."

"You be honest with me first, then." Brysen stared at her and waited. She stared at him and waited. The cavern felt heavy with their waiting, like silence could thicken the air the way cooking an egg too long hardens the yolk.

"Oh, for sky's sake!" Grazim butted in and walked right between them, knocking Brysen out of the way as she walked to their sleeping pallet. "Just take the damned egg from him!"

On her left fist she carried a juvenile tailor's hawk, unhooded, each brown-and-red feather outlined in white, like the chalk markings a tailor might make to pattern a robe. The hawk wasn't leashed but wore jesses and a metal anklet that showed it was the property of the army of Uztar. The hawk ruffled its feathers and shifted its weight as it passed by Brysen, and he wondered why the army let Grazim take one of its hawks.

"Hey!" he yelled after her, following.

"Hey!" Kylee yelled after him.

Jowyn, who was standing in front of the pallet trying to look like a formidable wall of marble-colored flesh, turned at Grazim's approach, but he wasn't as white or as strong as when he had access to the sap of the blood birch forest. Exile from the Owl Mothers had meant slowly losing the effects that sap had on his body.

"Hand it over," Grazim snapped at him.

"How'd you get that hawk?" Brysen demanded.

"Hand. It. Over," Grazim repeated at Jowyn.

"I don't know what you're talking about," Jowyn told her. He wasn't a great liar, but he tried. "Like Brysen said, we just went up there to be alone. To relieve some tension after this morning's excitement."

"To relieve tension?" Grazim crossed her arms.

Jowyn tried one of his little sayings: "*Brittle branches break in blowing wind; sometimes it's better for a branch to bend . . .*" Only Jowyn would try dodging a question with a rhyme about a tree—a rhyme that was extremely dirty, when Brysen thought about it—but Grazim was not amused.

"We know what you found," Kylee said. "Kyrg Birgund knows, too. Ryven told him. He's been having dreams, just like you. And me."

Brysen clenched his jaw. She'd known the whole time, and now everyone else knew, too. And just like Brysen had feared, everyone who wanted power wanted the egg for themselves. Maybe Kyrg Birgund had made a deal with Grazim; maybe that was why she had one of his hawks.

"You can't give it to the general," Brysen said, moving past Jowyn to pull the egg out from under the blankets. It was still black and warm, and he had an urge to tuck it under his red tunic and feel its heat against his skin. Instead he held it at a distance where both girls could see it but not touch it. Though the cave was dim and the egg was black, it gave off a negative kind of light, a darkness that gleamed.

"Have you noticed what they're doing, Brysen?" Kylee asked him. "They provoked that riot this morning by luring you to the Mutes. I think they *want* us all to kill one another. That egg is a way to drive a wedge between us. They want us fighting."

Brysen shook his head. "They don't know what they want," he told her, although he found he didn't have the words to explain how he knew that information, and he didn't think his sister would take the same leap of faith that Jowyn had. Brysen had done little in his life to earn her faith, and he knew it.

"Anyway," he said. "I'm not fighting. I'm not the one trying to steal the egg."

"I'm not trying to steal it," Kylee said. "I'm *asking* you for it."

"It's my responsibility," he replied. "I found it. And I promised to keep it safe."

"You *promised*?" Grazim scoffed. "Whom did you promise? The ghost eagles?"

"It," Brysen said, looking at the egg. "I promised it I would keep it safe."

Kylee threw her hands up in the air, startling the hawk on Grazim's fist so that the other girl had to whisper calming words to keep it from launching. "You know what Birgund wants from me?" Kylee said. "He wants me to use that egg to control the ghost eagles so he can exterminate every single person in the Mutes. He thinks that will solve the village's hunger and violence problems in one go. He doesn't get that he's asking me to do the ghost eagles' bidding."

"So you don't want to kill those people?" Grazim asked her, sounding surprised.

"If you aren't going to do what the kyrg wants, what *are* you going to do?" Brysen asked her. "Why do you want the egg?"

"To destroy it," she said.

Brysen felt the creature in the egg stir, pressing against the shell. He couldn't tell if that was its beak or its foot moving around, but there was a sharpness against his palm. The bird might hatch at any moment, and if it did, if it hatched into danger, would it fight back? How much did they have to fear from a newborn ghost eaglet?

"When the ghost eagles speak into our minds, they speak as 'we,' right?" Kylee said. "They act as one. That's how they seem to know what's going on everywhere, how they move us around like pieces on a game board. They're one mind spread across hundreds of bodies. It seemed to me like the one in the net this morning wasn't the only creature feeling its pain; it shared that pain with everyone. And if our minds can catch pieces of its agony, imagine how much the other ghost eagles felt. So I'm thinking that, if we destroy this one, maybe we can hurt them all."

"Or maybe that would just make them angrier?" Brysen said. He remembered what the ghost eagles had shown him at his old home, how scared they were of him having the egg. Maybe Kylee was right; maybe destroying it would destroy them; maybe the egg was their greatest weakness.

But he couldn't let her destroy it, not after he'd promised to keep it safe. He didn't really care about the war between humanity and the ghost eagles anymore; he cared about protecting this one little thing that couldn't protect itself, even when everyone else hated and feared it. Maybe even *because* everyone else hated and feared it.

"I can't let you hurt this one," Brysen told her. "I won't."

Flecks of gold appeared on the shell again.

Kylee took a slow breath; her voice softened. "I know you're still hurting because of what happened to Shara, but this isn't just another helpless bird to protect. This is a fragment of death itself. This is a cyclone in a shell, and when it breaks out, it's going to blow us apart."

"You don't know that," Brysen said. "Maybe I can teach it to be different." He tried to show her the gold flecks. "If I protect it, I can show it what humanity *can* be. It's not evil—it's just scared."

"Good!" Kylee said. "It should be scared! You can't teach it a lesson, Brysen. You're being naïve. The ghost eagles don't care how *good* people are. I've been in their mind and they've been in mine. I *know* these creatures better than anyone alive, and I know they kill the good and the bad with equal glee. All they want is to kill. This egg is our first chance to truly hurt them since the attacks began, and it *cannot* be allowed to survive."

"No," Brysen told her again.

"I have to," Kylee said, and took a step toward him. He stepped backward, into Jowyn, who nearly tumbled onto their sleeping pallet. There was nowhere to go. They were cornered. The shell was matte black once more, the swirls and whorls of different shades blending into one mass of darkness. Grazim's tailor's hawk looked at Brysen with bright and furious eyes. "*Please*," Kylee pleaded.

"No," Brysen told her, his voice no more than a whisper.

"Come on," Nyck called from the other end of the cave. "Everyone just calm down, okay? We can figure this out."

"Who wants some lunch?" Ma called from the hearth. She was oblivious to the drama playing out in the chamber next door.

Kylee shook her head from side to side a tiny bit. She did not intend to compromise. Neither did Brysen. He stiffened his back, stood straighter, and held the egg tighter, showing her his resolve. He was prepared to argue with her for as long as it took, but she didn't argue any more. She turned away from him, toward Grazim and the tailor's hawk on her fist, and she did something she had never done before.

She called a hawk against her brother.

13

"*SHYEHNAAH!*" SHE BROKE OFF THE WORD LIKE A BRANCH STRUCK BY lightning, and the hawk launched from Grazim's fist. "Praal."

"Kylee!" Jowyn yelled. Brysen was too stunned to move. He saw the brown wings opening, traced the white tips of the feathers, watched the bend of the legs as it rose, its talons outstretched to seize the egg out of his hands.

At the last moment, he turned and crouched, curling around the egg to shield it with his back and arms, hugging it under him. He tucked his head to protect his face as the hawk dropped onto his back, flapping and screeching, its talons snatching at him. He felt light scratches against his back, but the bird didn't break flesh. Kylee had commanded it to get the egg, not to hurt him. The hawk harried him, flapping its wings over his head, diving at and bumping into him but inflicting no wounds. Kylee was holding back, but for how long?

This was the nature of the Hollow Tongue. It was a language of intent more than vocabulary. The speaker had to choose the right word, but the word alone wasn't enough. They had to mean it with all their heart, with all their memories, with the want and the need for which it called. The more powerful the word and the more powerful the bird, the more truth it demanded.

But the Hollow Tongue wasn't a passive language, either. It acted on those who spoke it and was the language of a predator. All its words hungered. Brysen felt it pressing on him now, burning in his lungs, roiling his stomach, and calling to him. The ghost eaglet stirred inside its shell; Brysen smelled smoke and heard the crack of a whip. It stung. Every wingbeat against his back was an echo of the whip that made his scars.

He'd been curled like this before, his body wrapped around a helpless hawk as his father's rage tore open his skin, then doused him in liquor, then burned him. He'd burned alive and lived, and so had that bird. He'd protected her and loved her, and she, in the way a bird of prey could, loved him. He would protect this one, too, not because it was useful or because it could change the world, but because someone had to.

He thought he saw a flurry of black feathers in the corner of his eye, a glance of giant wings. But there was no ghost eagle in this cavern—only the one in the egg and the one in his mind.

"Kylee, call it off!" Jowyn screamed.

"Give me the egg!" she demanded. Brysen could hear tears in her voice. "Please, just let it go!"

"No!" he yelled back, finding his own voice choked with tears, too. "I can't."

"If that egg hatches, it will kill us all," Grazim said. "Give it up."

"Call off your bird," Jowyn told Kylee, stepping around Brysen to get in her face.

"Everybody, please! Calm down!" Nyck yelled. "We're on the same side!"

The egg shuddered under Brysen. The creature inside pressed against the shell, eager to break out. The anger in the air was calling it. It was calling to Brysen, too. He wanted to let the egg hatch, let it unleash its fury—on his own sister, on Grazim, on the bird, on the whole world, the world that took his eye, his hawk, and his sister's love. *Eviscerate it all.*

His rage was overwhelming. His ears rang with it. He felt as though he was out of his body, like he was floating at the roof of the cave, looking down at his back through the hawk's eyes, tracing his own scars with a vision clearer than he thought possible. He could see the faintest hairs, the tiniest fissures in his flesh, every blood vessel. He could rip that flesh to shreds . . . or he could turn the hawk on Kylee.

He began to move, straightening a little, ready to fling her own attack at her with ten times the fury. But Kylee moved faster, saw an opening and rushed him, snatched the egg out of his grip and rolled with it across the floor, holding it tight. The hawk rose away from him, screeching, confused.

Brysen felt like a piece of him had been cut away. He saw only white, like his remaining eye'd been cut out. Then his vision cleared, and he saw Kylee had the curved black-talon blade raised above the egg. Brysen anticipated the pain, felt the tiny hairs tingle on his neck, saw the shell shudder. He watched her wind back, preparing to stab, hard, to slam the blade through the shell and sever the baby bird's head from its body before it hatched.

But the knife glanced off.

The egg was unharmed. The knife went skittering away, out of Kylee's grip. She grabbed the egg and lifted it, slammed it down on the rocks, but still she couldn't hurt it.

"Break!" she yelled, pounding the shell on the rocks over and over.

"Stop it!" Brysen yelled.

"Just die!" Kylee screamed at it. Tears of frustration streaked her face as she threw it into the cave wall, watched it fall onto the floor again, then kicked it against the sharpest stone she could find. "Just die! Just die!"

The egg was as solid as ever.

"*Kraas!*" she commanded the hawk, which dove from the cavern's ceiling and attacked the egg full force with its talons, tried to grab it but couldn't. A tailor's hawk could catch a leaping river salmon without slowing, could crush a goat's skull in its grip, but this one stumbled and slipped right off the black shell. It screeched in frustration.

"Stop it!" Brysen pleaded with his sister, and she looked up at him, and he saw her mouth forming a word, saw her breath rising. She was about to send the hawk for him again, but this time there would be no holding back. This time it would tear skin. Brysen knew this in the way night knows dawn: Kylee was going to hurt him now. He also knew that he would let her, because that was the pattern in their family, that was what always happened. He was the boy who failed and who suffered for it, and she was just like his father, the instrument of his suffering. She hadn't killed their father; she'd become him.

"*Shyehna—*" she began, when she was cut off.

"*Shyehnaah-tar!*"

Ma's voice sliced the air, and as suddenly as it had attacked, the tailor's hawk broke off, circled, and flew back to Grazim's fist. The eaglet calmed in its shell, no longer responding to their worst impulses.

Brysen looked at his mother, standing in the opening of the chamber, lit from above by a slash of sunlight from a skylight. Her arms were open, though one hand held a wooden spoon that was dripping thick porridge onto the floor. Her other hand was clenched into a fist. She was panting, as though she'd just run up a mountain.

"Ma?" Kylee said.

Their ma lowered the spoon and her fist.

"Ma?" said Brysen.

She looked from Brysen to Kylee and then shook her head. "You don't speak these words," she said. "They speak you. Look at what they've done. This is not who you are—either of you."

She was Altari, like Grazim, a believer in the holiness of birds of prey, believing that they were made unclean by any consort with humanity, that training or trading or commanding them was deep blasphemy, and that the Hollow Tongue was never meant to be spoken from human mouths. Grazim, who had a gift for the language, had long ago renounced the faith of her people, but Ma, as far as they knew, never had. And yet she had just spoken words to call off the hawk and to calm the baby bird in the egg, words that were stronger than Kylee's or Brysen's.

"Ma?" Kylee said again. "How?"

"I left my home and my people for the same reason Grazim left hers," she said. "How do you stay in a community that hates what you are? But I took their hate with me, and I buried the Hollow Tongue as deep as I could for as long as I could. I prayed it would vanish from the world. I lost myself in those prayers." She looked from Brysen to Kylee and back again. "The wounds we suffer when we're young can draw the map of our lives if we let them. I let mine. But you two, you're more than what you've suffered. *Be* more."

At that moment she seemed to remember the spoon in her hand, because she looked down at it, then up at them again. She glanced around at the stunned battle boys, at Grazim and the hawk, at Jowyn, and at the twins. "Food is ready," she added as she left the chamber. "None of you eats enough."

Kylee hesitated, then picked up the egg and held it out to Brysen. He flinched. He didn't mean to, but his nerves were still raw.

"I'm sorry," she whispered.

He took the egg but wasn't ready to take the apology. He wasn't sure she deserved his forgiveness. She was only returning the egg because she'd failed to destroy it, and they both knew what had almost happened, who they had each almost become. His sister had acted as a predator; he as prey. They were just what the ghost eagles always thought.

He glanced down at the blackness in his hands. He had the egg back now, and he might be able to keep it safe, though he knew he couldn't keep it safe in the cave.

Kylee was belting her knife and whispering with Grazim. They were having some kind of quiet argument, their foreheads inclined toward each other, though Grazim was taller and had to bend slightly to keep their faces close. Brysen could tell they were on the same side even in disagreement—whatever side that was—and he knew he couldn't trust them. They might try to kill the eaglet the moment it hatched. Besides, with the kyrg knowing about it, they wouldn't just let him hang on to the egg. The general would defintely want to take it for himself. Brysen had to go somewhere else with it if he was going to make sure it hatched safely—somewhere no one would follow him . . .

He turned to look at Jowyn. He didn't need to speak. Jowyn knew what he was going to ask.

"That's not a good idea," he said. "The Owl Mothers shut themselves away in the blood birches for a reason. They kill uninvited strangers."

"We're not strangers," Brysen reminded him.

"We're worse," he said. "I'm an exile who betrayed them, and you're a boy they hate."

"Okay, sure," Brysen agreed. "But the point is, we're not strangers."

"Brysen," Kylee interrupted, and he stopped her.

"You know I have to go," he said. "Don't try to argue with me."

She flinched this time. "I wasn't," she said. "I was going to tell you to be careful and to pack better than you usually do. Bring more food. Hunting won't be easy now."

"Wait, you think this is a *good* idea?" Jowyn said.

"You're just going to let him go?" Grazim said.

Kylee met Brysen's eye. She smiled sadly, and though he knew she was hurting, too, and was looking for some sign he'd forgiven her, he couldn't offer her any. Not yet.

"He can't stay here," Kylee confirmed. "He has to go before Ryven and the general come searching for that egg." She cleared her throat. "Look after him, okay, Jowyn? Don't let them hurt him."

"We're two feathers on the same wing," Jowyn said. "He falls, I fall."

Kylee laughed and wiped away a tear. "That's not how feathers work," she said. "But you have to go before it's too late."

Except it was already too late.

RED-HANDED

"AND WHY SHOULD WE TRUST YOU AT ALL?" AALISH ASKED.

The handsome young man in front of her leaned back on his small stool. Even with the bruise on his face and the over-size robes of a long-haul trader draped over him, he looked too fine to be in their shack in the heart of the Mutes. His voice was too polished, his skin too clear. Aalish knew his kind of handsome didn't happen to the sorts of people she knew. She'd been on the march since she was born, first with nomadic Altari herders and then with the Kartami horde, sacking settlements and burning bodies. That kind of life didn't leave much room for skin balms and ointments. This man didn't even have any visible scars. What kind of person had no scars? A life made scars. Aalish did not trust this man.

"You shouldn't trust me," he said, looking from her to Dhona. "I have my own agenda, as you have yours. But right now, our interests are aligned. You want to survive. I want you to fight. You can't do the former without the latter, so I'm here to help."

"And why would a kyrg want us to fight?" Dhona stood, towering over him and setting her red-wrapped fist on the small table between them. She had a way of looming over anyone she chose, even though she was not a terribly large person. She was raised in the Kartami horde, a child of one of the first warriors to join the cause, and she'd been fighting ever since. She had a way of figuring out people, and judging by this dapper young man's silence, she was right: He was an actual kyrg, here, in the Mutes. Aalish considered taking him hostage right then, but Dhona was the leader between the two of them, and Aalish had learned to defer to her judgment.

When Dhona was first paired with Aalish to infiltrate Uztari towns and recruit spies, she'd balked at the idea of putting down a blade and being matched with someone she described as "pale and soft as a cloud." But Aalish had proved herself a skilled companion, and they both discovered that recruitment and intelligence-gathering suited them. Love came later, but when it did, it was complete. They knew each other and trusted each other and were prepared to die for each other, but, even more important, they wanted to live for each other. The Mutes were a sky-cursed place, filthy and hungry and cramped, but every day with Dhona was its own brutal joy. Aalish, being honest, saw no reason for it to end.

During the war, spying saved both their lives. When the ghost eagles came and tore every Kartami kite from the sky, they were on the ground, disguised as Uztari soldiers. They even managed to slit a few throats.

Though the battle ended, the war never did. The last fortnite had been a respite, and now here was this kyrg trying to start it up again. The question Dhona was after: Why? Aalish didn't really care. She'd have happily sent him on his way and let things go on as they had been. It wasn't like the two of them would starve. No one good with a blade and unsentimental about strangers ever had to go hungry.

"My name is Ryven," the young man said. "And I was a kyrg—you're correct. But I was removed from the Council. For treason."

Dhona laughed.

"An uprising from your lot would go a long way toward bringing me back into power."

"After you squash us with Kyrg Birgund's soldiers?" Aalish said.

"After Kyrg Birgund fails to squash you, and I step in and

negotiate a truce," Ryven offered. "Of course, some will die in the fighting, on both sides . . . but have you noticed how crowded it is in here? A little thinning of the flock wouldn't be the worst thing, would it?"

"I can see you aren't much of a compassionate ruler," Dhona said.

"Hawks don't cry for rabbits," Ryven said. Aalish flexed her fist and made sure he looked closely at the red kerchief she wore around it. The red was faded to brown, because the dye she used had come from an Uztari falconer's jugular. She didn't want this delicate man to forget he was at her mercy. Somehow, though, Dhona's stillness seemed more threatening to him. Aalish was always in awe of that woman, how she managed to be so formidable with such ease.

"So you're proposing to arm us so we can fight long enough for you to play peacemaker?" Dhona finally said.

"If you can survive that long." Ryven laced his fingers together and rested them on the table, his body loose and relaxed. He was not intimidated. "Either you start this fight very soon with weapons I provide, or you wait and Birgund and his little fledglings let the *talorum* inside to tear you apart."

Aalish shuddered at the Hollow Tongue name for the ghost eagle: its true name. Even Dhona flinched. They'd gone to war to rid the world of these monsters in the sky, but Ryven invoked them with such casual ease.

"We have eyes on the hatchlings," Aalish said. "We can handle them."

"The two you sent up after the boy are already dead," Ryven told them, as though describing yesterday's weather.

"How do you kn—" Aalish began, but Dhona stopped her.

"The *talorum?*" she said, her voice catching on the word. *Bound to death*, it meant, and even speaking it could cast death upon you.

Dhona wasn't superstitious like that, though.

Ryven nodded. "They tell me things."

"This all so you can get back on the Council?" Dhona tapped her fingers on her knees. "I don't believe you'd do all this just to be back on the Council of Forty. They're hardly in control of anything these days, and you seem like someone who doesn't bet on a losing pigeon."

Ryven chuckled. He had a compelling smile, warm and open—and false. It was like a good story: You want to believe it, even though you know it's a lie. "I can have more than one goal at time," he said. "As long as Kyrg Birgund is kept busy for a while, I will bring the fighting to an end and make sure you have a place in whatever new order emerges."

"And you'll be in a position to do that?" Aalish raised an eyebrow.

Ryven rolled up his sleeves to show tan lines from his

falconer's glove, staring at both of them, daring them to show offense. When they didn't, he spoke. "I will have control of the ghost eagles by then, so yes, I do think I will be able to dictate a few terms for the way peace will look. Help me by helping yourselves, and you'll get say. Turn me down and . . ." He let his voice trail off, then cleared his throat. "I'm a better friend than enemy."

With that, he stood, raised his cowl to hide his face, and stepped out into the afternoon light. Hunched over and limping in the narrow lanes of the Mutes, Ryven looked to all the world like a broken old soldier—and not at all like a treasonous, deposed ruler of Uztar who'd just proposed to give weapons to his enemy. He moved away from them very quickly, however, and Aalish and Dhona agreed it would be wise to follow and learn what he was really up to. He said it himself: They shouldn't trust him.

They didn't.

KYLEE

UPDRAFT

14

IT WAS AMAZING HOW QUICKLY ONE MISTAKE COULD CHANGE everything your friends thought of you. Brysen made mistakes all the time, but no one ever looked at him like they were looking at Kylee now. The injustice of it tasted like ash on her tongue.

"Anger took over." She tried to explain herself. "You know how the ghost eagles can get in your head."

"There isn't a ghost eagle here," the young battle boy, Lyra, said, rushing to a peephole by the door to scan outside. She wasn't thinking about the eaglet inside the egg. Kylee wondered if the ghost eagle could get into her head before hatching, or if the violence she'd unleashed had been purely her own.

Kheryn, the battle boys' muscle, stood next to Nyck, dismantling Kylee with their eyes. No one would ever look to the battle boys for lessons on morality or gentleness, but they did have a code. They fought for one another, not against one another, and they'd never, ever, ever call a hawk against one of their own.

Only Grazim didn't look at her with disgust, which wasn't the best endorsement of her actions. When they first met, Grazim sent a hawk to torture a prisoner of the Owl Mothers, just to provoke Kylee into a mercy killing.

Although she was glad for Grazim now, their friendship was fraught and more than a little bloody. Those were, when she thought about it, the only kinds of friendships she'd ever known. What kind of world only made bonds like blood clots? Was it really a world worth fighting for?

"Soldiers are coming up the hill!" Lyra warned them.

"Ryven told Kyrg Birgund all about the egg," Kylee said. "I promised I'd bring it back."

"Guess he figured out you were lying," Kheryn said with some judgment in their voice. "And you let yourself be followed back here."

"Guess so," Kylee said, projecting whatever defiance she

could. She was not going to be judged for doing what she thought was necessary to protect all of them.

"They'll try to breach," Nyck said.

"We'll need to stall them while Brysen sneaks out," Kheryn said. "He'll need to take one of the tunnels we can lock behind him. Preferably one that doesn't lead straight into the Broken Jess. Your ma know of any others?"

"I can ask her," Kylee replied. Kheryn had the most fighting experience of all of them, so it made sense to let them take over. Also, Kylee figured none of them was inclined to let her lead right now, anyway.

She still didn't feel like herself. The fury she'd unleashed on her brother unsettled her. She knew the ghost eagles couldn't create new thoughts in her mind—the eagles could only twist and provoke what was already there, show her the worst version of herself and make her believe it was her whole self. It was a lie that used a person's jagged pieces to hurt them and, apparently, to hurt people they cared about.

We will tame you all, the ghost eagles had sworn.

She had, at the time, looked into the dreadful, swirling convocation and simply told them, "No." What a fool! She'd done exactly what they wanted. They'd tamed her more easily than a child tames a flycatcher. The ghost eagles knew her too well. They knew just how to get in her head. If she was going to beat them, she had to find ways to surprise them.

Going to her ma for help would definitely be a surprise.

"Ma?" she said, stepping into the hearth chamber, where her mother was putting a stopper into a bulbous waterskin.

"Your brother will need this." She held the heavy waterskin out to Kylee. "It's a hard climb to the blood birches."

"The soldiers are coming," Kylee told her. "We need a way out. Have you found any other tunnels?"

She nodded, pointed to a wall of the hearth chamber where broken pots and bowls and shards of pottery were piled. "You should go with him," she said. "Look after each other."

"He doesn't want me to go with him," Kylee said. "He's got Jowyn now. And after what I did—"

"Some birds fly the same circles over and over every season," Ma interrupted. "But you are not birds. The breeze doesn't tell you where to go."

"Ma, I don't have time for Altari folk wisdom right now. Brysen's going, and there will be a fight here. Maybe you should go with him."

She shook her head. "This is where I belong."

"You could help him," Kylee said. "Use your . . ." She wasn't sure how to describe it. "Use your gift for the Hollow Tongue."

Her mother let out a rueful laugh that reminded Kylee of Brysen's. "I hated myself for this 'gift' for so long," she said. "I was taught that it's sin, and I believed it. I believed it was a curse I'd never be free of if I stayed where I was. So I came to the Six Villages, looking for acceptance. Instead I found your da, and I rebuilt the misery I fled. It was a misery I felt I deserved. And when you had the same gift? That seemed like a punishment designed for me. I put it all back on myself again. It wasn't on purpose, though I chose it, I suppose." Her eyes found her daughter's. "I guess, Kylee, what I'm saying is that I can't fly where either of you are going. Much as I'd like to help, I know myself now. I've carved the same circles in the sky for so long, my wings don't bend any other way. You need to go without me. Fly new circles."

"You don't *have* to do what you've always done," Kylee said back. "You can change."

Again came the rueful laugh, and as if in answer, Ma held out the waterskin for Kylee to take to her brother. Kylee was like her mother that way: A retreat into the practical was better than saying the wrong thing when words failed. Maybe there would be time to find the right words if they all survived, but there was no time now. Kylee took the waterskin to Brysen and pointed out where to go.

"Thanks," he said quietly.

"Thank Ma," she told him. He just coughed a little. "I'm sorry, Brysen," she said again. There were wounds you could make that only you could heal, and then there were wounds that only got worse when you tried. Sometimes it was hard to know which was which.

Brysen nodded, but that didn't tell her much. He moved for the tunnel entrance. She didn't want this to be the way they parted, but she had no other choice. She watched him disappear into the dark.

"We've got six falconers coming up the slope!" Nyck yelled from the door. He and Lyra chose blades from a cubby that was meant to hold cloaks during the colder seasons.

"Arm yourself!" Kheryn yelled at Kylee. She was standing halfway between the hearth chamber and the large, round entry room. Before Kylee could act, Grazim was beside her, presenting her with the curved black-talon blade in its sheath.

"I can't believe you're going to let that feather-headed mope run off to the Owl Mothers with the egg," she said.

"Who would I be if I made him stay?" Kylee replied as she took the sheath and belted it around her waist.

"Someone much smarter than you," Grazim suggested. It was nice having a friend who didn't lie to her. Grazim was unarmed but had the tailor's hawk on her fist—a better weapon than any blade.

"Smart's overrated when it comes to family," Kylee said. "He's my brother. I can't take it from him just because I think I'm right."

"But you *are* right," Grazim countered. "That thing has to

be destroyed. What if the Owl Mothers take it? We can beat Birgund *and* the ghost eagles if we find a way to use that egg against them, but it's no good to us if your brother walks it right into the enemy's hands."

"No," Kylee said. "But I won't force him."

"You're stronger than he is!" Grazim objected.

"That why I have to let him go."

Grazim clearly didn't understand, but Kylee knew she had power, and power demanded she find another way. Her father had been a weak man, and he took out his weakness on Brysen. She'd almost done the same. Only the weak needed a whip. She was going to find the strength to do something new. She just didn't quite know what that was yet.

"How did I end up tied to such a finch-brained friend?" Grazim shook her head and took Kylee's hand. She squeezed their fingers together with a smile. "The things I do for your mud-munching family."

"Open the door!" a muffled voice called from outside. It was Ser Ygeva, the officer from that morning.

"Prepare to open the door," Kheryn said.

"Wait . . ." Kylee was puzzled. "Why are we going to open the door for them?"

"We want them coming for us, right?" Kheryn said. "So Brysen has time to get away. We gotta give them someone to fight so they don't start looking for him."

Made sense. Kylee was glad she'd deferred to their judgment.

"Knew I'd end up shedding blood for Brysen today," Nyck said, spitting a green glob on the ground and adjusting his footing as Lyra prepared to release the mechanism holding the boulder in front of the cave entrance.

Kylee touched the handle of the knife on her belt. She thought about what Kyrg Birgund wanted her to do, the massacre he thought she would commit for him. He thought of her the same way the ghost eagles did: as a vehicle for rage. Maybe they weren't wrong. After all, she'd nearly torn her own brother to shreds. But she'd also found a way out of an encounter without bloodshed, just that morning. She didn't *have* to shed blood to get what she wanted. She could find other ways, if given the chance. She wondered if Kyrg Birgund's soldiers would give her that chance. She looked from Nyck to Kheryn to Grazim and then back at Ma, in the hallway behind her. She'd have liked to make peace for all their sakes, but she was ready to make war for their sakes, too. She'd do what the situation demanded—no more and no less.

"If they want blood, they'll get it," she said as she drew her blade. "But let's be clear: If it comes to it, this isn't about Brysen. This blood's for us."

15

NYCK STEPPED BACK FROM THE PEEPHOLES BY THE ENTRANCE, AND Lyra released a rope from the cleat where it was tied. With a nod, Kheryn signaled Nyck, and the large, round stone began to move, rolling ponderously in its groove in the floor. It was like staring at the sun as an eclipse ended. Golden daylight flooded the antechamber, and Kylee was blinded for a moment by the brilliant afternoon. She saw the bright blue sky divided into uneven rectangles—blocked into squares by the net bolted into the stone just above the entrance.

The net cast strange shadows across the cavern floor, and Kylee knew why the soldiers had chosen this moment to attack. Peregrines prefer to attack their prey in the same way—with the sun at their backs, so the unfortunate prey can't see them diving until it's too late.

Kylee saw the first attack just before it struck: two kestrels racing for the cave's entrance.

Grazim saw them, too, but looked to Kylee for orders. Kylee, however, looked to Kheryn. Sometimes leadership meant knowing when to step back. She'd let the fighters lead the fighting.

"What are you waiting for?" Kheryn yelled at her. They weren't used to command. Gang fighting had different rules and expectations, but it was mostly hit first and harder.

Grazim snapped a command at her hawk, which launched from her fist and flapped out of the cave and into the daylight. The two dragonfly-fast kestrels turned wide to flank the hawk from opposite sides, and on the ground, their tamers ran wide in the opposite direction, bolting for the cave's entrance.

Kylee saw the other soldiers fanned out down the slope in a half-moon shape. Their commander, Ser Ygeva, stood in the center, directing fighters on both flanks. Their positioning made it hard to see the entirety of the force without stepping from the safety of the cave. Kylee imagined they'd have archers prepared at either side of the opening.

The rest of the falconers had their small birds—all kestrels—tethered but not hooded. Kestrels were a smart choice. They were slight and maneuverable enough to fight well under the netting but too small to do severe damage if Kylee and Grazim turned them on their masters.

The kestrels sped toward the bigger hawk, but it dove for the ground just before they collided, forcing both birds to dodge away from each other. They'd been so close, their wings touched. Another reason to use kestrels: They were one of the few birds of prey to hunt in groups. They knew how to work together to snare their prey. They wouldn't so easily be outsmarted by a juvenile tailor's hawk, even one commanded by the Hollow Tongue.

The hawk madly flapped away from the two little birds, flying so low its feet brushed dust. The kestrels pursued, weaving figure eights as they herded the hawk higher, toward the underside of the nets, trying to tangle it. Kyrg Birgund's soldiers had clearly trained their birds for just this sort of attack. The Redfists in the Mutes wouldn't use birds to fight, so the only reason to have trained for this was in order to combat Kylee and her friends. Birgund expected Kylee to resist, which meant he was ready for the counterattack. They'd need to be smart here.

Nyck, who had better taste for action than for planning, simply rushed from the cave entrance with a katar clutched in each fist. The handle of a katar was perpendicular to its short blade; stabbing with a punching motion could, in the right spot, be followed by a rib-cutting twist. Nyck wasn't shy about violence—you didn't grow up around hawk battle pits and end up squeamish about blood—but he also wasn't a fool, and killing Uztari soldiers was extremely foolish. Either his double-bladed charge was a bluff, or the combination of soldier's ale and hunter's leaf had made him stupid.

Kylee sighed, certain it was the latter.

A falconer unleashed her kestrel and tossed it at Nyck, the bird flying fast from the fist. It stretched its talons and rose above him as high as the nets would let it, preparing to dive. Lyra ran from the cave, a war hammer in both hands, a war cry screaming from her mouth. She charged one of the falconers, using the slope of the hill to gain skull-crushing momentum.

"*Toktott!*" Kylee yelled, and one of the kestrels pursuing the hawk broke away, veering close enough to Nyck to knock off course the bird about to attack him. Meanwhile, Lyra's attack on the falconer just missed, and her own wide swing's momentum made her fall forward. The closest soldiers simply scooped her up and disarmed her. One of them pressed a stiletto blade to a pulsing vein in her neck. Just as quickly as it started, combat halted.

"Hurt her and you'll die," Nyck shouted, eyes locked on the soldier holding Lyra. He tended to get grandiose under the influence of hunter's leaf. It was harmless enough in the Broken Jess, where brawls over half-bronze bets ended with broken bones and bloodied noses. But such bravado could be deadly in a standoff against the falconers of the Uztari empire.

"Your agreement with Kyrg Birgund isn't even as old as the sweat on my neck and you've already gone back on it," Ser Ygeva shouted at Kylee.

"Brysen's his own person," Kylee replied. The longer she talked, the more time Brysen had to get away. She had to keep stalling. "We disagreed about what should be done, and he made his own choice."

"You didn't stop him?" Ser Ygeva asked.

Kylee shook her head in an exaggerated way. "Did Birgund really think I was going to fight my own brother over an egg?"

Kheryn and Grazim glanced sideways at her. That was *exactly* what she had done.

"The kyrg thought you would honor your agreements," the officer said. "However, if your brother is going to make us chase him, then we will."

"You don't need to!" Kylee told her. "I'll honor our deal, just without the egg. I can . . . I can still do what Birgund wants, in the Mutes . . ."

"You can't be serious," Grazim whispered to her.

"I'm buying us time," she said through clenched teeth.

"No deal," Ser Ygeva replied. She scratched at her cheek, as though her scar itched. "The terms were the egg. Without it, the kyrg has no interest in your services. He has other ways to handle the Mutes. This was more a test of your loyalty and reliability, which you, of course, failed, as I assured him you would." She scanned the group, then gave a curt nod. The falconers began unleashing their kestrels. "Neither he nor my officers are interested in you, your family, or your abilities anymore. You have been a thorn in Uztar's side for some time, and your continued freedom is no longer desired, nor is your survival necessary. Surrender or die."

"I don't love those options," Kylee replied.

"There are no others," the officer snapped back.

So they've chosen blood, Kylee thought. *So be it.*

She didn't wait for them to make the first strike. She seized the moment.

"*Kraas*," she said so quietly it wouldn't have startled a mouse, yet the kestrels heard, and their oldest instinct ignited at the word. They shrieked and whirled on their tamers, talons up, scratching and tearing and harrying the soldiers, who stumbled backward, desperate to unleash the birds and get away. Some didn't even bother with the knots; they just pulled off their gloves and tossed them, diving to the dirt and covering their heads.

But Ser Ygeva didn't retreat, not even as her falconers were bloodied by their own birds. Her infantry soldiers charged.

At the same moment, the solider holding Lyra went to draw his blade across her neck—but Lyra was too quick for him. He sliced a bit of skin, but she stomped his toe and rolled her head away, then delivered a sharp blow to his ribs. With that, she was free—on the wrong side of the soldiers, yes, but drawing some of their attention.

Nyck thrilled into action, meeting one of the soldiers blade for blade. He moved with the cunning of a pit brawler, dodging the man's blows and punching with unrelenting fury. But the soldier had training enough to parry every attack, even though he couldn't land a body blow, either.

Nyck laughed through the fight, as if the soldier weren't actively trying to kill him. At one point he even dodged a thrust of the soldier's rapier, twirling to the side and entangling the man's arms. Locked close with their heads together, Nyck gave the soldier a kiss on the cheek. The move was so unexpected, the solider even laughed, disarmed first by Nyck's insouciance and then by Nyck's elbow to his gut, which doubled him over. Nyck took the opportunity to kick away the soldier's rapier.

He didn't kill the soldier, though; Nyck simply crossed his blades in an X in front of the man's neck, daring him to move from where he knelt.

He didn't dare.

Kheryn picked up the fallen rapier to intercept another soldier, who slowed her run and then stopped, looking up at Kylee and Grazim. They were still standing in front of the cave's mouth.

"You haven't trained in tactics, Kylee," Ser Ygeva called to her. "If you had, you would realize that this grouping you see is not the size of a normal Uztari platoon." Ygeva whistled, and suddenly emerging from the boulders all around them, above and below and to the sides of the cave, were two dozen soldiers, crossbows aimed at her and at the battle boys. And marching from inside the cave, held at swordpoint, were Jowyn and Brysen, each with cloths stuck in their mouths to gag them. One of the soldiers had the bag that held the ghost eagle's egg. Ma wasn't with them. Had she hidden? Had she run?

Ser Ygeva looked at the soldier Nyck still held on the ground. "My soldiers are all prepared to die for their mission," she said, "though it would be a shame for one to die so pointlessly. We would still prevail, and you, little chickadee, would be buried so deep in the mud your soul would forget there was ever such a thing as sky."

Nyck looked ready to keep fighting, and so did Kheryn and Lyra, but Kylee knew when she was beaten. She couldn't even see the kestrels she'd turned on their handlers; they must have flown somewhere in the Villages, still obeying her order to attack, and they wouldn't be able to hear her call them back.

She nodded to Nyck to release the captive soldier. Nyck pulled away his blades and Kheryn held out the soldier's sword to him but dropped it just before the soldier took it back, so the man had to bend down to Kheryn's feet to pick it up. Kheryn even smiled as the soldier bent. Nothing humbled a battle boy.

"Looks like you don't have to say good-bye to your little brother after all," Grazim noted.

"He's actually older than me," Kylee replied.

"I always forget that," Grazim said, "with the way you coddle him."

"Are you really gonna do this now?"

"Reminding you to not act like a sentimental idiot seems like a good use of my time," Grazim said, "until I can figure a way out of this."

"I got us into it, I'll get us out," Kylee said.

"Oh, no, Kylee." Grazim shook her head. "You and your family have done enough. I think it's time you let someone else lead the way, someone who hasn't accidentally incurred the wrath of everyone on the ground and in the air. You're a pretty terrible leader, you know?"

Kylee looked over at her brother. He was bound and gagged; his eye was fixed on his bag, which was in the soldier's hand. Kylee looked at Jowyn, whose eyes were fixed on Brysen.

The battle boys were looking at one another as though deciding how much more difficult to make their surrender.

Battle boys didn't like surrendering their weapons without someone paying in groans.

"You're right. I'm a terrible leader," Kylee told her friend, "but there's only one way to improve."

Grazim waited.

"Practice." Kylee grinned.

Grazim actually laughed, which made the approaching soldiers nervous.

They should be nervous. Kylee didn't plan to let this go unanswered.

"Make sure to gag those two also," said a voice within the cave. Stepping out from behind the soldiers who held Brysen and Jowyn was Kyrg Ryven.

"Ryven—" Kylee began, but she was cut short as a ball of cloth was shoved into her mouth and tied in place. Ser Ygeva did this herself, her face close to Kylee's.

"Just cooperate," she whispered. "You can all survive. The empire will need you when this is all over." Ser Ygeva met her eyes, nodded once to make sure she was understood, then stepped back as Ryven came up to her. She kept her eyes on Kylee.

"I know you're angry with me, Kylee," Ryven said. "Although I'm the one who *should* be angry at you. You betray me every chance you get, and yet, like a vulture overfeeding on the corpse of a camel, I come back to pick at you again and again. I do wonder if your brother, perhaps, would make a better meal." Ryven rested a hand on Brysen's shoulder, and Jowyn tensed in response. "He seems more reasonable."

Through her gag, Grazim laughed.

"Of course, we've all learned something today." Ryven dropped his hand from Brysen. "And I have a feeling Kyrg Birgund will want to know how you—"

Ryven stopped short, looking up just as a spear erupted through Ser Ygeva's chest and splattered blood onto Grazim. Ygeva was still looking at Kylee as she fell forward into the mud.

A moment later, two riots of Redfists erupted from two sides: the first from a neighboring cave up a hill, just beyond the netting, and the second from the Villages below. Their spears and arrows and swords cut down the soldiers of Uztar faster than they could muster a response, and they quickly seized the prisoners for themselves.

Ryven raised his hands in surrender without the slightest hesitation.

"Well, this is turning into an interesting day," he said, almost like he'd been expecting the attack.

One of the warriors balled her red-kerchiefed fist and doubled him over with a punch to the groin, then turned to Kylee, all smiles.

"My name is Dhona," she said, and then she pointed to another soldier, who strode up the slope wiping Uztari soldier blood off her blade. "This is Aalish. And you, Kylee, have made a lot of enemies for someone so young. I like it."

She smiled at Kylee, but there was no warmth in it.

16

THEY WERE HERDED THROUGH THE STREETS IN A CONFUSING procession, doubling back, passing through sympathizers' houses, and accessing hidden passageways in storage rooms and latrines, until they reached a nondescript shack, one of many in the center of the Mutes. Here Kylee, Brysen, Jowyn, Grazim, and the three battle boys were pressed onto the floor, their hands bound to stakes in the ground behind their backs, forcing them to sit.

"Welcome to your new home," Aalish said.

Ryven was taken elsewhere, which disappointed Kylee. She'd have liked to see him suffer alongside her. They took Brysen's bag, which held the ghost eagle egg, somewhere else, too. She worried what Ryven would do if they let him get too close to the egg.

Kylee studied the light coming through the slats of the shack, trying to figure out how long they had until sunset. She wondered whether the ghost eagles would come to get their egg or if they wanted Ryven to have it. In her experience, birds of prey were ferocious when it came to protecting their hatchlings, but the ghost eagles weren't normal birds of prey. She wasn't even sure they laid eggs. She considered that no one had any idea what this egg actually contained or what the creature inside would do when it hatched. *How very like us,* she thought, *killing one another to control something we haven't even begun to understand.*

Still, if it was killing they wanted, she could give it to them.

The eagles will come, and I will use them and their rage to free us. Birgund wants a massacre? I'll give him one. I might even turn it back on him when I'm done in the Mutes. And then we can finally—

She stopped herself. This was the pattern: feeling helpless, getting angry, and then lashing out in fury. Like Ma said, she'd flown this same circle over and over before. The eagles kept setting her up—setting up all of them—to kill one another. She considered that the egg itself might mean nothing to the eagles; maybe it was simply a way to ignite humanity's violent rage against itself. Or it might mean everything to the eagles, and then whoever controlled it could control them. Kylee closed her eyes against the throbbing in her head. Either one thing was true or its opposite, and all she knew was that she knew absolutely nothing.

Well, not *nothing*. She knew that she was a prisoner.

Solve that problem first, she thought. *No sense borrowing trouble from the future when the present has plenty on offer.*

"No birds to worry about here." Aalish pulled the gag out of Kylee's mouth, then did the same for Grazim and Brysen. "Water?"

Kylee tightened her jaw, determined to accept nothing from these people, but she changed her mind when she watched the others drink and realized how very thirsty she was. You could reason with captors or overpower them, but there was no argument against thirst, and if she and her friends did manage to escape, who knew when they'd be able to stop for water again?

"So." Aalish crossed her arms. "We have some questions."

"There's an herb that will clear that rash right up," Brysen said, which earned him an elbow nudge in the side from Jowyn.

"AHHH!" a man's scream came from somewhere nearby.

"Sounds like Kyrg Ryven is resisting our questions," Aalish said. "It'd be wise for you to be more cooperative."

Brysen fell quiet, looked down.

"So tell us about this egg," Aalish said.

"You know what it is," Kylee told her. "And you know what the eagles do to whoever has it."

"And yet your brother was going to walk straight up the mountain with it?" She eyed Brysen. "Were you not worried the ghost eagles would rip open your fragile little body and take their egg back?"

Brysen clamped his mouth shut.

"No clever reply?" Aalish turned her gaze from Brysen to Kylee. "We know you betrayed the kyrg by letting your brother try to run off with the egg."

"How could you know that?" Kylee asked. Her voice came out softer than she'd wanted it to.

Aalish shook her head. "I ask the questions. Tell me: Whose side are you on in this war with the sky?"

"Ours," Kylee said, meaning her friends and family. She hoped the answer was vague enough that Aalish might think she meant humanity, even if she didn't.

"Good," Aalish said. "Because I need you focused on what is important here, not on petty squabbles from the past."

"I wouldn't call laying siege to our villages and murdering falconers by the thousands a petty squabble," Nyck cut in. "I seem to remember going to war against your army."

"That was before," Aalish said. "You need to think about the future."

"What about this morning?" Nyck replied.

"That was a *mob* surrounding you," Aalish calmly told him. "I won't pretend to apologize for any discomfort they caused, and I won't pretend your well-being is any concern of mine. I will, however, tell you that it will not happen again. I can also promise that it is in all of your interests to cooperate with us."

"I'm listening," Kylee said. She'd learned that the most powerful weapon wasn't a sharpened blade or a keen falcon; it was knowing what your opponent wanted.

Previously she had thought she understood what everyone around her wanted. She thought Birgund wanted to clear out the Mutes to exert stronger control on the Six Villages. She thought the Redfist rabble in the Mutes wanted to rise up and kill every Uztari they found, seizing the dwindling resources of the Six Villages for themselves in the process. And she thought the ghost eagles just wanted them all dead by whatever means necessary.

But the ghost eagles' egg changed everything. Now everyone wanted *it*.

"We want to know what's going to happen when this egg hatches," Aalish said.

"How should we know?" Kylee told the woman.

"Brysen?" Aalish turned to him. "Where were you going with the egg?"

"On a quiet walk in the fresh mountain air," he said back to her.

Aalish wasn't going to accept his sarcasm this time. Another muffled scream from Ryven made them all flinch, and then Aalish lifted Jowyn from the floor.

"I suppose Dhona would like a chat with this boy next," she said. "I hear that the longer these exiles from the Owl Mothers go without the sap of the blood birch, the more acute their pain response becomes. I wonder if that's true?"

"Don't you dare," Brysen told her, though his voice was about as menacing as a vole's squeak.

"Tell us where you were going," Aalish replied.

"To the Owl Mothers," Brysen answered before Kylee could stop him. "I saw a vision of the blood birch forest."

Kylee closed her eyes, disappointed. She'd seen it, too. Right after they'd left Kyrg Birgund, while she and Grazim were walking back to their cave, she heard the eagles' distant shrieks. She'd seen the blood birch forest from above, its many thin white branches swaying slightly in the wind, the whisper of its leaves, the creak of branches like arthritic bones. She'd been hit with a wave a sadness at the image, but she hadn't known why. The world was so full of sadness these days. Who could parse one cause from another?

But this sadness, she now knew, belonged to the ghost eagles. Something about the blood birches made them mourn.

The door opened and in came Dhona, followed by Ryven, who looked completely unscathed. Of course his screams had been lies. Ryven was, to his core, a deceiver. But why would he help the Redfists when he'd been with Birgund that morning?

"If we try to take the egg to the blood birch forest ourselves," he told them all, "the ghost eagles will tear us apart before sunrise, right?"

Brysen shrugged. "Find out for yourself."

Ryven grabbed Jowyn's jaw in his palm, turned the boy's head to the side, looked at the tattoos on his neck, and pursed his lips. "I always wanted to understand these images the Owl Mothers make," he said. "Perhaps I should take off the boy's skin so I can bind them into a book for later study."

Brysen whimpered, which made Ryven smile. "Relax," he said. "I'm not a monster. I simply want your cooperation." He let go of Jowyn and looked at Kylee. "Birgund doesn't care whether or not you massacre the people living in Mutes," he told her. "He wants to keep you all busy while he dismantles the nets and takes them to cover his army on a march to the Sky Castle. He figures the ghost eagles will be so focused on the slaughter here that he can get some distance before they catch on. I don't think he even cares about the egg."

"You're lying," Kylee said flatly. "Birgund wants power. He wouldn't just let it slip through his fingers."

"He's stuck in the past," Ryven said. "He still thinks power comes from the Sky Castle. He wants to go home. He's packing at this very moment."

"But not you?" Kylee asked. "Don't you want to go home?"

"That egg is everything," Ryven said. "I want to unlock its secrets."

"Like my brother said." Kylee shrugged. "Go for it."

Ryven pulled the egg from a satchel and raised it between his hands, turning it this way and that. Kylee was mesmerized by the swirls of black on black, and she felt her heartbeat pick up as the egg moved in his hands.

"I've studied the *talorum* for a long time," he said. "Do you know how their eggs are made?" He didn't wait for a reply. He wasn't really asking. "We have ancient texts that describe how an egg knit itself from the shadows of a torture chamber. Another says they rise from the mud beneath a mourner's processional. One says an egg was found in the arms of a frozen child on the slopes of a high mountain in the ice-wind season." He snorted, considering the grim image. "There's some truth to all those accounts," he said, "but to get the whole truth, one must go to the source: the eagles themselves."

"You asked them?" Kylee wondered.

Ryven cleared his throat. "Not exactly. But I see the same dreams you do. I, however, have a lifetime of study to add context to their meaning. The eggs, I believe, are born from pain. While it is true, as far as we know, that ghost eagles kill their mates, they don't do it *after* the act of creation; they do it *as* the act of creation. A ghost eagle's grief creates the egg, and what could be sadder than killing your own mate?" Kylee tried to keep her face blank, but Ryven knew he had her attention. This was just like when he'd given her lessons in the Hollow Tongue. He used her hunger for knowledge like a falconer uses morsels of meat. He was keeping her keen, perched on his every word. "Perhaps, I suppose, being tortured by your own parents?"

Kylee sucked in a breath. She saw the darkness on the eggshell swirl, waves of deeper darkness roiling over one another. The shell itself was a kind of living thing, and it responded to her mind and to her brother's. Ryven looked down at the egg in his hands and a smile brightened his face. He was getting the reaction he wanted. He was provoking them.

"I've come to believe," he continued, "that this egg called to you both because of *your* pain, Kylee. Your family's pain. I think this egg was created just for you, from your grief. The eagles couldn't help it. Like a tether binds an untrained falcon to the fist, this egg binds them to you, and you to them. It's as much yours as theirs." He held it out toward her, as if offering it, though her hands were still bound behind her back. The surface was swirling with her anger, but she saw flecks of gold in it, too.

She looked at Brysen, and his eyes were wide and damp. He wasn't angry. He didn't even look surprised. The corners of his mouth twitched, and no one else might've noticed, but she knew her twin's face better than her own. He was *delighted*.

"It's ours," Brysen whispered, like Ryven had just granted his greatest wish in the world.

"It's bound to you," Ryven clarified. "But it is very much their egg, and they want it back."

"Are you going to . . . ," Brysen began to ask, the same whimper in his voice as when Aalish had hoisted up Jowyn. "Are you going to give it back to them?"

Ryven took a deep breath, thinking. "Not yet," he said, and nodded at Aalish.

"First," she said. "We had to pick a fight."

He grinned at Kylee. "You're right, of course. I was lying about Birgund running away. He'd never leave unfinished business behind, and you, little chickadees, are his unfinished business."

At that very moment a chorus of shouts and whistles erupted outside as Kyrg Birgund's soldiers stormed the Mutes. Thanks to Ryven's treachery, the Redfists were ready for them.

17

AT THE FIRST WAR CRIES FROM THE BATTLE OUTSIDE, THE SHELL shuddered in Ryven's hands, the tiny flecks of gold that Brysen's excitement had created vanishing at once. The ghost eagles had wanted a bloody fight between people, and they'd gotten it. From the sounds that made their way through the thin walls of the shed, it was an ugly encounter, and Kylee just knew that if Ryven was telling the truth, this would be the moment the eagles would try to retrieve their egg, even though it was now full daylight.

Dhona and Aalish stepped outside to check on the fighting, and Ryven moved to peek through the doorway, the egg still in his hands.

Grazim had removed the gag from her mouth, and she whispered to Kylee, "We can't fall back into Birgund's hands. He'll kill us."

"I know," Kylee said.

"We can't just sit here and wait for Ryven to use us, either," she said.

"I know," Kylee repeated.

"We need to do *something*," Grazim insisted.

"I. Know!" Kylee shouted, and sprang to her feet with her arms still tied behind her back. The violent motion loosened her restraints, but it wasn't enough, and she fell back onto her behind again, landing with a painful thud. It was enough to bring Ryven and a guard back over to her.

"Secure her," Ryven ordered. "Whatever happens, keep the twins safe and in our control." He looked Kylee and Grazim up and down, then added, "And restore the gags. Birgund will have brought birds with him."

"Smart," Kylee told him, as the guard took a stinking piece of reddish-brown cloth—it looked to be dyed with some kind of animal blood—and shoved it into her mouth.

In order to tie it, however, the guard had to put his back to Kheryn. The strong battle boy used their knee to knock the guard forward, into Kylee's lap. The force of his fall loosened the stake in the ground behind Kylee, and she was able to wriggle her hands free.

"Guards!" Ryven called out the door, keeping his distance with the egg still in his hands. "Help!"

Two more Redfists burst in, but Kylee rolled on her side, kicking one's legs out from under him and then kicking over Kheryn's post. They slid their hands from behind their back and went to work.

The best fighter the battle boys had went up against all three Redfists at once. It wouldn't be long before they made short work of the opponents.

With Kheryn's release, Ryven realized that the fight had turned against him, and he rushed out the door. Kylee let him run with the egg while she untied Nyck and Lyra, then Grazim and Brysen and Jowyn.

Before the fight with Kheryn was over, Nyck leapt onto the back of one Redfist and used the gag from his mouth to choke her out. He didn't like to miss a brawl, even if his violent contribution wasn't fully necessary.

"Miscreants," Grazim muttered. She was just as committed to violence as the battle boys were, but only when she thought it was necessary.

"We have to get the egg back," Brysen said, a desperation in his voice. "It's ours."

"Ryven's a liar," Kylee said. "We don't know he was telling us the truth, or the whole truth, at least."

"You saw the egg change," Brysen said. "You *know*. When I

first found it, the eagles were angry and scared, but they couldn't just take it from me. It was like something was stopping them. If they get through the nets, I have the feeling nothing will stop them taking it from Ryven."

"I mean . . . so what?" Nyck asked. "They'll kill him and get their egg back. What's one more ghost eagle when we're already up against hundreds? Let's just get out of here while we can."

"No," Kylee said. "My brother's right. That egg needs to be with us. It's the only leverage we have."

She could tell Brysen didn't like hearing the egg referred to as leverage, but he didn't complain. The others agreed, and Nyck accepted the consensus and bounced on the balls of his feet, eager for the fight. "Well, okay then, we hunt down that scuzzard. Let's do it."

Kheryn pushed open the door.

The narrow streets were overrun with people fleeing. Fighters rushed against them, heading in the opposite direction. Ryven was wending his way through the torrent of bodies, toward the entrance to another narrow street.

"Them!" someone yelled from the other direction. Dhona and three of her Redfists were pushing their way back toward the shack. "Get them!" Dhona shouted.

"Nyck?" Kylee asked.

"On it!" The battle boy grinned and turned to face Dhona

and her guards, whistling a little birdsong to taunt them. He was shifting from side to side like a bowerbird looking for a mate. "Let's play."

Overhead, three red-tailed hawks flapped just below the nets and then dove at the first red-wrapped fists they saw, attacking with talon and beak.

"Clever," Grazim noted. "Birgund trained their birds to attack anyone wearing red cloth on their fists."

"What happens when the Redfists figure that out?" Kylee wondered, even as she saw fighters untying the cloth and letting it fall to the ground, then targeting the birds of prey with arrows and spears as the birds dove on their less astute compatriots.

Dhona and her guards were far better fighters than Nyck and Kheryn and Lyra, and far stronger. Lyra had already taken a punch to the teeth without landing a single blow back, while Nyck was doing his best just to dodge Dhona's blades. He was tiring.

"Must I do everything?" Grazim sighed, and then called out to the nearest bird of prey, a black-shouldered kite. These birds were known for their dexterity when near the ground—a good choice for fighting in narrow lanes below netting, and an even better choice for Grazim to command. "*Pleu-wiit*," she whispered to it, and it turned from harrying a bloody-faced man with red cloth wrapped around both his fists—missing the point of the symbolism, Kylee thought—to fly straight for Dhona. Its talons raked through her short hair, tearing at her scalp.

"Let's go!" Kylee yelled at the battle boys, who used the moment to retreat and rejoin the group, all of them chasing after Ryven, Brysen faster than any of them. Brysen took a turn too early in his haste, though, bumping into a corner, which saved him from a spear. Clearly aimed for him, the weapon slammed into the wall just before him, at the turn he would've taken had he not misjudged the distance. He stopped short to stare at it, shocked. Jowyn pulled him down and under it, dragging him around the turn just as the Redfist who'd thrown the spear charged.

Kylee was on the Redfist first, tackling them into the wall and trying to throw them to the ground. They fought back, though, and flipped her with her own momentum, then pressed their knee into her throat. She gasped, saw stars. She felt like her windpipe might collapse, but a bird suddenly alighted on the hazy face of her attacker, screeching. A pigeon hawk, the brass anklet of the Uztari army around its ankle catching the late afternoon light with a gorgeous gleam. The bird flew away as the attacker fell off Kylee—Lyra and Nyck had dispatched the Redfist without even slowing their run.

"This way," they said.

"Nice work," Kylee said to Grazim as they ran, nodding at

the three birds following them. Grazim had commanded them to cover the group.

"I've discovered a real love for the language," she replied, a kind of focused glee in her eyes. The blond girl had a gift for battle that Kylee never would. They'd only been on the run for a few moments and Grazim had already commanded half a dozen birds of prey from the Uztari falconers. Kylee hadn't called down a single bird. But there was a flaw in their plan: The moment a bird didn't follow its falconer's command, the soldiers would figure out they were under control of the Hollow Tongue. The soldiers could just watch the bird's path to determine where Kylee and Grazim were headed. She had no doubt Birgund sent these birds deliberately, to find them out.

"They'll notice the birds and follow us . . . How do you say 'confuse them'?" she asked Grazim.

"*Shaalit! Shaalit!*" Grazim chirped, and several Uztari birds broke in different directions over the Mutes, weaving and flapping in no discernable pattern. This bought them time before Birgund would be able to tell which birds were with his targets and which were leading him on a wild-hawk chase.

They followed Ryven down an alley. The path ended in a fork, and Ryven disappeared into a triangular shack set right at the split, Brysen just behind him. They piled in. It was one of the gin counters that bought thirdhand gin from the black market at ridiculous prices; its shelves were mostly bare.

Ryven stood behind the counter, holding a sharp hammer over the ghost eagle egg.

Brysen stood in front of him, arms up, begging the kyrg not to harm the egg.

Except Brysen had already seen Kylee fail to hurt the egg back in the cave. He knew it couldn't be broken with a hammer. Her brother was stalling, waiting for the rest of them. He was also, it appeared, trying to avoid more violence.

"Please," Brysen pleaded. "That egg isn't even hatched. It's not a ghost eagle yet. It hasn't done *anything*. Let it go. Let me take care of it."

As Brysen spoke, flecks of gold floated through the black swirls on the shell.

"Not one move, or I crack this thing and swallow the animal inside," Ryven threatened, and the gold faded. Brysen glanced over his shoulder at Kylee. Kylee's anger was turning it black.

"He's lying," she said. "He loves the ghost eagles more than anything. He doesn't want to hurt this one."

"Of course I don't, Kylee," Ryven said. "But I do want to survive. So we all get out of here together. Me carrying the egg, and you protecting me from them, or I *will* crack it."

"And then?" Kylee asked him.

"I come with you to the blood birches," he said. "I've

reached the limits of what I know, and I need to know more. I want to discover what this egg means along with you."

"You are incapable of saying anything true," Kylee said. "So let's stop the games. You're not going to break that, *and* you're not going to let us take it to the blood birch forest."

Ryven stared at her a moment longer. Their eyes locked, and she truly had no idea what he would do next. She did not expect him to break into a smile and laugh full, deep-throated, belly-born laughter.

"We could be great together," he told her. "More power than anyone could ever dream, but you just won't cooperate, will you? I chose you for my side, you know? And yet you never go along with my plans. So I chose a different side."

"What did you do?" she asked him. He didn't answer.

Or rather, if he did answer, she didn't hear him, because that was when a huge ghost eagle tore off the roof.

"REEEEEEE!" it yelled, flapping its wings, blotting out the sky. Pieces of shredded wire and netting dangled from its talons like entrails.

In her mind, Kylee saw crumbling towers hewn from black stone. She saw a nest surrounded by at least a hundred ghost eagles, all looking toward its center, where a shadow swirled, forming the shape of an egg, pulled together from the sound of screams on the wind. She smelled fire.

Inside her was a great swelling of . . . not peace, exactly, but homecoming, a feeling like her feet hitting the ground after a dangerous but successful climb, when she still existed in two places: part of her on the high rocks above and part of her on the ground to which she'd returned. It was a feeling of wholeness, and it wasn't hers.

It was the ghost eagle who, upon seeing the egg, felt whole.

Redfists and the Uztari soldiers hacking at them in the alley fled in the same direction together, running away from a terror greater than either side. The battle boys ducked and held one another, their bloody hands grasping to keep their friends safe. Grazim shielded herself behind Kylee, and Jowyn let Brysen shield him this time.

Only Kylee and Brysen and Ryven didn't cower.

The massive eagle's wings beat the air into whirling currents, holding it in place like a kestrel hovering on a breeze, and the angle of its shadow painted its elongated image across the three buildings next door. They also lost their roofs when the ghost eagle tore the netting free.

"I got this for you, like I promised!" Ryven yelled up to the eagle, holding the egg aloft. "*Eeefa!*" he yelled. "*Eeefa!*"

Kylee didn't know the words, but she saw their meaning in her own memories. The cold kindnesses she and her brother gave each other at the start of each ice-wind season: candied ginger, a new leather hawk lure, a fur blanket. She remembered Grazim fighting at her side to protect her and Brysen, whom Grazim neither liked nor understood. She saw Ma ducking down a tunnel when the soldiers arrived—not running away but rather freeing Kylee of the burden of her mother, letting her go.

"Gifts," she said out loud, understanding the words now. "You're giving the egg as a gift."

The ghost eagle didn't move to take it from Ryven. Instead, it screeched.

Kylee saw rats stealing the candied ginger, a haggard hawk ignoring the lure, their father stealing the new fur blanket. The gifts that failed.

"They know you're lying," she told Ryven. "A gift isn't a trade. They know you want something in return."

Ryven glanced at her without turning his head, then quickly returned his gaze to the huge hovering ghost eagle. "Take it," he yelled. "I got this for you! *Eeefa!*"

Kylee felt heat in her lungs, the ghost eagle's want, the ghost eagle's anger that Ryven would try to lie to it in its own language. The pressure built. She knew the ghost eagle could just kill Ryven and take the egg, but it was waiting for her. The ghost eagle didn't want to just snatch Ryven in its talons and break his delicate body in two. It wanted Kylee to command it.

I think this egg was created just for you, Ryven had said. It was bound to her and to Brysen, and it responded to them. They commanded what it might become. She wondered why the ghost eagle wanted her rage so badly, why Brysen's gentleness scared it.

"It wants me to kill you, Ryven," she said calmly, watching the swirls of black form eddies and whirlpools on the egg. "But I won't." Streams of gold bubbled up on the shell. The eagle cried again.

"REEEEE!"

She wanted to scream. She remembered every frustration, every failure, every loss she'd ever experienced all at once, in a blur. Over and over, all she could think was: *Unfair. It's unfair. It's unfair!*

She exhaled slowly.

"I won't," she told the ghost eagle calmly, in her own words. "Do what you must, but I won't be the one to command it. My rage is not yours to borrow."

The heat died in her lungs. She wasn't going to be an instrument of this creature's will, and now it knew. When she unleashed her fury, it would belong to her alone.

She looked at Ryven. "If I were you, I'd run," she said, just as the eagle screamed and tucked its wings, diving for him.

The deposed kyrg was fast. He jumped to the side, tossing the egg in the opposite direction, straight at Brysen, so the ghost eagle's attention split. The bird altered direction and tried to catch the egg before Brysen did, but it missed, then turned and caught Ryven by the back, hoisting him up with one clawed foot. Its talons dug into his back and stomach.

"AHHH!" Ryven yelled as he rose with the eagle, and the mighty bird flapped, carrying him over the Mutes and away from the Six Villages. Ryven struggled and screamed and shouted commands in the Hollow Tongue, but the ghost eagle paid no attention. He was taken away in agony, but he was alive.

"Why didn't it just kill him?" Grazim whispered to Kylee, resting a hand on her back as they watched the eagle fly off with its prisoner into the copper sky.

"I don't think it's done with him—or us—yet," Kylee said. "We have to get to the blood birches. Whatever's going on, that's where they're afraid we'll go. I want to know why."

"Um," Brysen interjected, his gift for words unmatched as ever. Kylee turned to him and saw that the egg he held with both hands was glowing gold as sunset.

Kylee gasped. "We have no idea what we're dealing with, do we?"

"We have to hope the Owl Mothers will," Brysen said.

"We have to hope they don't kill us all on sight," Nyck added.

"Now's the time to go if we're going," Kheryn told them, drawing their attention back to the scene around them. The fighting in the Mutes continued, Redfists and soldiers of Uztar chasing one another through the narrow lanes and cutting one another down without mercy or hesitation.

Grazim held up her fist and closed her eyes, then shouted a word and waited.

And waited.

And waited.

And then the tailor's hawk she'd taken from Kyrg Birgund flapped into the shack to alight on her fist. She didn't open her eyes until she'd tucked one of its talons beneath her thumb. She smiled and whispered a thank-you when she thought no one was listening. Kylee smiled at her friend. Sometimes when everything you knew was broken, you needed to see that you still had one thing in control.

"Good thinking," she told Grazim, who pretended to ignore the compliment but couldn't hide her satisfaction.

They made their way quickly back toward the cave to get supplies for the journey into the mountains. Kylee hoped to find her mother there safely, too, at least to say good-bye. She might even ask Ma to come with them, she thought. She hoped the Owl Mothers would provide an explanation for the things Ryven had revealed, but if not, then at least a place of sanctuary.

18

NO ONE FOLLOWED THEM INTO THE MOUNTAINS, OF COURSE. NO ONE would dare. Even the battle boys had lost a bit of their bravado since cowering beneath the ghost eagle's wings, and now that they were out from underneath the protective nets, they were all on edge.

"Maybe I should've stayed behind with your ma?" Nyck suggested. "Someone to look after her. She's all alone in that big cave now, hiding out. What if the Redfists come back for her?"

"She's a survivor," Kylee said. "She'll be fine. Anyway, she didn't exactly want company."

When they returned to the cave to pack up for the

journey, their mother had come out of a tunnel, where she'd hidden herself. She told them she was going to stay, that she was too old for a journey like theirs.

"You're not that old," Kylee had said.

"I'm old enough that I'm not going to change my ways," she'd said. "But I'll pray for you." She'd looked over at the battle boys, at Jowyn and Grazim, too. "For all of you."

Kylee had almost snapped at her, almost insulted her return to prayers—as if prayers had ever done any of them any good—but instead she'd closed her mouth and surprised her mother with a hug. Ma was doing her best. It was far from good enough, and it never had been, and they both knew it. Wherever her children went now, they would go without her. Ma was letting them go, untethered.

Kylee couldn't explain all that to Nyck, so instead she just said, "Why are you so worried about her? You miss her cooking that bad, or are you afraid?"

Nyck puffed up. A good way to keep Nyck brave was to insinuate that he wasn't. It worked every time.

"And anyway," Kylee added, "the Redfists aren't coming for her. Birgund's keeping them busy."

"What if Birgund comes after her when he's done with them, then?" Lyra asked.

"He won't," Kylee said.

"How can you know that?"

"Because he'll be coming after us."

They all looked at the Six Villages, down the slope behind them. In the Mutes, fires blazed and soldiers fought. People screamed, people fled, some fought back. It was a mess. But the bulk of Birgund's forces weren't even engaged in the massacre. They were at the Broken Jess, breaking down the protective nets and turning them into a kind of mobile fortress, so they could march during the day and hide under them at night. They still believed the ghost eagles only attacked at night, even though a ghost eagle had just flown away with Kyrg Ryven screaming so loud everyone in the Six must have looked up to see it. They had to cling to some belief that they might be safe, or they'd all have lost their minds.

It was a magical kind of thinking, but everyone had a personal kind of magic. It was something they believed in just to keep going. Her mother's tunnels, for instance. Brysen's belief, despite all the evidence of his life, that he had a grand heroic purpose. Grazim's trust that, despite everything the kyrgs had done to her, she would be one of them one day, the first Altari on the ruling council of Uztar.

Kylee wondered what magic belief kept her going. The Owl Mothers would not be happy to see her. Since Ryven had escaped the Sky Castle's dungeon, it was likely that Üku, leader of the Owl Mothers, had, too. Üku wasn't going to welcome her former student with open arms and a warm cup of tea. Kylee was just as likely to feel a talon pierce her spine before she ever even saw Üku's face. And yet she needed to believe that she would somehow find the words to save all their lives. Her magic belief was in herself.

"So," Nyck said, "you think the Owl Mothers and I will get along, like? They're pretty set in their ways. And me, I'm not about to apologize for mine. And, you know, arguments with them can get kind of . . . what's the word?"

"Murdery?" Lyra suggested.

"They're not murdery," Jowyn objected. "They simply have strict laws that keep their part of the mountain safe and preserve their way of life. They've guarded the blood birch forest and the words of the Hollow Tongue for longer than history knows, so something about their methods must work, right? You have to respect that."

"I don't have to respect anything," Nyck said. "At least the Redfists I can understand. Violent, enraged mobs are simple. Murderous, matronly mountain mystics are not a flock I can fathom."

"They're not 'murderous, matronly mountain mystics,'" Jowyn said. "They're the fearsome protectors of ancient wisdom. They preserve balance and memory in our world."

"They *are* pretty murderous," Kylee interjected. Grazim nodded in agreement. She'd never given up on the Owl Mothers the way Kylee had, but still, it was hard to argue with the facts. The Owl Mothers killed just about anyone who set foot in their territory without their permission, and they reserved the right to revoke their permission at any time.

"You wouldn't call an owl murderous," Jowyn said.

"Yeah," Kylee said, "I would."

Nyck laughed and touched his forefinger to his cheekbone, just below his eye, one of the Owl Mothers' gestures. Jowyn spat, which was one of Nyck's.

Kylee was glad that, despite what they'd gone through, everyone was still themselves, jabbing at one another in whatever ways they could think of. The little fights they had bonded them for big fights with others.

Only Brysen didn't participate. He'd pulled away from Jowyn's side and was walking the steep trail on his own, ahead of them, the bag with the ghost eagle egg slung over his shoulder. He'd grabbed a stick, both for balance and to probe the ground in front of him. It was a pretty clever adaptation to his new way of seeing. Kylee trotted up beside him to tell him so.

"It is what it is," he replied coolly. Maybe she and Brysen weren't as okay as she thought. She understood if he was still angry, though she wished he'd just tell her instead of being all sullen about it. She preferred open aggression to passivity. "Did you come up here just to compliment my walking stick?" he asked.

"No," she told him. "When Ryven said the egg was made for us, by our pain, you looked . . . happy."

"Is that a question?"

Of course it is, you infuriating finch-face! "Were you?" she asked.

"Yeah," he said.

"Why?" she asked him. "I don't understand what there is to be happy about here."

Brysen paused for a while, thinking. "Because it means there was a point," he said. "Everything we've been through, everything we've lost . . . maybe it wasn't meaningless. Maybe it mattered."

She saw it again: a slight smile at the corners of his mouth. She felt a great swell of love for her brother at that moment. He was reckless and selfish and foolish most of the time, but he was so eager for his life to have meaning that even the possibility of it could make him smile at a storm cloud. He was, in spite of everything, clinging to hope. It was hard not to be affected by it, too. It gave her hope.

"So what do you think it means?" she asked. "How this egg responds to us? The gold and the black colors?"

"I think it feeds on our rage," he said, "but also on our mercy. Mercy changes it."

"I'm not sure we *want* it to be merciful, with the world being as it is," Kylee said.

"I'm not sure we can *survive* its rage," Brysen replied. "You've seen what that can do."

"Yeah, but if it's doing it for us, then maybe it's a blessing," Kylee said. "We're not strong enough to fight all these armies alone."

"Maybe we have to be strong enough not to fight them at all?"

"How?" Kylee wondered. She'd had the same thought, but you couldn't force peace on people wedded to violence. Prey that refused to fight didn't turn a predator gentle; they just made for an easier meal. Kylee wasn't going to be eaten. "We can't just will people to stop killing one another or to stop trying to kill us. If we could, I'd have done it already."

Brysen shrugged. "It's as dark here for me as it is for you," he said, and he wasn't talking about the oncoming night. "I'm just trying to feel my way forward without falling over, like everyone else." He looked at the stick in his hand. "There's no walking stick that can help with *that*."

He smiled at her, and his smile was a promise of forgiveness, that he could forgive her for what she did, and that she could forgive him, too. She reached out and touched his hand, startling him. He nearly pulled away but caught himself. He took her hand, their fingers interlacing as easily as when they were little children, when their whole world was each other. *This* was her magic. It wasn't just faith in herself alone. That was a necessary faith for her, but it was not sufficient. Family was what she had to believe in to keep going. Whether it was one you were born to or one you chose, family wasn't the promise of painless love; it was the promise of healing. She and Brysen would heal, and that was reason enough to put one foot in front of the other, come what may.

They held hands as they walked the next steps on the trail. The sun set and night came on, stars appearing in the blue-black sky like pinpricks on a blanket. They climbed and hiked and nearly crawled up narrow ridges and steep inclines, bouldering together to reach the first of many cliffs they'd have to scale to reach the blood birch forest.

"Maybe we should wait until morning to try this?" Nyck suggested.

"We need to get as much distance between us and the Six as possible," Kylee told him.

"Yeah," Nyck said. "I just don't want whoever chases us up here to find our bodies in a pile at the bottom of this cliff because we lost our handholds in the dark."

"That's a fair point," Grazim said. It took a lot for her to agree with Nyck on anything, which gave Kylee pause. If they had to make camp, then this was a good, defensible position in which to do so, up against a wall of solid rock. They'd see anyone approaching from below, and they'd have the high ground in a fight. Kylee would also worry about Brysen's night vision and depth perception if he had to scale a cliff in the dark, but she didn't want to say anything lest he take offense, try to prove himself, and die in the process. That'd be a very *him* way to die.

Suddenly the fine hairs on the back of Kylee's neck stood up. She felt a chill, sensed something move on the air. Her eyes shot upward.

"REEEEEE!" A screech scratched the sky and a shadow the size of a horse dropped in front of her—black wings wide, back upright, the crown of feathers on its head preened and puffed. A ghost eagle, prepared to strike.

This would be a very *her* way to die.

19

KYLEE NEARLY FELL OVER AS THE GHOST EAGLE'S CRY STOLE THE AIR from her lungs. "REEEEEEE!"

She saw visions of the Owl Mothers chasing her through the forest, great gray owls and brilliant snowy owls and blunt-headed barn owls diving and tearing at her. It was a memory of her first escape from the Owl Mothers, when things had not gone to plan. She saw Brysen grab his left hand, no doubt caught in the memory of when Üku had threatened to cut it off.

The ghost eagle stepped toward her, pushing her away from the cliff face and out into the open.

"Watch out!" Kheryn leapt over Kylee, pulling their knife in midair and charging for the massive ghost eagle.

"No!" Brysen yelled, whether to Kheryn or the bird, Kylee couldn't tell. But no sooner had Kheryn's feet hit the ground, knife thrusting for the ghost eagle's shoulder joint, than another eagle dove behind them. Scything a piece of the dark from the night sky, the second ghost eagle slammed into Kheryn's back, knocking them forward so hard they lost their grip on the blade. The eagle swooped down to the trail, landing with its head cocked sideways, onyx eyes devouring moonlight.

Kheryn rolled forward with the force of the blow. The battle boy didn't even have a chance to grunt or scream or yelp before a third ghost eagle appeared, talons outstretched, and snatched them by the skull and shoulders, heaving them skyward, their neck snapping. After gaining some height, the eagle tossed Kheryn's body halfway down the slope.

"REEEEEEE!" the eagles screeched together, and Kylee saw avalanches in her mind, rockslides and floods—every manner of obstacle that nature could inflict on a traveler in the mountains. She saw Nyck and Lyra, gutted and devoured by the massive birds. Grazim's body, lying untouched in the mud at the bottom of a gully, a single slash opening her from forehead to waist, her innards splayed to the stars like a blooming flower. She saw Brysen and Jowyn, alone on the snowy peaks, shivering and freezing in each other's arms until the last breath left their lungs, turning to ice that sealed their lips, forever just a feather's width from each other.

These tragedies hadn't happened—they were the ghost eagle's threats. And as far as Kylee knew, ghost eagles didn't make idle threats. They could share nothing they didn't believe was true.

But Nyck and Lyra were still behind her, doubled over, no doubt seeing the same terrible images she was. Jowyn had tackled Brysen and covered him with his body, as if some fragile flesh and bone could protect him from the eagles' hunger. Brysen, to his credit, was struggling out from under Jowyn.

Lyra came to herself and bolted from where she crouched, turning back in the direction they'd come. At first Kylee thought she was fleeing, but that wasn't the battle boy way. Lyra was trying to go wide, to circle around and reach Kheryn's body.

"Leave them alone! Don't you dare eat them!" Lyra yelled.

A ghost eagle dropped in front of her from the sky, flapped its wings, harried her back up the slope, but it didn't strike.

"REEEEE!" the eagles cried, and now there was a sunrise in Kylee's mind. Kylee felt the warmth on her skin. She saw the sun burning high, sending gold over the plateau, its brilliant light shining on a crumbling black structure tucked into a jagged mountain. She'd seen this before: This was where the ghost eagles had perched around an empty nest in another vision, but this time the view was from far enough away that she could recognize the location.

The Talon Fortress. It had been abandoned long ago, but it still loomed on the far side of the plateau.

When her eyes refocused, Kylee found herself still standing in the dark. The three massive ghost eagles blocked the path in front of her. One of them launched into the air and flapped to the top of the cliff they'd been set to scale. Its talons gripped the upper lip as it leaned down over them and screeched again. It was hard to distinguish between the pain of the pitch and the horror of the visions it carried. One of the eagles took two hopping steps to the side and lowered its head nearly to the ground, where a thin trail wound away through the rocks, heading in the opposite direction of the blood birch forest.

And then the birds waited.

"This isn't an attack," Brysen said, catching his breath, sitting up. "They're telling us where to go. They're . . ."

"Herding us," Kylee finished his sentence.

"But Kheryn?" Nyck groaned, eyes flitting between the terrible trio of monstrous birds blocking their way.

"That was self-defense," Brysen said sadly. "If this was an attack, why'd they stop?"

The two eagles turned their heads to him, then turned as one to look at Kylee.

"They want us to go to the Talon Fortress," she said. "Not to the Owl Mothers."

"And we're just going to do what they want?" Nyck cried, fists balled. He took a step toward the birds, sliding a blade from his belt, like he was being subtle. The ghost eagles had the ability to see his heartbeat; they could definitely see the knife in his hand.

"No, Nyck," Kylee told him. "Don't."

"Calm down!" Brysen warned. "They'll kill you if you give them reason to. Stay calm."

He pulled out the egg, showed it to the eagles and then to Nyck. Its shell was still gold, but there was more black than before, like storm clouds forming on a sunny day, and they were growing.

"The only way to beat them is to let go of that rage," Kylee said. "They're creatures of violence. They can't understand its opposite."

"I can't just forgive them," Nyck said.

"That's the point," she said. "It's impossible to forgive them, which means it's the only way to stop them. They're not expecting it."

"You want me to weaponize forgiveness?"

"Yes," Kylee said. "No other weapon we have can possibly work."

She took satisfaction in the idea that it wasn't really forgiveness if it was being used to thwart them. She hoped that would satisfy Nyck in some way.

He looked back at her with tears in his eyes. Battle boys were not the forgiving sort, and Nyck had just lost a friend. Kheryn had been one of the very first battle boys. They'd been around when Nyck first formed the gang out of street urchins. Nyck had left home, abandoning sisters who wouldn't see him for who he was, and found Kheryn. Kheryn, who was so sure of themselves, it seemed perfectly natural for them and Nyck to join together. Nyck and Kheryn met Nyall later, and the three of them scraped and scrapped and scavenged for survival for half the seasons of their lives.

In an instant, the ghost eagles had ended that story. Kylee could see it all. The ghost eagles were *showing* it all. They didn't want Nyck to forgive them. They wanted Nyck to attack. They were hungering for it, even as they hoped the group would simply follow the path they'd pointed out, the path away from the blood birch forest.

They're torn, Kylee thought. *What they want and what they need are tearing them in different directions. They're longing for violence, but they're confused by peace.*

"Stand down, Nyck," she urged him. "Take a deep breath and stand down."

Nyck whined. "But—"

"I know," she said. "But it's the only way."

Nyck hesitated but unclenched his fists. The black clouds on the egg's surface lightened. He put his blade away and took a step backward. One of the ghost eagles lunged at him, and for a terrible heartbeat, Kylee thought she'd been wrong. But Nyck didn't move.

The ghost eagle's beak snapped closed hard enough to tussel his hair, but it didn't touch him.

"We won't fight you," Kylee said. "If it's death you want, you'll have to take it from us, because we won't give it to you."

The ghost eagle shuddered, then swung its head toward Brysen. There was a terrible silence as the ghost eagles thought without screaming, shared nothing of their thoughts, and then, the two of them as one, charged at Jowyn, launching from the ground and flapping toward him.

"No, please!" Brysen cried as their talons stretched for Jowyn's pale skin, and Brysen dropped the egg to protect him. Kylee dove on top of the egg as one of the eagles broke away and tried to snatch it. She felt its sharp talons graze her back and slice her shirt, cutting her open like a whip cracking across her skin. She screamed and saw flashes of her father bringing his talon-tipped whip across Brysen's back.

The eagles wheeled away from the attack. The egg was out of their grasp, beneath Kylee, and the only way to get it would be to finish ripping her open.

And yet they didn't.

And they hadn't.

They were bluffing, and she'd called them on it. Ryven was right: The eagles were bound to the twins through this egg, and they wouldn't hurt Brysen or Kylee as long as they had it. They were safe with the egg, but she wondered how safe their friends were. Kheryn was already dead, and the others were just as vulnerable. She and her brother couldn't shield them all for the whole journey, especially if they went against the ghost eagles' wishes and continued for the blood birches.

She looked up at the three giant eagles. They were circling above the group now, only visible by the shape of the stars they blotted out. She held on to the egg, a swirl of gold and black in her hands. She looked at Brysen and Jowyn, who were shuddering and clinging to each other, and then back at Grazim, her hand on the hilt of her knife, prepared to attack these harbingers of doom to protect a pale boy she didn't even like. She looked at Nyck, who was struggling to keep himself together after watching his dearest friend be murdered. Kylee felt a swell of pride for these people, a swell of hope. They were going to win, because they could do one thing the ghost eagles hadn't figured out. They could love one another in infinitely more complex ways than the huge birds' tiny brains could fathom. That was how they would defeat these birds of prey: by being human.

"We'll take your egg where you want us to take it," Kylee said. "We'll go to the Talon Fortress—"

"Kylee, no," Brysen said. "We have to go to the Owl Mothers."

"We'll never make it," she told him. "Not all of us, anyway." She nodded toward Grazim and Nyck and Lyra, and Brysen understood. She was going to make a deal with them.

"You don't touch any of us on our way!" she shouted up at the dark.

The sky was quiet. Like owls, the ghost eagles had serrated feathers and could fly without making a sound. Kylee wondered if they'd understood her, tried to think of a Hollow Tongue word with which to command them. But finally they screeched their agreement and flew toward the Six Villages and whatever grim meals awaited them there.

They did, however, leave Kylee with a parting image.

She saw Nyall, her oldest friend, ragged and tired and surrounded by ghost eagles, a prisoner in their nest at the

Talon Fortress. With him, dropped by rough talons, was Ryven.

Then the image vanished. The ghost eagles were gone.

"Did you see that?" Brysen asked her.

"What?" Nyck asked. "What did they show you?"

"They showed us where they took Ryven," Kylee said. "And that they have Nyall."

"They . . . what do you mean?" Nyck grumbled. "They *have* him?"

"He's a hostage," she said.

"What kind of bird takes hostages?" Lyra groaned.

"One that learns from us," Kylee said, clutching the egg, whose shell had gone black again. If they did anything to hurt her friend, she wasn't sure she would be able to take the advice she'd given Nyck. She wasn't sure she could forgive.

"So we're not going to the blood birches anymore?" Grazim asked.

Kylee took a long look up the cliff, toward the distant mountain forest. "No." She sighed, doubting the wisdom of following where the ghost eagles wanted them to go, but knowing it was the only way to keep her friends safe.

"If we're lucky, maybe the Owl Mothers will find us on the way," Grazim suggested.

"Or if we are very, very unlucky," Kylee replied.

EXIT STRATEGY

SOMETHING HAD CHANGED BEYOND THE WALLS OF THE SKY CASTLE. Kyrg Bardu could feel it in the same way she could feel a storm coming. She always had a good sense of shifts in weather—and of shifts in power. Those two talents helped her rise to become proctor of the Council of Forty, the highest authority in Uztar.

From her earliest days on the Council, she'd directed the nobility to fair-weather hunts and warned them when the rains or winds might turn on them, and she did the same for their political fortunes. She knew precisely when to ask for favors and when to call a favor due, when to cultivate a friend and when to cut a friend loose. She didn't often commit violence herself, but she had no qualms about deploying it with precision.

None of those skills was helpful to her now. She was barely hanging on to order in the city now that it was cut off from the rest of the plateau, its gates sealed and strong nets hung over every open street and courtyard. Some districts were already in open rebellion. Her army was stranded in the Six Villages along with her most loyal kyrg, and the treasonous Kyrg Ryven had escaped. She'd had to deploy her personal guard to keep order below the nets, as food stores were running low and the ghost eagles picked holes in their defenses nightly. Outspoken dissidents were left tied on the wrong side of the nets, and their screams carried from one end of the city to the other, though it was the sudden silences that had the greatest impact on maintaining order.

The other kyrgs were growing restless, and she needed to do *something* to hold their loyalty. Fear alone couldn't tame them for long. One trained a hawk by feeding it just enough to stay hungry, and one managed subjects in the same way. How could she keep her council keen to obey when she had so little to offer and their people needed so very much? And how could she do anything at all when she didn't know what was happening, when she couldn't get a message in or out because those cursed ghost eagles snatched any messenger pigeon she posted?

She was in a tough spot, but she was not helpless. She just had to look for help in unsavory places.

And that was why she'd had Goryn and Yves Tamir brought to her. They were the only living heirs to the Tamir clan, and they were trapped in her city, far from their home in the Six Villages. Goryn had escaped her dungeons but didn't make it far, and his sister had been living quite openly in the city for some time before the ghost eagle attack, building her own criminal network. Bardu had kept her brother prisoner as a favor to his sister, in fact. Yves didn't want the competition. Now that Goryn was free, he didn't seem to know that his sister didn't have his best interests at heart. Bardu held on to this knowledge like precious bronze, and Yves knew it. That was the tether that kept the criminals bound to Kyrg Bardu, what allowed her to trust that they would do as she wished. She could turn them against each other any time she chose. She felt, in that sense, as powerful as a ghost eagle herself.

"You've got smugglers' routes into and out of the city?" she asked the Tamirs.

"We do," confirmed Yves.

"But no one is foolish enough to take them," Goryn said. His cruelty was legendary, but he wasn't terribly bright. His sister looked irked that he'd volunteer that information, and

Bardu shared a knowing look with her. Bardu had no younger brothers herself, but she was familiar with the concept. They could be quite a nuisance.

"*Someone* is," Bardu said. "After the Council meeting tonight, I'll have someone who I need you, Goryn, to escort outside the walls."

"But it's death out there," the petty gangster began. "I wouldn't even—"

Bardu cut him off. "You will be protected," she said.

"How?" he asked. "Who can protect me from the ghost eagles?"

"I can," said Üku, leader of the Owl Mothers, who was entering the chamber behind him. "And I can even give you a chance for revenge, if you do exactly as I say."

Goryn Tamir nodded and didn't say another word in objection. Bardu admired him for that bit of wisdom, at least. He knew when to keep his mouth shut and obey a powerful woman who knew so very much more than he did. She almost felt a pang of guilt that his reward for obedience would likely be death all the same, but she left that decision entirely up to the Owl Mother.

That was the first part of their agreement.

The second part would happen when the Council assembled one last time.

. . .

The Council of Forty was much diminished. Kyrg Bardu had appointed her nephew to replace Kyrg Ryven, so their number was steady at thirty-nine, but she didn't dare try to replace the absent defense counselor, lest she provoke dissent from his remaining soldiers, most of whom were still loyal to him and eagerly awaiting his return. While absent, however, Kyrg Birgund could neither aid nor threaten her current plan, which suited her just fine. When it was done, if he returned, he would fall in line for the good of Uztar. He was noble that way. He did whatever he thought Uztar needed, and as long as Bardu ruled Uztar, Birgund would serve her. If he didn't, she'd find a way to discredit and destroy him.

"Thank you for coming," Bardu told the bedraggled council. They'd been mostly holed up in the central citadel itself, as the city was no longer safe for nobility to wander unescorted. There was anger in the air, rumors that the Council was hoarding food and weaponry. These rumors were, of course, true, but Bardu intended to use them to justify the extreme course of action she was about to take. "I know this last moon's turning has been hard on all of you. I'm aware of the challenges you face."

"We're unable to keep the nets of my district patched! I lose people every night!" one of the kyrgs said, an earnest, older man whose district was rather pitiful but who'd amassed quite a fortune in fixing hawk battles—a fortune that was largely worthless under the present circumstances.

"There's violence in my district all day," another councillor whined. Her district was filled with well-equipped merchants and falcon dealers, and Bardu knew the Tamirs had built much of their new criminal gang by extorting those very businesses. Clashes between them and the kyrg's constabulary were regular and bloody, and Bardu had to repeatedly assure the kyrg that she'd put a stop to the violence.

"You'll be glad to know I've made arrangements that will end that bloodshed," she told the angry kyrg. Then she addressed the older man, saying, "And while the repeated attacks from above are unfortunate, I can promise they will not be a problem for you much longer."

"How so?" the kyrg demanded, rapping his fist on the table.

"Tell us about food rations!" a third kyrg objected. "None of these problems matter if our people riot because they're starving!"

"How you allot your dispensation from our food stores is up to you," Bardu told him.

"By the time I feed my family and staff and guards and their families, there's hardly any left for my district," he objected.

Bardu shrugged, and the kyrg threw his arms into the air. "You don't care?" he groaned, then he stood, addressing the thirty-eight kyrgs seated around him. "Perhaps it is time to choose a proctor more prepared to meet this unprecedented moment in our history. I propose a no-confidence vote. Do I have a second?"

"Aye!" Four or five different kyrgs seemed to concur, though Kyrg Bardu couldn't be sure how many; she wasn't looking at the Council table. She was looking at the window, where no one had noticed that the protective net around the tower had fallen away. The sun was setting, red behind the mountain range.

"It's not unprecedented," she said casually, admiring the growing dark.

"Excuse me?" the disloyal kyrg said.

"It's not unprecedented," Bardu repeated. She smiled without opening her lips. "I've recently been told an interesting story by an old"—she paused, searching for the right word—"ally." That word sounded right, she decided, and welcomed Üku into the chamber.

"This is not the first time the flock of ghost eagles has attacked," the Owl Mother explained to the group around the table, who still believed themselves rulers of Uztar. "Every few generations, they return and provoke and massacre and attempt to bring forth the destruction of, well . . ." Now the

Owl Mother appeared to be searching for the right word. "Civilization," she said at last.

"This has happened before?" one kyrg asked. The kyrgs were incredulous. "Why is there no record?" another objected.

"There are many records," Üku scoffed, though Bardu herself knew of none, and nor did any of the other kyrgs. Until Üku had presented herself in Kyrg Bardu's private chambers, free from the dungeons and with a host of new information, Bardu had never heard nor read of anything like the current troubles they were living through. The Owl Mother did not, however, elaborate. She simply continued.

"For more generations than history has recorded, my people have stood watch and protected civilization," she explained. "We have preserved the Hollow Tongue and controlled those who speak it as best we can. When the time comes—as it now has—we take steps to return the ghost eagles to their distant peaks and restore the balance of Uztar. We shall do so again, once I am at liberty to return to the blood birch forest."

"She is a traitor to Uztar," a kyrg announced. "Why should we believe her?"

"Why should we let her go?" another added.

Üku looked to the proctor. It was her turn to speak now.

"You should not," Bardu told them. "You do not need to

believe her, and letting her go is not up to you. *I* believe her, and I have chosen to let her go."

"You don't have the authority!" the kyrgs objected, with much table-pounding and chittering, like a flock of finches.

"We shall take the no-confidence vote right now!" the leader of the mutinous kyrgs proposed, opening her arms wide as all hands around the table rose together. There wasn't a loyal counselor among them.

Bardu smiled anyway. "Do as you must," she said. With that, she turned and left the room, Üku trailing behind her. Just before she crossed the threshold, the Owl Mother spoke a command.

"*Kraas*," she said, and then Yves and Goryn, who were waiting in the hall, shut the door to the council room and barred it behind them.

"The nets are down?" Bardu inquired.

"Every window," Yves confirmed.

Through the heavy doors, she heard muffled shrieks and screams as the Council was torn to pieces by the silent birds that stalked the night above the Sky Castle.

Someone pounded on the door from the inside, and their scream for help was high as a kestrel's screech, but it was quickly cut short. Goryn looked nervously at the bar across the heavy wood, which was bending and straining.

"I did as you asked," Üku said. "Now I must get home."

Bardu nodded at the gray-haired woman who, with a word, had rid her of the burdens of politics and given her complete control of the reins of power. She'd need Yves Tamir's help to maintain control, but she would no longer have to massage the egos of thirty-nine petty despots. Bardu could rule as she wished from now on.

"Take her back to her people," she told Goryn, and then Bardu addressed Üku one last time. "You are sure you can bring these ghost eagles under control once more? It does me little good to rule an empire that's been torn to shreds by birds."

"I will do as the many Mothers before me have done," Üku said. "It's a simple matter of burying their egg beneath the dirt, where its cries will fade and die before it ever has a chance to hatch."

"But what if it does hatch?" Goryn asked.

"That's where you come in." The Owl Mother patted his unshaven cheek. "We'll need to kill the twins, who are trying to protect it." She shook her head. "It's a pity. I had such hopes for the girl to join us, but she chose her friends and family over the fate of civilization . . . yet again. Poor, stupid girl."

"And the brother?" Goryn asked, almost salivating at the idea of getting his hands on Brysen.

"He'll be with her," Üku said. "Do what you like. Our history depends on the twins dying, as it always does and as they always do. It doesn't matter much if they suffer in the process."

Goryn smiled.

"I said you'd have your revenge," Kyrg Bardu told him, glad he was leaving her castle for good and glad the twins who'd plagued her for so long would soon be dead.

BRYSEN

THE SAME ROUND RANGE

20

KHERYN HAD BEEN THE BEST FIGHTER AMONG THEM, AND NOW KHERYN was dead. Their death was Brysen's fault. He found the egg; he carried it. Everything that happened since he first declared he would capture a ghost eagle was his fault. Now everyone he cared about was, yet again, in grave danger and, yet again, trekking through mountains to an uncertain future. And the only advice he could offer them was: *Don't fight back.*

He never meant for anyone to get hurt because of him, and yet his villages burned and his friend's body lay broken on the mountain behind them. Nyck wasn't philosophical or sentimental about death, but he'd lost a friend on this quest of

Brysen's making, and Brysen felt like he had to say *something* about it.

"Just let him grieve," Jowyn urged him as they walked, but he couldn't let Kheryn's death seem meaningless.

"Ancient Uztari thought it was a blessing to be carried off by a ghost eagle," Brysen said, matching Nyck's pace. "Kheryn would've appreciated the drama of their last breeze. They always liked to go big, right?"

Nyck glared at him, neither looking for nor accepting his comfort.

"I'm sorry, all right?" Brysen said. "I won't let their death be for nothing."

"Maybe it isn't up to you," Nyck said quietly. "Maybe what their death meant or didn't mean isn't up to you. Could you just . . . not talk to me?"

"Uh . . . um . . . okay," Brysen said. "I'm just really sorry this happened. Just—"

Nyck cut him off. "I mean, like, right now." He sped up his pace, and Brysen let him go, feeling worse. He wanted to do something to fix this, but how did you ease a person's pain when they didn't want it eased?

"That was an *Altari* belief about the ghost eagle, by the way," Grazim corrected Brysen. She didn't have much patience for anyone being wrong in front of her. It wasn't nice, but correcting people was Grazim's way of being kind.

She truly believed people wanted to know better than they did, and since she considered herself smarter than everyone else, she felt it was her duty to educate those around her.

At least, that was Brysen's interpretation when he wanted to be generous. She might've just been a vicious raven with a short blond haircut and resentment piled higher than she stood, but life was violent and uncertain, and Brysen decided to choose generosity whenever he could.

"To be killed by a ghost eagle was considered a sign that the sky accepted your repentance for the blasphemy of Uztari bird taming," she continued. "Ancient Uztari stole that belief from us and appropriated it for themselves, I guess to make themselves feel better when a ghost eagle took someone."

"I never believed it," Brysen said quietly, so that Nyck wouldn't hear. "If it were a blessing, they'd have never taken my dad. He was a scuzzard's meal while he lived."

"Try not to be like him, then, right?" she said. "Just leave Nyck be."

When his ex-boyfriend, Dymian, tried to kill him, Brysen thought he'd lost what small faith he had in people, but then Jowyn was there, waiting for Brysen to let him in. And when his hawk, Shara, was killed, he thought he'd never find room for gentleness again, but then this egg appeared, and with it came a purpose.

He wasn't stupid; Brysen knew the ghost eagles were

dangerous. Whatever they wanted him to do with the egg was likely cruel, but choosing the hopeful path, choosing to protect something vulnerable even if it didn't deserve protection, was the only way he could think to fend off the despair he'd battled all his life. He had nursed every wound, setback, heartbreak, and disappointment he'd ever felt. He'd fed and raised them to be stronger than he was and received only more suffering for it.

You can't train a hawk on grouse and then expect it to hunt rabbit, and Brysen had decided to feed his soul finer food than self-loathing and mistrust. So he trusted Grazim, he forgave his sister, he let Jowyn love him, and he'd leave Nyck be. But he also vowed to protect this ghost eagle's egg until it hatched, no matter what. He knew to keep the ghost eagle's egg out of Nyck's sight for a while. Battle boys mourned in their own way, and the process usually involved breaking things.

Jowyn stayed by Brysen's side, keeping pace all night and helping him grab for handholds when he needed them, but otherwise he didn't say much. This wasn't a route through the mountains that any of them knew, and they were trusting whatever signs of a trail they could make out. Caravaners took the plains route from the Six Villages to the Talon Fortress, so none of their markings would exist this high. But hawk traders and trackers traveled this way, and they did leave signs to look for—etchings of their logos on markers, bits of leather tied to scrubby trees to show the way home again. If you knew what to look for, you would find maps in the landscape, and together the group found ways to read them, even if they sometimes disagreed about what markers meant. They took more than one fork in the wrong direction, and whenever they did, they found the ghost eagles screaming overhead, guiding them back to the right path.

Jowyn made up a nervous rhyme: *"When death has drawn your map of days, best take your feet some other ways."*

"I like your dirty rhymes better," Brysen told him.

"Me too," Jowyn agreed.

It was nearing sunrise when they stopped to take their first rest. They were in a boulder field, where huge stones sat heavy and overgrown in lush green grass. Nearby, another cliff wall stretched straight up to the sky. The field would have been neck-deep with snow during the ice-wind season, but now it made for an easy place to rest. The plan was to hike at night, when no one was likely to follow them.

So far, they hadn't actually seen anyone following them, and Brysen wondered if maybe the ghost eagles got their wish: Maybe the people in the Six Villages all killed one another. Or perhaps Kyrg Birgund left for the Sky Castle, like Ryven said he would, trying to get home against long odds.

Alternately, maybe everyone was following them and they simply were not well-trained enough to see it. It wouldn't make much difference. If the ghost eagles wanted them to make it to the ruins of the Talon Fortress, they'd make it there. *When death has drawn your map of days,* he thought, *you'll walk the path that it has laid.*

His rhyming wasn't as good as Jowyn's, and he decided not to share it.

He sat next to Jowyn with his back against a large boulder they had to themselves. Grazim and Kylee sat together, drinking from their waterskins and gnawing on some of the food Ma had sent them off with. He watched the two girls sitting together, not talking but content in each other's company. He was glad Kylee had a friend. He knew he'd taken up too much of her attention for too long. Like their mother was letting them go their own way, he thought about how he might let his sister go, how he could break the tether between the two of them so she didn't find herself in the middle of his messes anymore.

Then again, it wasn't his tether to break. His sister would do what she chose, and if she chose to keep caring about him in spite of the trouble he got them in, then the best he could do was try to be worthy of her care.

And to listen when she gave good advice—like now, when she was shouting over to him: "Stop staring at me and eat something!"

He knew he had to eat but found he wasn't very hungry.

The sun showed itself over the peaks behind them, and Brysen gazed down onto the plateau. It was a strange experience to watch the sunrise in the mountains and not hear any birdsong. When the ghost eagles crushed the Kartami army, they unintentionally succeeded in achieving the Kartami's dream: They emptied the sky. Most birds fled over the mountains into the unknown lands beyond, places from which the original Uztari fled. Where they perched and nested and hunted now, no one knew. Were there other people there to hear them singing, civilizations Uztar didn't know, who thought the sudden arrival of every sort of bird was the most beautiful blessing?

The thought made Brysen smile. What looked like a storm under one sky could be a rainbow under another. Once you realize all the skies are the same sky and the curses and blessings offered depend on where you stand, the billows and blasts of life become easier to bear. This was what he'd learned from the ghost eagles. They seemed to share one mind across hundreds of bodies. Every vision they showed him said one thing, over and over: We're all so much more than our fragile, failing bodies. We're all shards of everything.

The body still made demands, however, and Brysen stood to meet one of his in privacy.

"Need help?" Jowyn offered, half standing, and Brysen frowned at him. Even love had its limits, and this was one of them.

"I think some things are best done alone," he said. Jowyn look relieved.

The others watched Brysen step away. He had to mime the particular act he was about to do so they wouldn't follow him. He found a secluded spot behind a boulder at enough distance that they wouldn't be able to hear or smell him, either.

However, had he chosen a closer boulder and been less shy about the normal functions of the flesh, one of his friends might've heard the Owl Mother drop down in front of him, her great gray bird blinking on her fist in the daylight.

"Go back," she warned, her eyes as wide as her owl's. "Go back while the sun still covers you."

She reached for the bag that held the eagle's egg, and before Brysen could shout, another Mother had her rough hands clamped over his mouth and his head locked in a chokehold.

At least they'd waited for him to finish and pull up his pants, otherwise the moment would've been as embarrassing as it was perilous. The great gray owl opened its wings.

21

"TRY TO SCREAM AND YOU'LL LOSE THE OTHER EYE," THE OWL MOTHER whispered in his ear. "We're not here to hurt you, but we're not opposed to hurting you, either, got it?"

Her hand smelled like oiled climbing rope. They were days from the Owl Mothers' territory and headed in the opposite direction. Brysen hadn't known them to come so far down the mountain. This wasn't right. But most things hadn't been right since he first found that egg. He wanted to wriggle free of their grip and call for help, but he asked himself, *What would Kylee do?* He figured his sister would play it slow, hear them out, and not take any reckless action before she understood the situation.

Be like Kylee, he thought. *Just be more like Kylee.*

He nodded in the woman's grip as best he could. He wished his sister had been there to see him being reasonable.

The Owl Mother released her grip on him, but the great gray still had its eyes locked with his. He'd never move fast enough to escape an attack if the conversation took a bad turn. Brysen hoped, were he gone long enough, that Jowyn would come looking, but he'd made it pretty clear that in the shared heights and plummeting crags of their relationship's landscape, he'd prefer to leave some parts of the map unexplored.

To put it another way, Jowyn wouldn't interrupt him pooping.

"So," he asked, pulling his belt straight and doing what he could to regain his composure, if not his dignity. He tucked a stray hair behind his ear, then remembered he hadn't had time to wash his hands or anything. He decided not to think about it. "What brings you down the mountain in daylight with your nocturnal friend?"

He nodded at the owl. The owl panted, blinking one eye, then the other.

Stupid creatures, owls were. You had to have some sense to let yourself be tamed, and owls didn't have much. They were beautiful, of course, with astonishing hearing and eyesight, along with powerful talons. They had serrated feathers on the fronts of their wings that let even large owls like the great gray fly silently, but no bird of prey was perfect. Most of an owl's skull was taken up by its impressive eyes, leaving little room for brains. They were quite easily confused, and it was no wonder the Owl Mothers relied on the Hollow Tongue to train them. The mundane training methods of regular falconers rarely worked well on owls. The Owl Mothers were the only ones who could reliably deploy them.

"You have to come with us," the first Owl Mother said.

She was young, probably not much older than him, but her face was already creased with lines from a hard life at high altitude. While Owl Mothers had access to the sap of the blood birches, which could heal them and toughen their skin, they never used it on themselves. They claimed it was because their scars, scabs, and wrinkles were sacred signs of full lives. Brysen suspected they had other reasons, ones they didn't share with outsiders or even with the boys of their covey, who lived on the sap. Jowyn didn't even know why, and he spent most of his life with them. When Brysen thought about the augur in that alley, about his ranting and raving, he did wonder if that had something to do with it. Jowyn had looked pretty shaken afterward. Did the Owl Mothers keep the boys addicted to the sap to control them?

"I'd love to go with you to the blood birches, but I can't," he told them. "The ghost eagles want me to go this way, and they're holding a friend of mine hostage. So unless you want to argue with them, you should probably just let us go on our way."

The young Owl Mother in front of him raised her eyes to the one still holding him tight. She let go and turned him around to face her. She was strong enough that she could spin him with one hand and keep him in her grip with the other. He might as well have been a feather doll in her arms.

Her skin was dark and her eyes bright. The coils of her hair were tied up in a crown, decorated with white owl feathers. She wore gray-and-white climbing clothes with a slew of brown-and-white scarves. This made her blend into the landscape of the mountain, and before she even spoke, Brysen felt the ripples of her authority. She was someone accustomed to being obeyed.

"The *talorum* has lured you through every step of your life, boy," she told him, using the old word for the ghost eagle. "And what have you gained by it?"

"It hasn't been all bad," he said. "I kinda like my new look." He waggled the eyebrow above the bronze patch as best he could. The Owl Mother was not amused.

"We were always fond of Jowyn," she said, "and would hate to see him hurt, even in exile."

"Are you *threatening* him?" Brysen dropped his pretend playfulness. "Because that would be a very big mistake."

"Oh no," the older woman said. "We are threatening *you*. He accepted his exile on your behalf, and it would break his heart to lose you, which will happen if you continue on this path."

"So you came all this way down the mountain to protect Jowyn from a broken heart? Thoughtful." Brysen didn't believe it, but he still didn't know what they were after. If they wanted to steal the egg from him, they could've already, and if they wanted to bash his skull on a rock, they could've done that, too.

"Just bring the egg and come with us, and everything will be fine," the younger Owl Mother told him. She tried to soften her voice, to sound reassuring, but reassuring wasn't a natural tone for an Owl Mother. It still came off like a threat.

"Nope," Brysen said.

"You don't have a choice," the older Owl Mother told him.

"Of course I do," he replied. "You could've ambushed us and killed me for the egg, but you didn't. We're having a chat. That means there aren't enough of you to ambush us and you two are on your own, or you're afraid to hurt me for some reason but you think threatening me will get you what you want. Threats are only for the weak, and since when are Owl Mothers weak?"

The women looked at each other, each waiting for the other to reply. Brysen's confidence soared. He was holding his own, pushing back against them, seeing through their deceptions. He felt pretty good about it.

Until the older one spoke.

"You're right," she said. "We can't kill you or your sister, and if we took the egg from you right now, the ghost eagles would easily take it from us. But, like them, we have no problem killing your friends, including Jowyn, whom we truly do hold dear. That is how important it is that you bring the egg to the blood birches yourself. We came to you first, to ask that you and your little questing party follow us up the mountain. We won't ask again; we will compel."

Brysen glanced back toward the camp. He could hear the murmurs of Nyck and Lyra talking. He wondered if there were other Owl Mothers watching them right now, preparing to strike.

"The ghost eagles will not just let us go with you," he repeated.

"You have more power over them than you think," the older Owl Mother said. "And if you come with us, we will do our best to protect you. We would die to protect you, in fact."

"So you'll either kill my friends or die to protect me? You really know how to make a guy's head spin."

"Is this really fair to the others?" she asked him. "Putting them in danger, knowing you are safe?"

"They know it's dangerous. They chose to come," he said. "And I'm hardly safe just because the ghost eagles won't kill me and you say you can't."

"You've been here before, on this mountain, passing our way against our wishes. We thought you'd have grown wiser by now."

"I've never been accused of having wisdom."

"Enough with the sarcasm, boy!" the younger one snapped. "You let everyone risk themselves for you over and over again, flying the same doomed path. We continue to be amazed by your selfishness."

"*We?*" He felt a small swell of pride. He was a topic of discussion among the Owl Mothers.

"We find your antics tiresome," she added. "Every single one of us. But even the tiresome aren't hopeless. Do the right thing now, and you can protect your friends and loved ones from what awaits them on this path. That is a choice you have to make for yourself. An entire civilization is at stake!"

"So you say," Brysen told her. "Maybe you should explain it to me before I make any promises."

"We don't have to explain anything to you," the older one said. "We don't require you to understand. We require you only to obey." She raised her fingers to her lips as though to whistle; this was likely a signal for the Owl Mothers Brysen couldn't see, the women hiding somewhere in the mountain mist rising off the boulder field. Brysen was an expert in seeing when he'd used up someone's patience, and he had used up theirs.

245

"Wait!" he shouted.

The older one paused.

"Promise me that if I cooperate, if we follow you, then you won't just protect whoever has the egg. Promise me you'll protect all of us. Nyck and Lyra and Grazim and Jowyn, too."

"Fine," the older Owl Mother said.

"Swear on your owl."

"That is a sacred oath," the younger Mother snarled at him, "not to be wasted on presumptuous boys who—"

"We will swear it," the older woman said, cutting off the younger. "Although you do not deserve it."

"If help was given only to those who deserved it, civilization would've collapsed a long time ago," Brysen said.

"Look at your world." She sighed. "It *has* collapsed."

Brysen bent down and picked up the bag with the egg. Peeking inside, he saw swirls of gold on the shell.

"Change is not collapse," he said.

The younger Owl Mother looked at the older one, who looked at Brysen in stony silence for a long time.

"So I guess I need to tell the others we're changing course and you're our bodyguards?" he said. "They are going to have some questions of their own." He thought about Nyall, wondered what would become of his friend when they defied the ghost eagles' plan. Could he really risk one friend's life to protect a few others? It was bleak math, and he never was great with numbers. He just had to hope the ghost eagles needed Nyall alive. As long as Brysen had the egg, they probably would.

He hated that so many lives hung on that uncertain word: *probably*. It was a flimsy branch to perch their hopes upon, but it was the only one he had.

"Hey, Bry!" he heard Jowyn call. "You okay? Or did your ma's cooking do something unmentionable to your—" Jowyn froze when he saw the women in front of Brysen.

"Clava, Siwoo," he gasped. "What are you doing here?"

The younger Mother, Clava, looked glad to see Jowyn, but the older one, Siwoo, didn't take her eyes off Brysen. She tapped the tips of her index fingers together before finally answering.

"We've come to escort you safely on your way," she said, at last looking at Jowyn and giving him what seemed like a genuine smile. She returned her gaze to Brysen. "I hope none of us comes to regret it."

22

GRAZIM AND KYLEE STOOD THE MOMENT THEY SAW THE OWL MOTHERS step around the boulder behind Brysen and Jowyn. Brysen tried to gesture at his sister that it was okay—they weren't all about to get murdered by owls. He hoped he was right.

The tailor's hawk on Grazim's fist cried, and she had to whisper something to calm it and keep it from bating away. Hawks and owls were of the same family but were not much fond of each other, like cousins who only meet at cliffside funerals and poorly organized weddings. They'd endure each other's company but not without compulsion. Brysen would've just hooded the hawk, but the Hollow Tongue was more effective.

Nyck was lying down with one arm over his eyes, and Lyra had her head on his stomach. It was a point of pride among battle boys that they could fall asleep anywhere. Brysen had once seen Nyall fall asleep on a table at the Broken Jess and stay asleep while Nyck and Fentyr used his back and some cooked noodles to plan out their battle pit strategies. He only woke up once to complain that the noodles were cold before going right back to sleep. Brysen floated a wish to the bare, blue sky that Nyall was still alive and would stay that way.

"Kylee, Grazim," Siwoo greeted both girls. She cast her gaze over the sleeping battle boys with the indifference of an owl flying past a potato. "It has been a long time. I trust you're well?"

Kylee just eyeballed the two Owl Mothers, but Grazim broke into the biggest smile Brysen had ever seen on her. Her whole body leaned forward like she was about to run and hug them, but then she caught herself, reset her face to its usual statuesque scowl, and touched her index finger to the cheekbone below her eye.

"An honor to see you both so far down the mountain," she said. "We did try to come to you, but . . ."

"The boy explained," Clava confirmed without looking at Brysen. She returned Grazim's gesture with her index finger. "So we have come to escort you up personally."

"Up?" Kylee said. She glanced at her brother. "But we have to go to the Talon Fortress. The ghost eagles—"

"Have your friend, yes," Siwoo said, cutting her off. "We know. However, many more people and their friends will suffer and die if you do not get that egg to the blood birches. It cannot be returned to the *talorum* and allowed to hatch."

"Wait." Brysen stopped her. "You didn't say anything about it not hatching."

She looked at him sideways but returned her attention to Kylee. Now that Siwoo had seen Grazim and Kylee, Brysen felt the Owl Mothers' old indifference to him return. He was only of interest to them because he had the egg.

"We have ways of preventing it from hatching," Siwoo explained. "But only in the forest. If you come with us, we can put an end to it. When we do, the convocation will depart."

"How do you know?" Kylee asked her.

Brysen regretted cooperating. He had to get the egg away from the Owl Mothers, but doing so would endanger everyone else. He felt like a leaf fallen into a rushing river, pushed on by too many currents, pulled this way and that, half drowned but never dragged under.

"Because," Siwoo told her, "it has happened before."

That stopped him cold. He and Kylee looked at each other, confused.

"You aren't the first children to have called a ghost eagle's egg into existence," Siwoo said. "And as long as people cry out in weakness and want, you won't be the last. But *we* have always been there to prevent catastrophe. We have always made sure these eggs do not crack open."

"Why?" Brysen whispered.

"How?" Kylee asked.

"As I told your brother," Siwoo said, "you do not need to know. You need only come with us. If that egg is allowed to hatch, I promise worse terrors than the ghost eagles will be unleashed on this world."

"Is that why they're afraid of us having it?" Brysen asked. "Are the ghost eagles afraid of it hatching, too?"

"Yes," said Siwoo. "They fear it more than anything, and they want it to hatch more than anything." She almost smiled at a thought that crossed her mind. "I suppose like all parents."

Brysen didn't find it funny. The colors on the shell's surface swirled wildly now, gray blacks crashing into red blacks, mixing with blue blacks. He saw his sister shifting her weight from foot to foot, ansty, feeling the pull of the shell as it called to her. It was calling out to him, too. It wanted to hatch. It *needed* to hatch but didn't know how. It also knew it was in danger. It knew because Brysen knew. Kylee looked at him.

She tried to signal something, but he didn't understand.

The two of them used to share an entire unspoken language, but ever since they'd each taken different pieces of the Hollow Tongue, it was like they'd lost parts of their own language. Knowledge, like family, was not a static thing; it changed and moved and blew away with the consistency of clouds. At least Brysen had Jowyn now. He worried his sister was a lone cloud, adrift in endless sky. Although she'd shove him to the ground for thinking about her like that.

He tried to signal something back to her, which she did understand.

He was going to run.

At the first chance they had, he wanted them all to run.

Kylee shook her head no.

She looked up at a large boulder, then opposite it, at a steep cliff. There were stones out of place, areas of slight discoloration.

Camouflaged Owl Mothers, watching. If Brysen and the others ran, they wouldn't make it far. He'd rather climb freely than as their prisoner. So, he would have to bide his time.

"Okay, well, the sun is up, and we better make some distance before nightfall," he said, talking quickly. He went over to Nyck and Lyra to wake them.

"Wha? Huh?" Nyck rubbed the sleep from his eyes. Lyra lifted her head off him, leaving a strand of drool.

"We're going up to the blood birches after all," Brysen told them. He bent down to help Nyck up and whispered in his ear. "When I say run, you run."

Nyck didn't have time to respond, because Brysen moved on without looking back. There was a steep cliff between them and the fastest path to the blood birches, and scaling the cliff face would take them most of the day. He wondered if maybe, when they got to the top, more of the Owl Mothers would reveal themselves. Or maybe, when night fell, the ghost eagles would return and send them all back on the path to their nest. He knew now why the image of the blood birches made them sad. It was where their children went to die. Brysen would not let this egg get there.

"*Zasaase*," he whispered to the egg again. "You're safe with me."

Jowyn gave him a funny look. "They're here to help us," he said. "They know what to do with that thing."

Brysen didn't reply. The boy still believed in the Owl Mothers, even though they had exiled him. He didn't need to know they'd threatened his life to get Brysen's cooperation. If he could get Jowyn safely away from them without breaking his heart, that's what he'd do.

"Time to climb," Clava announced.

Among their group, Kylee was the strongest climber, and while Brysen was confident in himself, he hadn't done any free climbing since the Kartami took his eye. He was pretty sure Jowyn could climb, having lived so long with the Owl Mothers, but Nyck and Lyra were more the sorts to climb onto pub tables than steep mountains. He didn't know what experience Grazim had, growing up on the flat plains of the plateau, but she lived with the Owl Mothers for a time, too, and must've learned something.

He reached into his bag for the coiled rope he'd packed. He and Kylee could rig a simple belay system, so the others could climb with a little more confidence that they'd all reach the top alive.

Kylee caught up with him and Jowyn at the bottom of the cliff while the others were gathering their things and making their way on the narrow path.

"What's going on?" she demanded. "You're acting strange."

"No, I'm not," Brysen told her. "This is just how I act."

"So you *are* acting?" She cocked her head at him. It was so annoying how she laid these verbal traps for him. They both knew she was smarter than him; she didn't have to prove it all the time.

"I'm just . . . ," he started, before he knew what he was going to say. "I don't think we should trust them."

"Who said I trust them?" Kylee replied. "We both know the ghost eagles are afraid of the blood birches, so if we get there, we'll be in a stronger position."

"You're not worried about Nyall anymore?" he asked her.

"Of course I am!" she said. "But they won't hurt him as long as we have the egg. And maybe, along the way, we can get the Owl Mothers to tell us more about it. Having more information is never a bad thing."

"I can't let them destroy the egg," he told her.

She sighed. "I know," she said. "But we'll hear them out, okay?"

"They won't explain anything to me."

"*I'll* hear them out," she clarified. "But we'll decide what to do together. No sudden decisions. Just don't——"

"What?"

"Don't do what you usually do," she said, and he knew just what she meant, but she said it anyway. "Don't be reckless."

Before he could argue about the relative merits of reckless-ness, she took the ropes from his bag and began tying them into a climbing harness and belay lines. She was always better with knots than he was.

"You want to make sure this side goes *under*." She showed him. "Or else it could slip and you'll be meat paste on jagged rocks." She shoved the rope back into his hands.

Siwoo and Clava strolled past them, putting their hands against the sheer rock and then looking back at the twins. "I suppose you *would* need ropes," Clava grunted, reaching for a handhold and starting the climb, sure-footed as a mountain goat. Siwoo was right behind her, and their owl circled overhead at the top. They climbed so fast, Nyck and Lyra were still throwing things into their bags by the time the Owl Mothers were halfway up.

Kylee didn't wait for Brysen but followed close behind, hauling one end of the rope with her. Grazim followed, tossing her hawk skyward with a command to wait-on, so that he and Jowyn had to belay for the battle boys and go up last themselves.

Once they were alone at the bottom of the cliff, Brysen and Jowyn had a chance to talk.

"You're hiding something from me," Jowyn said. "You have that look."

"I'm just worried about you," Brysen said. He hated to lie to Jowyn, but he hated to hurt him even more. A little lie could be like a stitch in a wound, something to keep a person from bleeding worse. "You're exiled, and going to their territory scares me. What will the rest of the Owl Mothers do when they see you again?"

"Well, exile made me like any other outsider," he said. "So they'll treat me just like you . . . They'll probably try to toss us both in a crevasse if I make them mad."

"Wouldn't some of your old friends try to protect you?" Brysen wondered. Jowyn had been a member of the covey since he was small. If anyone still held affection for him, it was likely one of the Mothers, although, as Jowyn had made clear, his affections flew as wild as the winds and could just as well have felled one of the fledgling Owl Mothers.

"That's not how it works," Jowyn said. "When we're in the covey, we sublimate ourselves to the Owl Mothers collective. Our own desires are always subordinate to the needs of the community. No one would choose one exile over the verdict of the group, even one as absolutely charming as me."

"And humble, too."

Jowyn grinned. "What good's a peacock who won't show his feathers?"

"So there isn't even one person among the Owl Mothers who wants you back?" Brysen asked, knowing he shouldn't keep pecking at this but unable to stop himself.

"Oh, I assume they *all* want me back," he answered, "but now I'm snared in an entirely different trap." He squeezed Brysen's bicep.

"All traps can be unsprung," Brysen countered.

Jowyn chuckled as he composed his rhyme. "*But not a trap that's so well hu—*"

"Get moving!" Clava shouted down at them, her focused voice sharp as an arrow.

"Well, here we go," Brysen said. "Just promise me that if I say run, you'll run. Promise me you'll trust me over them."

Jowyn frowned at him. "I trust you," he said. "I run when and where you do, whenever and wherever that is, got it?"

"Got it," Brysen said. "For now, that means up." He reached for the first handhold, grasping and coming up short. He tried not to feel ridiculous. Who reaches for a mountain and misses?

Jowyn took Brysen's hand, put it gently to his lips and then placed in on the rock face as gently as setting a baby bird in a nest. "I've got you," he whispered, and Brysen knew he meant it. They'd climb side by side.

"Left leg up, out to the side—there!" Jowyn told him. "That grip's still an arm's length above . . . Go for the one on your right. See it?" Jowyn guided him, and with Brysen's skill and Jowyn's depth perception, they made it up the cliff. It took only three times longer than everyone else.

"That was *not* pretty." Kylee smiled down at him after he finally hauled himself over the ledge and rolled onto his back to catch his breath. "But it was impressive."

"That's how I want to be remembered," he wheezed at her, clutching the bag holding the ghost eagle egg to his chest. "Not pretty, but impressive."

"I think it's more likely to go the other way," Jowyn joked in between gulps of air. He was beside Brysen, just as breathless.

Both their knuckles were bloody, and Brysen's face was red from where he'd smacked into an outcropping he thought was farther up than it was, but otherwise, he felt elated. He hadn't climbed anything larger than a boulder since losing his eye, and scaling this first cliff was a triumph worth celebrating.

He forgot himself and whooped.

Siwoo grunted.

"Waiting for these boys is taking too long," Clava said. "Jowyn used to be better than this."

"Life is change, Mem Siwoo," Jowyn said to her as he pushed himself up off the ground and extended a hand to help up Brysen.

"We fly and fly the same round range,
And turning, and turning, change and change."

"This is not the time for your poetry," Siwoo snapped at him.

"That's not my poetry," Jowyn said. "That's an old prayer I used to say as a kid."

"Well, it's no time for prayers, either," Siwoo grunted.

"You're not in charge of him anymore," Brysen defended Jowyn, who put his hand on Brysen's arm to stop him.

"It's fine," he said. "Let it go."

"But—"

Jowyn locked his eyes on Brysen and shook his head. He didn't want this argument, didn't want Brysen talking back like this. It was a reminder that the pale boy had a full life in the covey of the Owl Mothers before he and Brysen glided into each other's lives, that Jowyn hadn't chosen to leave but instead had been exiled for choosing Brysen. Just because he was on Brysen's side didn't mean he wanted to antagonize the Owl Mothers. Suddenly Brysen's fears of bloodshed and battle and the death of an innocent bird were perched beside new but familiar sensations: anxiety and jealousy. What if Jowyn remembered that he liked life better with the Owl Mothers than with Brysen? What if he had an ex in the covey? What if he regretted choosing Brysen in the first place?

Siwoo removed a bulbous waterskin from her belt and passed it to Brysen. "You are too slow. This will move you faster."

Brysen took the pouch and studied it skeptically. "Distilled hunter's leaf?"

"Sap of the blood birches," she replied. "All of you should drink. You will climb faster and farther."

Jowyn stared at the bulbous skin of sap as though it was a rock snake. He neither moved toward it nor away from it, but he looked like he might do either in an instant. "You're not allowed to share this with us," Jowyn said. "Especially not with me. The sap is forbidden to outsiders."

Brysen held it tightly but didn't drink.

"And yet there it is," Siwoo said. "Drink."

"I've always wanted to try this." Nyck took the pouch from

Brysen and knocked back a gulp. After he wiped his lips, he seemed to realize something and, looking at Jowyn's unnaturally white skin with poorly masked concern, asked, "This isn't going to, like, transform me, is it?"

"You will always be what you always were," Siwoo said cryptically, and offered no more, which Nyck took as no comfort. Siwoo likely hadn't meant it as any.

Lyra drank next, warily, then Grazim. Brysen watched the waterskin move among them. Kylee hesitated, then drank before passing the container back to Brysen. He thought about Jowyn's tattooed skin, how hard it had been when they met, how quickly its wounds healed.

"Will it—?"

"No," Siwoo grunted at him. "It will not restore your eye, but it will sharpen the vision of the one that's left, and bring back the strength in your sad, tired little body."

Brysen prepared to drink, but Jowyn put a hand on his wrist, stopped him.

"Don't," he said simply, almost pleadingly.

Jowyn's sudden earnestness was odd, but Brysen gestured toward the two Owl Mothers in front of them. "They gave it to us."

Jowyn leaned in close and whispered, "We're not meant to. Neither of us."

Brysen frowned. He looked out across the plateau, in the

direction of the Talon Fortress. It was still days away. He looked back at Jowyn, so worried about permission and rules.

"Sorry," he said. "I've got to. We need to climb." He knocked back a gulp. As it hit him, he could find only one word to describe it: "Whoa."

23

BRYSEN HAD INGESTED THE SAP WITH FOOD THE LAST TIME HE climbed up this mountain, and he'd drunk it, distilled through Jowyn's hot blood, after nearly dying of cold in a frozen lake, but he'd never had it pulled pure from the tree. The taste was something uncanny—familiar and mysterious at the same time. It was sweet like white walnut, bitter like dandelion, and metallic like fresh blood. There was something he couldn't quite place, too, a cold taste that made him think of hungry wolf pups crying on frozen steppes, of a vulture circling over bare rock, of death and helplessness. There was also a hint of cherry.

That was the flavor that blew his mind.

When the cherry taste hit, so did a rush of warmth, and the light around him sharpened. The outlines of the mountains, the scrubby trees, even the people popped into greater focus, and he could see depths and distances with dizzying clarity. He could see details in the dirt and the stone. He could spy a pattern in the wind, movement of the sky, and even the difference in temperature compared to the plains below. With this sight and sense came a burst of energy that was both calm and ecstatic. He wanted to scale the nearest cliff and the one after it. He felt he could climb all day and all night.

Jowyn took the sapskin from him slowly, reverently, and passed it back to Siwoo without drinking. Brysen saw what passed between the Owl Mother and Jowyn—a tiny, respectful nod—and he saw Jowyn dart a nervous glance at him and then look away. And in that look he saw every moment since they'd known each other bound like a pigeon in a snare. His thoughts squirmed.

"Onward, then?" Siwoo suggested, and then they were moving. Brysen had to force himself to slow down so he could walk with Jowyn.

"Is it always like this?" he asked.

"No," Jowyn said in a tone Brysen didn't recognize, but it was one he understood. It was the voice ice would use if it could speak. "It gets more intense."

Brysen put a hand on Jowyn's shoulder and, to his surprise, didn't miss on the first try. The sap worked. "Are you *mad* at me for drinking it? Because I had to."

"Listen, the sap is not like hunter's leaf," he said. "It changes you. Look at that augur we met in the alley. Without it, he went mad."

"You're worried I'll lose my mind?"

Jowyn didn't answer.

"Are you worried *you're* going to lose your mind?"

Still Jowyn didn't answer, but his mouth twitched briefly. Brysen never would've seen that without the sap's vision.

"Loneliness and bitterness drove that guy mad," Brysen said. "Neither of those things are in your future, not while I'm around."

"It's not that," Jowyn snapped at him. He'd never snapped at Brysen before. "This isn't about *you*. Drinking it means something. Drinking it is *supposed* to mean something, anyway. It's not just supposed to be useful. It's sacred. Or at least, it was."

Brysen felt dizzy from the tension. His senses were sharp and his muscles loose and lively, but despite that, he felt like he was falling. He'd been so focused on his own sense of what had to happen, he hadn't even noticed that he and everyone around him had just stomped on something sacred to Jowyn. There was so much about the Owl Mothers he didn't know, and no matter how close he and Jowyn were, he could never know what it was like to grow up in their covey in the blood birch forest. He'd let his needs of the moment drown out Jowyn's, and he didn't have to understand why what he'd done was wrong to know that it had hurt the person he cared about. He wanted to make it right.

"I'm sorry," he apologized. "I just thought it's the only way to move fast enough . . ."

"It is," Clava interrupted them. She'd fallen in at the rear of their march and showed no interest in their privacy.

"It's fine," Jowyn said coolly. "I'm an exile, after all. I don't get to have an opinion about this anymore."

Clava looked like she wanted to add something, but instead she nudged Brysen forward. "We have to keep up," she said, and they kept walking.

By sunset, they'd hiked a distance that usually took days and scaled another two cliff faces. Brysen tried to help Jowyn, even offered to carry him, but the boy refused for as long as he could. When his legs finally gave out, Brysen caught him in his arms, but it was Siwoo who lifted Jowyn and carried him the rest of the way.

They reached the opening of a cave, high enough that, in the distance, they could see the edge of the blood birch forest in one direction and the high black spires of the Talon Fortress in the other. Brysen thought he could even make out the movement of large black-feathered birds among the spires, but it could've just been a trick of the light and the sap and his own racing mind. The ghost eagles had left them alone so far, even though they were now going the wrong way. He wondered what they would do when night fell.

The Owl Mothers had considered it as well.

"We won't be in the open when night falls," Siwoo told them as she whistled her owl down from the sky. Grazim's hawk cowered on her fist, clenched its feet tighter and tried to bury its head into its own feathers. "By the time the sixth star appears, the ghost eagles will come."

"They won't hurt us," Brysen said, patting the egg in his bag.

"They won't hurt *you*," Clava replied. "We won't take our chances."

Once they were inside the cave, the two Owl Mothers covered the opening with a large boulder using a mechanism. It looked to be engineered just like the entrance in the cave they left behind in the Six Villages. Everyone knew the Owl Mothers kept caverns and tunnels all over the mountains, but Brysen was surprised at how well-stocked this one was. The floor was smooth dirt, and there were thick furs hanging to use as bedding. There were sturdy barrels of food and water along the rear wall, and perches for at least a dozen owls inside smooth, carved niches. He could even hear the trickle of water from a subterranean stream they used as a latrine. This cave was nicer than the one they'd left.

As Brysen settled down to sleep, with the straps of the bag holding the ghost eagle egg wrapped around his arms, he turned toward Jowyn, who lay beside him. He could see the boy clearly despite the dark. It wasn't like Jowyn was torchlit but rather as though the dark itself was a different kind of light. Brysen wondered if this was how nocturnal birds saw the world at night, if this was how the sap made Jowyn see. He wondered how Jowyn had seen him when they first met.

Jowyn was radiant. It was like Brysen could see the vitality pulsing in him, the tight coils of every muscle, the heat coming off his skin. But there was also anger flapping behind his features. His eyes were open and damp, staring straight up at the ceiling.

"Do you want to talk?" Brysen whispered.

"Shh!" Siwoo hissed from the other side of the cavern.

"I want to sleep," Jowyn said, and rolled over with his back to Brysen. The tattoos up his side rippled with energy, like the story they told was itself alive. For the first time, Brysen was afraid he'd just cut himself out of that story. He thought he'd known the right thing to do, but it had hurt the love of his life.

I had no choice, he thought, although of course he did. He had a choice, and he made it. He hoped Jowyn would forgive him eventually. He hoped they lived long enough for Jowyn to forgive him. Between the Owl Mothers and the ghost eagles, he wasn't sure how long their survival was guaranteed.

As night came on, he watched the other boy's side rise and fall with sleeping breaths, unable to fall asleep himself. There was some darkness no light could break, and Brysen still saw it when he closed his eyes. Outside the cave, he heard the ghost eagles shrieking.

24

HE MUST HAVE FALLEN ASLEEP, BECAUSE HE WAS WALKING THROUGH snow with his sister, somewhere on a high mountain pass. They were barefoot, but the cold didn't hurt, and when he looked down at his feet, worried they'd gone numb from frostbite, he saw giant bird's feet with great black talons. He looked at his sister, but he saw double. She was his sister, but she was also a ghost eagle. Her large eagle head dipped up and down, taking in the sight of him. He, too, was a ghost eagle and himself.

Dreams are strange, he thought, and then wondered if it was strange that he was aware he was dreaming.

He cried out in the eagle's voice, "REEEEEEE!" and

launched from the snow in unison with his sister. Together they flew, skimming just above the icy slopes, flapping over jutting peaks, then catching a breeze and gliding high in the air current, seeing the world below like mapmakers looking down at stretched paper, sensing every brushstroke that made the world. There was no division between the earth and the sky, nor between Brysen and Kylee. The wind that carried them was the same as them, and they were the same as each other, and that feeling of unity was pure, blissful joy, as thrilling as the flight itself.

And then a scream tore through him, and suddenly Brysen's thoughts were solely his own and the world below looked alien and strange. The great bird beside him looked just as strange. There came another scream, and he found himself diving in its direction, certain that if he could just stop the screaming, then he could fly free again and find his joy again and be one with everything he saw.

So he dove, and the scream grew louder and louder, and there he saw the Six Villages. He dove for them, and he saw his house, and he aimed for it, and it stood like it had before it burned.

In the yard, he saw that the door to the house was open, and somehow he knew what he would see if he looked in. His eyes snapped to the hawk mews, where all the falconry equipment was stored along with the birds to train and sell, and he couldn't see inside, but he knew by the screaming what he would see.

Himself.

The scream again. It called him, it pulled him down.

His father was there. Brysen was curled over Shara, his hawk, protecting her, and his father stood over him, whip in one hand, torch in the other.

He tried to turn away, to fly anywhere else, but still he dove for the mews, and beside him his sister dove for the house, where she had been the night he burned, and they were each being pulled, relentlessly, mercilessly down, down, down into their past, into themselves, into the worst moment of their lives.

I don't want to go back there, he thought. He could smell the smoke, the fire getting closer. The scent of burning hair, burning feathers, burning skin.

Burning and burning and burning.

Stop flying. Please. I don't want to feel this again. Stop it. Stop it. Stop it!

And he was awake, gasping, in the cave. He was wrapped in Jowyn's arms, smelling like sweat and like moss on the mountain and like himself, a smell that told Brysen he was safe. There was no smoke. No fire. He was gasping and his heart was racing, but he was safe.

"You're okay," Jowyn whispered to him. "You're safe. You're here. You're safe."

His eyes opened fully now, and he came back to himself in the dark cave. He wondered why the ghost eagle had showed him this. Why was he seeing it?

He remembered then that he was not the only person who dreamed through ghost eagle eyes.

"Kylee!" He sat up and jumped from the floor, rushing across the room to his sister, who was awake already, sitting alone, cross-legged, facing the stone that blocked the cave entrance. He knelt in front of her. Tears streaked through the dirt on her cheeks, but her eyes were fixed forward, through him, her jaw set tight. "Are you okay? Kylee? You're here. We're here now. We're okay. We're okay. I'm okay."

She blinked and looked at him, surprised he was in front of her.

"I stayed," she said quietly. Brysen noticed the others were awake in the cave behind her, listening but keeping their distance. He focused on Kylee. "I stayed with them as they dove." It sounded like she was apologizing.

"That's all right," Brysen said.

She shook her head. "No," she said. "I mean . . . I dove with them, and I lived it all again. I couldn't resist it. I *felt* it all again, everything I felt then, but also what you felt. What Ma felt." Her voice caught. "What *Da* felt, too. I whipped you. I burned you. And I watched you burn."

"It's okay," Brysen said again. "It's not your fault. And look . . . I'm okay now?" He wished it hadn't come out like a question.

"*That's not it!*" his sister said, her voice rising, trying to make herself clear. "I was the ghost eagles. I mean. *They* watched you burn, and *they* felt it all, and they didn't want to, but they couldn't help it. It's like Ryven said: They're bound to us and they have no choice. A falconer calls a falcon to the fist with a whistle. A ghost eagle is called by pain. They're not hunting us. They never have been. We've called them, over and over and over. Ma called them. You and I, we called them . . . but it hurts them."

"It hurts them?" he asked, but he knew what she meant instantly, in the way someone points out a face in the clouds and you stare and stare but don't see it until suddenly, by catching one billowy feature, the whole face snaps into focus just before the cloud blows away or darkens to a storm. "Memory," he said

Kylee nodded. "I think we remind them of something, something they want to forget. Something they cannot forget."

"It's not our pain that calls them," Brysen said, understanding more now. "It's that our pain is like theirs. It's like . . ."

He looked back at Jowyn, who was watching him, worried but patient, giving them space. "It's like our pain and theirs rhyme," he said.

Kylee nodded again. "I think that's why we can talk to them. I think that's why we've always been connected. They think we understand each other."

"But we don't," Brysen said. He still didn't know what it was they wanted or what it was that hurt them.

"We *do*," Kylee insisted. "We're the same. All your life you chased the greatness that Da never thought you'd achieve, and it's only left death in its wake. All my life I've tried to control things that I can't control—Da's rage, you, an entire war— and it's caused nothing but misery. You and I were trying to heal ourselves with the same tools that wounded us, just like the ghost eagles. They are in pain, so they inflict pain."

Every word she said was true. Brysen had sabotaged himself his whole life, trying to get what he thought he wanted only to wreck what he had. Over and over and over again.

"What are we supposed to do?" he wondered.

"We need to know what they're trying to forget," she said. "Like how we can only heal ourselves by knowing where we're hurt, we need to know what's hurting them."

"And then try to heal them," Brysen said. "The Owl Mothers say they're keepers of history, right?" he prompted. "So maybe they know."

They turned in unison toward Siwoo and Clava, who were watching them.

"Do you know what's drawing the ghost eagles back to us over and over again?" Kylee asked them.

"And why are they afraid whenever this egg turns gold?" Brysen added.

"These are not things you need to know," Siwoo said.

"But you *do* know?" Kylee stood. She took a step toward them. Brysen stood up behind her, ready to back whatever she decided. He caught Nyck's eye. The battle boys were ready. Grazim was ready.

"It will all be explained when we get to the blood birches," Clava said.

"If you want me to go any farther with you, you'll tell us now," Brysen declared.

"You forget our agreement," Siwoo told him. "Your friends stay safe as long as you cooperate."

Brysen nodded even as he saw surprise flit across Jowyn's face. The boy hadn't suspected he was in any danger from the Owl Mothers, and the moment he realized that Brysen had only agreed to go with them *because* they'd threatened him, he gasped. The dark tattoos the Owl Mothers gave Jowyn stood out on his pale skin, and he wrapped his arms around himself, covering them. They marked Jowyn as theirs even in exile, and he'd just learned they were using him as a hostage to get

Brysen and Kylee to do what they wanted. It couldn't have felt good.

"I'm sorry," Brysen said to him.

"We're sorry, too," Siwoo said. "We're fond of you, Jowyn, but this is more important than our own personal desires. That egg must not be allowed to hatch."

"*Thaa-loom*," said Clava, and her owl launched itself for Jowyn.

"*Tatakh!*" Grazim snapped from the shadows, and her tailor's hawk screeched as it shot from its perch like an arrow leaving a bow, talons bolting up. It snatched the owl from the air and pinned it to the cave floor, squeezing it so hard it panted but not yet killing it—not until Grazim told it to.

"Stop!" Jowyn pleaded. "No one has to hurt each other. We can all cooperate."

"They made their choice," Kylee said.

"They were going to hurt you," Brysen said, flinting his voice just as hard as his sister's.

"You're outnumbered in here," Kylee told the Owl Mothers as the battle boys fanned out to flank them. "So if you want to leave this cave alive, you'll tell us what you know."

"That's an unwise threat," said Siwoo. "You're on our mountain, and you won't make it far if we don't walk out of here with you come sunrise."

"Sunrise is a long way off." Kylee stepped toward the two

women, drawing her knife. Brysen couldn't tell if she was bluffing or not. "Talk."

"If the egg hatches, humanity will not endure," Siwoo said. "That is all you need to know."

"No," Kylee said. "I need to know *why*."

"We need the whole story," Brysen added.

Clava looked at Siwoo, deferring to the elder Owl Mother. Siwoo licked her lips once, and then cracked the heavy quiet of the cave with a laugh. "Oh, children," she said, slapping her palms together. "Oh, but you've had the story all along."

Brysen looked at his sister. She looked back at him, shrugged. She didn't know what the Owl Mother meant any more than he did.

But Siwoo wasn't looking at either of them. They followed her gaze to Jowyn, to his tattoos.

Brysen first looked at the tattoo depicting the two of them together. Jowyn got that in the Villages after his exile. The rest were from the high slopes of the blood birch forest, made by the Owl Mothers' ancient art.

"They tell my story," Jowyn said, doubt creeping into his voice.

"And can you read them?" Siwoo asked.

Jowyn looked down at his own chest, looked along the length of his left arm. "Some of them," he said.

"But not all?" Brysen wondered.

"No." Jowyn shook his head, looking at the Owl Mothers desperately. "Not all of them."

Clava smiled.

"Wait?" Jowyn whispered. "All this time? My skin?"

"We carry a long history," Siwoo told him, "and we need to record it. Every boy of the covey carries a piece of it with them; their stories are parts of the larger story of us all. It's the blessing we give you. That's why only they are supposed to drink the sap of the blood birches. That's why only they are allowed to stay with us. We bless their skin with the truth. Your truth. Our truth."

"What language is it?" Brysen asked, though he feared he knew the answer already.

"It is, as best as we can render, the Hollow Tongue," Siwoo said.

Jowyn hugged himself harder, and Brysen knew what it was like to feel betrayed by your own body, like part of it didn't belong to you. For so long, he'd thought of his scars that way, like a story his father wrote about him, lash by lash. But Jowyn taught Brysen to love all of himself. Maybe he could do the same for Jowyn.

He crossed the cave to Jowyn, put his hand on Jowyn's arms and gently opened them. He looked back at the Owl Mothers.

"Can *you* even read it?" he asked.

"Some," Clava said.

"Most," Siwoo said.

"But not all?" Brysen asked.

"We all carry fragments," Siwoo told him. "None of us carries all."

Brysen thought about the way the ghost eagles worked: a single mind spread across many bodies. It made sense that the ghost eagles' history would also be spread across many bodies, too, a human approximation of the mind the story tried to describe. But if he and his sister were truly bound to the ghost eagles, then maybe they were the ones who could read it all.

He rested a hand on Jowyn's neck, touched the swirling lines, let his fingers trace them down to Jowyn's collarbone. "May I?" he asked.

Jowyn nodded. Brysen breathed in and out as slowly as he could, and he reached out with his thoughts, tried to listen in the way he listened to his dreams, in the way he listened to the ghost eagles' screeches. His fingers traced the patterns on Jowyn's skin in the way his ears traced patterns of birdsong.

The egg seemed to make a noise in its bag, though really it was only in Brysen's head. His sister nodded. She heard it, too.

Brysen saw fields. He saw people hunting with birds of prey, speaking to them and being spoken to in their own language.

"I can understand it!" he announced, a swell of pride rushing through him.

"This is not right," Siwoo said.

"No one should read this," Clava said.

"What good is preserving the story if no one can read it?" Grazim wondered.

"We are lost without our history," Siwoo said. "But that doesn't mean we should relive it."

Jowyn shuddered. Gooseflesh rose on his arms and chest. Like Brysen explained to him, the Hollow Tongue wasn't just a language you spoke and heard. Its words became what they described. To read in this language was to create what it described, and whatever it described was what made the ghost eagles scream. Gooseflesh rose on Brysen's arms, too.

"Give them privacy," Kylee snapped at the Owl Mothers, and she tore one of the furs from the wall and rushed to them, holding it up. Grazim came over and held the other side, so the two boys were somewhat alone.

"I made a mistake with the sap," Brysen said once they had this tiny bit of privacy. He needed to restore Jowyn's trust before reading the text on his body, before bringing the story on his flesh to life. "I'm sorry. If you don't want me to do this, I won't."

"No . . . ," Jowyn said, looking Brysen right in the eye in the dim cave. "I want to know. I want *you* to know."

"I'm gonna need to read all of it," Brysen said, looking the other boy up and down.

Jowyn didn't even make a dirty comment like he normally would've. He just let his pants fall, showing the tattoos that ran from his left ankle all the way up his torso and to his neck. They stood out in deep blacks against his pale skin, swirls and dots and lines; some shapes looked almost like people, others like birds. Some were thick and some thin, and they rose and fell and shifted with his breathing, with his shivering. The very acts of living made them change, and Brysen sensed that was part of the language, too. How else could you write the language of the birds but with text that bends with air and blood?

Brysen moved his fingertips down Jowyn's neck, traced the shapes and images, and his mind stretched between Jowyn and the egg and his own thundering heart as he read the story from top to bottom. Jowyn quivered as Brysen's fingers moved along his collarbone, as history threaded the skin between them. Brysen touched barely a finger's-width of skin at a time, but each point of contact brought an image alive in his mind, more vivid than a memory. He saw the story of how their world began, how it changed, and how it broke.

"There were people here before the Uztari," he said quietly. His thumb traced a pattern like the season's changing winds over the round ball of Jowyn's shoulder muscle.

"Speak up!" Grazim said, but before Brysen could, his sister spoke.

"There were other people here," she said. She saw what he saw. As he read, she saw it, too. "There were people here on the plateau before the Uztari came."

"The Altari," Grazim said from the other side of the furs. "My people. We know this."

"No," Brysen said. "There were no Altari here. These were falconers . . . but they were . . . not any of us. And our people . . . the people we call Uztari, they were lost on the other side of the mountain, in the Frozen Lands."

He felt cold shudder through him, saw Jowyn's bicep twitch. Brysen ran his hand along it, then lifted the arm to see the images that formed a cloud at his underarm and on his upper rib cage. Forty curls formed a kind of flock that led across his ribs to his back, where a small group of lines clustered.

"The people wandering on the ice were starving. They were desperate and afraid, but they sent scouts to follow a flock of forty falcons from the Frozen Lands to this land, where they found the First Falconers living."

He moved down Jowyn's ribs, touched the soft skin of his side, of his stomach. He saw these scouts arrive on the plateau, bedraggled, afraid, hungry, and he saw the First Falconers greet them, unafraid. The falcons told them these scouts were coming. The falcons told them to prepare. They had one language, the birds and the people, and they spoke it freely. They fed the newcomers, and though they couldn't speak their language, the falconers taught them to train birds of prey, which let themselves be trained. Kylee orated the story on the other side of the blanket as Brysen read it. Their minds were tethered to each other through the text, the language of the birds, and also to the past, as though it were happening right now. Brysen felt sudden warmth as he saw their ancestors descend from the frozen mountains to the fertile plateau that would become Uztar.

In the story, it was not yet Uztar.

"What happened to the people who were here?" Jowyn asked, his voice barely a whisper.

Brysen ran his hand along Jowyn's hip to a vicious pattern etched onto his thigh.

"There was a war," Brysen said, shocked by the sudden image of blood and terror that filled his mind. Bodies falling, children screaming, birds of prey stabbed in their sleep beside their falconers. The feeling was nauseating. He had to hold Jowyn's body to keep himself from falling over. He skipped something, ran his hand back up to the space above Jowyn's heart. He saw a time of peace, when the Uztari scouts and the First Falconers got to know each other, were curious. Some argued. Some people had misunderstandings that became violent, but most learned to communicate, formed friend-ships, fell in love with each other, and even started families together. The story was told out of order. Again Brysen ran his hand down Jowyn's stomach, back to his legs, where the war burst out. He smelled smoke. It nearly knocked him over.

Naked in front of him, Jowyn shook. He saw a change in Brysen. "What is it?" he asked. "What do you see?"

Brysen looked up at Jowyn's eyes. "I . . . There were mur-ders," he said. How could he explain? "The First Falconers were killed . . . *all of them*."

"By the ghost eagles?"

Brysen shook his head. The whole story wasn't there. Jowyn only carried fragments. He couldn't be sure, but he'd seen no ghost eagles. They may not have existed yet.

"By us," he said, just as the fur in front of them fell. A par-liament of owls, flying silent, harried them back toward the center of the chamber, and a crowd of Owl Mothers stepped forward, their white-haired leader, Üku, coming right up to Brysen.

"These stories are not for little boys to tell," she said, yank-ing Brysen away from Jowyn by the collar of his shirt and tossing him onto his back in the dirt.

25

"ÜKU, I . . ." JOWYN SOUNDED LIKE HE WAS ABOUT TO APOLOGIZE, BUT the Owl Mother held up her hand to silence him.

"Put on your clothes," she snapped, refusing to look at him further. She had exiled him herself, and her dismissive wave hit Jowyn like a punch. Brysen wanted to defend him, wanted to shove Üku to the ground and tell Jowyn that she wasn't worth getting upset over, but she'd been Jowyn's first chosen family, and the pain of losing that wasn't one Brysen could heal with a shove. Also, he'd have been killed before her backside even hit the ground. A large group of Üku's clan flooded the cave.

They came in from every direction, and with them was a

host of phantom-white boys from their covey. Brysen's eyes darted all over their bodies, seeing their tattoos but unable to read them all at the same time. He realized he had to be focused to do it, one at a time, with his sense of touch and sight and smell all bent toward the images. Just as speaking the Hollow Tongue demanded your full self, so too did reading it. He wasn't sure how he'd be able to read it, but gathered in this cave, at this very moment, was the entire history of the ghost eagles and Uztari civilization. His head spun with the echoes of the fragments he had just read on Jowyn.

He saw flashes of scenes. Arguments between settlers, fights breaking out, children being born, birds screeching, blades clashing, and then pools of blood in the moonlight, so deep and dark they looked black. And from these pools formed swirling patterns that merged and congealed into the shape of an egg . . .

A white snow owl screeched at Brysen, breaking his concentration. It fluttered onto Üku's fist, and its brilliant yellow eyes locked on him. In his distraction, he was too slow to see two pale boys from the covey lunge forward and grab Jowyn, pinning his arms behind him.

"Let him go!" Brysen yelled.

"Or what?" a cruel voice snarled. Plowing through the dozens of thin, pale boys and fearsome Owl Mothers came a face more familiar than the rest: Goryn Tamir. The eldest

Tamir son stepped up behind Jowyn, his long-estranged little brother. The blood birch sap had changed Jowyn's complexion, but he still looked a little like Goryn, and seeing them together startled Brysen. He'd nearly forgotten that Jowyn had fled to the Owl Mothers as a child because of the cruelty of his siblings. "I've waited quite awhile to see you again, little magpie." Goryn tapped a finger on Jowyn's neck but kept his eyes on Brysen. "I'd like to see you beg for his life, I think."

"Not yet," Üku snapped at Goryn, and much to Brysen's surprise, Goryn lost his sneer and lowered his head. The gangster heeded the Owl Mother. It appeared he was even afraid of her. Brysen would've liked to make him choke on that fear.

Then he saw that Üku held the ghost eagle egg.

"I promised Goryn that when the killing blade slides across your throat, he will be the one to drag it," Üku told Brysen. "But we have things to do first. And our *sisters*"—she cast a hard glare at Clava and Siwoo—"will face consequences for allowing you to read what you have read."

"We had no choice," Clava said.

"You always have a choice," Üku replied. "You could have fought."

"We would have died," Clava answered.

"Some battles are worth fighting, even if you lose," Üku

said, and Brysen wondered how keeping him and his sister from knowing the truth about the ghost eagles could be worth death.

Outside the cave, the ghost eagles were shrieking. The egg in Üku's palm was deep black.

Brysen tried to ignore the new flashes he saw in his mind. Blood splattered across stone, fires burning in the Six Villages, his father hoisted into the mountains by great black talons, Nyall surrounded. He felt all of it just the same.

The ghost eagles were angry. Or maybe the anger was his. Either way, he liked it.

"Let Jowyn go," he snarled.

"Boy," Üku snapped in a tone that made him feel like a half-eaten grouse. "Do you think we've lasted as long as we have in these mountains by fearing children like you? Do you think we fear the ghost eagles?" She shook her head. "You think you have some great destiny because these birds are bound to you. You know so little."

"So tell us," Kylee said. "We only know so little because you're keeping knowledge from us."

"This isn't the first *talorum* egg I've held," Üku said, looking at the egg. "And you aren't the first young people to have been bound to one."

Brysen waited for her to go on, to explain. For a moment

he was afraid Üku would leave it at that, that she'd simply call her owls to strike and he'd die not knowing the rest of the story, but she finally spoke.

"Do you know how the blood birches grow?" she said.

"They grow from the blood where a murder victim falls," Grazim said.

"That's the myth," Üku said. "The truth is that *we* are how they grow. Each tree hatches from an egg—an egg that's been buried in ground that we fertilize in blood. Can you guess whose blood?" She looked at Grazim, but the girl didn't have the answer this time. Üku provided it. "Whoever called forth the egg. Whoever is bound to it, as you two are bound to this one, must bleed out their life in the dirt above it. And from that come the life-giving blood birch trees."

"But . . ." Brysen was confused. Even Jowyn and the pale boys in the covey looked confused. "There are hundreds of blood birches."

"Thousands," Üku said. "And we"—she gestured at the Owl Mothers around her—"have been burying them for tens of thousands of years. Every generation or so, we bury another. No matter how many eggs our unique human capacity for pain calls forth into the world, we find a way to bury each before it hatches. The ghost eagles always try to stop us, and they *always* fail."

Jowyn looked at Clava and Siwoo. His pale skin had taken

on a greenish hue. "Did you know? You were leading Brysen and Kylee to die?"

The Owl Mothers looked at their feet. They knew.

Jowyn suddenly doubled over and threw up on the dirt. The other pale boys still held him, but they were gentle. They let him heave himself empty, and Brysen so badly wanted to rush to his side, to rub his back, to comfort him, but any sudden movement would be dangerous. Besides, he wasn't personally all that surprised. The Owl Mothers had never held his life in much regard. Still, he'd have liked to understand why burying the egg and killing him and Kylee was necessary. He also wanted to keep them talking. As long as they were talking, everyone would remain alive. When the talking stopped was when things would get ugly.

"Why do this?" he asked Üku. "What's one more ghost eagle hatching when there are hundreds already?"

"Because the ghost eagles are not born from eggs," she told him. "Their convocation exists as it was first created. Their eggs are different. They are a union of humanity and its monsters. Only once before has an egg been allowed to hatch, and it nearly destroyed everything. Us and them."

Brysen looked at the egg Üku held, seeing the black swirls on its surface in a new way. He and his sister were bound to this thing, as the ghost eagles were, but it didn't belong to either of them. It was something different. *That* was why the ghost eagles wanted it to hatch at the same time they were afraid of it. The egg was . . . *change.*

"Why would they want the egg to hatch?" Grazim asked. "If it's dangerous to them, too, why are they trying to make us bring it to their nest?"

"People destroy themselves for all sorts of reasons," Üku said. "Why should ghost eagles be different?"

Brysen tried to catch Kylee's eye. They'd been right. The ghost eagles were in pain; they were both scared of the egg and drawn to it. They wanted the end of the world because it would be the end of their hurt.

And Brysen had nearly given it to them.

"What happened the first time an egg hatched?" he asked.

"REEEEEEE!" the ghost eagles shrieked outside the cave, and Brysen saw Nyall again, surrounded, in danger, looking up in desperation at the starry dark. They were growing impatient.

"*Shessele!*" Üku yelled so loud her voice echoed through the cave, and the screeching fell silent, though the silence made Brysen shudder. The ghost eagles knew that Üku had their egg, and they were afraid of what she would do with it, like they'd been afraid of what Brysen might do with it. There was no gold visible on the shell's surface this time.

Their silence was like a rock python coiled, poised before a boot comes down either to flee or to strike.

"It doesn't matter what happened before," Üku said. "You'll come with us, we'll bury this, Goryn will get his earned revenge, and history will move on, as it always has and as it will again."

"No," Jowyn squeaked out, looking around at the other Owl Mothers, desperation and disappointment dancing across his face.

Goryn laughed, but Üku shushed him.

"If you truly love this boy, Brysen, then you can protect him with your death." Üku nodded at Jowyn, and the boys of the covey held him tighter. "It would pain all of us to do Jowyn harm, but it would pain the whole world to let this egg hatch. So the real question is: How selfish are you?"

"I . . ." He didn't have an answer, and he couldn't see a way out of this. He'd been selfish all his life. Maybe the Owl Mother was right. Maybe he had to do something to serve humanity, instead of just himself and his feelings. Maybe what he wanted wasn't most important after all. He wondered if his blood would be enough, if he could sacrifice himself to save both Jowyn and his sister, and—he felt a swell of pride as he thought it—*the world.*

Of course, his sister wasn't about to let him make that choice.

"Enough of this," Kylee snapped, and Brysen didn't need a soothsayer to know what would happen next.

His sister swung her arm to the side and released a knotted rope that held the mechanism to the cave entrance. The boulder rolled aside. Moonlight flooded the cave just before a fury of black feathers burst in.

Kylee didn't need to command the ghost eagles; the killing fury they unleashed belonged purely to them. All Brysen and his sister had to do was stay out of the way.

As six eagles filled the cave, their talons aimed for the flesh of Owl Mothers, Brysen felt emotion swell from their screeching cries. It felt like a pit fighter's battle roar, like a kiss on the wrong person's lips, like a leap from too high a ledge into too cold a lake, a joy that wounded. When the first ghost eagle tore off Goryn Tamir's head, Brysen wasn't sure if he'd commanded it or not.

"REEEEE," they cried. Brysen thought both *you're welcome* and *thank you* at the same moment, and he didn't know which thought was his.

26

THOUGH ÜKU SHOUTED HER OWN COMMANDS, THE GHOST EAGLES didn't heed her. The ghost eagles flapped through the cave, their wings so wide they brushed the walls on either side, but they were dextrous, moving as skillfully as a goshawk through scrub brush. They aimed directly for the Owl Mothers, knocking everyone else from their path. The owls fluttered and tried to escape but had nowhere to go. Grazim curled her entire body around her tailor's hawk to protect it.

As Brysen dove to the floor, he saw his sister still standing, her back pressed to the wall just beside the door, her face bent into a grimace, like she was hauling herself up a boulder with the last strength she had. She was fighting the rage the ghost eagles were flooding into her. Brysen knew he couldn't fight it; he simply let it wash over him like a wave. The Owl Mothers had threatened his life. They'd threatened Jowyn's life and the innocent egg's, and still they refused to tell him the whole truth of why. Whatever wrath the eagles felt toward them, they were right to feel. Brysen found the emotion bearable if he simply let it blow through him, like wind through a whistle.

"REEEEEE!" the eagles screamed again. His fists balled. It was hard not to grab on to their anger and hold it, but he didn't dare.

He saw one of the pale boys holding Jowyn throw him down and dive on top of him just as the first black eagle reached them. Üku vanished behind a veil of black feathers. The owls still hooted and cried and tried to hide themselves in every corner of the cave. Their wings fluttered as they were yanked down, one by one. The Owl Mothers tried to shout commands in the Hollow Tongue, but that language belonged to the ghost eagles.

Brysen didn't know where to look. He saw flashes of pale white flesh and black feathers, splashes of red. He heard cries and screams, but the voices were indistinguishable, and the boys of the covey all blurred together in the general panic. He couldn't lift his head too high off the cave floor to get a clear look. The air above him was nothing but talon and claw.

Then, like a murder of crows leaving a tree in one sudden burst, the eagles rose. Brysen saw a huge black foot wrap around the egg in Üku's hands, and just as quickly, he saw a pile of three owl boys where Jowyn had fallen, backs bloodied, unmoving. His eye darted between Üku, who was trying to tug the egg from the ghost eagle, and the pile of boys, where Jowyn lay. The eagle yanked the egg away and knocked over Üku.

Everyone else lay flat on the floor, covering their heads with their hands. Even Kylee had finally taken cover. The birds screeched and screamed, heading for the entrance with their prize, and Brysen knew that if they took their egg, he would lose any influence he had over them. Nyall would be doomed. If Üku was telling the truth, then humanity would all be doomed, along with the ghost eagles. He saw it all: a world strewn with bones, an empty desert, and lifeless frozen steppes. He *felt* it all, because that was what the ghost eagles felt. Emptiness.

In the vision, there were no wings overhead. There was nothing. By destroying humanity, the ghost eagles would destroy themselves. And that's what they wanted most of all.

As long as humanity endured, so would they. As long as they endured, so would humanity. Their goal was oblivion.

Brysen looked again at the pile of bodies where he thought Jowyn lay. He didn't know if the boy he loved was still alive.

He could crawl to him and find out, but then what? If Jowyn was gone, would he welcome the ghost eagles' oblivion? Would he let the world end because his had?

No.

He wasn't ready for oblivion. One thing he had learned from Jowyn was that even the deepest wounds can heal. A broken beating heart was better than no heart at all. He had to stop the ghost eagles. He had to stop them from killing him, from killing the world, from killing themselves.

He didn't know how, but he knew that Üku's way couldn't work. Burying the egg only to have it return, generation after generation, solved nothing. The ghost eagles would never stop tormenting humanity, and humanity would never stop tearing itself apart over them. It was the same cycle over and over, and it had to be broken.

He and his sister had lived like that. They fell into patterns, hurt each other and themselves in the same exact ways, time and time again. They were learning how to do something different now. They were learning to change, and if they could learn, so could the ghost eagles.

Üku had said that the egg's hatching once before had nearly destroyed everything, but those with power easily confused change with destruction. He didn't know what would happen if this egg hatched gold, and he figured no one else did either. He knew he'd like to find out.

"I love you," he whispered toward the heap of bodies where Jowyn lay, and then he shot to his feet and jumped for the egg as it passed over him. Talons scraped his flesh. He felt a sharp pain in his shoulder as the great eagles sliced past, and they screamed. He saw the whip crack against his back, he saw everyone he'd ever loved die or turn from him, or both, leaving him alone. He felt every selfish thing he'd ever done to deserve his loneliness roll over him like an avalanche. He let it roll. He felt all of it, and he kept after the egg anyway, hands up, grasping the foot that held the egg, and it pulled him off the ground.

He rose from the cave floor, holding on as tightly as he could. He'd never get the egg loose from the eagle's taloned grasp, but wherever it went, he would go, too. As he clung to the huge eagle's ankle, he looked back. The boy lying on top of Jowyn was still. But, in just a fleeting glimpse, Brysen thought he saw Jowyn. His scalp was cut, bright blood against white-blond hair, and his eyes were closed.

If they killed him . . . , he thought, squeezing the ghost eagle's ankle tighter. They flew from the cave's entrance into the dim dark of dawn over the sloping mountain range. The eagle flapped, rising with the convocation just over a ridge. Brysen's toes brushed stone. They were flying straight for a large boulder. The eagle was going to break him on the rocks. Close to him, the black egg nearly hummed with darkness.

"Brysen!" Jowyn's voice called after him. Brysen looked back to see him, a tiny pinprick standing in the cave entrance. "Brysen!"

His body flooded with warmth. Jowyn lived! Jowyn lived and was about to watch Brysen's body be slammed into the rocks and turned to paste. The boulder loomed toward him, filling his horizon. His pulsed thrummed so loud in his ears that he couldn't even hear the wind or the shrieking birds or his friends calling him from far off.

"*Tuslaash*," he said to the ghost eagle above him, the Hollow Tongue word for *help*, but he wasn't asking—he was *offering*. To them. To the egg. To the entire wind-blasted world. "*Tuslaash*," he said again, and he meant, *If I can heal, then so can you.*

And the ghost eagle screamed, and the egg gleamed gold as the talons opened. The egg fell, and Brysen fell with it, hurtling toward a snowbank on the slope. He hoped the powder was deep enough to break his fall.

SURVIVORS

ÜKU, MUCH TO HER SURPRISE, TOOK A BREATH.

She lay against a wall. Every part of her hurt—or, rather, she hurt in her entirety, and every part of her told her so. Her lungs rasped with inhalations and wheezed with exhalations, but the painful movement of air meant she was still alive.

Morning light drew a sharp line on the ground ahead of her, where the door to the cave cut the sun's angle. Nature's geometry always awed her, the lines that shadows could slice so sharply, the way a jagged peak could stand against an icy sky, even when both were clothed in the same cold snow. She kept her eyes on that line of light on the cave floor. She didn't want to turn her head to one side or the other, knowing what she would find there.

Her sisters. Her owls. Her boys. Her entire community, or nearly all of it, wounded, dead, or dying.

She took in a deep breath and felt like her ribs were snapping through her skin, and she used that physical pain to harden herself against the grief that pressed down on her. She was known for being callous and unsentimental, because she had killed and she had watched others kill, and not all the victims were guilty of anything more than bad luck or bad timing. But she was not callous; she simply knew that no single bird matters more than the flock. She knew her history; she carried it in her bones and in her blood. She knew that no one's life mattered all that much in the ever-turning gyre of time. People lived and they died, but history flew on. Like a single mind stretched over countless bodies and across endless seasons, each life was just a small tale in the larger story that made the world.

In spite of that, individuals were the ones who grieved. History doesn't grieve. It simply turns and turns and turns without mercy.

Üku grieved. She grieved for her friends, and she even grieved for her enemies. She even grieved for that stupid boy, Jowyn, whom she had exiled, and for the boy with whom he'd fallen in love. She didn't *want* anyone to suffer, but the only way to keep Uztar going was through this suffering. When she was a little girl, she'd been taught that it was necessary. She was initiated into the Owl Mothers before getting all her adult teeth, and she learned the truth of their place in the world then, along with her role in guarding it. It was up to her, and to all Owl Mothers, to maintain balance. Watch the world for those who had commerce with the ghost eagles, and if an egg was found, bury it. The flock would retreat. It was simple, if not easy.

She'd always done her best to honor her role, but it was hard to serve both her community and the demands of history. It took tremendous effort to keep the world from tilting out of balance, like a boulder set on a ridge that is battered by ever-shifting winds, longing only to roll. She'd always been up to keeping that boulder in place, unmoving . . . until now.

To her side she heard a soft fluttering of wings, and she turned her head enough to see the bright yellow eyes of her snow owl. The creature was standing in shadow, watching her. It hopped forward a step, then back, dipping its head and bobbing from side to side, curious but wary. It was the last survivor.

"*Shessele*," she told it. *Be calm.* The bird relaxed. She wondered what she should tell it now. Fly free, or stay with her? If it left, it might immediately fall victim to the ghost eagles. If it stayed, it might fall victim when they returned.

Would they return? Where had they gone? She was alone, so they must have all left in a hurry, chasing that wretched egg.

She sighed. She'd surprised herself, allowing them to escape with it. Maybe, in her advanced seasons, she had grown too sentimental. She hadn't moved quickly enough to kill those twins. She'd tried to spare at least one of them, tried to bring them around, to make use of them. That was foolish.

She'd expected them, of course, and so she'd prepared. She'd trained Kylee and baited her and let her drag her magpie-minded brother along. She'd done her best to keep the wars going at a steady pace, to keep everyone focused on their old enmities and never questioning the history they knew . . . but she hadn't expected Kylee to become so strong, nor her brother to try his hand at healer. They'd surprised her, and she'd done her best to adapt, but now the flock had returned in its hundreds, and if she didn't find a way to bury that egg . . . if it hatched and sang its song . . .

No Owl Mother before her had failed, and she feared to be the first. *If only I could move my legs!* Maybe she should call the owl against herself, end this misery. Let the world's turning troubles become someone else's problem.

"Üku," a feminine voice whispered. She turned her head away from the owl to see young Clava crawling toward her in the dark. "They left, went after the boy, Brysen," she explained. "He fell from the eagle's talons. He has the egg. It was gleaming gold when it fell."

Üku smiled. Moving her lips made her aware that she'd broken several teeth. "So all is not yet lost," she said.

"If it hatches—"

"We are doomed," Üku finished the thought for Clava. "But you can move. You can stop it."

"I don't think so," Clava said sadly.

"I believe in you, Clava," Üku reassured the young Owl Mother. "You might be the last of us to live. You must carry on."

"I'm sorry, Mem Üku," Clava said. "I don't think I want to is what I meant to say. I think I might *want* the egg to hatch."

"No," Üku groaned. "You can't. The last time it hatched, it was—"

"I know the stories," Clava said. "But perhaps something different will happen this time. We only know the story that came before. We don't know that the future will look the same. A history that circles and circles like a hungry hawk is hardly one worth repeating. I want to see what might happen if the circle breaks."

Üku grunted. "So you'll defy the community that raised you. Defy our entire purpose, because you know better than history?"

"I want to see a future that doesn't look like the past,"

Clava replied. "The twins might be that chance. We've never seen the egg gleaming gold before."

"You're young," Üku told her, patting the girl on the hand. As she did so, she slid her other hand underneath her own body, finding the small knife she kept on her belt. She was capable of grief but also of justice. She wrapped her fingers around the handle. "You can be forgiven for daydreams. I only wish Siwoo had taught you better."

Clava shook her head and rested her other hand on top of Üku's, holding it gentle as she might an injured sparrow. "No, you've got it backward. *I* taught *her*," Clava said. "Breaking history's circle will require the young to lead the old. She is wise enough to see that. I wish you were as well, Mem Üku."

"The arrogance." Üku sighed. She pulled the knife from beneath her and swung it for Clava's neck but found her wrist stopped short before the killing blow could be dealt. A dark hand squeezed the pressure point so hard, the knife fell from Üku's grip. She looked up to see Siwoo standing over her, holding back her hand.

"Apologies, Mem Üku," Siwoo said. "But history is not a fistbound hawk. It can't be kept tethered forever. It must fly. We think it's time."

"You can't," Üku said, and felt—for the first time she could truly remember—fear. "If that egg hatches . . . if the eaglet sings . . . there is no telling where it will lead."

"What frightens you thrills me," Siwoo said. "I want to hear a new song in this world. I'm not so old as you."

Üku closed her eyes, prepared herself to grieve again. "And you never will be," she said, then she called the last surviving owl. "*Avakhoo mejeej*," she said, and kept her eyes closed as she listened to the sudden fury of shrieks and screams and then the silence that followed.

When she opened her eyes, Clava and Siwoo were dead, the owl's white feathers splattered with blood. Her owl had cleansed the community, as she'd commanded. Now, if she could just find a way to stay alive a little longer. She might yet stop those two nestling twins from cracking history's shell wide open.

KYLEE

THE BIRTH OF THE DARK

27

KYLEE NEARLY TACKLED HER BROTHER IN A HUG WHEN SHE FINALLY reached him. She'd thought for certain he'd be dead. She was so relieved he *wasn't* dead that she forgot for a moment how exposed they all were under the open sky.

"We need to take cover," she warned, but Brysen just shook his head and held the egg to his chest. It was gleaming gold in the morning light. He started laughing.

"Did you crack your head?" Grazim wondered.

Brysen looked at her, then back at his sister, then up at the empty sky. "They're terrified," he said. "They're terrified for the same reason the Owl Mothers are."

"*Were*," Kylee said grimly. "I don't think . . ." She lowered her voice; Jowyn had finally joined them from the cave, and she didn't know how upset he'd be. "I don't think any of them survived."

She could still feel an echo of the rage the eagles flooded her with when she opened the door. It was a thrilling kind of numbness, a rush she imagined a battle pit fighter might feel, a cold pain that masked a hotter one. Even remembering the feeling gave her chills.

"Were." Brysen nodded quickly, then fixed his face and embraced Jowyn in a deep hug. The pale boy buried his head in Brysen's shoulder, which was awkward because Brysen was much shorter.

Grazim interrupted their tender moment. "So what do you think they're terrified of?"

"The truth," Brysen said. "They got really upset when we were learning pieces of their story. Think about it. The Hollow Tongue only works with the truth, right? Like, you can only speak it if you mean what you say and believe it and if it's your truth, right?"

"Yeah," said Kylee, unsure where he was going with this.

"And the Hollow Tongue comes from the ghost eagles, right? Like, it's their language."

She nodded again.

"Why do they obey commands in it, though?" he asked. "Think about what we just saw. No one commanded them to attack, and they're powerful enough to do whatever they want, whenever they want. But when they're commanded in the right way, they obey us. They can't help it. The truth has a hold on them, a hold not even they understand."

"There is some truth they fear," said Kylee. "Something they're trying to tell us and trying *not* to tell us at the same time."

"Like when I used to get angry at you for trying to help me," Brysen said.

"*Used to?*" Kylee raised an eyebrow. Her brother clearly thought he'd matured so much more than he actually had.

He let her comment go with a quick frown. "So they're burying some pain of theirs that's coming out as our nightmares and as violence against anyone around them, and even when they hurt themselves, they can't stop. Just like me. Just like Da."

"And Ma," Kylee added. "And me."

Some people, when they hurt, turned inward, like her mother did, while others lashed out, wreaked havoc, hurt anyone they could just to push their own hurt away. The ghost eagles weren't so different from people in that way. They craved destruction because they didn't know what to do with their pain. They were drawn to Kylee because she fed that destruction. Her anger was easier to obey than whatever hurt they were hiding.

"What if we can find out what's hurting them," Brysen suggested, "and, like . . . help?"

"You want to help the ghost eagles?" Grazim threw up her arms. "The ghost eagles who've killed thousands, who abducted your friend Nyall, and who nearly just dropped you off a mountain?"

"Yes," Brysen said flatly.

"How?" Grazim asked.

He looked at Kylee as if she'd asked the question. "I have no idea," he said.

"We can ask an Owl Mother," Jowyn said, his voice rising a little.

Brysen rested a hand on Jowyn's neck. "I don't think the ghost eagles spared anyone, Jo," he said, pulling the boy close in anticipation of his grief.

"No," Jowyn told them. "Look."

He pointed to a rocky outcropping above them, and Kylee saw what at first just looked like a lump of snow, until it turned its head to show bright yellow eyes. Üku's snow owl was watching them. The sun was up, and a snow owl would not sit out in the open like this unless it had been commanded.

"*Cawfa*," Grazim called at it, before Kylee could think of a word that might be useful here. The bird took off and flapped back toward the cave, and they all followed it.

"Nicely done," she told Grazim as they climbed back up the hill. "What'd you say?"

"You really should spend more time studying vocabulary," Grazim chided her. "It means *reveal*."

"I learn better in context," Kylee said. "Anyway, if I studied more, then what would you have to do? Isn't it nice to be needed?"

Grazim let out a rare and genuine laugh, which chased the last remnants of the ghost eagles' rage from Kylee's mind. Rage, like pain, was felt alone, but laughter thrived in flocks.

When they followed the owl back into the cave, it landed silently along a slash of light on the floor, where the angle of the sun was cut by the mouth of the cave. The white bird was half in light and half in darkness, and it stood, surrounded by bodies and limbs, waiting.

"Symin!" Jowyn rushed to one of the pale boys on the floor, a member of the covey who was lying faceup with both his pale hands clutching his stomach. The red was bright against his bone-white skin. The boy had been torn open by a talon and by all rights should've been dead already, but the sap of the blood birches gave him a fragile perch on life.

"I'm sorry," he said.

Jowyn bent over the boy, weeping, and Kylee wondered at that sort of affection. What history allowed Jowyn to cry for someone who, moments before, was willing to kill him at Üku's command? Interestingly, she noticed that he ignored his own brother's headless corpse. People thought the minds and feelings of birds of prey were inscrutable, but any human heart was just as much a mystery.

Jowyn held Symin's head in his hands until the boy's last breath rattled the air between them.

Brysen had the good sense to stay back and let the two of them have their moment together. Watching Jowyn weep for a stranger reminded Kylee that whatever story they were living out right now, there were countless others being lived alongside them, some cut short because of her and Brysen's actions, some indifferent to their existence altogether. No one was a minor character in their own lives, and every death that Kylee's and Brysen's decisions unleashed altered the lives of others immeasurably.

"Kylee and Grazim, my wayward students," Üku called to them from the shadows at the back of the cave, near whatever hidden passage had led her in. She was alive, but she hadn't fled or chased them. She'd sent her owl to bring them to her. Kylee reached for the knife on her belt, then stopped herself. The day was new and had seen enough blood already.

"Why can't the egg hatch?" she demanded. "What happens?"

The white-haired woman leaned forward but didn't stand. Kylee suspected she couldn't.

"History unravels," she groaned. "We've made sacrifices along the way, taken risks, played politics and stirred wars, but we've always done so with one goal: to keep worse horrors than these from being born. To protect our civilization from itself. All Uztari history exists because of our efforts. If that egg hatches, it will sing a song no one can bear to hear."

"Maybe it's time," Brysen said. "Maybe it's a song we need to hear."

Üku shook her head, grimaced. She was in a lot of pain. "You cannot let it hatch. Bury it," she said. "And do as I say. Shed your last blood on the soil above. You'll be a hero, boy." She met Brysen's eye. "Isn't that what you always wanted?"

Brysen took a sharp breath, and Kylee was surprised how well this woman understood her brother, but she didn't think he'd be persuaded. Maybe the old Brysen would, but this Brysen wasn't on a quest for glory anymore.

The woman looked at the golden egg he held, and her dry lips cracked into a smile. "Don't let its beauty fool you," she said. "You cannot bear what it will do when it erupts from this shell."

"We deserve the chance to find out," Kylee said. "We are not going to let you, or *them*, decide for us."

"Oh, Kylee." The Owl Mother sighed. "I admire your strength; I thought I could harness it. It turns out that's not going to work, is it? Maybe without you, your brother will make the right choice."

"I'm not going anywhere," Kylee said.

"No," Üku agreed. "You are going to die right here." She looked to the tailor's hawk on Grazim's fist and to her own white owl, still perched near the entrance, and she shouted, "*Kra—*" but her command was cut short. Jowyn leapt from the body of the boy he'd been weeping over and grabbed Üku by the throat, squeezing. His arms strained as her eyes widened. She flailed and clutched at him, scratching the pale skin of his taut forearms, pulling and slapping.

"Jowyn!" Brysen cried out, trying to pull him off with one arm, the egg cradled under the other.

"I loved you," Jowyn cried at Üku as he squeezed the life out of her. "You were family to me. All of you were family to me, and I left you because that's what was best for all of us . . . and you still wouldn't leave us alone. Why wouldn't you let us be?"

His voice cracked through the cave. The egg was turning black again as life left the last living Owl Mother. Jowyn, the gentlest boy Kylee had known, killed Üku in front of them all, then collapsed on top of her body, screaming. Her owl screeched once and flew from the cave, flapping madly for the horizon, unthethered from all it had ever known. Gone.

"Why, why, why . . ." Jowyn pounded Üku's lifeless chest, then dropped onto her and held her tightly, like he was hugging her.

Brysen tried to comfort the boy as Kylee stood, mouth agape, wondering what they were supposed to do now. She felt nothing for the dead Owl Mother, who would've killed them all, but she did feel a deep sadness at the uncertainty of their position.

They had no answers. They had no plan.

All they had were cryptic comments from a dead mountain mystic and an unhatched egg still finding ways to push them toward death and destruction. Maybe Üku was right— maybe burying it deep was the only thing to do. Though that would leave Nyall hostage with nothing to offer the ghost eagles in exchange for his return.

"Well, that was no help at all," Nyck grunted, looking at the body. "We go back toward the Talon Fortress, then?" He was already headed for the cave opening.

Kylee waved her brother over where she stood and lowered her voice. "We need to know the rest of the story," she said.

"I told you," Brysen whispered back. "It's fragmented on Jowyn's skin. It's not the whole record. Besides, I don't think I should ask him to let me finish looking at his naked body right now, you know? Not a great time."

Jowyn moved to kneel over Üku's corpse, crying quietly.

Kylee shook her head. "Not his," she said, and Brysen frowned, puzzled. His eye widened, horrified, when he realized what she was asking of him.

There were dozens of dead, tattooed boys around them, each one's skin telling a different piece of the story Üku had refused to share.

"You want me to . . . *read* the dead?" he said.

"We'll do it together," she said. "It'll go faster that way."

Her own voice was hoarse, as though she was afraid to be heard asking what she was now asking. It was one thing to see death; it was another to run one's fingers over corpses, trying to steal the last bit of knowledge that they would ever hold.

Brysen leaned over to whisper so only Kylee could hear. "I don't know if Jowyn can bear to see us do that," he told her.

"He'll have to." She felt like a monster, but what other choice did they have?

"I vowed . . . ," Jowyn said, and everyone looked to him. Nyck and Lyra and Grazim had kept their distance but now moved closer to hear. Jowyn's eyes were locked on the lifeless body of the Owl Mother. "I vowed never to kill anyone ever again, but I did it. I was so angry about Symin dying that . . . my vows meant nothing."

"It's okay," Brysen said. "You were defending all of us. She was about to kill us. She would've killed you, too."

Jowyn shook his head. "I didn't *have* to kill her. I could've just covered her mouth, restrained her," he said. "But when I was choking her, I didn't just want to stop her speaking. I didn't even just want her to die. *I* wanted to kill her."

"That was the thing in the egg," Brysen said. "It was goading you. That wasn't you."

"It *was* me, though," he said back. "I didn't hear voices or see things that weren't there. I was there. I was choking her, and I liked it. She put this story on my skin, lied to me about what it meant, and I . . . I hate her for it. I'm a monster, just like Goryn and the rest of my family."

"No!" Brysen said, grabbing Jowyn by the chin and tilting up his face. "You are nothing like your family. You are kind and gentle and loving. You saved me. You keep saving me."

"I didn't save *her*," he said, trying to looking back down at Üku.

"No," Kylee interrupted. "You didn't save her. But you can still save us." He looked up at her, his eyes wet. "We'll lay the bodies outside for the sky burial. You can say whatever rights you like, but Brysen and I need to look at them. We have to face the truth of whatever it is the Owl Mothers have been hiding. It's the only way to know what the ghost eagles are afraid of. It's the only way any of us will survive them."

Jowyn looked at Brysen, then back to Kylee. He nodded, and together, all of them began carrying the bodies outside, one at a time, the pale boys and the Owl Mothers, and they laid them on rocks in a row, side by side, arms intertwined, eyes open and staring at the day's rising sun.

Jowyn prayed over them with words he found comforting.

> *"We fly and fly the same round range,*
> *And turning, and turning, change and change.*
> *Bodies fall and bodies rise,*
> *From mud to air to feed the skies . . ."*

While Jowyn prayed, Brysen and Kylee moved from body to body and began reading as quickly as they could. Any vultures left in the sky would be circling soon.

28

IT WAS GRIM WORK, BUT BEFORE LONG, KYLEE DIDN'T REALLY SEE THE corpses as she moved along them, nor did she hear Jowyn's chanting or Nyck's warnings to hurry so they could leave this "creepy place." She didn't even hear her brother, though he was speaking to her, filling in the gaps of the story as she read her part.

They told the story together, to each other, though most of what they told was unsaid, carried in the unspoken language that stretched between them like a falconer's call to a hawk in the distant air. The story bound them and erased any distinction between them. At times Kylee wasn't even sure which of them was speaking; it was as if they were one voice in two bodies. They were as close as they had been since childhood, closer even, though the story they shared now was far from a child's fantasy.

Kylee saw it all and felt it all and knew every piece of it was true.

"The scouts who had followed the flock of Forty Birds on the plateau gladly took help from the people who were there before, these First Falconers. Over time, these newcomers learned techniques from the First Falconers to fly birds of prey after the food they wanted to catch. And in gratitude for the meat they ate, they sang odes to the birds, built shrines, told stories and jokes. Words entered their language that paid homage to the sky and to the creatures who ruled it. A few even learned some words of the First Falconers' language, formed bonds with them, made friends, fell in love. The newcomers and the First Falconers formed families, built partnerships, braided their futures together. The newcomers learned words and sayings in the First Falconers' language, learned how some birds mated for life and these pairs were called *vaas*—meaning, simply, *us*. Suddenly that *us* meant more than ever before, as the community grew. *They* became *we*, *we* became *us*, and children were born, and these new children were part newcomer and part First Falconer. They were something new.

"*Eeefa kai'ee*, the people called them. Gifts of the New.

"Some newcomers and some First Falconers were wary of

these mixed pairs and warier still of their children, who were something the sky had never before seen. The older generation did their best to understand the younger one, as all parents do, as all parents must. They did not always succeed."

Kylee paused, looked up, and found her brother looking at her. They thought of their ma, hiding back in the Six. The mother who failed to understand them and whom they failed to understand. It was a kind of comfort to know this struggle was as ancient as it was common.

Brysen returned to reading the bodies. "Of course, feelings were wounded and rules were broken."

"Fights erupted and were left half settled, grudges nursed and gossip spread. They were a community now, and such things happened in communities," Kylee continued.

"But the newcomers had the memory of hunger in their blood," Brysen said. "They carried their people's hunger from the Frozen Lands and they carried their parents' hunger and their parents' parents hunger, and that kind of hunger is not so easily sated in a season or two. They wanted more and feared losing what they had so recently gained."

"The First Falconers grew nervous about the newcomers," Kylee said. "The more the two peoples coupled with each other and learned from each other, the more they feared their cultural traditions were being lost."

She saw meetings in round stone homes on the mountain

slopes, arguments between parents and children. Some asked why they should fear a ragged flock of wandering souls who couldn't tell hunter's leaf from itching vine. Others wondered why they should fear change. Were they not learning new things, too? Some thought they gave too much, shared too freely.

"But the newcomers were also afraid," Brysen said. "These falconers were more powerful than they. What if the falconers changed their minds? What if their welcome wore out? *We live at their mercy,* they said. *It's fine now, but what if we anger them? They could turn their birds against us. They could turn our birds against us.* They feared being overpowered. When the rest of their people arrived over the mountains a few generations from now, they'd be at the mercy of these First Falconers. The only way to be safe was to strike first, to overpower them by surprise, lest the newcomers lose everything."

It was true that birds who let themselves be tamed could turn at any time. It was true the First Falconers had more power, living as they did in shared communion with the raptors. It was true that all their children were changing—giving up old traditions, creating new ones. The newcomers were not wrong to fear. They were wrong in what their fear made them do.

Kylee's fingers traced a horrible series of jagged lines on the cold body of a boy not much older than her. His brown, lifeless eyes looked up at the sky, and his expression still looked surprised. Somehow that was the face she saw first in her mind as the newcomers sprang an attack on the First Falconers.

After the sun set one night, under cover of dark, when the sixth star appeared in the sky and as the First Falconers slept near the branches where their birds were perched, the newcomers ambushed. They came with knives, and rocks for bludgeoning, and fresh-forged swords from the new metals the mountains gave them.

But before they struck, they took chunks of meat and used their training to quietly call the birds away, to cage them. Their most powerful allies subdued, the First Falconers woke to murder. None were spared, and their blood soaked the hard dirt and turned it to mud.

Kylee felt like her hands were wet with blood. She pulled away from the grim text and looked at her fingers, dirty from climbing but dry. And yet she could smell blood on them.

She heard Jowyn still reciting, "*Turning, and turning, change and change,*" moving along the bodies after her, grieving for each and every one of them. There were too many. How much grief could one person hold? How could she be expected to hold all of history's grief?

"Kylee?" Brysen asked, looking across the row of corpses at her.

"I don't want to read any more," she said. She pressed her palms into her eyes, as if she could shove the suffering she'd seen back inside. She had seen enough death. She'd *caused* enough death. Why did she have to see this story? What good could knowing it do? It was too brutal, too real, and it was too old. If Kylee couldn't change the past, why should she have to relive it?

But she remembered her dream from the night before. Streaking down from the sky, watching her brother's torture. Watching herself watch it. The ghost eagles made her relive the hardest parts of her own life, and she understood that what she was reading now, from corpse to corpse, was their life story, the story they feared most, the worst day of their lives, the moment they were created.

The story was power, and without it, she'd be at their mercy again and again. Maybe if she knew all of it, they would be at hers.

She placed her hands back on the cold skin in front of her and returned to the gruesome tale, trying to remember to breathe until it was over.

"Not all the lines were so clear," Brysen said.

"Not everyone died so easily," Kylee said.

Some of the First Falconers woke in time, fought back. Birds clashed above them and feathers fell. Some of the First Falconers and some of the newcomers ran together, tried to

save one another, tried to save their lovers and their children.

Most were found. Most were cut down. The extermination had been well and cruelly planned.

"Is this the memory that hurts them?" Brysen wondered.
"The death of an entire people?"

Kylee felt light-headed. Her toes and fingers were colder
than the rest of her. Her heartbeat raced like a hummingbird's
wings. "We have to keep reading," she said. "There are no
ghost eagles yet."

Brysen swallowed, nodded, and put his hands back on the
tattoos of the nearest body.

"There were two survivors of the massacre," he said.
"Twins."

She saw them. Younger than her and her brother, but with
dark hair, like them, and light eyes. They were both small.

"Siblings from a mixed family of newcomers and First Falconers," Kylee said.

"*We're* from a mixed family," Brysen pointed out, and Kylee
thought about Ma with her faltered Altari faith and Da with
his brutal Uztari devotions.

"The twins fled into the mountains," Kylee read. She didn't
need to point out the similarities. She and her brother, more
than once, had fled into the mountains to escape some horror
or another.

Kylee saw what these ancient twins had seen: their friends and families slaughtering one another.

Kylee's hands paused at an oval tattooed on one boy's wrist. It belonged to Symin, the one Jowyn had wept over. She almost thought she should let Brysen read this body, but her fingers had already begun to speak, and she looked down at the oval shape—an egg, she realized—and Brysen narrated what she saw in her own mind. The link they shared through this strange text was dizzying, but somehow it made the burden of the story easier to bear.

"They huddled together in the lonely cold of the high mountains," he said. "Freezing and frightened in the waning light, they held each other, and that is where they found an egg, knitted from the darkness where their shadows met. It terrified them. It called to them from within its shell."

"It was deep black," Kylee said. "And it began to hatch."

"One of them wanted to protect it," Brysen said.

"One of them wanted to destroy it," Kylee said.

She looked at him again. This story wasn't the same as their own, but it rhymed with theirs in the way distant lives sometimes can. She was scared to know more, and she needed to know more.

"As they argued over the egg," Kylee said, "it hatched. The creature that emerged looked at them, at their fear—"

"And it screamed," Brysen said.

"And they screamed," Kylee said.

She saw this huge bird so clearly. It was larger than a ghost eagle. Its crown of feathers grander and somehow also blacker, like it was not a color but the absence of all color. The ghost eagles were a night sky; this hatchling was oblivion.

"When it screamed," Kylee continued. "It was a kind of word. One final word in the language the birds and the First Falconers shared, part curse and part prayer and part command. It had no meaning that can be understood by living ears, but the dead heard. The bird called and called and called to them."

"The bodies of the First Falconers that were strewn across the plateau began to stir," Brysen said. "Their bones hollowed out. The blood around them pulled itself into their skin, which transformed into feathers. Their faces stretched, became beaks. Their arms turned into wings.

"The ghost eagles were born from the dead," Brysen said, his voice a whisper. "From blood." Brysen gasped, breaking the spell of the story.

"And from a word," Kylee said to him. "Blood and language and the grief of the survivors made them."

Kylee felt a hand on her shoulder, startling her. Grazim had come up behind her and gently pulled her back from the body. "Let me," she said. "Maybe I can read, too."

Grazim knew more words of the Hollow Tongue than

Kylee, so perhaps she could read it. It was a relief to rest, even though it was a burden for Grazim to see what Kylee saw, to know what she now knew.

"The ghost eagles attacked," Grazim read, and Brysen startled at the new voice. The power was in the text, though, and not in the twins, because soon the two of them fell into a rhythm while Kylee simply closed her eyes and listened. "The gleaming black bird from the egg kept calling to them, and they attacked any murderous newcomers they could catch. The terrified twins on the lonely mountain watched their own community hunted into caves and barricaded shelters. The survivors were starving, desperate . . ."

She fell silent and Kylee opened her eyes to see Grazim looking between her and her brother. "Unlucky the ones forced to repeat history," she told them both, and sounded like she was quoting something, though Kylee didn't know what.

"But a few years later, others arrived to save them," Brysen said, carrying the story forward. "A second party had set out a generation after the first."

"They'd been lost," Grazim explained. "Only the shrieks of the ghost eagles had guided them to this place."

"They'd wandered for countless seasons," Brysen said. "The children had grown and had children of their own. They were surprised to find their kin alive after so long."

"And in a moment they thought would be a triumphant reunion," Grazim said, "they instead found death and despair."

And Brysen continued: "But a warrior among them saw one eagle on the mountain that was different from the others; the larger one, the terrible new hatchling."

Kylee could see it from the ancient warrior's point of view—a huge bird the size of a house, hovering and calling the ghost eagles below to their brutal purpose. She watched, not even hearing her brother's or Grazim's voices, as the warrior notched an arrow and shot it through the giant hatchling's throat.

"The song stopped," said Grazim.

"The bird fell," said Brysen.

The ghost eagles hesitated.

"And another egg formed in the night," said Kylee. She hadn't meant to, but she'd begun reading the bodies again, her fingers drawn to images on the cold skin around her. "The same warrior who killed the bird also grieved for it, and their grief and regret at that killing, despite its necessity, created a new egg."

"The twins ran to it," Brysen said.

"One wanted it to hatch," Kylee said. "Wanted it to finish the slaughter, end the world that could be so filled with pain, finish the job of killing the people who had killed the First Falconers."

"The other wanted to stop it from hatching," Brysen said, "to save the last fragments of humanity in the hope they might heal."

"The twins fought, and the egg was buried on the spot where one twin"—Kylee's voice caught, but she forced out the words—"killed the other. The ghost eagles, having lost their song with the death of the hatchling, fled."

She shivered and found that Brysen had come to her. He took her hand. "We aren't them," he said. "We aren't them."

"I'll finish this," Grazim told them both. "You two just rest."

She read the last of the story from the bodies that surrounded them while Kylee held her brother's hand and he leaned his head on her shoulder. On the other side of the great row of bodies, Jowyn continued his ardent prayers.

"We fly and fly the same round range
And turning, and turning, change and change.
Bodies fall and bodies rise,
From mud to air to feed the skies."

His prayer, Kylee thought, *is just another way of telling this same story.*

"The second scouting party who'd just arrived were horrified at what the original newcomers had done," Grazim said.

334

"But they were glad to learn from them how to catch and train small birds of prey. They called themselves *Uztari*—those bound to the sky and its gifts. They exiled the surviving newcomers, the ones who killed the the First Falconers. They called these cousins of theirs *Altari*—'bound to the mountain.' They forbade them from touching a bird of prey again, though those Altari swore off birds of prey altogether, claiming they wanted nothing to do with them anyway, that their absolution would come through self-denial.

"So the two communities grew apart, as communities do, two branches off the same trunk, and there were fights and gossip and births and deaths and weddings and tragedies and ideas both new and old. And so it went, on and on and on. In the night, they heard the scattered, confused convocation of ghost eagles screaming from the mountains."

"What happened to the twin who survived?" Brysen asked. Though his head rested on Kylee's shoulder, he was far from relaxed.

Grazim's hands searched across the images. "She renounced both Uztari and Altari ways and stood sentry over the place where she killed her sibling. The warrior who shot the bird stayed with her, and they watched a blood birch grow."

"She became the first Owl Mother," Kylee said. She didn't need to read the tattoos to know the truth: The warrior became the first of the covey. The warrior and the twin protected the true memory of what happened, even as the civilizations growing in the valley forgot.

"Time passed," Grazim read. "And sometimes whispers came in the night or nightmares flourished among the young. It was to be expected. And if a child sometimes heeded the voices in their young blood and ran off to a wilderness in the mountains above, well, that was to be expected, too. In the Frozen Lands, leaving your group meant death, but many thought that perhaps they might stand a chance of surviving in this new land. Although those who left never did come back. They joined the Owl Mothers in the mountains, who still knew the truth and who tried to remember whatever words in the Hollow Tongue they could.

"The Uztari trained birds of prey to serve them, though the birds were wilder and less obedient; no one could quite make them do what they wanted. Leashes and gloves and hoods were developed to compensate for the loss of the language. The ghost eagles came back from time to time, to hunt and stalk and seek revenge. They tried telling their story to those who they thought might understand . . ."

People like Kylee and her brother.

And their mother before them.

People who had wounds they couldn't quite heal, people whose pain echoed their own.

"When new eggs appeared, they were always discovered by new twins who had new stories of their own. The Owl Mothers in the mountains, and the runaways who joined them, always intervened, always buried these, and the first shoots of new trees broke from the ground where they were planted. In time, they formed a forest, because life is persistent."

"But so is memory," Kylee said. "The ghost eagles carry the memory, and they will not let it be forgotten. They want this egg to hatch and destroy us all."

All Uztar was a graveyard. All Uztar was built on a lie. Its truth as the eagles understood it was an empty land and sky filled with the unforgiving dead.

"They'll do to us what we did to the First Falconers," Jowyn said, surprising Kylee. She hadn't thought he was listening. He knelt at the end of the row of corpses, beside the body of Symin. One finger lay on the cheekbone below Symin's eye. The other hand rested on the tattoo of the egg. "They want us to kill one another, as we killed the First Falconers. And then they want this hatchling to create new ghost eagles."

"They don't want to tell their story," Brysen gasped, understanding what Jowyn meant. He sat up, looking at Kylee. She understood, too.

"They want us to relive it," she said.

Nyck spoke up for the first time that morning. "So, um . . ." Kylee had actually forgotten he was there. "Can we, like, not do that?"

She couldn't argue with the battle boy's suggestion. They had to do something new. They had to change the story.

29

"I VOTE WE BURY THAT EGG," GRAZIM DECLARED, CROSSING HER ARMS and refusing to move farther along the path that would lead them to the ghost eagle's eyrie in the Talon Fortress. "Maybe it'll work and they'll go away even if one of you doesn't kill the other."

"You *vote*?" Kylee turned to her friend. "When did we start voting on things?"

"Now," Grazim said. "We're starting now." And she raised her hand into the air.

Nyck and Lyra did the same. Jowyn looked at Brysen, wiped the tears from his eyes, and raised his hand. "I'm sorry," he said. "Look at what they've done." He gestured over the row of bodies. "If burying the egg will send them away for a while, how can we not do it? It'll save lives."

Kylee stood at Brysen's side. "We don't know it will work. *And* they still have Nyall."

"I'm sad for your friend," Grazim said. "But if you take that thing to its flock, you might be dooming all of us. I do not want to be torn apart by a vengeful ghost eagle *or* turned into one by some ancient bird's song."

"I can't believe you want to bury it!" Kylee threw up her hands, angry that she had to argue about this with an Altari girl, especially after what they'd learned. "Our entire civilization is based on a lie and you want to go on hiding that history, just like the Owl Mothers did?"

"Not *hiding*," Grazim said. "But not letting that history kill us, either."

"Everything Uztari and Altari think they are and all the wars that have come from those beliefs are based on a crime," Kylee said. "Maybe this egg hatching will bring justice."

"It was a crime our ancestors committed and got away with," Grazim said, acknowledging that they did share common ancestors after all. "The victims are all dead, and so are the perpetrators. What would justice even look like?"

"I don't know," Kylee said quietly. "But there was nothing in that story about the egg gleaming gold. Maybe if we don't act just like everyone who came before us, something new will hatch. Something different."

"*We fly and fly the same round range,*" Brysen quoted Jowyn's prayer. "I think this egg is a chance to break the pattern. I'm with Kylee. We take it to them, we keep it gold, and we let it hatch."

"Even though it might end the world?" Grazim shook her head.

"The world doesn't end," Kylee said. "It just changes. That's what the Owl Mothers were afraid of: change they couldn't control."

"They weren't wrong," Grazim snapped at her.

"They were wrong to hide what they knew for thousands of seasons," Kylee said, and felt a familiar heat in her lungs, the familiar rage. "They hid the truth from all of us. Every bit of oppression your people suffered, they enabled. Every war fought over who belongs on this land, they provoked. They could've told the truth at any time, but they hid it. Letting this egg hatch will be the start of justice too long denied."

Kylee took a quick glance at the egg in Brysen's hands. She saw its surface swirling with black and gold. She wished Brysen would put it back in a bag. Her brother looked down at the egg and then at her, hesitating. If they were wrong and gave in to the rage the ghost eagles provoked, this story would go as it had the first time—they would doom everyone. If they could control their anger, manage to keep the egg gold, then . . . well, she had no idea. They were either marching toward terrifying death and desolation or toward uncertain justice and transformation. It was a hell of bargain, but it was the only one they had.

She addressed the others: "If we just bury this egg, they might leave. Or they might not. We're not going to murder each other on the spot. If we go to the Talon Fortress, I don't know what will happen—but I do know they have one of ours. Nyall is our friend, and if we leave him to them, he's dead." She looked at Nyck. "Nyall was one of the first to join your gang after Kheryn, when you were frail little urchins at the Broken Jess, wasn't he?"

Nyck nodded.

"Battle boys stick together, right? So we can make this journey and give the eagles what's theirs in order to save one of ours. Or we can sacrifice our friend and maybe pass this off to some other twins who'll be born in some other time. You heard the story. Like a hawk circling familiar hunting ground, this will happen again and again until the ghost eagles are satisfied. I'm tired of living in circles. I don't know how this will end, but . . ." She gave Brysen a small smile. "Let's do something reckless and find out."

"I've always wondered what came first," Jowyn said,

stepping to Brysen's side and taking his hand. "The bird or the egg. Guess this is one way to find out."

"Fine," said Grazim, giving in to the consenus. "We'll do this your way . . . but it looks like we won't be the only ones headed in that direction." She pointed down the slope toward the plains below, and Kylee saw a column of tiny figures marching along the river's edge, on a quick course for the Talon Fortress. They marched in formation, which made her think they weren't a gang of Redfists from the Six Villages, but Kyrg Birgund's army on the march. Why wasn't he going to the Sky Castle like he'd planned? Why was he headed the same way she was?

"Scuzz," she muttered. The ghost eagles wanted people to go to war against one another, so they *must* have pushed Birgund's army right into Kylee's path. Did they show him visions? Did they harry him back? It didn't matter. They wanted this fight. They didn't want to give her a choice in the matter. Just like always, they wanted Kylee's rage and would do whatever they could to provoke it.

When she and Brysen lived in fear of their father, Brysen longed to impress him, while Kylee wanted him dead.

The ghost eagle killed him.

When Brysen promised to capture a ghost eagle to free his scuzzard of an ex-boyfriend from the Tamir clan and Kylee wanted freedom from those who'd exploited them, what happened?

The ghost eagle bound itself to her and killed her enemies without mercy or distinction.

And when Brysen wanted to stop the war against the Kartami and Kylee wanted to call destruction down upon them all, the ghost eagles did her will. They stopped the war, but only after crushing both armies in their massive talons.

At every turn, the eagles made themselves instruments of her rage, though she now knew she was an instrument of theirs. But she didn't believe *her* story was written already. She was not a twin from the story and she was not destined to forever serve the ghost eagles' rage just because she had before. She was not who they thought she was. She would rather choose than be chosen.

As she watched the army march for the fortress, she felt certain Ryven was among them. The ghost eagles would use him just like they used her, and she wondered how she'd find a path out of the destruction they longed for.

"We need to get to the fortress before that army," she said. "We'll hike through the night."

"How?" Nyck objected. "The ghost eagles—"

"They'll let us pass," she said. "They *want* this conflict. They want us going this way with the egg. They'll only stop us if we shy away from the fight."

"But we *should* shy away from it," Brysen told her, raising the black-and-gold egg to her eye level. "If this hatches in the middle of a battle, we know what will come out. We need to keep it as far from violence as we can."

"That's why we're going to do whatever we can to stop a battle before it starts," she said.

"And we'll just hope whatever comes out of that thing isn't worse than what the story told?" Lyra asked. "How do you know *gold* equals *good*? Why do you just assume that?"

Lyra crossed her arms. Now she wasn't going to move.

"Hey . . . yeah." Nyck planted his feet. "That's a good question."

Kylee really didn't want to argue with the battle boys, and she didn't have a good answer for them, but their question was fair. "I don't know," she said. "I have to believe in something right now, and this is what I'm choosing. Call it faith."

She walked past them, to what she thought was the trail, making for a pass that would cut toward the Talon Fortress nestled in the far foothills. She didn't look back to see if the others followed; she just had to have faith. It was thrilling and scary at the same time. She could be wrong about everything. She didn't even know what she didn't know, and she felt a bit like her brother, leaping into the unknown and hoping she could learn to fly on the way down.

30

A CITY ABANDONED IS LIKE A BODY WRACKED WITH ILLNESS. THE same basic structure exists, but its systems have turned against itself, and its decay is uneven. Some pieces continue to function—even thrive—while others irreparably fall into ruin. In a city, like in a body, sewage is one of the first systems to fail. The Talon Fortress was no exception.

It was an old structure, older than Uztar. Kylee now knew it once belonged to the First Falconers, a temple and shrine to birds of prey. It was used for much of Uztar's history as a southern garrison, standing watch opposite the northern Sky Castle. Its outer walls were curved black stone and seemed to erupt from the mountainside, like talons breaking through the earth, grasping at the sky. Those who served the Talon Fortress were rougher, harder soldiers than those of the Sky Castle, but when the great convocation of ghost eagles arrived, the soldiers fled or were slaughtered.

In the dreams guiding her, Kylee saw visions of the days after the ghost eagles took the fortress. They made the structure their nest. Kylee couldn't help imagining what would happen if the hatchling sang its song again. Would the left-behind dead turn into ghost eagles themselves?

It took Brysen, Kylee, and the others four hard days to reach the fortress, with each day's climb leaving them exhausted and sore and frightened. Brysen calmed the egg as they hiked, restoring its golden gleam, but his and Kylee's nightmares grew worse the closer they got to the fortress, and the gold and black colors swirled together whenever they inspected the egg's shell. It gave them no indication of whether they were making a giant mistake. It only pulled them forward.

But now, the morning of the fifth day, it looked like they might have actually beaten Birgund's army to the fortress. The group had lost sight of the plains-bound army while climbing above a cloud bank, because they'd been moving at such a relentless pace and had descended so quickly. Kylee let herself feel a glimmer of hope that they had time to set an ambush for Birgund's forces. That would give them the chance to talk sense, to negotiate, just as long as the ghost eagles didn't attack either side before a conversation could start.

Having had no time to bathe on the hike, they all smelled ripe, but it was nothing compared to the gurgling stream around whose mouth they now stood. Jowyn looked a little less bone-white and little more grass-green at the smell. They'd stopped to rest and catch their breath by a sewage outlet just beyond the high central gate.

The black fortress was quiet. The sun blazed, and there was no sign of a single ghost eagle, nor any bird but the tailor's hawk on Grazim's fist. Nyck tried to scan down the slope for any sign of the approaching army.

"I don't see them," he said. "They're not coming up the main road."

"They can't hike the trails like we can," Lyra pointed out. "Too big an army with too many supplies."

"You think they stopped farther back on the plains?" Jowyn wondered.

"Or maybe the ghost eagles took them out already," Nyck suggested. "To keep them from interfering."

"No," Kylee said. "The ghost eagles *want* them to interfere. They want us fighting so they can harness our anger for their hatchling."

"Also," Brysen added, "we didn't beat the ghost eagles.

They're here already." He pointed at the fortress's architecture, and Kylee wasn't sure what he was looking at, but then she saw streaks of white painting the black stone all along the parapets. Fresh bird scuzz.

Brysen, for all his foolishness and grandiosity, was a decent hunter and a very good trapper of hawks. He knew how to spot signs of a nest, knew the different ways hawks and falcons and owls and eagles built nests for mating and found perches for hunting, how their mutes looked streaking down branches or the sides of boulders. Part of giving every piece of his heart to falconry for so long, even if he'd never been great at the actual training, was that he knew how to spot details while tracking that others might miss.

"Someone set up nets to keep out the ghost eagles," he added, pointing to a line of posts carved into the stone walls. Heavy ropes and nets looped around the posts. None of them were the same color as the rest of the fortress, but they looked familiar . . .

They were made from supplies taken from the Six Villages . . . which were now undefended.

Kylee felt a pang of doubt. "If the army *is* in there," she wondered, "where are the ghost eagles?"

They all scanned the bright blue sky. It was empty save for a cottony puff of cloud dissolving in high wind.

"Sleeping?" Lyra suggested. "It is daylight."

"Watching," Brysen said. "They're hunters first and fore-most. They're watching their prey to see what we do."

"What *will* we do?" Grazim asked. "What's your plan, Kylee?"

"First, we'll sneak in so Birgund's sentries don't see us coming," she said. "And we'll get an audience with Birgund before night falls."

"He'll just take the egg from us," Brysen said. "We can't let that happen."

"We'll have to hide it somewhere safe," she said.

"If we aren't carrying it, then won't the eagles just take it?"

"We'll hide it inside, under the nets," Kylee said. "Buy ourselves time."

"Wait," Nyck cut in. "If the Uztar army got here first and the ghost eagles aren't here to kill them all, then . . . where's Nyall?"

That one stumped Kylee. She understood that the ghost eagles made way for this confrontation because they wanted people to destroy one another, but she couldn't be sure how they intended to use Nyall. Did they lie that he was their prisoner? *Could* they lie in their visions?

"I honestly have no idea," she admitted. "But the answers aren't out here. We have to go in."

"How?" Grazim asked, and Kylee pointed to the stream of sewage trickling beside them.

"Oh no . . ." Nyck groaned.

"Gross." Lyra wrinkled her nose.

Jowyn just threw up.

"You want us to crawl in through *that?*" Grazim gaped at the drainage tunnel emerging from the thick rock face below the fortress's outer wall. Remnants of weeks-old sludge and filth oozed out.

"It's the only way in," Kylee said.

Brysen gave Jowyn a cloth to wipe his mouth. "You okay?"

Jowyn nodded, gave a weak smile, and offered a rhyme: *"We all have bodies; they all make waste. To reach new heights, we're first debased."*

Brysen pulled Jowyn to him but chose, wisely, not to kiss the boy who'd just puked in the scrub brush. Kylee was glad to see that romantic love hadn't turned her brother into a *completely* disgusting person.

"I'll go first," she offered, bracing herself not so much for the smells—odors were to be expected when crawling through a sewage tunnel—but for the textures, which no nose plug could guard against.

But on hands and knees she crawled forward into the dark, climbing the tunnel where it bent up at an angle and listening for the squishing, squashing, sploshing noises of the others following behind her. From the sounds of Brysen complaining, Nyck and Lyra gagging, and Grazim mumbling curses, she figured they were all keeping up. The deeper they went, the darker it grew, and Kylee was grateful for the dark. She didn't need to see what was floating around her legs and forearms. She sloshed on, thinking as she went about how to deal with Kyrg Birgund in a way that didn't involve showing his guts to the sunlight, as much as she'd have liked that.

The thought made her shudder. She knew she had to squash those urges, but if ever a man deserved a violent end, it was a man who ordered the violent end of so many others. If he was granted mercy, how could he be served justice?

He can't, she thought. *He has to die.*

She wondered if the ghost eagles were in her head at that moment, even though she was deep underground. Or perhaps it was the unhatched eaglet putting such thoughts into her mind.

Or maybe this was just who she was and the thoughts of death and despair were all her own. She'd have to resist acting on them, no matter how hard she was provoked.

When the group emerged into light again, they found themselves at the bottom of a drainpipe, which let rainwater flush the sewers. It was deep as a dozen houses and blocked by a grate at the top, but it was narrow enough for each person to press their back against one side and their legs against the other in order to "walk" up horizontally. Anyone who grew up in the mountains would have no trouble with such a maneuver. Grazim, however, grew up on the flat plains of the plateau, and though she'd lived with the Owl Mothers, she never ventured far from their camp. She balked at the height of the smooth walls.

The tailor's hawk fluttered off her fist, flew up, and flapped near the overhead grate, anxious to be free. Thankfully hawks didn't have a good sense of smell. If Grazim had carried a turkey vulture, the bird might've been overwhelmed by the stench. Although to a vulture it might've smelled overwhelmingly delicious.

"Relax," Kylee reassured Grazim, whose blond hair had been painted black by the sewage and whose ruddy skin was reacting irritably to something. Red hives covered the muck-slathered skin on her face and neck. She bore it all with stoicism, though her eyes were locked on the bird above with something like jealousy. "Verticals aren't as hard as they look," Kylee explained.

"We won't let you fall." Brysen stepped up behind Grazim and clapped her on the shoulders with a wet slap, splashing filth from her shirt onto her cheeks. "You're one of us now, signed and sealed in the great goo river beneath the world."

Grazim glared at him but was too nervous to snap back, and besides, he clearly meant what he said, though his tone was obnoxious. Obnoxiousness was usually how Brysen expressed sincerity. He was not going to let Grazim fall. He'd already started tying a rope around his waist, and he passed it to Kylee so she could tie it around Grazim. Grazim raised her arms up over her head to help, giving Kylee a nervous smile.

"Brysen's good at this," Kylee told her. "I'd trust him on any rope I was dangling from."

"He's probably the reason you'd be dangling in the first place, though, right?" Grazim said.

"She's not wrong," Kylee told her brother, with a small laugh.

"Fair," he said, adjusting the bag on his back. The weight of the egg pulled at the leather straps. It was hanging heavier, and Kylee wondered if it would hatch soon, now that they were at their destination. Did it know where it was? Was it, like the ghost eagles themselves, biding its time?

Kylee tied off the other end of the rope, and started up the narrow chute with Grazim below her and Brysen below Grazim. They were all three tied together, so if one fell, the others might stop their fall.

Or they'd all fall together. This method had a way of focusing the mind. Every foot placement was a careful one. Together, they rose.

When they reached the top, Kylee found the grate was hinged. One strong shove with the top of her head pushed it up enough that she was able to haul herself up, then reach down and help Grazim and her brother out. Nyck, Jowyn, and Lyra needed no rope assistance; they all climbed out on their own and looked around. The tailor's hawk fluttered up from below and perched on the top of the open grate, darting its beady eyes around its new surroundings.

Jowyn stood up to his full height, coughed once, then doubled over and heaved again. They were each covered, head to toe, in mixed runoff from the fortress. The only clean spots on any of them were where their backs had rubbed against the wall of the pipe and where their sweat had painted clean streaks on their faces.

"We should rinse off," Nyck suggested.

"We need to find cover," Grazim warned, looking around the small courtyard where they stood.

They were in some kind of air well between two large buildings. A net was strung from the rooftop ledges, stretching over the gap above them. No one could spring an ambush from up there, and there was only one entrance into the small courtyard: a narrow arched doorway.

"I guess we go this way?" Kylee said. Grazim whistled her hawk down to her fist, and the small, filthy party moved on, heading down a narrow alley that opened onto a parade ground.

Kylee signaled the others to stop. They hung back in the shadows and watched as a platoon of soldiers marched through a pair of wide double doors. Their formation was six rows deep and six soldiers across, with two falconers on the ends of each row and infantry in the center. When they reached the middle of the parade ground, they stopped, and turned, facing the alley entrance. Kylee flinched and ducked back.

"Did they see us?" Brysen whispered urgently.

"Shh," she told him, and waited, barely breathing, as the formation split apart, revealing two prisoners. Their hands were bound behind their backs, their heads covered with decorative leather hoods like those of newly caught peregrines. Kylee didn't need to see their faces to know who they were.

"Ma," she whispered. "Nyall."

At Ma's side stood Ryven, as cocky as ever. Though his left arm was in a sling, he stood like a peacock displaying its plumage, crisscrossed by patterns of shadow and sunlight under the netting. He was dressed in a black silk tunic trimmed in bronze and a formal black kilt with bronze clasps. It was the sort of outfit he'd worn to his fancy parties back at the Sky Castle. He was dressed, Kylee realized, for a special occasion, like a funeral or a birth. He had a nasty bruise on his face, like he'd landed on it from what Kylee hoped was an unpleasant height. He should, however, have been more than bruised. He should have been dead. She'd seen the ghost eagle take him away. She wondered now why they'd let him live and what of their history he knew. She also wondered what game he was now playing.

"Yeah, they know you're here," a voice said from behind the group.

Kylee whirled around to find Aalish, the Redfist warrior. Her face was scratched and scabbed.

She wasn't alone.

Four more Redfist warriors stood with her, though her stout partner was notably absent.

"They know we're here, too," she told Kylee. "They sent us to fetch you."

"For what?" Brysen growled, holding tight to the bag with the egg.

"GET THEM CLEANED UP FIRST!" Kyrg Birgund's voice echoed from the parade ground, shouting in their direction.

Aalish shrugged. "These noble types are so squeamish. Follow us."

"Fetch us for what?" Kylee repeated her brother's question without moving. She wanted to negotiate with all of them. She did not want to just walk into a trap.

"The kyrg will explain. And you won't be harmed," Aalish added, "yet . . . Anyway, what choice do you have?" She paused, looked at the nets, then at the one bird in their possession: Grazim's hawk. "You'll lose any fight you start."

"We don't want a fight," Kylee said.

"Good." Aalish nodded. "Then you get a bath. This way."

Kylee let them be led into the sunlight, and they marched, filth-covered but with heads held high, across the grounds. The buildings around the parade ground were newer than the outer walls—round stone buildings and towers in the Uztari style—though here and there were black stone ruins, curved and shiny. These made Kylee think of the First Falconers and how their black blood glistened in the moonlight before they were transformed into ghost eagles. She looked at the prisoners the Uztari army held as they walked past.

I'm here to save you, she thought in their direction. *Just stay calm.*

She was telling herself the same thing. She had to stay calm if she was going to keep the sky from falling on all of them.

31

HOT SPRING BATHS WERE TUCKED AWAY IN A TILED COURTYARD between two squat stone buildings, just across from a round tower surrounded by high outer walls and an iron gate: the central keep. The fortress's newer architecture mirrored the Sky Castle's, but the baths were old. The tiles were smooth and black, and Kylee imagined the First Falconers sliding across them on wet feet, laughing and lounging in good times, or resting from a hard day's hunt.

They were gone now, every one of them, and she and her group of friends were now the only people who carried their memory. She wondered what she owed them. Should she let the egg hatch in vengeance and turn the dead into a new flock against the living, let that sort of justice be done? Or should she try, with her brother, to hatch the egg as something new and hope that healing was somehow possible? Was there a song any bird could sing in any language that could make amends for what had been done?

"We don't have all day," Aalish barked. "Clean yourselves."

The water in the one large pool steamed and gurgled, heat issuing from its source deep in the mountain. The baths had fallen into a bit of ruin. Broken bricks and pieces of stonework had fallen into the water, littering the floor with jagged shrapnel, but the stench on Kylee's clothes overwhelmed any hesitation she might have felt for bathing under so many threatening glares. Soldiers from Birgund's army and warriors with their fists wrapped in red cloth stood watching them.

Nyck wasted no time; he jumped in fully clothed, instantly befouling the crystal-clear water, and the others realized they might lose their chance at cleanliness if they didn't jump in, too, and quickly.

Only Jowyn bothered disrobing first—so he could scrub and wring out his clothes before putting them back on clean—and he rolled his eyes at the rest of them for their bashfulness. Brysen gave in to the eye roll and copied Jowyn, stripping down, but no one else followed their lead, and the two boys kept to themselves on the far side of the pool. Brysen still held the bag with the egg in it, washing himself and his clothes one-handed. He kept the bag above the water with his free hand.

Kylee waded over to him.

"I can hold that for you for a bit," she suggested, glancing at the opposing groups of soldiers watching them. "Unlike the twins in that history, *we* can share."

"Are you sure?" Brysen asked.

"Yeah, I mean, of course I'm——" And then she understood what he was really asking. Was she sure she could hold the egg and not unleash a slaughter? Was she sure her own hunger for vengeance and control wouldn't take over? Was she sure the ghost eagles couldn't get inside her head?

"No," she admitted. "I'm not sure. But"——she lowered her voice——"we have to keep this thing safe *somewhere*. I think I know best how to do that."

She prayed he understood her now. She prayed he knew what she was trying to do.

He hesitated, and then she saw a glimmer of recognition in the curl of his mouth. He understood.

"It's mine," Brysen said a little louder than necessary, loud enough for the soldiers to hear. "You can't take it from me."

She stood so her back blocked the soldiers' view of her brother.

"I can keep it safer than you," she said. She sensed the

soldiers' eyes on them. "The ghost eagles spoke to me first, anyway. I should be the one to hold it."

Brysen's mouth actually hung open. "Are you kidding?" he scoffed. "How old are you? *They spoke to me first* is not a good reason."

"It is so," she said.

"Is not," he said.

"Is so," she said, stepping up into his face and nearly tripping on a jagged piece of black stone hidden in the cloudy water. They both looked down at it as she regained her balance. He nodded a tiny bit.

"Is *not*," Brysen said, stepping up to her, resting his foot on top of the stone.

The rhythm of their bickering took on a chantlike quality.

"Is so."

"Is not."

"Is so."

"Is not." Brysen dropped his voice, glanced toward the soldiers at the water's edge with a quick smirk.

"Is *SO*." She pushed him.

"Is NOT!" He pushed her back.

"Hey, calm down!" Jowyn tried to get between them, play the peacemaker, because he didn't speak their wordless language or know their soundless tunes. He didn't know what they were up to. They'd been bickering and playing and hurting and healing each other since the womb. They didn't need to explain themselves to execute a plan. However a flock of starlings know which shapes to form in the sky, Kylee imagined she and her brother shared a similar language, and she hoped Jowyn was sensitive enough to notice and to play along.

"Why can't you grow up?" she yelled at Brysen.

"You're always stealing *my* glory!" Brysen yelled at her, shoving past Jowyn. "Not this time!" He tried to dunk her, but she dodged and dunked him instead, diving onto his back as they plunged underwater. Jowyn, finally having figured it out, jumped on top of them, kicking and splashing the water into a foam.

The others, not in on the ruse, rushed over, but she and her brother were already under the water. Her hands found the bag as her brother opened it. He reached for the black stone as she slipped out the egg and wedged it behind another piece of rubble before breaking the surface and sucking in a huge gulp of air. Brysen followed soon behind.

"ENOUGH!" one of the officers yelled. "You're all clean. Out of the water! And you two!" She pointed her sword at Jowyn and Brysen. "Put on some clothes! No one wants to see your hummingbird beaks."

Jowyn and Brysen looked at each other. Kylee thought she saw a tinge of color hit Jowyn's cheeks, and Brysen shouted back, "Hey! A hummingbird's beak is the longest part of their body!" but the soldier had already turned away. As they climbed from the water, Brysen still clutched the bag, which hung a little heavier off his shoulder, and Kylee quickly glanced back at the water to make sure the egg was well hidden. She'd have to find a way to come back for it, but first she had to convince Kyrg Birgund to form a truce, though Ryven would work hard against it. She had no doubt he was serving the ghost eagles' desires now and would do whatever it took to bring that egg to a terrible hatching.

She made sure to stand next to Grazim as they dried off and whispered at her, "Stay keen."

The girl gave her a puzzled look—not because she didn't understand, but simply because, at this point, staying sharp should have gone without saying. Kylee nodded. Just like with her brother, she and her friend had their own unspoken language, too. You don't have to be born family to become family, after all.

They were escorted into the central keep, where Kyrg Birgund was waiting. He welcomed Kylee, Brysen, and the others and offered them heaping plates of beans and vegetables and fermented breads, along with stoneware cups of bubbling cloudgrass tea.

He did not, however, have any birds of prey in the room, and he asked that Grazim's be caged for the duration of their talk. A blanket-covered birdcage stood behind him.

"It's only polite, for the more devout Altari among us,"
Birgund said, which made Kylee snort with derision. Birgund
never cared about offending the Altari before, and he also
clearly didn't know that the distinction between Altari and
Uztari was entirely an invention of false history. They were all
the same: heirs to a genocidal empire.

Ryven stood at the kyrg's side. He eyed her with a smirk.

"I saw the ghost eagles take you," she told him. "And yet
here you are. With Birgund." She nodded toward the kyrg.
"And with the Redfists." She nodded toward Aalish. "Playing
all sides at the same time is bold, even for you."

"By the sky's mercy, our black feathered friends let me
live," Ryven replied, with such insincerity that he had to be
mocking her. He looked down at his arm in the sling. "They
brought me here, where your friend was already being held. I
have skills that he does not, and I commanded the ghost eagles
to leave us. They obeyed."

"Just like that?" Kylee asked. "They brought you all this
way to let you go, just like that?"

"Just like that," Ryven confirmed. "We both know why." He
held out his hand; he wanted the egg. "We're pieces on their
game board, as you know, Kylee," he said. "They've put us all
where they want us, and now they expect us to play. I explained
that quite clearly to Birgund and to Aalish. There are only two
sides. Ours and theirs. Surrender the egg and we foil their plans."

"Let me keep it and we foil their plans," Kylee countered.

"So we all agree: We want to foil their plans," Kyrg Birgund interrupted. "It's a good place to start. Kylee, give us the egg and you'll get your mother and your friend Nyall back safe and unburden yourself of this monstronsity. It's the prudent thing to do."

"What do you think you can do with this egg?" Kylee asked him. "Do you really think these birds let you come here, alive and with hostages that I care about, just to give you control? They know me better than that."

"I won't pretend to understand their motives," Birgund said. "But I see an advantage, and I intend to use it. That egg, Ryven assures me, will give me some power over them— power to protect our empire and all the people in it—and I will not allow you to squander it."

"So you trust Ryven now?" Kylee asked him.

"Not at all," the kyrg confessed. "But you made it here alive while carrying the egg, which means it must provide some protection."

"How do I know you won't just kill us all once you have the egg?" Kylee asked.

"You don't," Birgund said. "But trust has to start some-where."

"Agreed," said Kylee. As much as she wanted to call him a

duck-defiling pile of dung, she needed him to trust her, too. She needed him to see they were not enemies here.

"How did you get Nyall?" she asked.

Birgund tapped his fingers together, considering her question. Finally, he answered, "He was here with Ryven when we arrived. Starving and thirsty, I might add. We saved his life." He side-eyed the dapper deposed kyrg beside him. "*Both* their lives."

"The ghost eagles left them for you," Kylee said. "Did you ask yourself why?"

"Just because the ghost eagles want it to happen doesn't make it wrong," Birgund replied.

"I agree," Kylee said. "You just don't know their endgame. I do."

"And what's that?" Birgund held a patronizing smile on his lips.

"They want me to kill you," she said. "They want me to use the Hollow Tongue to rip you and your army to shreds."

Birgund's expression didn't change at all. "I assume you want the same."

"Just because the ghost eagles want it to happen doesn't make it wrong," she said back to him.

His smile widened. At least she'd earned a little of his respect. "So we are going to have to want something more than these birds want us to kill each other, I suppose."

"I suppose so," Kylee said.

"If we control the egg, we control them," Ryven said, and Birgund held up a hand to silence the man.

"You've made your position clear," he said.

"And what about us?" Aalish added, speaking up from behind the group. "We agreed to a truce, to focus on a common enemy, and so far I have not heard any of our concerns mentioned. The egg should be destoyed."

Birgund tented his fingers in front of him and locked his eyes on Kylee's. "So you see what everyone here wants," he said. "You are in a good position right now. You have an item that's valuable to all of us. The sun is up; the nets are secure. I don't imagine your position will get any better as time goes on. So tell me now: Aside from the safe release of your friend and your mother, what do you want?"

"It's not about what I want anymore," Kylee said. "It's about what the ghost eagles want and about what they don't even yet know they want."

"She's stalling," Ryven grumbled. "Just take the egg from her."

He thinks he's safe, Kylee thought, which was what all the cruel men she'd ever known had thought right up to the moment she called death down upon them.

32

"I WOULDN'T DO THAT," KYLEE WARNED TWO REDFISTS. THEY'D BEEN moving toward her brother and his bag. "We're all talking right now, but if it comes to fighting, none of us will win."

"The ghost eagles can't get to us in here," Birgund said.

"Unless they're here already." She looked around the table, imagined the fight to come, the needless death. And then she imagined every dead body transformed into a new ghost eagle, pained, afraid, and bent on vengeance. Ryven's brow furrowed.

"You only know part of the story, don't you?" Kylee asked him. "You're acting as if you know it all, but your knowledge is flimsy as the moth-eaten blanket I grew up with."

"That was my blanket," Brysen interrupted. "Yours was nibbled by rats."

"We didn't have rats," Kylee said. "The hawks ate them all."

"Well, *my* blanket was the moth-eaten one," he said, killing time. How long did they need to stall? How long until the egg was ready to hatch?

"Was not," Kylee said back to him.

"Was so!" Brysen said.

"Was not!" Kylee said. Poor Jowyn looked like he was about to explode at the return of their hijinks, while Grazim, who had no idea what they were doing, was trying and visibly failing to keep her cool. In that way, she matched Kyrg Birgund. His face had turned red as sunset.

"Stop this before I have you both bound and gagged!" he yelled at them. "You are here because you have this egg. You can pretend you have some noble motives all you like, but you didn't bury the egg when you had the chance, so I know you want to see it hatch as much as I do."

"Bury the—" Brysen gasped, all pretense dropped. "How do you know about that?"

Birgund rapped his knuckles on the table and smiled. He nodded to a soldier behind him, who pulled the blanket off a cage at the back of the room. One snow owl perched inside. A scrawled note lay on the cage floor. Kylee couldn't make out the writing, but she knew the ink and she knew the bird. The owl belonged to Üku, and the note was written in her blood. Her last command in that cave hadn't been an attack; she'd prepared herself to die and then sent word to Birgund. He knew the ghost eagles could be stopped and he knew how: Bury the egg and soak the ground in Kylee's and her brother's blood. The only reason he hadn't killed them yet was because he didn't have the egg, and the moment he got it, Kylee feared, would be the moment they died.

"The Owl Mothers were fools," Birgund said. "They had access to the greatest weapon imaginable and they squandered it because they were afraid."

"Fear can be a source of wisdom," Grazim said. "Only a fool ignores the voice of fear altogether."

"And only cowards heed it," Birgund countered.

"She didn't tell you what will happen when this hatches, did she?" Kylee asked. She looked at Ryven. "Do you know? Did the ghost eagles whisper it into your mind? Or is yours a more one-sided friendship?"

Ryven looked away from her. He didn't know, and he didn't like to be reminded that she knew more than he did. If Kylee thought she'd chastened him, though, she was wrong.

"This is tiresome!" Ryven thundered. "Take it from the boy."

"No one move unless I order it!" Birgund thundered, but

the Redfists were on Ryven's side, and one of them moved for Brysen. One of Birgund's soldiers went to stop them as Jowyn rose to protect Kylee's brother. The room was balanced on the edge of bloodshed.

"No!" Kylee pleaded.

"REEEEEE!" a ghost eagle cried. Its call was answered by hundreds more. The volume alone told Kylee they loomed just on the other side of the nets. They weren't waiting for nightfall. Violence was coming, and they had come with it.

Brysen offered what little resistance he could without actually throwing a punch: He went limp, forcing the Redfists to wrangle the bag free and toss it across the table to Ryven, who caught it just as a soldier knocked a Redfist down with a kick to the back of the knee.

"Everyone stop!" Kylee pleaded.

Ryven licked his lips as he opened the bag one-handed and turned it over. The heavy black stone rolled onto the table with a thud. It was still wet from the baths. For a moment, Ryven stared at it, puzzled that it should look so little like an egg. Then it dawned on him: They'd made a switch.

"Search them!" he ordered.

"And search the sewers where they came in!" Birgund echoed. "Find it!"

Redfists and soldiers raced from the room, trying to be the

first to the sewers to find and control the egg. At least they'd start looking in the wrong place, which bought some time.

"That was very stupid," Birgund said, though he was talking to Ryven. "Very, very stupid."

For once, Kylee agreed with him.

"They're going to find it," Brysen warned. "They're going to fight over it."

Kylee nodded. She knew. She feared they were about to fail.

"REEEEEE," the ghost eagles screamed, eager for the pain of their own creation—the only emotion they knew—to rise again.

"We have to try before it's too late," Kylee said.

"Try what?" Birgund glowered at her.

"Try what?" Ryven whispered at her.

She looked at Brysen. "Together?" she asked.

He nodded.

Kylee closed her eyes. She thought of her mother, of the pain she must have felt to see her children suffer all their lives, of the broken places inside her that *let* her children suffer. She thought of her father, of the wound he carried and passed on to his children through violence and hurt, of the pain and rage he must have felt when he died, knowing it was his children who killed him. And then she thought of the ghost eagles, created and wounded by the cruelty of human history and still so drawn to its pain that they were unable to break free, unable despite all their power to imagine anything other than that pain, tethered to their own agony like an addict to hunter's leaf.

She thought about how hard it is to break the patterns you've always lived by; how you fight, like a hatchling struggling to crack free of its shell. And she looked at Ryven's face and thought of words she'd heard him speak, words she'd read in the history written on bodies, words she could use now, words she hoped were true enough to crack open an egg.

"*Eeefa kai'ee*," she said. Her voice became a shout: "*Eeefa kai'ee!*"

Brysen shouted the words with her, and outside the ghost eagles screamed, and she and Brysen felt it happening, even if they couldn't see it, couldn't know for sure. They cried out in the same words the First Falconers and the newcomers had called their own mixed children. A gift of the new.

Neither Kylee nor her brother nor the ghost eagles knew what would emerge from that shell when it cracked. Not all gifts are easy to receive.

HATCHED

THE SONG WAS MUFFLED AT FIRST, THOUGH THAT WAS NOT THE SONG'S fault. There were layers of bone and blood and flesh and shell to get through, and the eaglet's ears weren't very developed, and there was also a howling mountain wind and the shouts and cries and moans and laughter of an entire civilization. And there were history and memory, which were louder still.

But there was always the song, a call on the air, the same pattern, repeating.

We're here, We're here, We're here.

The eaglet didn't know who or what a "We" was or where to find "here." It did not yet know distinctions, not between itself and the world, nor between places. All it knew was that it existed now and this song was calling it.

We're here, We're here, We're here.

Sometimes the song had the lilt of a parent embracing a child, and the little baby bird in its shell felt safe and warm. Feeling safe taught it something new. If it could feel safe, then there was such a thing as unsafe. If it could feel warmth, then it could feel cold.

Sometimes the song was filled with the quick breaths of lovers touching, and the eaglet felt a thrill through its body. It could feel that its body was distinct from other bodies, that they were not one, and if flesh could be touched, it could also be pierced.

And then it heard the song filled with anguish. With pain, isolation, fear.

We're here, We're here, We're here.

Each note was a plea, and the eaglet in its shell heard them and felt agony and felt the shell that held it back, and knew it was not strong enough to break out. It raged in its shell, felt its thoughts turn black. If there could be pain, there should be rescue. If there could be pain, there should be revenge. If there could be pain, it should be stopped.

Powerless, the baby bird in its thick shell screamed without a voice, and over time, its screams grew louder, but they were trapped inside. The eaglet had everything and its opposite with which to answer this song. It didn't know why it existed or how it had come to be. It knew only its purpose: answering the song. It had been sung for so long without an answer. When would the eaglet find a voice and reply?

It was jostled. It was handled. It felt itself protected; it felt itself endangered. It didn't know why. It did nothing to earn the screaming pain that filled its waking thoughts and sleeping dreams; it did nothing to earn the warmth and love that sometimes washed over it. Neither could be predicted, both came and went without warning.

And still there was the song, crying out, demanding answer.

We're here, We're here, We're here. It sang and screamed and cried and raged. *We're here, We're here, We're here.*

And the eaglet in its shell tried to answer.

I hear! I hear! I hear!

It screamed for so long, it thought no one would hear . . . but someone heard. The eaglet felt them—other minds floating in other bloods, so different from its own, but hungering as it hungered for something they did not understand.

How long had it been since anyone heard? A heartbeat? Ten thousand seasons? The answer erased all time. There was only now. Only this moment.

And then the song changed.

You're safe, it said. *Stay calm*, it said. And finally, after an instant that could have been an eternity or perhaps the other way around, it said, *Become. You are a gift. Become.*

The eaglet found its voice. The eaglet found its strength and pressed against its brittle shell.

It hurt. The shell was hard, and the eaglet fully filled the egg, but the voice still called to it, and it called back.

I hear! I hear! I'm coming!

The shell pressed against its skin, pushed back, resisted. The stress and strain were too much; the little eaglet would never get out. The call would go unanswered. But it pushed and wriggled and finally the surface cracked and light shone in. But there was only the smallest hole. How could it get through?

And then water roared in.

The eaglet gagged. The eaglet choked.

A new song rushed in along with the water, a song like the eaglet had never heard. A song that was life. A song that was need. A song that was rage and promise and hope and bloody, violent death. A song that was everything it had ever felt inside its shell as well as a promise to feel more, but the song drowned in the water filling the shell, and the little baby bird was choking.

It thrashed and rolled and cracked the shell wider, and more water rushed in.

At the moment of its birth, death was coming fast.

The eaglet broke from its shell and was free, and it spread its wings, but the world was water and light, and the water was heavy and the light was blinding, and it tried to chirp its song at last—the long-awaited answer to the eternal cry of its days and nights—but its beak opened and water flooded its fragile lungs and the baby bird's light dimmed, and though it tried to flap its newborn wings, it sank and sank upon smooth tile and rough black stone.

The eaglet wasn't born for this watery sky, but it was buried beneath it, never taking one clear breath or singing one solid note. The song that called it into being would never hear its answer, and the baby eaglet learned, just before death, what sadness was.

It drowned.

BRYSEN

THE WEIGHTED WORD

33

THE MOMENT THE SHOUTING STOPPED, BRYSEN FELT DIZZY. HE GAGGED and coughed, and then he spat out . . . water.

"Hey, Bry." Jowyn rested a hand on his back, patting him, and Brysen tried to turn to him, but he lurched forward again and heaved crystal-clear water onto the floor.

Kylee, too, was spitting up water.

Brysen looked at her, then at the puzzled warriors opposite them and the soldiers halfway out the door to search for the egg, and then at Ryven as realization dawned.

"Idiots!" Ryven shouted at them. He ordered his soldiers to the baths before rushing for the door himself. "An egg can't hatch underwater!"

Brysen knew they had summoned the hatchling from its shell, finally found the words and the intention to call it out, but that they'd called it to its death. It was drowning.

He righted himself to standing and looked at Jowyn. "I need to get back there," he said quickly, and Jowyn understood. Kylee nodded at Grazim and at the battle boys, and there was no hesitation. They didn't have birds of prey to fight beside them, but they all immediately charged, rushing the nearest soldiers they could see, tackling them, whaling on them. Even gentle Jowyn took out one Redfist's legs, toppling them to floor and trying to pin them down.

"What is this!" Birgund bellowed, but Brysen was already through the door. He leapt past two guards who tried to block him and sprinted down the winding steps of the keep to the bright sun, racing across the parade grounds to the entrance of the baths. Ryven was behind him, but the man's injuries had slowed him, and he was falling farther and farther behind as Brysen sprinted faster and faster ahead.

I'm coming, he thought. *I'm coming. Hang in there. I'm coming. I'm right here. I'm coming. I'm here.*

He saw Shara in his thoughts, felt her soft brown and gray feathers against his cheek, saw what he'd come to believe was a gentle fury in her red-rimmed goshawk eyes. She'd always been a contradiction—a partner who didn't really need him, a friend who was indifferent to him, a wild animal that let itself be tamed by him. All Shara ever looked for from Brysen was safety: the one thing he failed to give her. She was dead and gone, but she was here with him, too. In every footfall against the smooth stone, in every thundering breath as he ran, she was there. *I'm coming. I'm coming. I'm coming.*

He leapt into the water the moment he reached the pool, again soaking his already-wet clothes up to his waist, sloshing through the hot spring, sweating in the steam, until he saw it: a bird's body, the size of a full-grown hawk but featherless, floating halfway between the bottom and the surface, unmoving, with wings spread.

He sucked in a breath, dove under, and wrapped the creature in his arms, then stood with it cradled to his chest, his sopping-wet gray hair hanging over his eye so that he had to shake his vision free before he could look down at the baby bird. The sun shone on both of them, and the bird's fresh, raw skin glistened from the water. A few puffs of waterlogged, downy feathers ringed its neck. The texture of firegrass and itchy to the touch, they were the same color as Brysen's hair—the gray of storm clouds, the gray of smoke. They weren't black. They weren't gold. They were nothing.

A newborn bird's chest should heave with labored breaths from the strain of hatching. This bird's chest was still, its eyes closed, its body cold even in the sun's afternoon blaze. Brysen looked down at the bird and whispered, "I'm sorry . . . I brought you here . . . I'm so sorry . . ."

Suddenly the sun blotted out, like the moon itself had eclipsed the day.

Brysen looked up and saw the ghost eagles, in their hundreds, perched on the nets above, looking down with their black eyes, their black bodies pressed so close to one another that no light could get through. They watched, as silent as owls. The only sound he heard was the creaking of the nets under their weight.

Then came the footfalls of the soldiers running after him, some from the keep, some from the sewers. He saw his sister and Jowyn: Uztari soldiers had Kylee. Two Redfists held Jowyn. Nyck and Lyra and Grazim were headed in his direction, fighting every step of the way. Ryven ran up and stood by the edge of the water, too, catching his breath. Blood seeped through the fabric of his sling.

Good, Brysen thought. *I hope it hurts.*

He looked down again at the bird in his arms. No change to its downy feathers, but he found he wanted there to be. He wanted it to transform, to come back, to lay waste to everything.

The thought nibbled at him. It was like a tick biting his grief, glutting itself on his emotions but infecting him with something else. The ghost eagles wanted his rage and were transforming his regret.

Look at your friends, all prisoners, he thought. *Jowyn. Nyall and Ma. Your sister. They will all die unless you stop them. There can be no healing. Only death. Forever death.*

Hundreds of ghost eagles looked down at him with grief and anger, longing for him to unleash his emotions. Their hatchling was dead, but they remained tethered to Brysen and they wanted only to do what felt familiar. They wanted to kill.

You know the words to heal it, he thought. *This is your purpose. This is your gift. Heal it and we will have our revenge.*

He looked up at the people around the baths. All of them were pitted against one another, ready to strike one another down to claim what they thought was their due. All of them thought they had power, but he knew, at that moment, the only power that mattered was his.

The eaglet was dead, far past hearing any falconer's call, but Brysen had a gift. Brysen could heal it. He was suddenly certain of it, certain that this was his purpose, the reason he suffered, the reason he learned to speak the language of birds, the reason for everything. All his choices brought him here, to this moment, with talents only he possessed.

Call it back, the dread flock above pleaded in his mind. *This is your chance for greatness. Show them all who you are.*

He felt the word forming on his lips. He felt pride swell inside him. He'd done all he could, followed every sign and obeyed every instinct that led him here, but all that followed him was death. From the moment he first swore he could capture a ghost eagle, he'd tried to prove his greatness, and it brought nothing but grief. And now this bird he swore to protect was drowned because he thought he could outwit armies and defy history, and yet, like a fool, he'd left it to hatch underwater. He was too reckless. Nothing good ever came of chasing power, and that was what the ghost eagles wanted. They wanted him to do what he always did: chase a glory that was beyond his grasp and sow chaos all around him.

If this bird returned to life, everyone would die and then be transformed into death itself. More ghost eagles crying out in a pain they didn't understand; more people struggling to control them. The cycle of pain and destruction would go on forever. He had to break it. He had to let go.

Standing waist-deep in steaming bathwater, surrounded by soldiers looking down at him and silent ghost eagles above them, he let go of the baby bird. Its wide wings splayed in front of him on the water's surface, and he stepped back, turned away from it, and sloshed through the water to the bath's edge. As he wiped his eye, he looked up at his sister. The soldiers holding her had dropped her arms, more frightened of the flock above them than of disobeying orders. "I won't give them they want," Brysen said.

He'd sought glory and greatness for so long in as many forms as he could imagine—falconer, then trapper; warrior, then healer; protector and peacemaker—and none of them worked. None of his grand schemes *ever* worked. He was no hero, and this wasn't his heroic tale. This was just his life, striving and reaching and never grasping, and he'd had enough. He was done. His pain was his own. He wouldn't let the ghost eagles use it, not anymore. No one else would suffer because Brysen hurt.

"We're different," he said out loud. "A hurt animal attacks. Hurt people don't have to hurt people. I won't anymore."

The ghost eagles looked down at him, their black eyes invisible in the shadows of their faces. Some of the soldiers around the pool had their weapons raised, but they stood totally still. No one dared move with so many ghost eagles overheard. Brysen's was the only voice, and his shouting was not answered.

"You understand?" he yelled at the ghost eagles. "I'm not one of the twins in your history. I'm done! I will not summon death for you!"

The ghost eagles' heads all tracked him as he waded to the water's edge and pulled himself out. He looked straight up at them. They weren't leaving. They weren't attacking. They were just . . . waiting. And then their heads turned.

The flock of ghost eagles screeched as one.

"*Oh, merciful sky* . . . ," one of the soldiers in front of him whispered, and the Redfists holding Jowyn let him go, dropping to their knees and pressing their foreheads to the ground. He heard splashing and the fluttering of wings behind him. He spun around.

Across the pool, the hatchling burst from the water. *Alive!* And bigger than before, its new feathers gleaming gold.

He felt a surge of pure joy, and a smile wider than the horizon cracked across his face. He'd changed the story. All he ever had to do was let go.

34

THE RISEN EAGLE'S FEATHERS SEEMED TO BLOSSOM AS BRYSEN watched. Its wings beat the air, and water fell away. It was exactly like the hatchling in the history they'd read and it was nothing like the hatchling in the history they'd read. Its beak was black, like the beaks of the ghost eagles above, but every wingbeat seemed to change the color of its plumage. Like wind swirling through grass on the plains, the feathers gleamed gold, then black, then gold again with dizzying speed. The newborn bird looked down at Brysen. Its wings kept it hovering in place, and its eyes darted around the scene, taking in everything. They were a crystalline blue, like

Brysen's own. Pride puffed inside him, but as it did, the feathers blackened.

He exhaled. This was not about him. Whatever this bird would do now, Brysen could not be the one decide it.

"REEEEEEE," the ghost eagles shrieked again, and the golden bird cried out in answer, louder than they were. Brysen saw the newcomers on the frozen steppes, saw the moment of their arrival on the plateau. The bird was going to tell their story.

The ghost eagles panicked. They didn't want to hear it. They screeched and scrambled, pulled at the nets, began to tug them loose.

"This can't be," Ryven muttered. "This is not the way."

"It's not up to us," Brysen told him. "Their words were never ours to speak. They have to face this in their own way."

Ryven looked up at the huge bird, then back at Brysen. "No," he said. "You are too weak to serve them, but I am not. I still have a destiny." He closed his eyes, and when he opened them again, they were black from lid to lid.

"Oh no," Kylee gasped, pulling Brysen away from Ryven.

"*Vayara!*" Ryven shouted. "*Vayara!*"

The great golden bird's song stopped. It looked down at them all, and its eyes locked on Ryven.

Ignore him, Brysen thought. *You're bound to me. Don't listen.*

But Brysen knew he had let go, and in letting go, he freed

the bird from him, and freedom was a dangerous thing. The bird could choose for itself what to hear and what to obey. Brysen knew, from reading the history of the ghost eagles on so many corpses, that hearing this story was hard.

Destroying one another was easy.

The hatchling chose what was easy. It obeyed Ryven. Its feathers blackened.

Ryven had commanded it with one word: *apocalypse*.

The black-feathered hatchling sang a new song, and the ghost eagles cried out with dreadful joy, like the instant when a climber falls, just before the rocks loom up to pulverize him.

They got what they wanted—history would not repeat. It would end.

The hatchling swooped underneath the nets, flapping straight along the fortress's black stones and crashing into where stakes held the nets in place.

In an explosion of dust and stone, it tore a corner of the netting and ripped away the stake that held it, breaking out into the open sky. It was on the same side of the nets as the ghost eagles.

"REEEEEEE!" the flock screeched, and in his mind, Brysen saw himself cowering in front of his father, pleading for his little injured goshawk's life.

"REEEEEE!" they screeched, and he saw himself curled around the egg, as the hawk his sister called battered his back.

"REEEEEE!" they screeched, and he saw Jowyn crying out, weeping for his friends, unable to save them, and then he saw his sister, helpless, gagged, and pulled into the shadowy doors of a black stone building with a stiletto blade against her windpipe, and—

These were not visions. This was happening now. Kyrg Birgund himself had grabbed her and pulled her away.

A rain of black blood began to fall from above as the huge hatchling tore into the flesh of the first ghost eagle it reached, driving its talons into the larger bird's underside and ripping it open.

The ghost eagle did not fight back. It let its own offspring rip it open. The others screamed, "REEEEEEE!"

They welcomed death.

Brysen's vision clouded. He saw other sets of twins— twins he'd never known, children from the past—as they were hunted down, torn apart, the eggs they carried buried in the mud. Wars erupted. The ghost eagles saw families turn on one another, saw families torn apart, saw lovers perish before they could make families. Generations bloodied; generations broken, over and over.

It was all finally ending. Their future would wipe away their past.

The vision knocked him to his knees.

The hatchling tore from eagle to eagle, leaping and fluttering across their backs and ripping them wing from wing. Black feathers fell and black blood spread like ink in the baths. Pieces of the net settled on the surface and the bodies of ghost eagles tangled in it as it sank, some of them still alive, some of them drowning.

And the hatchling's feathers were pure black. It had grown and was still growing, and sunlight streaked down through gaps in the crowd of eagles above, spaces forming where it tore its elders from the air.

Brysen screamed for his sister, but she'd been pulled back to the keep, away from the sky's reach.

"*Tuslaash*," he yelled, asking for help, but the baby bird couldn't hear him over the ghost eagles' screams, and the ghost eagles were too fixated on their own destruction to heed him. The young bird they'd created with Brysen and Kylee now carried within it their same rage and their same wound. That was their gift: They passed a new generation their pain. Ryven had unleashed it for them.

The handsome former kyrg stood at the bath's edge, looking up, letting ghost eagle blood coat him as he laughed. "I tamed them!" he cried. "I tamed them." As if he had any control over this, as if they hadn't used him in the way they wanted to use Brysen and Kylee.

Brysen felt a surge of anger. He was going to throw this man into the water and drown the life from him. He began to lunge, then stopped himself.

No. It wasn't *he* who stopped.

Jowyn had his hand. Jowyn had found him. Jowyn shook his head. "This isn't you," the boy said.

"REEEEEE!" the ghost eagles screamed, and swirled in the sky.

On the ground around them, the Redfists had begun to fight with the Uztari soldiers, goaded to shatter their fragile alliance by the visions of self-destruction that filled their heads with every dying ghost eagle's cry. Brysen saw the first soldier fall, a Redfist's spear through their chest. Their body fell into the baths, surrounded by the inky-black blood of the ghost eagles, which congealed around the body and began forming feathers. And then, from the water, a new ghost eagle rose, and it tore the head clean off the soldier who killed its human form. And that soldier, too, became a ghost eagle.

The hatchling couldn't kill them fast enough.

The eagles thought their destruction would end their pain, but no justice was served by destroying themselves, and nothing was healed. The cycle would go on and on, even if no humanity survived.

The new ghost eagles couldn't stop themselves. They

screamed as they flew, and their screams filled everyone's thoughts. Brysen saw every petty act of discrimination the Uztari had ever inflicted on the Altari, every massacre the Kartami had committed in their war to empty the sky and destroy Uztar.

He saw his own history, too. The misplaced love, the reckless wounds. How he'd hurt others by flinging himself into grand dreams, how Shara's death was his fault, how the Six Villages' collapse was his fault, how his sister's current capture was his fault. How this horror was his fault. All of it. He was responsible.

He collapsed.

Jowyn caught him, held him. "Are you hurt? What's wrong?"

His voice sounded far away.

"They took your sister to the keep," he said. "We have to help her."

Brysen just shook his head. To move in this world was to break and be broken. He didn't dare do anything else.

A ghost eagle screeched as it fell, its body thumping on the stone tile in front of him. There was still some life in its black eyes, and they met Brysen's gaze. It let out one quiet whistle, and Brysen felt its miserable contentment. Its pain was past; a new generation would carry it now.

"This isn't what I wanted . . . ," he told it, grimacing.

"Believe me," he pleaded with the dying bird, and he knew his voice was echoing across all their minds. "Please stop."

Brysen found he couldn't say a word of the Hollow Tongue anymore, not even the most basic command. Even though he found he could recall the sounds, he couldn't make his mouth form them. The words had left him.

They were never mine.

Like the Altari said, the Hollow Tongue was never for people to speak. Like the Kartami said, birds of prey were not on humanity's side. But like the Uztari said, birds of prey were everything their civilization was built upon.

Each civilization carried a shard of truth, because they were all broken pieces of the same shattered mirror. Brutality and lies had shattered it, and Brysen feared it was beyond repair.

Jowyn helped him stand. Brysen saw Grazim running toward the keep, dodging groups of brawling soldiers. She had no hawk on her fist.

"We need to help your sister," Jowyn said. "Maybe she can stop this."

"Ryven," Brysen said back. "Ryven can stop this."

Jowyn shook his head and pointed. "It's too late for him."

The handsome man was still laughing, but he was no longer standing on the ground. A ghost eagle was lifting him, higher and higher, as he laughed and laughed and laughed.

"I tamed them!" he kept shouting. "I did this! I tamed them all!"

And he kept laughing as talons pierced his heart and his laughter turned into an eagle's shrill cry. He began to fall and transformed in the air, one more predator in a sky full of them, indistinguishable even at the moment the hatchling ripped him in half.

35

JOWYN AND BRYSEN CAUGHT UP TO GRAZIM AT THE GATE LEADING INTO the central keep. It was closed, and there were soldiers on both sides.

"Let us in!" the soldiers outside screamed, looking back at Grazim, Brysen, and Jowyn like they were ghost eagles themselves. Behind them, giant birds shrieked and black feathers swirled down from the sky like a nightmare of snow. Brysen saw Nyck and Lyra sheltering under a stone arch. They saw him and made a run for it in his direction.

"Following orders!" the soldiers inside the gate yelled back. They poked their blades through the metal slats, pushing their own people away. "Defend your posts!"

The soldiers who wanted in turned to Brysen, drew their weapons . . . and threw them to the ground. "We don't want trouble," they pleaded. "We're not your enemy."

They knelt, covering their heads. Two even pressed themselves flat on the ground, like Altari supplicants begging for the sky's forgiveness. But faith born from fear never finds a strong perch in the soul, and when Brysen took a step toward them, they rose and scattered, scrambling on top of one another to run anywhere else in the fortress, pounding on barracks doors and hiding in outhouses. Some of them tried hiding where Redfists were already sheltering, and Brysen could hear the screams as one or the other was cut down.

It was a gruesome scene, and it echoed the story he and Kylee had read in the tattoos.

We fly and fly the same round range, he thought.

He had to get to Kylee. He prayed that he could free her and she could stop this. He prayed she was still alive and hadn't already become one of the terrible birds.

"Open the gate!" Brysen bellowed, trying to sound as terrifying as possible. His voice cracked. He was never very good at terrifying. "Open the gate and you'll be spared," he said, as if that were a promise he could make. To amplify the threat, he held up his fist as though calling a bird to it, but the guards behind the gate simply ran deeper into the keep.

"We won't get in this way," Grazim said. "This gate's triple-reinforced. We're gonna have to climb."

Brysen looked up into the brutal day. The nets had all fallen now, and the high walkways around the keep, which were normally posted with archers, were unguarded. All that stood between Brysen and entering the keep was a two-hundred-span vertical climb up the outer wall and a scrum of newborn ghost eagles shrieking and flapping and attacking one another as the hatchling attacked them.

As their bodies fell, some splashed into the baths, vanishing below the blood-black water, while others hit the stones and stretched like shadows at dusk. They lost all substance, leaving no flesh or skeleton behind—just patches of shadow. What would happen when it was done? he wondered. What would happen after it killed them all and found itself alone in the world?

Just then, the hatchling looked down at him for a moment.

Its screams stopped, and he saw something uncertain flicker through it. It didn't know what would become of it after it finished killing.

It had grown. It was now larger than an adult ghost eagle, but there was something different about it. The crown of black feathers on its head was still flecked with gold, and its feet were gold, and its eyes were still that uncanny human blue. Brysen realized it might not yet be fully lost to its own agony.

"Yeah," Brysen agreed with Grazim. "We have to climb."

"Before we go up there," Jowyn told Brysen, looking straight into his eye, "I want you to know I am still here."

Brysen sniffed. "Okay," he said, his voice scratchy from shouting.

"You don't have to have some historic destiny to be the best thing in my life," Jowyn told him. "Whatever happens up there, I need you to know that. You are enough just as you are."

"Yeah . . . ," Brysen said, as uncomfortable with Jowyn's sincerity as with his timing. "We need to climb a wall now, though, okay?"

Jowyn squeezed his shoulder, looked up at the high wall and then back at him. "I just needed you to know that."

Brysen swallowed. The bodies of ghost eagles were falling all around them; the shrieking of the ghost eagles was flooding their minds with every unpleasant memory they'd ever had and dead soldiers were turning into ghost eagles too quickly to count. Jowyn wasn't wrong to think something bad might happen. Things were . . . not great.

In case the worst did happen, Brysen didn't want to leave anything unsaid, either.

"I hope I make you as happy as you make me," he told Jowyn. It was a strange thing, talking about happiness right now, but he wasn't a poet, and that was all he could think to say. Happiness was the only armor he had against the eagles' screaming. It worked.

"I, for one, am going to keep thinking about a cold glass of sweetroot ale and your mother's chili bread," Nyck said, putting his hands on the wall beside Lyra's and beginning to climb.

"Boys, I'm really glad for you both." Grazim put a hand on each of their backs. "But if we don't get up the wall and stop this, your happiness will be worth less than the scuzz on the bottom of my boots."

"Just wondering," Jowyn asked. "Mocking us is keeping your mind clear, right?"

She smiled at him. "You're smarter than either of you look," she said, looking from them to the high, round wall of black stone. There were gaps in the grout between the stones, places for a toe or a fingertip. It would be precarious climbing.

"You gonna be able to do this without a harness?" Brysen asked her.

In answer, Grazim backed up and, with a running start, launched herself to grab a handhold higher up than she was tall, then braced herself with the rough soles of her boots. She pressed the entire width of her body against the wall, using the smallest handholds and a good deal of friction to keep herself up. She couldn't look down at him, but he was sure that if she could, she would stick out her tongue. She started moving up like a spider, and an old children's rhyme ran through Brysen's head.

The canary-killing spider went up the tower grout
Down came the hawk to snap the spider out
Out came the snake to scare the hawk away,
And so the deadly spider could climb another day

He had no doubt Grazim would make it to the top and would do what she could to free his sister when she got there. Of course, she had no special fondness for Nyall or Ma, so she wasn't likely to make them a priority unless Brysen was there to remind her to.

"You up for this?" he asked Jowyn, who was watching the carnage of the hatchling and the ghost eagles with his mouth half open. Brysen had to squeeze his arm to get his attention.

"Uh, yeah . . . yes," Jowyn said, going first so Brysen could watch his hands and toes a little easier. Brysen was the stronger climber between them, but he didn't want to take a chance with his depth perception. Even one mistake on this climb would be the only one he'd get to make.

The higher he went, the more cracks and fissures he found

in the wall of the tower, which made the climbing easier. His arms burned, while his legs were numb, but Grazim had nearly made it to the top, so he urged Jowyn to quicken his pace.

"I can go fast, or I can go carefully, Bry," Jowyn grunted at him. "Which would you prefer?"

"Never mind," Brysen said. "Carry on."

"Anyway, Bry, it's gonna take some time. Might as well take in the view," Jowyn called down as he picked his way to the next gap in the grout, lifted a leg to a stone that stuck out slightly farther than the ones around it, and used the strength of his legs to lift himself.

Brysen looked at the flex of Jowyn's leg, the way he pushed from the wall with his entire lower body kept taut, then thrust himself close against the stones again. "Not bad," Brysen smirked, glad for the distraction.

"I meant the view out there!" Jowyn yelled.

Brysen felt his cheeks flush but turned slightly to look over the outer wall of the Talon Fortress and down to the plateau. The sky was clear and empty all the way to the far mountains, all the way to the Sky Castle itself. He wondered what was happening there. Was the hatchling's cry loud enough to echo across the known world? Were the dead transforming there, too, flooding the sky with ghost eagles? Were they screeching enough terror into the rulers and the ruled for civil war to erupt, or was it life as usual, with the well-protected and the powerful living as though none of these distant battles concerned them at all?

In answer to his thoughts, the hatchling shrieked, and he saw the first shoots of a tree break from dark soil, a blood birch beginning. This was a memory. He didn't know if it was one of the ghost eagles' or the hatchling's or if it belonged to one of the unhatched eggs beneath the trees on the mountainside. But the vision moved quickly, as though time had sped up, and he watched the tree grow and strengthen and ooze its sap and feed generations of Owl Mother coveys. He even saw Jowyn. He saw a memory of young Jowyn drinking the sap, young Jowyn growing paler by sipping, not knowing the horror that planted the tree in the first place. He saw Jowyn, older, meeting him, saving his life time and again.

The hatchling shrieked. The ghost eagles shrieked with it, and Brysen understood what these images meant: The Sky Castle would fall.

Brysen had survived because of Jowyn, who was only able to save his life because of a tree that had grown generations ago to cover up a crime, and only because he had survived had he been able to bring the hatchling to life, so it could now avenge that crime.

The ghost eagles knew how to bide their time.

He craned his neck around to look for the terrible bird he

helped call into the world. Had it really known he would meet the boy above him one day? Had it all been planned, every tremor of his heart and the longing in his skin? And if that was the case, what choice did he ever have? Had he been tamed the moment he fell for Jowyn?

The hatchling looked at him, flapping in place midair. It let go of the great black eagle it held, let the bird fall into the baths, where it spread like spilled ink in the steaming water and vanished. Was it . . . laughing at him?

"On second thought," he called up to Jowyn, "you better try to climb careful *and* fast!"

"Like I said, I'm doing my—"

And that was when a ghost eagle sliced past them in the air, brushing Jowyn with its hardened flight feathers and, in surprise, Jowyn slipped.

Brysen felt dust fall onto his head before he looked up and saw Jowyn's legs dangling, both hands clinging like grappling hooks to a gap in the grout. He looked down at Brysen, the soot and dirt streaking the sweat on his pale face, and his mouth formed a surprised O. Brysen felt the invisible tether that tied them to each other stretch, a figure eight that looped around their hearts like an infinity sign. He felt it snap in half.

And then the love of Brysen's life fell, kicking out from the wall to avoid knocking off Brysen on his way down to the unfeeling stones below.

36

BRYSEN DIDN'T THINK AS JOWYN'S FLAILING LIMBS FLEW PAST HIM; he let go of the wall with one hand and reached out to grab the boy, which of course wasn't possible. The attempt threw off his weight, and he slipped and slid down three body-lengths of stone, scraping the side of his face and both his palms before catching himself.

"NO!" he yelled, as if he could scold gravity for taking Jowyn from him, and then, with the last breath he had before Jowyn's body smashed into pulp—the last breath before breathing became as pointless for him as it was impossible for Jowyn—he shouted at the birds above him in his own plain language. "NOT HIM!"

And then he snapped out a command, doubting it would work but needing it to anyway. "*Li-li!*" he said, meaning *trade*. What he meant, with every beat left in his heart and every thought left in his mind was, *Take me instead. Save him.*

The hatchling's black-feathered head snapped toward him, its blue eyes locking on the falling body, and then it dove, feathers gleaming slightly more gold than black. With one foot, it caught Jowyn just before his skull cracked on the rocks, and it tossed him like a child's doll over its head so it could flap up beneath him and carry him on its back.

"Hold on!" Brysen yelled.

"Yeah!" Jowyn yelled back. "I got that part!"

The huge bird flew straight up the wall and snagged Brysen by the arm, wrapping its great taloned claw over his shoulder and yanking him away, into open air. He had to grip its foot and ankle with both hands to keep his arm from being pulled out of its socket.

"Ahh!" he managed to yell, really hoping he hadn't just peed a little. He'd asked for a trade; if the bird was obeying him, then he was likely to drop any moment.

"Jowyn, no matter what," he said, "I think you—"

But the bird screeched, and Brysen remembered every time his hands had ever touched Jowyn's, every dirty joke he'd ever laughed at, every breath of air they'd ever shared when their lips were close, and he knew it wasn't going to drop him.

Still rising, the black-and-gold bird snatched Grazim by the back of her shirt with its other foot, lifting her up and over the parapet and onto the archers' walk. All three of them tumbled onto the hard stones, bruised but very much alive.

The bird landed on the walkway behind Brysen, standing twice his height and looking down, head cocked to the side. Its feathers were mostly golden now, and Brysen put a hand above his head to touch its heaving chest.

"Thank you," he told it. "But why?"

The golden bird let out a small sound, like a chirp. He didn't understand it. Then again, maybe he didn't need to. He'd needed help and he got it, and that just might have to be enough.

"Where's Kylee?" Nyck asked, panting as he pulled himself up onto the ledge, then looked at the huge golden bird. "Thanks for the ride, by the way," he told it as he helped Lyra up. The bird swung its head toward him, and Nyck raised his hands. "Just kidding!"

Two dozen black eagles circled above them, screeching, crying out for their own destruction. The hatchling looked up at them, some of its feather taking a darker tint.

Brysen felt a churning in his gut; the hatchling was still

conflicted. It wanted to finish what it had begun, but it felt something new now, something that wasn't destruction. It wanted more of that, too.

"Stay," he urged it. "Sing the harder song."

"Prrrpt," it let out, a tiny chirp that showed Brysen images of his Shara, the gray-and-brown goshawk, cradled in his arms. Shara falling from his fist and getting tangled in her leash until he could right her again. Shara preening and fluffing her feathers as she settled to perch at the foot of his bed. He smiled at the huge bird, and he felt a tear trace a straight line down his cheek. He'd never *not* grieve for his lost bird. He'd never not grieve for the childhood of wounds he'd endured, or for all the pain his quest and this war had caused. But he could grieve while living.

The ghost eagles above screamed down at him, trying to shatter his calm, but they could not provoke him or the hatchling. He didn't need their voices anymore.

They didn't want to grieve.

They wanted death. They wanted destruction, his and theirs, a fury of feathers and blood that would erase the world. He would not give it to them.

But Kyrg Birgund would.

The kyrg stood with two of his soldiers under a stone archway that led inside the keep, their ears all stuffed with wax. Each held a blade to a hostage's throat: Nyall was at

Birgund's left, Ma at his right, and Kylee was held firm in his own large hands. A third soldier came forward, sword drawn, but hands shaking. Bloodshot terror loomed in all the soldiers' eyes.

"What now?" Brysen yelled in his direction, hoping his voice was loud enough to get through the wax. The huge bird behind him spread its wings, and the feathers now alternated black and gold on the underside. Its legs bent as it tucked its wings again, preparing to launch. It held, though, waiting for Brysen. It *wanted* to be commanded.

He met his sister's eyes, shook his head no. He hoped she understood. They could not kill their way out of this. Brysen knew what it was like to have your best intentions shredded by your worst impulses; how your past pain called you to its fist over and over again, no matter how hard you tried to break free. The hatchling and the ghost eagles were still caught in that cycle.

But the hatchling wasn't waiting for Brysen's command anymore. It was waiting for Kylee's.

Kylee, however, wasn't the first to speak.

"Enough of this," Grazim said. "Release my friend."

Birgund stared her down. "Call off this bird."

"It's not my place," Grazim said, then looked at the ghost eagle, frowning in thought. "Or maybe it is . . ."

"Grazim, careful," Brysen urged, but she snapped out a command.

"*Bost!*" *Release.* The hatchling sprang off the parapet, shoot-ing straight for Kylee. Kyrg Birgund dove to the floor and rolled, tossing Kylee away and losing his blade. The third guard tried to catch her again, but the hatchling knocked him aside so hard he cracked his head on the stone wall and fell still.

The hatchling cried, its feathers blackening, and the corpse began to transform.

"Why did you do that?" Brysen yelled at her.

"The moment demanded it," Grazim replied, rushing to Kylee's side to help her up.

The hatchling turned on the two guards holding Nyall and his ma. "Leave them," Brysen shouted, trying to warn the sol-diers to let their hostages go, but they couldn't hear with the wax in their ears. They were still holding Nyall and Ma when their heads hit the ground, disconnected from their necks. Their bodies began transforming as well. Nyall grabbed Ma and pulled her into the relative safety of a corner.

Birgund fled into the dark hallways of the keep, and the hatchling folded its wings and slipped right in after him. The newly created ghost eagles followed, shrieking, longing for the hatchling to destroy them.

Brysen rushed to where Grazim was helping Kylee.

"Are you okay?" he asked his sister. Grazim had a hand on her neck, which bled from where the blade dug in, but it was just a surface wound; her throat hadn't been cut. He grabbed the knife that Birgund dropped and cut a piece of fabric from the bottom of his tunic, then tied it around Kylee's neck as a bandage.

"That is *so* not clean," she said, laughing and hugging him.

"Call them off," he told Grazim. Then to Kylee, he pleaded, "We have to call them off. No more killing. It only makes things worse."

Kylee shook her head. "We can let them go a little longer."

"What?" Brysen leaned back. "How can you say that after what's happened?"

"That thing is destroying the ghost eagles," she said. "We should let it finish."

"It'll never be finished," he replied. "That hatchling is going to create more ghost eagles than it destroys. We have to get it to stop."

"Why do you think I can do that?" Kylee asked him, and he hesitated. He looked at her, at her wounded neck and matted dark hair, her blue eyes rimmed red with exhaustion.

"Because you're the best person I know," he told her. "And if you can't do it, it can't be done."

She smiled slightly. "That's the nicest thing you've ever said about me."

"It's also the truest," he said.

KYLEE

A MOUTH TO SPEAK

37

ALL HER LIFE, KYLEE HAD WANTED THE POWER TO CONTROL WHAT happened to her and her family. She tried to manage everything and, more often than not, failed. Now she had real power, and she had no idea what to do with it.

Her brother was looking at her like she had all the answers. Grazim, who took a hell of risk to free her, was, too. And there was her ma, her forehead pressed to the floor, praying for Kylee, too. Nyck and Lyra stood ready to do what she told them, if she had any orders to give.

And then there was Nyall. Sweet Nyall, who'd been caught up with her since they first met and had done little but suffer for it. She hugged him, and he smiled as if he hadn't just been hauled across the world by giant zombie birds and held hostage by an entire army.

"Thanks for coming to get me," he told her.

"No problem," she said. "Now I need a favor."

"Anything," he told her.

"Look after this crew." She gestured at Brysen and the rest. "I've got to go after those birds and . . . talk them down." She picked up the old black-talon blade from where it lay on the ground. Brysen frowned at her. "In case some of the people I run into aren't about talking."

"You can't kill anyone," Brysen said. "You've seen what happens to them."

"Sometimes having a blade keeps you from needing to use it," she said.

"And sometimes having one convinces you that you need it," he replied.

"I'll do my best," she told him as she turned toward the corridor. Nyall scooped up a knife from one of the dead soldiers and walked to Kylee's side.

"Sorry," he said. "I'm not losing you again. Where you go, I go. Your fight is my fight."

She reached up and squeezed his shoulder. "It's really good to see you again," she told him. "I'm sorry for what you've been through for me."

He squeezed her fingers where they rested on his

shoulder, looking down into her eyes. "No apology needed," he said. "I'd do it again in a heartbeat." Then he paused and sucked his teeth. "Except the getting kidnapped by giant birds part. That was not the best day I've ever had." She laughed at his gift for understatement. "Anyway, when this is over and you're safe, it'll have been worth it. But you do owe me an ale at the Broken Jess . . . or whatever gets built in its place."

"Deal," she agreed. She knew Nyall loved her, and she felt almost as close to him as she did to her brother—but without all the weight of worry. She appreciated that he always tried to be someone she didn't have to worry about. She hated that she was about to put him in danger again, but there was no one she'd rather have at her side in a fight. She was not going to talk him out of coming with her.

"Same," Nyck announced, and Lyra stood with him. "We go where you go."

They all flinched as a scream and a ghost eagle's shriek issued from deep inside the tower.

Grazim stepped up beside the battle boys. "We've come this far together. Can't let you get all the glory."

Kylee appreciated the loyalty. She felt like she did on the morning when, together, they'd rushed into the Mutes: overwhelmed with love for this motley flock of friends who risked everything for one another and for a cause bigger than any of them. "I don't know how much glory there will be," she told them. "But we might just save humanity."

Nyck shrugged, and Grazim rolled her eyes.

"Sometimes you're as dumb as your brother," Grazim said.

"Hey!" Brysen objected.

"We're not doing this for humanity," Grazim told her.

"We're doing this for you," Nyall said.

Kylee bit her lip. Her eyes swelled with tears. She would do whatever was necessary to keep these people safe.

"Stay behind me," she said, when suddenly, soldiers and Redfists rushed at them from every doorway, blocking every path except the archers' walkway and the long fall off it. With the ghost eagles and the hatchling somewhere in the keep, there was no help to call upon here.

"Drop your weapons and you'll be spared!" Kylee bluffed.

The soldiers didn't make any move to drop their weapons. Their eyes were glazed, their hands shaking. The ghost eagles were in their heads, and they had no intention of backing down.

"You don't have to do this," she urged them, leaving her knife sheathed, showing her empty hands. "We can end this right now. All we have to do is *not* fight each other."

Somewhere, another ghost eagle shrieked, and the soldiers of Uztar charged forward.

"*Oh, scuzz*," Kylee whispered as the first of their blades

lunged for her, forcing her to dodge and draw her knife in self defense. She parried the next strike, which hit with enough force to send a ripple of pain up her arm. The impact nearly tore her shoulder out of its socket, and the knife flew out of her hand. She was basically useless in close combat, and the next swing of the soldier's blade would take off her head. She leaned back just in time and felt wind whistle past the tip of her nose.

"REEEEEEE," a ghost eagle cried, and she pictured her friends being slaughtered all around her, but she stayed focused, didn't let fear provoke her. She would dodge and defend but would not attack.

The soldiers didn't feel the same. Another charge came.

Nyall knocked her out of the way and slashed at the soldier until they retreated, then spun on another, parrying their sword away in a burst of sparks. He caught a Redfist in the chest with a long-legged roundhouse kick, slamming him into two soldiers who'd charged forward. Nyck and Lyra rushed into the fray and held their own. The Uztari and the Redfists hadn't trained together, so their attacks were chaotic; they kept getting in each other's way, and that bought Kylee time to pick up her knife from the floor and get back to her feet.

"Don't kill anyone!" she commanded. "Just hold them off as best you can."

Grazim had retreated outside and was calling with her fist

raised, trying to summon the tailor's hawk, but the hatchling and the ghost eagles had scared it and every bird clear out of the sky.

"That one!"

One of the soldiers pointed at Grazim, and a Redfist raised a spear to throw. Brysen and Jowyn were the only ones close enough to intervene.

"Bry!" Kylee warned, and both boys leapt together to tackle the assailant. They held the Redfist down by the arms. The Redfist dug their teeth into Brysen's forearm, and he screamed. Kylee had the urge to charge over and slit the scuzzard's throat while they were held down, but she dismissed the gruesome urge. She felt strong, parsing the ghost eagles' bloodlust from her own. She'd never felt more in control. Her anger was a tool that belonged to her, not them.

Another soldier stepped into her path, and she had to block his sword as it swung for her side. She stepped close so he couldn't get leverage with the long blade, raising her knee hard and doubling the man over when she connected with his groin. She was about to knock him down when Nyall shouted a warning. A second soldier charged, swinging a mace straight for her skull. She ducked the blow, and the mace swung wildly, crashing across the incapacitated soldier's face, sprawling him out in his own blood.

The blood began to congeal even as it poured out of him, started to spread across his skin and turn feathery. His limbs changed shape, his face stretching into a beak.

The soldier with the mace froze, shocked at having brained his own comrade, horrified at what was happening to him. In a moment there would be an enraged ghost eagle among them, and the bloodshed would get a lot worse.

Somewhere from within the deep recesses of the keep, Kylee heard the echo of the hatchling's wrathful shriek and the answering cries of the ghost eagles. They were feasting.

Nyall met Kylee's eyes just as he drove his blade through the shocked soldier's heart.

"No!" she yelled, but a killing glee was blazing out of him that made her skin crawl. This wasn't Nyall. He'd never smiled at violence, not even when it was necessary. The ghost eagles were in his head now, and he was not at all in control.

"Nyall," she said, trying to call him back to himself. And then, as a Redfist lunged behind him, she shouted, "NYALL!"

"REEEEEE!" the new-formed ghost eagle cried, even as the one Nyall created began to rise.

Nyall half turned, but not in time. A blade dragged across his throat, and a thin red line beaded on his stubbly neck, then poured down his chest. His eyes glazed, but he never looked away from Kylee as he fell first to his knees, then forward onto his face.

Kylee looked up at the Redfist who had done it. He was already charging her.

"*Talorum!*" she screamed, calling the two new ghost eagles with as much pain and fury as she ever had before. They launched themselves at Nyall's killer and dragged him into the sky, throwing him over the wall.

Kylee turned and thrust her blade clear through the neck of a soldier who'd been sneaking up behind her. Then she spun without slowing down and slashed the knife across another soldier's face before driving it down through the skull of a third with all the force her arms had.

"Kylee!" her brother called from somewhere far away, and she wanted to answer him, but her voice was lost in the scream of the new ghost eagles being born all around her.

"REEEEE!" they yelled, and the soldiers and Redfists ran, scrambling to escape the roof now that Kylee's wrath was unleashed. Most of them ran for the door Kyrg Birgund had taken, though one of them, in a panic, ran straight off the edge, realizing too late that there were no more nets to catch him.

He screamed on the way down, and the ghost eagle shrieked with him, but Kylee didn't feel any joy or righteousness in her rage.

As the ghost eagle screamed, she saw what it couldn't help but show her, and both she and it were powerless against the memories that mantled over them.

38

SHE EXPECTED TO SEE NYALL IN HER MIND, TO SEE SOME MEMORY OF their friendship that would drive her on to do what the ghost eagles longed for anyway, but instead she saw two people she didn't know.

An older couple, holding hands at a parade ground in the Sky Castle. They were in a crowd, watching soldiers march past. Uztari soldiers. They felt some kind of sadness and anxiety and pride, and Kylee felt it with them.

What is this? she wondered. *Who are they?*

And there, in the phalanx, one soldier looked up at the couple, smiling toward his mothers, and Kylee felt their hands squeeze together, fingers interlaced. She felt nothing but love, pure and absolute love, just like she felt for her brother. Just like Nyall felt for her. She knew it all at once, felt their feelings and her own, as if memory, time, and people were all one beam of light refracted through a single crystal, breaking off into countless streams of color.

The face smiling at the older couple was the same pale face staring blankly up at Kylee from the floor. She had just driven a knife through hard bone and into his brain. In her mind, the older couple smiled and waved, so proud.

"No . . . ," she whispered. "Don't show me that . . ."

"REEEEEE!" the ghost eagles all around called, and she saw the Redfist who killed Nyall, saw the warrior when she was part of the Kartami army, saw her on the night before they attacked the Six Villages, when she lay beside her husband and whispered of plans for after the war was won. She saw another soldier—the person whose face she'd slashed—kissing their children good-bye in the Sky Castle. She saw another soldier—the one who'd fallen from the parapet—saw him set his best friend's body out for a sky burial only a few days after the ghost eagles returned, then saw him look up and pray for the vultures to come, but the birds were all too frightened and the body rotted in the sun, and the soldier cursed Kylee and Brysen by name.

"Stop it!" she yelled. "I don't want to know them!"

But it was too late. She felt their stories rush through her, felt their entire lives in the way the ghost eagles did, and she felt the moment they were each cut short by her blade. The world was full of life and death, and it was too much to feel it all, too much to be responsible for any of it. "Stop it!" she yelled again, banging the sides of her head. "I don't want this. I don't want this!"

"REEEEEE!" she heard. But the cry wasn't from the ghost eagle nearest her; it was the hatchling. She looked up to see the huge black bird fly back in through the doorway, holding Kyrg Birgund in its talons, and dump the injured general onto the ground so that he rolled in front of her. A convocation of ghost eagles fluttered in behind the hatchling, cawing and crying and trying to draw its attention back to them, to end their agony, but the hatchling simply watched Kylee, waiting to see what she would do.

Now she saw Nyall alive in her mind even as she looked over at his dead body, which lay next to the kyrg. His delicate mouth and nose had begun transforming into the beak of a ghost eagle. His face sprouted feathers and his eyes blackened. His long arms were thickening into broad wings. She wanted to throw up; she wanted to embrace him; she wanted this horror to end.

Beside Nyall's transforming body, Birgund's face was bloody, his eyes wide with grim anticipation.

"Kylee," Brysen pleaded, again sounding very far away, and she saw him but not as he was now.

Instead she saw Brysen as a child in their home, his expression terrified because a boy was singing outside their window. She was curled under a moth-eaten blanket too thin even for the warmer seasons of the year. She poked one finger through a moth hole, confirming. It felt as real as it had in life.

"I told you we didn't have rats," she whispered.

"Shhhhhh . . . ," her brother hissed, but not at her. He popped his head out the window. "SHHHHH . . . he'll hear you!"

Kylee tensed in her bed as their father's footsteps thumped toward their alcove.

"He's coming!" Kylee whisper-shouted at Brysen. "Get under the covers!"

How old was she here? How long ago was this?

As their father swept aside the curtain that separated their sleeping nook from the main room, Kylee jumped out of bed and stood at the window, like she'd been there the whole time. She saw Nyall below, grinning. He'd been singing a song to her, trying to woo her in a way he thought was charming. He was still short and smooth-cheeked, and they were at the age when a lot of people are just beginning to have new kinds of feelings for each other. It was only later that Kylee realized she didn't have those sorts of feelings at all.

It took a moment for Nyall's gladness at seeing her to register that something was wrong, and another moment before she felt her father's heavy hand yank her back from the window. He stuck out his head and saw Nyall and spat curses at him, told him to get out of there before he got his brains bashed in, and the little boy with the smooth dark skin and the crown of thick, dark hair went running from their yard, racing back to the Six Villages like a ghost eagle was chasing him.

How little they knew then of the ghost eagles or of being chased by horrors. How little Nyall knew of the horrors still to come.

"I'm sorry, Da," Kylee pleaded with her father. His scruffy blond hair was matted from sleep and his thick blond beard held streaks of green spittle. "I didn't mean to wake you," she tried.

"Shut it," he snarled, and yanked the blanket off Brysen, revealing the small boy, still with black hair, staring up at him, wide-eyed and wide awake. "I know it was this scuzzing sapling that songbird was singing for."

"No," Kylee told him, truthfully. "It was me. Nyall has this . . . crush . . ."

"No-good hummingbird-feeder. Little rat-catcher. Little broke-backed sparrow," their father muttered curses at Brysen, completely ignoring Kylee. He dragged Brysen from bed and took the six-talon whip from the wall above Brysen's pallet, tearing off her brother's raggedy shirt with one hand, pulling so hard the fabric at the neck choked him.

Somewhere in the high mountains over their house, she thought she heard the distant cry of a ghost eagle, but that had been when she still thought they were a myth. And the whip sliced fresh lines of crimson across her brother's bare, golden back.

I'm gonna kill him one day, Kylee thought, or remembered thinking. *He never listens to me! I'll make him listen.*

And then she was back in the keep, standing over the cowering kyrg, seeing her oldest friend reborn in black feathers and unending rage, remembering the moment her own rage truly began, the moment the ghost eagle first heard her, when it seemed like no one else would.

She was angry that her father hurt her brother, but she was angrier still that he hadn't listened to her. Angry that Nyall hadn't listened when she told him not to come singing at her window. Angry at her ma for covering her ears when Brysen cried.

She'd killed her father with the ghost eagle and gotten Nyall killed, too, but she hadn't done the one thing she'd always longed for, the one thing the ghost eagles wanted without even knowing it, what they had longed for in spite of themselves.

Killing was easy, she realized. Dying, too. Even the dumbest birds of prey could kill, and they all died eventually, but there was one thing she could do that they never could.

"*Shessele!*" she commanded the ghost eagles as forcefully as she could, and they obeyed, calming, waiting. "Get up!" she ordered the kyrg, sheathing her knife.

"Kylee?" Brysen asked her, and he sounded closer now. She was back on top of the keep, present in this moment again and clear in her head. Brysen left Jowyn to hold down a Redfist alone. The man was so scared, he wasn't moving a muscle anyway. "What are you doing?" Brysen said.

"Get ready," she told him, wiping her eyes, which she knew were red and puffy now. She addressed everyone. "All of you, get ready. You're going to have to trust me. This is going to be scary."

"What . . . what are you doing?" Brysen asked again.

"We're going to the Sky Castle," Kylee said. "And when we get there, we're going to make them listen."

"Who?" Brysen wondered.

"Everyone," Kylee said. "Them. Us. The flock. It's the one thing we haven't done. We haven't listened."

39

SHE BARKED A COMMAND AT THE TWO DOZEN GHOST EAGLES STANDING around them and at the giant black-feathered hatchling looming in the center of the flock. She'd never felt more in command of the Hollow Tongue as she did in that moment. She'd also never been more afraid of what would happen if they chose not to obey her.

"*Karik*," she said, which meant *carry*, and she climbed onto the huge black hatchling's back and gripped its firm feathers in both hands. It spread its wings and bent its legs, preparing to launch into the air.

"Will they obey us?" Nyck asked, warily looking at the ghost eagles, his face streaked with tears. He was searching the birds' faces, trying to tell which had been Nyall, but this kind of death didn't work like that. They were all the same. They were all a collection of conflicting urges, unfulfilled dreams, and voices silenced too soon. They were not who they had been any more than an echo of a question is its answer.

"Climb on or get carried," she said. "They're leaving that choice to you."

Brysen took Jowyn by the hand and led him to the nearest ghost eagle. Despite what she knew—that these birds weren't individuals; that what they became was not what they had been—she hoped it was Nyall they were now climbing on. Even his echo would never harm his friends. Brysen helped Jowyn climb onto the eagle's back before pulling himself up behind him.

"We trust this?" Jowyn asked.

"I trust her," Brysen said, looking at his sister.

Grazim climbed onto the back of another ghost eagle by herself, whispering the words for *calm* and *steady* and *us* and anything else that might keep a bird of prey from attacking a falconer. Kylee didn't even smirk. The bird might not heed Grazim's command, but that didn't mean it wasn't worth trying. Maybe Grazim's words would work to calm her own frightened heart, if not the eagle's.

Nyck and Lyra hesitated, but neither wanted to look like

they were scared, so together they climbed onto one of the other ghost eagles, scrambling to be the first person sitting. The huge bird looked at Kylee, and she thought for a moment it was rolling its great black eyes at the battle boys' half-baked bravado. Its look darted up and down the hatchling's body, though, not Kylee's, and she felt a pang of doubt, but the doubt wasn't hers and it wasn't about her plan. It belonged to the ghost eagles.

They were still afraid of the hatchling they'd helped create. It destroyed most of them and created more, and they weren't sure what they wanted from it. It was golden again, and this was something new to all the ghost eagles. This was the change the birds both longed for and feared.

"Ma?" Kylee asked, interrupting her mother's quiet prayers. "We can't leave you here."

Her mother stood. She looked up at Kylee, sitting on the back of the giant golden hatchling, and smiled.

"*Karik.*" Ma repeated the word Kylee used, but this was not a command—it was an offer. She was letting her daughter's wishes carry her. The nearest ghost eagle lowered itself so she could climb on. Brysen and Kylee shared a look. Their ma, it seemed, still had surprises left in her.

One of the great black birds took a few steps across the ground, its large talons clicking on stone, and it loomed over Kyrg Birgund. He was playing dead, but his chest still rose and fell, and he was slightly closer to one of the doorways leading back into the keep than he had been before. The fool was trying to sneak away.

"Here we go," Kylee said aloud, and then, with a touch of force, she repeated, "*Karik!*"

The hatchling launched from the ground just as Kyrg Birgund got to his feet and tried to run through the door. The golden bird caught him in its talons, driving them into his shoulders. He screamed, and the hatchling lifted him, carrying him and Kylee as it flapped and rose toward the clouds, high above the fortress walls and the last remnants of the fearful armies below. They soared over the wild edge of the mountains, heading across the plains with the sunset at their right, to the west, and the Sky Castle straight ahead.

Behind her, all the ghost eagles flew in formation, like geese migrating across a cooling sky. At one point the hatchling flapped higher than mountain range, and Kylee saw fields of ice and glaciers beyond the plateau: the Frozen Lands. The world from which her people had come. There was a haze hanging above it that blended with the vast, white snow, and she couldn't make out much of the shrouded landscape, save for the tiniest clouds of what might've been flocks of distant birds. Eventually she lost sight of them and turned her attention back to the world she knew, the craggy landscape below.

The hatchling bent its wings to dive, sweeping along steep

slopes and high ridges, racing for the flat plains. Kylee gripped its neck tight and felt a rush of speed that tingled against her skin. Moisture from the clouds beaded on her skin, dampened her hair, and prickled her skin. The air whistled as it whipped through the hatchling's hard black feathers. Her stomach lurched into her throat when the bird screeched and dove again, dropping with tucked wings toward solid rock. She hugged its neck, pressing her face into its feathers. Each feather's filaments felt like pins against her body, but she held on and felt her stomach swoop as the hatchling turned and beat its wings, rising once more on a high breeze perfect for gliding.

She heard a distant whoop and looked over her shoulder to see Nyck grinning, clutching the ghost eagle's neck, but she had to face forward again. The hatchling's body wobbled on the wind, and the motion was dizzying.

She looked down as the browns and grays and whites of the mountains gave way to the greens and yellows of the plains. She saw the muddy, pale brown waters of the Necklace and with her eyes traced it to the Six Villages, which still stood, miraculously, where she'd left them. She could see vast swaths of her hometown in ruins—but not everywhere—and she could see people scuttling, small as ants from this height but going about the business of living just the same. She began to imagine a world after all this, a future. She'd been in survival mode for so long that she hadn't taken time to consider what would come next. Would the Council of Forty resist her? Would she have them destroyed or remade? Once the truth of Uztar was widely known, would the Altari and Uztari be able to make peace with each other? Would they demand some kind of justice? Who would decide what that justice looked like?

And most important: Would the ghost eagles be free from the pain that created them? Would humanity be forgiven?

What if I'm wrong? she thought. *What if all this is for nothing and the killing begins again the moment we arrive? What if I'm still just a fool for trusting their fury?*

The hatchling's feathers seemed to darken at her thoughts, and she felt its flight wobble. It began to drop—not like a falcon diving but like a sparrow struck by a falcon, falling from the sky. Its whole body turned sideways as it plummeted, and she had to hug it harder to hang on, her legs flailing over its limp wing.

"Kylee!" her brother shouted from somewhere above.

"I'm sorry!" she yelled, not to him but to the hatchling. "I'm not thinking clearly!"

But, of course, the bird was thinking whatever she was thinking. Their emotions were bound to each other, and when she began to doubt, so did the bird.

As the ground rose to meet her, she saw jagged boulders

that looked like grinding stones for making flour. She imagined her and the hatchling's bodies powdered to bonemeal and wet with blood. She imagined the ghost eagles behind her following, diving to their own deaths, their human passengers made victims of her despair.

"AHHH!" Birgund shouted. She'd forgotten he was even there. The hatchling hadn't let go of him, at least, and his scream reminded her that she had work to do. There was still a bond between her and the hatchling; she had to trust there was a reason for it. She had to have faith in herself, the same faith everyone else had in her.

When this is over and you're safe again, it'll have been worth it. That's what Nyall said. He wouldn't want her to fall. If she couldn't think of a reason to keep going for herself, maybe his memory was enough reason for now. Someone had to tell his part in this story, too.

The hatchling caught itself, opened its wings once more, and flattened its body against the wind, flapping to gain new height. Kylee pulled herself forward so her face was beside its head.

"Don't ever do that to me again," she whispered. The huge bird flapped higher, rejoining the group, and they broke through a heavy cloud bank, rising above to where the air was thin and cold.

The flight smoothed out, time melted into an endless

present. Kylee felt like there was no before or after, only the wind and the air and the thrill of flying. She had no idea how long it had been when the towers of the Sky Castle suddenly peeked through the clouds, and the hatchling shrieked, ending their shared reverie. It dove for the top of a central structure at the heart of the castle: the Council's tower, where Kyrg Bardu held court over the Council of Forty.

The others still flew behind her, still in formation. No one else would die today because she couldn't control the predators she'd called from history's nightmares. She had no intention of killing the people of Uztar's great Sky Castle. She was only trying to wake them up.

However, she realized that, if they resisted, she might not be able to stop the carnage that would follow. The choice, however, would be theirs.

40

THE DARK-FEATHERED FLEET SWEPT ONCE OVER THE SKY CASTLE, shrieking their arrival, while Kylee hovered with the great golden hatchling above the city center. Nets were still strung over streets and courtyards, secured to the tops of guard towers, palace spires, warehouse roofs, and even high burial stones. Funeral rites, it seemed, were on hold during the ghost eagles' siege. Kylee shuddered to think of the number of stockpiled corpses and what might happen if the hatchling sang them into furious new ghost eagles.

"Time to sing a different song," she whispered, and gripped the hatchling's feathers tighter as it bent its wings and dove for the nets covering the Council's tower. There was no going back now.

The hatchling dropped Kyrg Birgund from its grip, letting him roll, screaming, over the rough netting. With both feet free, the hatchling's talons then tore open the net as though it was soft as a mouse's skin. Kyrg Birgund fell through, and the hatchling dove after him, snatching him from the air and tossing him, semi-conscious, on a high veranda atop the Council's tower, before circling once and landing beside him.

The tower was quiet, as were the streets below. The entire city had fallen silent in awe and fear of Kylee and her flock. Having the entire center of Uztari civilization in breathless wonder at her power was a good feeling for a Six Village girl. She understood the hunger some rulers had, the kind of hunger that made them do unthinkable things. Power was like hunter's leaf; the more you have, the more you want.

It was that very hunger that led her ancestors to massacre the First Falconers. It was that very hunger that led everyone—from the kyrgs to the Owl Mothers to the Redfist veterans of the Kartami war—to betray, fight, and kill one another over it.

The hardest part of training a falcon is teaching it to release its catch. The birds do the work, after all, and they expect to eat their prey. Kylee had no doubt that teaching the rulers of

Uztar to let go of their hoarded power would be just as difficult. But they would have to begin sharing power for any possibility of a future. She could try to force them herself, but
that would only incite more violence. The cycle would begin
again.

The other eagles swooped in soon after Kylee, their passengers dismounting with shaky legs.

The huge birds stood by, waiting for Kyleee's next instruc-
tion. There were dozens, all of them taller than any of her
friends, and yet they all looked minuscule compared to the
golden hatchling; it stood taller than Kylee and Brysen would if
one stood on the other's shoulders. Kylee wanted to keep it near
her now, in case the Council had some tricks left. Desperation
could make even a hen attack a wolf if it had no other choice.

"*Avakhoo*," she commanded the remaining ghost eagles.

The ghost eagles hesitated. The word meant *community*, and
Kylee focused her thoughts on the community she meant: the
citizens of the Sky Castle, the rulers of Uztar, the powerful
and the powerless. She wanted all of them. She wanted everyone in the city brought to the large plaza in front of the tower
below the veranda. She wouldn't operate in shadows; she had
promised the ghost eagles their story would be heard, and she
meant for everyone to hear it.

Still the ghost eagles were confused, but Grazim understood. She stepped to Kylee's side.

"There are kestrels that hunt in packs," she said. "They're the only bird of prey that hunts cooperatively. They herd their prey."

"Herding," Kylee said. The ghost eagles herded Kylee and her brother where they wanted them—to the Talon Fortress, to the destiny they thought they chose. They understood herding.

"The word is *ka-see*," Grazim told her.

Kylee smiled at her friend. "You want to try it?" she asked.

"They . . ." Grazim's cheeks flushed pink. "I'm not sure they'll listen to me."

"We're all going to have to learn to listen in new ways," Kylee said. "Try."

Grazim squared her shoulders, puffed out her chest. "*Ka-see*," she tried. The ghost eagles turned their heads sideways, dipping their faces up and down.

"Try again," Kylee said. "You want to rule here in the Sky Castle, right? This is your chance. Gather the people."

Grazim took a deep breath and let it out slowly. She closed her eyes. Kylee watched her face transform with the focus of it, with clear intention. Grazim had always been a girl who knew what she wanted; she just lost her way a bit. She chased power when she thought it could prove her worth as an Altari, and now that she knew the entire idea of Altari and Uztari was a lie, she had to find a new outlet for her ambition, a new purpose for herself. Kylee saw it happen in the flutter of her eyelids: the moment she knew, completely, who she wanted to be in this world.

"*Ka-see!*" Grazim commanded, and the ghost eagles bent their legs and flew, spreading out and diving into the streets of the Sky Castle, weaving among statues of ancient falconers, landing in courtyards to shriek into the minds of all who could hear and send them running from their homes. They herded the people, and before long, a great crowd was assembled in the plaza at the base of the tower and growing larger by the moment. The ghost eagles swept the city and brought every able body to stand in awe of the giant black-and-gold hatchling on the tower above them.

"What now?" Grazim asked Kylee. Brysen peeked over the edge at the huge crowd, then pulled himself back.

"Yeah," he asked. "What do you plan to do with all these people?"

Kylee cleared her throat. "Now we get the Council. *Tatakh*," she commanded, and a half dozen ghost eagles entered the tower on foot, heads bobbing, ducking themselves low to pass through the human-size doorways. It wasn't long before she heard shouts and objections and pleas, and then the birds were back, three walking in front, three behind, and between them were Kyrg Bardu and Yves Tamir.

"Where's the Council?" Kylee demanded.

"You're looking at it," Kyrg Bardu responded, defiant. She crossed her arms and scowled at Kylee.

"Prrpt," chirped one of the ghost eagles, and Kylee saw what happened, what the kyrg had loosed in the council room. She didn't merely see it, though; she could hear the screams, smell the blood. She even felt fingernails scraping along the heavy wooden door as desperate people tried to escape. That little chirp bore witness to the massacre.

Kylee's stomach turned, and she looked at Bardu and Yves with revulsion. They were coldhearted killers. They were usurpers and criminals. She should throw them from the tower immediately.

"Kylee, don't," Brysen urged her, standing back with Jowyn, holding his hand. "We can't keep repeating the same mistakes."

"Some people don't deserve mercy," Kylee said.

"That's when it's most needed," Brysen answered.

The ghost eagles were keen. The hatchling's crown of feathers darkened, and when it fluffed its feathers, some of them gleamed gold as the sun, some black as moonless midnight. It stood behind Kylee and lowered its head so its beak rested on her shoulder, staring at Yves, waiting for a command to attack.

"Don't pretend you grieve for the Council," Yves Tamir sneered. "They'd have happily murdered you and everyone you ever loved."

"Be that as it may, you had no right to take their lives." Kylee saw Kyrg Bardu take a step away from Yves, distancing herself from the gangster, as if she knew what was about to happen. Kylee was trying to resist, though. She didn't want to kill anyone else. "You're murderers."

"So you're judging us?" Yves scoffed. "You have more blood on your hands than anyone else alive. I will not be judged by *you*."

"I'm *trying* to make amends," Kylee said. "I'm trying to change."

"And I'm wise enough to know how the world works. Killers kill, and you are a killer," Yves said. "You can't change that and I've no interest in your so-called amends."

"I see that," Kylee said. Just beside her ear she could feel the hatchling's breath. Her senses were sharp; her heart beat in rapid time with the huge bird's, too fast by far. Its feathers blackened, and she saw through its eyes as Yves Tamir slipped a small throwing knife from the sleeve of her tunic. Kylee sighed and then added simply: "*Kraas.*"

The hatchling leapt over Kylee with one flex of its legs, opened its black wings and raised its feet, snatching Yves Tamir off the ground with such force, her throwing knife seemed to hover in the air a moment before clattering harmlessly onto the stones. Yves looked at Kylee one last time before the hatchling dropped her, and she smiled, as if in killing her, Kylee had proven her right. They were both killers.

In the plaza below, people screamed, and the hatchling circled once, coming back to land at Kylee's side. It was black from beak to tail.

"I'm sorry," Kylee said to Brysen.

He looked at her with sad eyes, disappointed eyes. It was almost funny. She'd given him that same look too many times to count as they were growing up.

"Well, that was dramatic." Kyrg Bardu laughed and clapped her palms together. "So, Kylee, tell me, what do you want here?"

"Justice," Kylee said. "I'm here for justice."

"Kill me or don't," Bardu sneered. "But I won't submit to your childish ideas of justice."

"I don't need you to submit to mine," Kylee said, and nodded at the hatchling next to her, opened her palms to the convocation of ghost eagles surrounding them. "Submit to theirs."

Then she gave the birds the last command she ever meant to give.

"*Salaa*," she said. "*Salaa*."

The word meant *sing*.

41

THE HATCHLING OPENED ITS MOUTH AND RELEASED A PIERCING NOTE. Kylee flinched and braced herself, fearing this was the same song as at the Talon Fortress, the song from the ancient story, the song that called forth the vengeful dead.

But instead it sang a golden song, a song that told their history just as Kylee and Brysen and Grazim had read it. Except this history was told from a bird's point of view—from the eyes of every hawk who lost its falconer, of every falconer who was killed and rose unavenged. It told the story so every living soul in the Sky Castle could hear—and see and feel—and when it finished, there was silence.

The hatchling had turned brilliant gold, brighter than ever.

It gleamed so bright, it was hard to look at, and Kylee wiped tears off her face and peered down over the plaza.

Murmurs rose. Suddenly, all the ghost eagles launched from the veranda and circled the city, trilling sudden songs, songs of mourning and regret. Songs of confession and songs of accusation. Songs for every human loss and songs belonging only to the ghost eagles, that Kylee didn't understand herself.

They were songs that had never been sung before.

Sections of netting still hung in a few places over the plaza, and people pressed toward those spaces. Kylee feared a panic, a stampede, a riot. The ghost eagles, however, made no moves to dive. They simply circled, dozens of wide-winged shadows rotating slowly in a darkening sky.

"Don't panic!" Kylee yelled. "Stay calm!" She was too high up, too far away. No one could hear her.

The people started shouting. They tried to get away from the plaza. Even though the masses had heard the ghost eagles' story, all they cared about was getting away. They didn't understand. All they had to do was listen, but they only wanted to run.

Bardu clucked and shook her head.

"There you have it!" she said. "What now? So we're all living on top of a crime. What would you have us do? Give up falconry? Throw ourselves off cliffsides? Let the ghost eagles tear us apart?" She opened her arms. "What did you come here for? You can't expect us to invent some retribution against ourselves for our ancestors' crimes?"

They don't care, she thought. *They know the bloody past, and they don't care.* And then came that same old thought, circling back to her like the ghost eagles circling above: *They deserve to die.*

The hatchling bent its legs, its feathers growing dark. She didn't know what to do. She thought that by making the people listen, they'd come together and figure out what to do. She thought listening would be enough.

She was wrong.

The ghost eagles above let out a shriek. "REEEEEEE!"

Kylee heard the sound of a six-talon whip cracking across skin, saw herself cracking it across the spine of the mountains. She was huge. She was a god. She was the sky's wrath itself, and she looked down upon the scuttling mass of humanity and found them a terrible disappointment.

She could call the predators to hunt now. It would be so easy. She knew the words—all the words she'd ever need. She could kill anyone who didn't beg forgiveness, anyone who felt neither shame nor guilt. The hatchling could even go back to killing its own kind, if only Kylee asked. She could destroy anything she chose. She could *be* the justice she hoped the world would provide. She had that power.

She looked at the dread convocation above her and at the gargantuan hatchling beside her.

They had no answers, only rage, and the people below had no answers, only fear. No one knew what justice looked like when there were no amends to make. No one knew how to ask forgiveness when forgiveness was impossible.

But she only knew what she had always known: People care for themselves and their own lives, and even when they know the truth, they won't do anything about it. *No one lives in history; we only have the present.*

"It doesn't matter," she said. She began to cry. Brysen came to her, took her hands. "I told them everything, and it doesn't matter . . . there's nothing else to do. I can't make them care."

"It's okay," Brysen said, holding her. Kylee felt so silly letting her finch-faced brother comfort her now, but it felt good to cry. She only had one word left to say—the bloodiest word she could ever speak—and those who did not kneel and weep would die, and she'd be the one responsible. But that was what the ghost eagles wanted. That's what they were owed, and she would give them their due. The only answer for this broken world of uncaring fools was to let the ghost eagles end it.

But first, before the slaughter, Kylee just wanted to cry

with her brother one last time and grieve for all things they couldn't change.

"*Akaa*," Brysen whispered in her ear.

"What's that?" she sniffled.

"*Grieve*," he told her. "It's the Hollow Tongue word for *grieve*."

Kylee held his face in her hands, and gazed into his one damp blue eye, where she saw her own reflected back.

She turned to the hatchling, keen for blood, and looked up at the ghost eagles, just as keen, circling under starlight now, and she saw their whole sorry history laid out in front of them and stretching out into their future in the same widening gyre. She was struck suddenly by something she had never done, had never allowed herself to do.

All her life, she fought and protected and avenged and survived, but she never once *grieved*, not properly. The ghost eagles had fought and provoked and killed and died, but perhaps they, like her, had never grieved for all that they had lost, all that had been taken. When the past was unforgivable and unchangeable, what else could a person do? What else could anyone do? It wasn't perfect, but it was a place to start.

"Grieve," Kylee said, and she let out a long breath, let herself cry with it. She found her ma's eyes across the veranda and spoke to her, too. "*Grieve*," she said, and she pictured Nyall. She pictured Brysen's hawk, Shara. She pictured her old friend Vyvian, and she pictured Kheryn and the covey of pale boys on the mountain and even Üku and the Owl Mothers. She tried to hold every story she'd heard or seen in her mind, and then she looked at the flock of wrathful and frightened birds above and around her, and she commanded them.

"*Akaa!*" she said.

With a cry as low and long as the wind through the mountains, as one, the entire flock obeyed.

42

THE KEENING OF THE GHOST EAGLES RUMBLED IN THE MARROW OF Kylee's bones. It was deeper than any birdsong she had ever heard. Though it made her think of mourners' crows, it sounded nothing like a crow's cries. It made her think of the rattle vultures made when descending on carrion, but it sounded nothing like vultures. It made her think of prayers—the ones her mother muttered when their father stayed out late, gambling in the battle pits of the Broken Jess, and when he came home sopped in foothill gin and disappointment—though it sounded nothing like praying.

It was not a sound the world had ever heard.

Kyrg Bardu gasped at the sound, her face ashen. The

people on the plaza covered their ears, but the wailing penetrated finger and flesh as easily as air, and none could escape the sounds or what the sound showed them.

Once more they saw the history the hatchling had sung, but now they saw every moment of it from every point of view, all at once. They also saw their own lives and losses, remembering every elder who fed the vultures at their time and every baby taken too young by cold or heat or fever or fate. They felt their hearts break and felt them break one another's. Kylee saw Brysen's first boyfriend betray him. She saw Brysen holding Shara after healing her burns and then again, cradling her on the battlefield, when he couldn't heal her. She felt what Shara felt—safe and calm in Brysen's hands—as her tiny heart beat its last.

And she saw Nyall die in front of her again, but this time she experienced it through his eyes, saw what he watched as the light dimmed around him: her own face, looking back. She felt his surprise and the rising cold, but also his sense of calm. Her face held him steady. His love for her didn't fade, not even as his vision dimmed and his thoughts dissolved.

She heard Jowyn's voice, praying over his dead companions:

"We fly and fly the same round range,
And turning, and turning, change and change.

Bodies fall and bodies rise,
From mud to air to feed the skies . . ."

She looked at Jowyn on the veranda here, where he held Brysen and Brysen held him. They each wept for their losses and their childhoods and their joy in finding each other and their knowledge that even that was no promise of safety.

She wept, and they wept, and the world wept together.

Brysen looked up at her, his blue eye bloodshot and pouring tears. He felt her grief, too—how she could never quite protect him, how she blamed herself for the beatings he took for so long, how she clamped shut her lips and quieted her voice, and how, when she finally spoke, she unleashed such death on the world that she feared ever speaking again. He saw that she was sorry and that she knew what she was responsible for and what she wasn't. He saw that the past only flies in one direction and cannot be changed.

She was harmed. She did harm. She was broken. She was whole. She was not afraid to speak anymore.

The ghost eagles cried again, and then they dove to the plaza, landing among the people—who didn't flee this time. The eagles sang of every life they'd seen lost or snuffed out themselves, of their lives before they were transformed by pain. The people held one another and held the giant ghost eagles among them. The sound of the song swirled around them, and there was nothing in the world but sound, and sound was all there ever had been.

We're all just birdsong, Kylee thought. *Air that vibrates through bone and flesh. Sometimes heard and answered, and sometimes carried away on a lonely wind or lost in thunder or ignored in haste. We're all the songs we've ever heard and all the songs we've ever sung, even at our worst, sometimes at our best. We're all a broken birdsong.*

She found herself smiling through her tears. As the ghost eagles sang, she looked at Grazim, and whatever the other girl saw in Kylee's expression made her smile, too. Brysen and Jowyn were smiling. Even Kyrg Birgund, who was bleeding where he'd been dropped against a wall and looked perched on the precipice of death himself, was smiling.

The ghost eagles launched themselves up from the plaza, their black wings flapping. As they rose, they simply . . . broke apart, like mist or smoke, and the entire convocation of them vanished into night.

They'd finally sung their song. They'd been heard. They were gone.

Only the hatchling remained. It stood at Kylee's side, its feathers gold as the midday sun.

Kylee swept her eyes across the battle boys and her ma, her brother and Jowyn, Grazim and Bardu and Birgund. All of them looked back at her expectantly, as if she knew more than she'd told them or had some plan for what to do now. She had no idea.

Nyck raised an eyebrow, broke the silence. "Well, I could use a drink!"

They laughed togeher.

Each of them had felt one another's grief and let themselves grieve, but the facts of their world hadn't changed. Like the gold feathers shining on the great bird beside her, this was something no one had ever seen before. There was no way to know what would happen when the people of Uztar began to face the past—and one another—with unrelenting truth. A hawk can circle the same patch of sky over and over again, but when it breaks that circle and dives, not even the sky knows what it might catch.

It was time for them to stop circling.

The hatchling bent back its head and screeched, high and shrill. In her mind, Kylee sat astride the golden bird, soaring through wide-open sky.

Whatever came next would be something new.

AN OPEN SKY

IT WAS THE DAY BEFORE THE SIX VILLAGES HELD CONGRESS, THEIR
last before the ice-winds came and the Necklace froze over.
People huddled by their hearths to share cold kindness and
warm drinks and each other. Kylee found Brysen exactly
where she thought he'd be.

"They said you'd come with birdsong and lamentation," he
greeted his sister as he stepped outside the front door to their
home to see her, footsteps clicking on the loose stones of the
path. He'd rebuilt everything, but those stones he left in
place. Kylee counted the clicks, just like when they were little, when their father came home.

Click click. Click click. Click click.

Behind her, the great golden bird puffed out its feathers. The tuft on the top of its head rippled, which made Brysen grin. The bird was showing off. The more time she spent with it, the more she realized it had little bits of her brother. He had a hand in creating it, after all.

Brysen looked healthy, which made her happy. He'd put on some weight, which he'd sorely needed, and he was proud of the work he'd done on the house, which was in better shape than ever before. The mews were rebuilt, and inside the house Ma was showing Jowyn how to make beans into patties—they were more filling than meat.

"The birdsong and lamention will come tomorrow," Kylee told her brother. "Today is for us . . . Who's that?" She pointed at a small goshawk Brysen had cradled in his arms.

"Nyallay," he said. An homage. "Little guy broke his wing. I found him starving on a crag over the river, but as soon as he's healed and up to flying weight, he'll be fierce."

"You aren't . . ." Kylee frowned at her brother, and a murmur of who'd they been passed between them both. "Going back to the battle pits?"

She didn't want to believe he'd become that boy again or that the pits would even be rebuilt. How could people who knew a raptor's grief, who'd been inside a raptor's mind, make birds fight for sport and profit?

The hatchling's feathers glimmered with black veins, but Brysen held up a hand.

"No, no, no . . . ," he said. "Racing. We race and hunt. The hares and grouse don't like it, but no one's battling hawks anymore. Nyck outlawed it."

"Nyck?" Kylee raised an eyebrow. She'd been gone awhile.

"An edict from the Sky Castle," Brysen explained. "Birgund and Grazim want to divest power by the time the ice melts. They want each territory to send a representative to a new council, and Nyck's got everyone supporting him. It doesn't hurt that he's bribing anyone he can with foothill gin and everyone else with free food at the Broken Jess."

Kylee laughed. They could do worse than a petty criminal like Nyck at the Sky Castle. He knew what it was to survive, to fight, and to transform himself on his own terms. The new kingdom could use that kind of experience if it was going to transform.

After the ghost eagles vanished, a new government had to be formed, one that included Altari *and* Uztari. One that still held authority and maintained order but that didn't act as if the crimes of the past had never happened.

In the short term, that meant giving someone with experience a role in ruling, and there was no way under the blazing sky that such a job would go to Kyrg Bardu. And so, instead of rotting in a dungeon, Kyrg Birgund was appointed temporary regent, with Grazim as an equal beside him. Once the government was sorted, he would retire to train a new military corps, while Grazim would become proctor until new electors arrived to choose their own leadership.

Kylee knew her friend would be pretty good at politics, even with a rock viper like the old general sharing power with her. Kylee had left them in charge together because Birgund, for all his cruelty, always put his soldiers and his duty first, and she trusted he'd do the same now.

And Grazim?

She'd been outcast, and she'd been feared, and she'd been lonely, and she'd found friends. Who better to rule than someone who'd never stood a chance at ruling before? Who better to fight injustice than someone who suffered through it for her whole life?

Kylee had every confidence in Grazim.

Bardu was imprisoned and awaiting justice for the murder of the Council, which would come just as soon as a system of just punishment could be devised. She might be waiting a long, long time. Every settlement council and potential elector was debating how, exactly, this justice should look, and Kylee traveled the breadth of the plateau, visiting merchant oases and mining towns, hearing them out. Everyone was struggling to rebuild; everyone looked to her with fear and wonder. She wasn't there to tell them what to decide or how to craft their futures. She was a barely educated Six Villages girl who'd made her own share of brutal mistakes. She'd never presume to tell them how to live.

But she did have a role to play in the rebuilding.

In each settlement and village, she gathered people to do the hardest work of all: to listen.

She and the hatchling told the tale she'd told in the Sky Castle, and then they opened so the people—every one of them—could tell their own tales. They spoke of their crimes and their kindnesses, how they were hurt and who they hurt. They sought forgiveness, and they debated the punishments.

The past couldn't change, but they could all hold one another to account in the spirit of community, with an eye toward mercy. That was the only thing Kylee asked of them. To hear one another. To hear her. To know their story and to speak it as truthfully as they could.

Those who did not want to listen, those who refused to speak or spoke in self-serving lies . . . well . . . the hatchling's feathers could turn black as well as gold. It had a way of keeping people honest and intentions generous. In time, that generosity and honesty would become habit, but for now, they were all still learning. And as much Kylee hated to admit it, a little fear helped them along.

"You aren't tired of hearing all those terrible stories?"

Brysen asked her as he carried his small, injured hawk to the mews.

"They're not all terrible," Kylee said. "Some people found ways to shield each other. Some people fell in love. Life went on while we . . ." Her voice trailed off. She didn't have the words to describe what they had done. Torn at a wound the world made; ripped open scars so they could heal better. "Anyway, most people are better than the worst things they've done."

"But not all," he said.

"But not all," she repeated, and glanced at the hatchling. She didn't want to share those stories with her brother.

Not everyone wanted to remember, and many tried to forget the stories that built them, but still Kylee traveled and told her stories and listened to theirs, because she'd lived the cost of forgetting. She'd nearly destroyed the world because of forgetting. This was her burden and her joy. She imposed this sentence on herself and she gave herself this reward. She carried the stories.

The hatchling, with its timeless mind and limitless wings, held those stories, too. Its voice could share them all, across time and tears. The more it heard, the richer its song became—not easier to sing and not easier to hear, but fuller. That was its burden, too, and its joy.

She changed the subject. "How's it going here?"

"I do what I can." Brysen pushed open the door to the hawk mews, where a flurry of flapping and screeching erupted. He'd built cages and perches for three dozen birds of prey, and they were almost all occupied. "People bring me their injured birds, and we mend them, train them when we can, release them when they're ready. It's . . . fun?"

"You sure about that?" Kylee said.

"Yeah . . . ," he told her. "I mean, it's not easy to let them go. It's not like the sky's any safer than it was before just because the ghost eagles are gone. I know they won't all survive this coming ice-wind."

"But you do it anyway," she said. It wasn't a question.

"But I do it anyway," he repeated. This was the life he'd chosen. He didn't long for glory anymore; he just wanted to be with Jowyn and heal what little creatures he could, even though they flew from him the first chance they got.

"Hey!" Jowyn called from the door to the house. "You two gonna eat?"

Jowyn's skin was a lot less pale now, his tattoos faded and blurred. His hair had grown into a longer white-blond mop, which was surprisingly curly; Kylee noticed a few stray strands on Brysen's shirt. When Brysen looked across the yard at Jowyn, he almost appeared to flutter.

"Coming!" Brysen shouted, then, to his sister, he whispered, "He and Ma are experimenting with *cuisine*. Brace yourself. Last week I had to sleep in the outhouse because of something that was meant to be a pancake."

Kylee had never seen anyone smile so wide when describing intestinal distress.

Brysen set the small goshawk onto a bundle of blankets in a cage and latched the door. They went toward the house, where the hatchling patiently waited. It watched as they walked up the stone path.

Click click. Click click. Click click.

"Why don't you fix that?" Kylee asked.

"It helps me remember," he said. "It's like my scars. They're a reminder of the wounds, but they're also a reminder that wounds heal."

"That's what all the stories I hear do for me," Kylee said, taking his hand as they walked, looking at the way his gray hair fell over the bronze eyepatch. He had to turn his head to look back at her.

"Wounds heal," she repeated, and it was the truest thing she'd ever said. She'd keep saying it for the rest of their long and wild lives.

ACKNOWLEDGMENTS

A LOT HAS HAPPENED IN THE WORLD AND MY LIFE SINCE I FIRST
conceived of this trilogy. We had an election and a series
of political, natural, and economic disasters. Somewhere in
there, I left NYC and moved to Philadelphia. Somewhere
in there, I became a father. And right now, as I write these
words, I—like millions of others—am locked down in my
house because of a global pandemic.

I'm someone who believes in the power of stories to make
all kinds of things possible, and if you've read this far, so,
likely, are you. I also believe in the power of so-called escapist
literature, though I think of it as escape-pod literature. It's
built from the same material as the wreck it is fleeing, and it's

essential to have enough on hand in an emergency. An escape pod can open up new possibilities in countless unforeseen directions by breaking from the planned route. That's what speculative literature at its best can do. Welcome to my TED Talk.

Carrying the overwrought metaphor to its conclusion, there are many people I'm honored to share this particular escape pod with, people who made this trilogy possible and who carried me through it all these years. Grace Kendall, Elizabeth Lee, Kayla Overbey, Elizabeth H. Clark and Aurora Parlagreco (who designed the gorgeous covers!), Morgan Rath, Katie Halata, Teresa Ferraiolo, Olivia Oleck, and the rest of the FSG/Macmillan Children's team, from the publishers, production staff, school and library marketing, digital marketing, conference planning teams, and the sales reps to the (underappreciated but absolutely essential) warehouse crews who have kept books going out to readers even in the face of a global health crisis. They deserve to be celebrated. I never would have been able to maintain this career without the advice and support of my agent for over a decade of publishing, Robert Guinsler. Thanks, too, to Danielle Bukowski and Christopher Combemale and the rest of the Sterling Lord Literistic team. Also: Libba Bray, Katherine Locke, Adib Khorram, Lev Rosen, Caleb Roehrig, Adam Sass, Cale Dietrich, Tom Ryan, Shaun David Hutchinson, Dhonielle

Clayton, Phil Stamper, Isaac Fitzgerald, Veronica Roth, Ally Condie, Brendan Reichs, Adam Silvera, Claire Legrand, Holly Goldberg Sloan, and Kiersten White, each for reasons they all know. Amanda Luken spent hours on the phone with me as I avoided writing and got me excited to go back to it. I'm also grateful to the teachers, librarians, and booksellers who've supported me more than I deserve and more than I can thank them for. They are too numerous to list here, a fact that remains a delight and an honor.

The escape pod's kinda crowded, but I need to leave room for my family—my parents; my sister, Mandy, who yelled at me about the ending of book two; her husband, Dennis, who likes to see his name in print; and my nephews, Ben and Dillon, who are too young for this series. And my husband, Tim. He's the best person and hardest-working teacher and parent I've ever known. I'm glad he's my co-pilot. Lastly, I want to shout-out our daughter, for being my favorite human. I make this promise every day: I'm gonna try to be worthy of her for the rest of my life. But I won't let her read these books for at least another decade. For now, I just love watching the sky with her and pointing out all the wild birds watching over us together.